HOPE

By B.R.M. Evett

Sleeping Dog Press

BOSTON

FIRST EDITION

ISBN 979-8-9883407-4-4

Library of Congress Cataloging-in-Publishing has been applied for.

Cover Design by Kerry Ellis

HOPE

To Spencer and Dash, my life's great Hope

PART ONE

Nos patriae fines et dulcia linquimus arva:
Nos patriam fugimus;

We are leaving the sweet fields and the confines of our homeland:
We are fleeing our homeland.

— Vergil, Eclogues 1, 2-4

Chapter 1

The rusting fender wards off the rain, but it's a poor place to hide from the man with the axe. Creek has his legs pulled up as far as they will go, his arms wrapped around the precious cube of brushed metal that got him into this fix. It pushes up against his chin, right on the spot where he struck the broken concrete when he fell. It stings like nobody's business. He tries not to breathe. He can just make out the main clearing between the junk piles, and Junkman moving in a slow circle around the far side, the blade of the axe glinting black now and then in the halogen glare. Junkman's mouth is moving, but Creek doesn't need to hear what he's ranting on about. Any deaf kid with half a brain could tell he's got murder on his mind.

The whole caper has gone wrong from the beginning. Despite what the Duke said, there was no place where the chain-link fence curled up so you could slip under, and Creek had to cut a way in. That took fifteen minutes because the clippers he had brought were for wires, not fencing. He damn near broke his hand trying to snap them closed. It worked in the end, but it wrecked the clippers. Then Junkman's shed was locked. That was expected, but what wasn't expected was that the lock was a Keytek three-phaser. How the hell Junkman could afford a fancy lock like that was beyond him. Probably bought it on credit, expecting a big payday for the cube. Creek was good with locks, very good *(the best)*, but that took another twenty minutes.

So, what was supposed to be a slick grab and go turns into a major operation, and just his luck, doesn't Junkman come strolling back through the gate when Creek has barely finished removing the cube from its armored case. Nothing to do but hide. Amazing how little space a scrawny ten-year-old can take up behind a trash bin.

Junkman puzzles for a minute about the open door, but Creek can see he's not sure he didn't leave it open. *Louchey old drunk.* Creek waits for him to crash down onto his little cot and pass out, but Junkman decides to cook himself a hot meal for a change. Forty-five minutes crammed under the sink trying not to make a move, and, lord, doesn't that trash bin stink.

Finally, Junkman finishes his meal and hits the toilet, and Creek can sneak out. Junkman has left the bathroom door open, but he's focused on his business, so Creek slides around the bin and tiptoes toward the exit. So far, he's kept it smooth, checking every box, but wouldn't you know it, he blows it on the final leg. His belly started growling, all that time under the sink, and Junkman can cook, nasty, slack-faced wheezer that he is. The smell makes Creek's mouth water and his head go soft. Just a little chicken leg, sitting there so inviting on the table.

Well, doesn't he reach out too fast and knock over the gin bottle.

Junkman whips around and Creek scampers for the door, Junkman right behind, pulling up his pants and hopping like a jackrabbit. That's when Creek's luck really goes, and he slips on the rain-soaked mud outside the shed and smacks his chin on the cracked slab that supports the crusher. Junkman grabs at his leg, and it's only by going all wildcat that he breaks free and skitters behind the body of a Sony Espera 230. Nice car, in its time. But now he's on the wrong side from the fence hole. Pretty soon Junkman hauls out his axe, and they're playing cat and mouse around the heaps of old auto parts, rusted-out med machines, and smashed up furniture.

Creek finally gets behind a big pile of car corpses and slips under a fender. Junkman walks right by — his big, ugly feet passing a hands-width from Creek's nose. Creek thinks maybe he's going to give up and go back inside, but Junkman decides to wait it out, patrolling back and forth across the yard. Pretty soon he finds the fence hole and stations himself in front of it. So much for squirreling out of here.

And that's where things stand.

Junkman's mouth is still working like nobody's business. Creek half wishes he had the Neural Ear instead of Kimo, but she needed the Ear to negotiate with the Lady. Of course, if he doesn't get out of here with the cube, there won't be anything to negotiate. Plus, he hates the Ear. It's stupid.

Anyhow, Creek can guess what Junkman is on about. "Lookee here, kid," he's probably saying, "You best come out now, return what you stole. I won't hurt you if you give it back." Yeah, right. *You got an axe, you big dimmo. You think I'm a dimmo, too? I'm not coming out no-how.*

Must be an hour that goes by. Creek's back screams bloody murder, but at least he's dry. Junkman shifts from foot to foot, wiping the runnels of rain off his head every ten seconds or so. It gives Creek a taste of satisfaction to see him get soaked through. Just give up and go inside. But Junkman isn't about to give up. Creek glances down at the cube in his hands. That box is too damn valuable.

How did he ever get talked into this caper? No good comes from joining up with other people. Creek has spent more than half his short life on his own, and he's got on just fine. Well, not that fine, but he's survived, hasn't he? Except for that brief stint at John Chaico's refugee camp (he only went because he needed that shot) he's been a rabbit on the run, making his own, quiet way through this rotten old world. Happy as a skimmer.

All this trouble started at the camp. That's where he hooked up again with Kimo, and met the Duke, and…Candela. And doesn't he go all soft and let himself get talked into sticking with them when the camp gets burned. And doesn't he let himself get talked into making a play for this stupid box. "Lady Fal will pay a fortune for something like that. We'll be rich!" said the Duke. Now he's stuck here in a junkyard with a psycho ready to chop him in half.

Creek can't stand it anymore. He steels himself to make a break for it, figuring that if he runs first for the gate, Junkman will come after him, and if he weaves and bobs enough, he can get back around him to the hole in the fence. He takes a firm grip of the cube.

He's just about to push off the fender when a pair of headlights appears at the gates. Wide and high. Some kind of ranger or terrain car. Junkman whips his head around, his mouth twisting into the biggest curse of all. He looks wildly back and forth, a last-ditch play to find his quarry, then stumps over to the gate and undoes the chain. Creek almost makes a bid for the hole, but everything happens too fast and he misses his chance, so he stays put. The car rolls into the lot, sheets of rain flashing white in the bright beams. Three figures get out. Big men with long coats.

They say something to Junkman. He drops the axe in the mud and starts to plead. They watch him, impassive as a stand of trees. He gestures this way and that, his mouth running like a coal car down a hill. One of the men goes into the shed, comes out a few seconds later with the container that once held the cube. He shows it to the other two men. They discuss it amongst themselves. Junkman watches them with a crazed look in his eyes, half terror, half hope. One of the men puts the case in the back seat of the car, while the second climbs into the passenger seat. The third man smiles a gentle, rueful smile, says something to Junkman, and shoots him in the head. He gets into the driver's seat. The car backs out of the yard and disappears into the night.

Creek lies there for a little while, the pain in his back forgotten. The rain subsides, then stops. At last, he pushes the fender off, gets up, and trudges through the open gate onto the rutty road.

Poor Junkman.

Chapter 2

Lucinda taps her COR, and her mind sings knowledge. The questions come hard and fast, jumping randomly from topic to topic. She just manages to keep up.

What year were the New States formed and when did they dissolve?

Tap.

What protein mutation made Hetara II so much deadlier than Hetara I?

Tap.

Explain the imagery in Reginald Gatson's "Songs of the Boiling Seas.

Tap.

What is the blast radius of a Leidos-NG Q34 incendiary grenade?

Tap.

She jerks her head slightly to the right every time she taps — a habit she developed as a child — but that is just a tic. The COR responds to her thoughts. She asks for information, and it floods her brain with everything she needs. She asks for something else, and she forgets the old and remembers the new in the blink of an eye.

She glances over at Tristram. He is twenty-two — two years older than she is — but she reads fear all over his pasty face as he struggles (and fails) to catch up with her. A smile tickles her lips, but she suppresses it. No need to gloat.

What treaty created the Association of Enclaves, and what are its Twelve Tenets of Purity?

Tap.

What are Napoleon's three principles of warfare?

Tap.

Outline the differences in architecture between the Prometheus X2500 processor and the X3000.

Tap.

Her heart pounding with happiness, Lucinda's hands fly over the interface — drawing, shaping, framing the information into elegant, precise responses. When the final question comes, it almost makes her laugh: *Diagram the neuronal interface between the brain and its Cognition Optimization Relay.* She could almost answer this question without her COR, but she taps it anyway, just to be sure.

A bell sounds, and Tristram slams his hand down onto his console. Lucinda pretends not to notice. Sergeant Campbell, seated at the desk in front of them, looks up from his monitor, folds his hands, and addresses them.

"Mr. Proctor, I'm sorry, but that's the end of the line for you." Tristram nods, a ridiculous pink blush suffusing his head and neck. He wipes the sweat from his forehead.

Campbell looks at her. "Congratulations, Miss Weston, we'll see you Tuesday for the practical." He rises and walks out of the room.

"Sorry, Tris," Lucinda says. He gives her a bitter nod — his mouth a hard, flat line — and follows the sergeant, leaving her alone.

She half wishes that some of her friends — Tanya or Tabitha or Ashleigh — were here with her to celebrate, but they don't really get her decision to join Defense. She taps her COR and sends a quick VM to her parents. "I passed the one-on-one!" Not that they approve, either. Nobody in her circle does. It's a job for Second Classers. "I'm going to Sheena's to study for the written. See you tomorrow." It's a lie, but they won't know that. She heads for the Arts Center.

Hours later, she leans over him, a little smile twisting her lips. The little prop closet is stuffy and cluttered, but she loves it. Their private little Eden.

She taps her COR and whispers to him:

"All thoughts, all passions, all delights,
Whatever stirs this mortal frame,
All are but ministers of Love,
And feed his sacred flame."

"What's that?" he asks. His chest glows deep gold in the dim light.

"Coleridge," she says. Lucinda knows the name means nothing to him, but she knows it all: Every word the poet wrote, his birth, life, death, friends, influences. The knowledge delights, excites her.

She takes his brown hand and entwines his fingers — her own hand, whelite pale, so white it almost looks dead to her. She envies his lusciousness. She pulls his hand to her breast. He doesn't resist. "Is that better?"

"It's weird." His voice is husky and thick.

"What?"

"When you do that. With your COR-thing. Like you're a different person."

"Don't you like it? Poetry?

"Yeah…I mean, it's weird. But yeah. It's pretty hot."

"Good. Just a sec." She leans back, cocking her head slightly as she looks into her COR space, her eyes dancing over the image in her mind. She chuckles.

"What?" he asks.

"Nothing. My friend Ashleigh just sent me a funny vidi. They pulled a prank on Roger Thornhill. Such a dougie."

"Who's Roger Thornhill?" He frowns.

"No one. Never you mind." She lowers herself down onto him, her head bumping softly against the wall of the closet. Her hair, red as fire, falls between their faces. He pushes it aside with his long fingers. They kiss. His hand finds its way under her shirt. Lucinda shivers as he draws it up her side. "Sebastien," she whispers, like a charm of opening.

"That's me," he says.

The sky is pale with the roses of dawn when Lucinda lets herself out through the door in the rear of the Arts Center. Sebastien and his family are still officially under quarantine, so the front is chained and taped, but security is lax. The Cantrells have performed in the Enclave twice in the last year, and everybody knows them now. The back entrance is unguarded. Lucinda slips quietly across the parking lot, checking side to side, pulls herself up onto the low concrete wall beside the loading dock, shimmies over the fence, and walks away as if it were the most ordinary thing in the world.

The Hamilton Arts Center is in the oldest part of the Enclave. She comes down the little grassy hill onto Clinton, then breaks into a jog as she turns onto Elm Street, skimming past the fine old Victorians where the Selectmen live – three hundred and fifty years old, some of them, but as new and brightly painted as if it were yesterday. Normally, running through this part of town makes her happy. This morning, her mood is as gray as the sky. She taps an architecture module into her COR, and tries to cheer herself up by naming the various frills and gewgaws on the porches as she runs by: pilasters, gingerbread scrollwork, architraves, pediments. It doesn't help.

They had a lovely time. Until the end. She can still feel the warm pulsing down deep inside her, and hear Sebastien's stifled gasps of ecstasy in her mind. But as they lay, panting in each other's arms in the dark, dusty prop closet, he had said, "It makes me feel stupid."

"What?" she asked.

"When you…you know." He reached up and touched the small slot behind her right ear, the access port to her COR. She never used it — everything was delivered through the clouds — but it marked the difference between them.

She laughed and teased and cajoled him until he smiled, but the memory rankles. She had said, "I don't need you to be smart, I just need you for your body." She had meant it as a joke, but he hadn't laughed, so she kissed his collarbones and nibbled his earlobes until he couldn't *not* respond, and they had done it again. But then he went all quiet and somber. They carefully disentangled themselves so as not to knock the heap of sticks and staves and wooden swords piled up in the corner of the tiny space. Sebastien's parents were just on the other side of the wall, sleeping on the stage, and there was the Enclave Defenseman snoring in the lobby. Still, Lucinda wished he would flash her his electric grin and let loose his magic laugh. Instead, he kept his eyes lowered, and barely brushed her lips as they parted.

She pushes away the stubborn dissatisfaction pressing on her heart. He's right, of course. He is below her. He is a nonalite from outside the wall — *and he's a musician, for heaven's sake.* She is an elite in her elite community. And, though she didn't like to admit it, she did mostly like him for his body. But that was saying a lot. His body was *amazing*.

It wasn't that she had no real feelings for him. She did. But he could get so moody, especially when it came to the differences between them — her COR in particular. She *loved* her COR, and what it gave her. It was more than a handy tool. It was her world. It *defined* her. COR-less, he could never understand. But she could see how it made him feel inferior. She knew he was jealous, and wished she could make him see that she didn't care that he had no COR, and didn't care about the Enclave boys who had one, either. She didn't care that they could load the history of the Crusades or the mathematics of quantum field theory, and he couldn't. It had nothing to do with him or them, or anyone. Lucinda just loved that *she* had that power. Besides, she really enjoyed having sex with him in the closet behind the stage at the Arts Center. One thing in her life she could control. One thing that belonged just to her. Maybe it wasn't love, but it was *something*.

She reaches the top of the hill. The clouds are hanging low and the visibility is poor, but she can still make out the jagged teeth of the ruined City hulking in the mist on the horizon. Just beyond it lies the sea, sending its searching fingers all the way up into the Back Bay, invisible in the gloom. Mornings like this, she can almost see the ghosts of the past swirling in the fog. Imagine: Seven million people once lived there. Now there are scarcely that many on the whole continent.

A salt tang bites the air. She wonders if a storm is coming. She tries to tap the weather, but the coastal stations are down again. Nonas must have scavenged them for parts. Waves of longing, irrepressible, indescribable, roll over her heart. What could be out there? *Something…Something… Something…*

No. She has everything she needs here. Safe within the walls of the Hamilton Enclave. Out there lies disease, and death, and violence. The fallen world. Sebastien has told her enough stories about it to satisfy any craving for adventure. Besides, he comes from out *there.* Her wandering troubadour. Her forbidden love. Just enough danger to satisfy the itch.

She turns away and heads down Park Street. As she reaches Defiance Square, Lucinda loads data on the history of the mandolin, in honor of Sebastien. A cockeyed proof that she does care for more than his body.

The first flood of knowledge flows in. But before she can focus, a jolt knocks her head like someone slapped her. A loud buzzing fills the space behind her ear. She cries out. The knowledge flickers away, leaving pain behind, and a sharp, throbbing nausea. She staggers toward the small gazebo in the center of the square, and leans against a rough wooden beam. She shakes her head. The buzzing stops. The pain disappears. Panic takes its place.

Not again. She assumed it was a fluke the first time, but this is three times now. She sits on one of the little benches, willing her mind to calm, focusing her attention on the little plaque commemorating the seat to one Gladys Hall, whoever that was.

It can't be Mindworm. Nobody has had it since they instituted the quarantine, and that was months ago. People have technical issues with their COR all the time. *It can't be Mindworm.* But her fear whispers, *it could,* and an icy shiver rolls up and down Lucinda's back. She knows what it would mean. She was in chem class when Lisa Barrett went into convulsions and flew at Mrs. Granger, screaming like her body was on fire. She watched the corpses burning on the lawn outside the wall, along with everyone else. *No, please let it not be Mindworm.*

As if in answer to her silent prayer, her COR kicks in again, right where it left off. With a jag of electricity like a punch in the ear, the information sweeps through her mind. But she doesn't care about the mandolin's antecedents in the gittern, the mandola, or the lute. She doesn't care about the influence of the Vinaccia family on the development of steel-stringed instruments. Relief. Relief is all she cares about. She feels whole again. *It's going to be okay.* The frightening emptiness within her head is full again. It's not Mindworm, just a glitch, and surely the last time, and she doesn't need to worry about it anymore.

She pulls herself to her feet and heads out of the square, just as the street cleaning robot slides around the corner, whooshing gently as its swirling brush cleans the already spotless pavement. Another message pops in from Ashleigh — more pictures of the prank. Lucinda wishes she had been there. *No, she doesn't.* She had a much better time with Sebastien, even if he got all moody. *It's going to be okay.*

Lucinda's automated timestamp tells her it is 6:07 when she comes down the side path of her house and enters through the kitchen door. No surprise, her mother stands at the counter, just finished emptying the dishwasher. "Morning, Mom," she says, as sweetly as she can manage.

Marigold Weston doesn't look at her daughter as she comes through the door. Her eyes — flawlessly placed between the flawless waves of her blond hair and the flawless blue collar of her flawless dress — focus on the last of the teacups, as she places them without a clink into the glass-fronted cabinet above the breakfast area.

"I was at Sheena's. She was helping me study. Long night!" Sheena's family worked at the fish farm, and she and Lucinda briefly got tight when Lucinda summer-jobbed there last year, but the friendship had not lasted. She felt a stab of guilt about it. Sheena was a nice girl who waved at her every time she went past the fishery, and uploaded sweet messages to her COR inbox from the post office far too regularly for comfort. It had been fun for a while to slum it with Sheena, but she was a Third Class —no COR — and pretty soon they had nothing to talk about besides fish and boys. Still, her unfailing goodwill provided excellent cover for Lucinda's secret trysts. God forbid her mother ever checked with Sheena's family, but that would never happen. She would never sink that low.

"How did studying go?" is all she asks.

"Pretty well."

"You're going to be ready?"

"I'll be fine. I still have another week before the written. You saw I passed the one-on-one?"

Her mother nods and moves to the sink, washing her hands unnecessarily and rinsing out the spotless basin. "And your practical is… when?"

"Day after tomorrow. That will be easy. We get a download for that, so you just have to be comfortable in tight spaces. Which I am. No sweat."

Silence.

"I beat out Tristram Proctor."

More silence. Lucinda plays "She Got Yaow" by The G Track Gurlss in her head while she waits to see if her mother is going to push her on where she really went. Marigold stares placidly at her, all the time in the world.

"Well," Lucinda says at last, "I'm beat. I'm going to bed. Don't bother breakfast."

She heads for the stairs, almost escapes, when her mother calls after her, "Just be sure to be up and dressed – and *pretty* – by 2:30."

Lucinda stops. Her heart thuds. "Why? Who's coming?"

"Tommy Gilchrist and his family are coming over for tea."

"Tommy Gilchrist? Why?" She knows why.

"You know as well as I do, Lucinda. You're almost twenty."

"But–"

"But nothing. Don't get your hair in a knot, honey. It's just tea. But we have to start somewhere."

"Do we have to start now? Especially with the Defense exam coming up?"

"Martin Gilchrist called your father. And he's not someone to ignore." Martin Gilchrist was Deputy Director of Infrastructure for the Enclave. Her mother moved to the foot of the stairs, looking up at her daughter with the implacable serenity of a Roman statue. "It's just tea. Get some rest. Just be ready by 2:30."

"And pretty."

"And pretty."

What could she say to that?

Chapter 3

It's still dark when Creek gets back to the others, but dawn is not far off. He's so tired he can hardly put one foot in front of another. The kids have set up camp under the ruins of a little bridge, where one old town road once passed over another. Kimo had shown it to them. She'd spent a few weeks here the year before. One side has come down, leaving nothing but rubble — most of which has been scavenged by homesteaders for their walls and bunkers — but the other half provides good shelter. There's even a little chamber in the wall where a water junction used to run. Candela has claimed it for herself and Baby. The rest of them bunk down under the curving half-arch of stone.

They've got some good stuff, including two mattresses they stole from a Niner camp by the river. What a great heist that was! Creek and Kimo get one mattress, and Candela has the other one inside. Lamarque sleeps on blankets on the ground, along with the Duke when Candela kicks him out of the chamber, which seems to happen every other day or so. He never complains. He's conked out there now, mouth hanging open like a largemouth bass.

Kimo rolls over when Creek collapses on the mattress. He meant to slide in all snakelike, but his legs are shaking so bad from the long night that he can't control his fall. She snaps wide awake in an instant, more awake than Creek. She switches on her little camp light so they can see.

They use the language he taught her, which he had learned from his mother when he was little. He can still barely believe the moment he first met Kimo — four years ago now — at the Steader camp by the lake. Someone like him! Well, not really like him. She had lost her hearing, while he never had it. But still. Somebody to talk to! She had gobbled up the shape language like she was born to it — they'd even added on to it as they got to know each other better — and they had become thick like thieves, until they got separated when the camp was overrun. Two years later — miracle of miracles — she shows up with the Duke and Candela at John Chaico's school. Like fate, or something. It was good to have someone you could trust, even for a lone fox like him.

YOU MADE IT, she shapes.

Creek nods. He shows her the cube.

YOU GOT IT! I WAS SO WORRIED ABOUT YOU. YOU SAID YOU'D BE BACK BY MIDNIGHT. ONE AT THE LATEST.

I HIT A SNAG. A COUPLE SNAGS.

Creek recounts the adventure of the night before. Kimo's eyes get all big when he tells her about the car and the men, and the flash of the gun.

POOR JUNKMAN, she shapes.

I KNOW. HE WAS A CUSSBUCKET SONOFABITCH, BUT I DIDN'T WANT THAT EITHER. STILL, BETTER HIM THAN ME.

WHO WAS IT, DO YOU THINK? Kimo looks worried.

NO IDEA. SOME GANG, I GUESS. THE SALAMANDERS, OR THE BAD BOYS. THOUGH LADY FAL HAS THIS AREA PRETTY WELL SEWN UP.

WHAT ABOUT THIS DOCTOR GUY?

WHO?

HE TOOK OUT BEDFORD ESTATES A COUPLE WEEKS AGO. THE DUKE WENT THIEVING AT NEWTON CROSSING TODAY AND HEARD ABOUT IT.

NEVER HEARD OF HIM. He's so tired, he doesn't have time for this. *DID YOU TALK TO THE LADY?*

YEAH. SHE DIDN'T BELIEVE ME. BUT SHE SAID IF WE DID HAVE IT, WE'D GET A GOOD PRICE.

WHAT PRICE?

SHE WOULDN'T SAY. FAIR, SHE SAID.

BETTER BE.

They stop talking for a minute. Creek starts to drift off. Then Kimo nudges him.

ARE YOU WORRIED SHE'LL JUST KILL US AND TAKE IT?

Creek shakes his head. *I DOUBT IT. BAD FOR BUSINESS. SHE'S STRAIGHT UP.*

THAT'S WHAT THE DUKE SAYS, BUT HE'S BEEN WRONG BEFORE.

DON'T I KNOW IT. BUT I THINK WE CAN TRUST HER. NOW LEAVE ME ALONE. I GOTTA SLEEP.

He rolls over, with his back to her. But sleep doesn't come for a while. He feels Kimo grow still, the slow rise and fall of her breath sending almost imperceptible vibrations through the mattress. Her doubts have shaken his confidence. Those men, killing Junkman for the cube. What have they got themselves into? He looks up, half-expecting to see the high, bright lights of a ranger come barreling out of the darkness, men with guns leaning out the windows. *Don't be crazy,* he tells himself. *We'll sell it to Lady Fal, and it'll be her problem.* Still, he can't relax.

Creek reaches into his pocket and pulls out a small silver key. The door it opened burned away years ago, along with the little house. He can't remember her pressing it into his hand, or what she told him, or why she had even given it to him. But that's not the worst of it. He can't remember her face. He remembers her arms enclosing him, snuggling into her soft body, and the tickling of her hair as it rubbed against his head. He remembers the shaping of her arms as she taught him to read the world. He knows she is gone forever, but perhaps if he holds the key, he will dream of her. He closes his eyes, and within two breaths, he sleeps.

HE SAYS YOU WERE LOOKING ON THE WRONG SIDE. Kimo has the Ear on her head so she can understand the others, and is translating for the Duke. The Duke can actually shape pretty well — he and Candela got Creek to teach them when they were at John Chaico's school — but he forgets to do it a lot, especially when he gets excited (which is all the time).

I WENT ALL AROUND THE WHOLE THING, Creek shapes back. *JUNKMAN MUST'VE FIXED THE FENCE.*

MAYBE, BUT I BET YOU WEREN'T LOOKING HARD ENOUGH. The Duke is sixteen, a whelite boy, pale and spotty, from an Enclave up near the Canadian border wall — outcast during one of the purges. He had been the head of the hearing kids at John Chaico's, so he's supremely confident and sure he's always right. Creek decides not to argue. Let him have his way, it's not worth the trouble.

They are sitting around the solar plate, making breakfast. Lamarque scored some sausages from a burnt-out homesteader's, so it's a feast. Creek hasn't eaten since the night before, and the smell is driving him wild.

ALL RIGHT, shapes the Duke, as they watch the sausage sizzle. *KIMO, YOU TOLD HER WE'D BE THERE BY NOON?*

YES. SHE SAID NOT TO COME BEFORE THEN, BECAUSE SHE WAS BUSY.

He mouth-talks to the others for a while. Kimo tells Creek that Lamarque and Candela are going to stay behind to guard the cube.

WILL THAT WORK? asks Creek. *SHE'LL WANT TO SEE IT. SHE WON'T NEGOTIATE UNLESS SHE KNOWS WE'VE REALLY GOT IT.*

Duke shakes his head. *Too dangerous.*

Creek thinks *I thought you trusted Lady Fal,* but keeps it to himself. Instead, he shapes, *WHAT IF WE MAKE SOMETHING WITH IT?*

SOMETHING WE WOULDN'T HAVE OTHERWISE. THAT WAY SHE'LL KNOW WE'VE GOT IT, AND WE WON'T HAVE TO BRING IT TO THE CAMP.

The Duke can't follow that, so Kimo translates for him. He doesn't say anything, but it's clear as crissle he wishes he'd thought of it.

Lamarque says something, and the Duke drops his hands, and they start talking. Creek figures he's catching Lamarque up on everything that was said, since he only got half the conversation. Lamarque just joined the gang about six weeks ago, when his folks got lost trying to cross the river. He's okay. He's got an honest face, so black it's almost blue. He can't really shape yet. He's trying to learn, but he gets lost easily.

The Duke picks up the cube and shoves it toward Creek. He backs away, raising his hands. *I DON'T KNOW HOW IT WORKS!*

Kimo intervenes. *I DO,* she shapes. *MY PARENTS HAD ONE.* Kimo doesn't talk about her family much, but Creek knows they were elites — doctors at one of the clinics around old Baltimore. He figures that's how they scored the Ear for her. Baltimore was one of the last cities to go. He knows Kimo's parents and her little sister didn't make it, but he doesn't know why. Maybe plague. Maybe a raid. Some say units of the Texas Confederacy still roam the South, more bandits than army. Some say they still have pocket nukes. She hasn't told anyone what happened, and he won't pry. She somehow made it up here, and that's good enough for him. She seems okay. So, she lost her family. Every last one of them has a story. Hers is happier than Candela's.

The Duke starts chattering away at Kimo, a mile a minute. Making plans, giving orders. The usual.

Creek can't take it anymore. His stomach is about to crack open with hunger. *CAN WE EAT FIRST?*

The Duke snaps out of his frenzy and looks at him like he's nuts. Then it clicks and he nods. They're all starving. They grab sticks and skewer a sausage apiece. They use tiles that have fallen off the wall of the pump room for plates. The Duke shouts over his shoulder, and Candela appears. Baby must be sleeping.

Creek's heart starts up pounding. She's so pretty — her plump body lush and soft under her loose dress, her dark brown hair falling freely around her round face and tapering chin, her skin warm as buttered toast. She makes Creek want to crawl into her lap and lose himself, though he's way too big for that now.

Creek lifts the sausage on its stick and takes a bite from one end. It explodes in his mouth, hot juices and salt, and the perfect snap of the skin. He laughs as the liquid runs down his chin. Kimo starts laughing too, and pretty soon the whole gang is giggling and chomping. The meal feels like a warm hug in their bellies.

When breakfast is over, Creek takes the cube out from beneath the mattress. It's about the size of Baby's head, its brushed chrome sides shining dully in the late-morning light. He puts it on the ground next to the solar plate. They all look at it for a minute. It's so beautiful. Magical. An artifact from another world.

WHAT SHOULD WE MAKE? asks the Duke.

IT WILL HAVE TO BE ORGANIC-BASED, shapes Kimo. She presses on the side, and an invisible drawer pops open, revealing a collection of tiny vials. *THESE ARE DIFFERENT COMPOUNDS FOR MAKING MORE COMPLICATED STUFF — CIRCUITS AND MEDICINES AND THINGS LIKE THAT. BUT WE DON'T HAVE THE OTHER MATERIALS TO MAKE ANY OF THOSE. WE COULD PROBABLY MAKE SOMETHING PLASTIC WITH THOSE ENERGY BARS WE FOUND ON THE DEAD GUY.*

They go back and forth, suggesting various ideas. It can't be something they could just find at a homesteader's or at the abandoned mall at Breezewood (it's pretty cleaned out, doubtful they could find much there, anyway). Kimo has the best idea, and they finally settle on something they hope will convince the Lady.

Creek goes inside and gets the bars, all individually packaged in foil. Nobody really likes them – they're old and dry and bland – but they are still edible, and food is food, so everyone feels a little solemn when Kimo breaks four of them out of their sleeves and drops them into the compartment at the top. She presses a corner, and a transparent touchscreen rises out of one side. The orange letters, floating in space, fascinate Creek. He wishes he could read.

Baby wakes up, and Candela goes in and brings him out, pressing him against her side. He looks around at them, chewing on his damp, tiny hands. They all get very still.

Kimo's fingers dance over the screen, pressing little boxes that make green check marks appear. Then everything disappears except for a square blue button.

She looks up. *Ready?*

The Duke nods. She presses the button and the screen slides back into the box. They wait. After about two minutes, the screen slides out again, displaying words in bright green letters.

ALL DONE, shapes Kimo. She presses the box down low, and one of the sides lowers down like a little stage. She reaches in, takes out a small object, and holds it up to the light. It's a flat disk, about as big as a daisy, made of clear plastic like you hardly ever see anymore. In the center is a perfect little filigree of a leaping deer, its head turned to look behind it. Underneath, letters run along the edge. Creek knows they say, "Lady Fal." It stirs a memory in his mind – cold, a fir tree, a strong hand holding his. He can't place it. Somewhere before…

Candela gasps when she sees the crystal ornament, and thrusts Baby into the Duke's un-expecting hands. She takes the ornament and turns it in the light. Her eyes sparkle. She and the Duke have a busy conversation. She wants to keep it, that much is clear, but the Duke keeps shaking his head. Creek turns to Kimo for a translation.

SHE THINKS WE SHOULD MAKE MORE AND SELL THEM, BUT HE SAYS WE WOULD NEVER GET AS MUCH AS WE WILL FOR

THE MACHINE. He's glad Kimo is here to keep him in the loop. These crazy hearing kids.

Candela frowns and takes Baby back. Then, shoving him up against her hip, she turns to Kimo and asks her something.

Kimo frowns. *I DON'T KNOW HOW MUCH POWER IT HAS. IT'S PRETTY OLD AND IT'S BEEN SITTING FOR A LONG TIME…*

Candela leans in, pleading.

Kimo checks with the Duke, who nods. Go ahead.

She takes the last four energy bars and drops them into the compartment at the top. She brings out the screen and starts tapping away. Then she gets Candela to lean into the device. Candela presses Baby's cheek against hers and smiles while Kimo presses a button. Then Kimo takes out a couple of the tiny vials from the side and inserts them one at a time into a little hole that appears on the top. She finishes inputting the instructions and starts the recombination process.

When it finishes, she pulls out another little disk. It looks exactly like the first one, except instead of the deer, a small photograph of Candela and Baby smiles from the center of a ring of little flowers.

Candela takes the little ornament and stares at it in awe, her mouth open. She wraps Kimo in a big hug, smashing her and Baby against her breast. Creek looks away.

Lamarque taps the Duke on the shoulder and makes a quick gesture with his head. The Duke nods.

LET'S GO, he shapes.

Chapter 4

"Lucinda, time to come down." Her mother's voice cuts through the music playing in her mind — music Sebastien gave her — like a hot poker behind her eye. She'd been distracting herself by exploring the ruins of the Acropolis — long lost now beyond the sea — to the accompaniment of his mandolin. With a sigh, she taps off her COR, takes one last look in the mirror at herself, and heads downstairs. They asked for pretty. Well, she looks pretty.

"Nonas wouldn't dare," Martin Gilchrist says, sipping his Scotch. Lucinda's father has pulled out all the stops, opening his last bottle of 130-year-old Glenfiddich. Rumor has it there were only eleven bottles in the Enclave. There would never be any more. "They know we've got the heat guns working again. They couldn't get within fifty yards of the wall."

Gilchrist holds court at the mantel, his ruddy face glowing with wealth and confidence. He looks up as she descends. "Here she is," he says, like he's considering buying her to display in his foyer. Lucinda scans the room. Mrs. Gilchrist perches beside her mother, ankles crossed and eyes on her hands, folded over the perfect pleats of her lilac skirt. Lucinda can't remember her name — something floral, like her own mom. Tommy slumps on the other side of her. He looks ill at ease, and keeps scratching behind his right ear. Lucinda hasn't seen him in a while and had forgotten how bad his acne was, and how sullen and insipid he always looked. She crosses to the armchair and takes a seat, trying to mimic the way the other women sit — not because she wants to please them, but because she wants to avoid her mother's repressed displeasure, and the inevitable dressing down she will get from her father after the ordeal is over. He stands behind her chair, like a prison guard ready to prevent an escape.

"No doubt about it," he says, picking up the thread like the toady he is. "Our boys can handle anything the Nonas throw at us." He says 'the boys', even though Defense has been mixed-gendered for almost twenty years. Lucinda wants to point out that she will be one of 'the boys' in two weeks, if all goes well, but she bites her tongue.

Still, she can't stay out of it altogether. "What about this new guy?" She says. "The Doctor, or whatever he's called. I heard he took out Bedford Estates, and they have heat guns *and* ion canisters."

"Where did you hear that?" asks Gilchrist, drawing himself up like an affronted praying mantis. "It wasn't on the COR Gazette."

Lucinda shrugs. "It was on some thread. People know things, you know."

Lucinda's mother frowns, and she can feel her dad tense up behind her. Mrs. Gilchrist leans in to dispel the tension. "The Doctor. Why these petty thugs need to come up with these ridiculous monikers, I'll never know. Pump themselves up, I suppose. So dramatic."

"Exactly," says Lucinda's dad.

Mollified, or at least distracted, Gilchrist changes the subject. "Your father tells me you're taking the Defense exam, Lucinda, is that right?"

"Next week."

He nods. "Interesting choice. Well, good luck with that." His tone asks, 'What are you thinking, young lady?'

Lucinda's father steps forward. "It's just the exam," he says. *Thanks for the support, Dad.*

Gilchrist puts his hand on his son's shoulder. "Tommy's going into the Finance and Trade department, aren't you, boy?"

"Yep," says Tommy. The room falls silent, waiting for him to follow up with something. Anything. He just stares at the floor.

Gilchrist breaks the impasse. "In any case, I don't think we need to worry about the Doctor, Lucy." Lucinda has never let anyone call her Lucy. Ever. But her mother snaps her a warning look, so she bites her tongue. The silence falls again, stretching out until it seems as if it has always existed, and will never be broken.

At long last, Gilchrist nods to his wife. She turns to Tommy and says in a voice like a little bird, "Don't you have something to say, Tommy dear?"

He doesn't answer for a minute, and Lucinda entertains a wild hope that he'll bolt from the room and kill the whole idea. But he clears his throat, and, without looking at her, begins to mutter in his dull, grating voice. "So, Lucinda, I wanted to ask you…" Her heart begins to thud. "Um, I was wondering, you know, I was thinking, like…" His father steps forward, amping up the pressure. "I'm twenty-one, and you're…what, like almost twenty, and they think…I mean, I think it's time to think about, you know, like settling down. So I'm wondering…" His mother touches his knee, delicately, as if it were an injured mouse. "I mean, I'm asking if you'll, you know, marry me."

She knew it was coming. As soon as her mother told her to make herself pretty. It was her duty, for the Enclave, to pair up and reproduce. She loves her home, and she feels proud to serve, but *Tommy Gilchrist?*

It's not that Tommy is *that* bad. He's good with his COR. They were on opposite sides of a mock debate in school on which contributed more to the Collapse — the Hetara Pandemics or Civil War Three — and he impressed her with his quickness and acumen. When he wasn't moping on the sofa, he had a biting humor and a wicked talent for cutting people down to size. But she feels the ghost of Sebastien's hot touch on the skin of her back, the ecstatic throbbing deep inside her, the image of glowing passion in his huge, dark eyes. Even if she isn't sure her feelings for him are real, they are more real than what she feels for Tommy Gilchrist. Which is nothing.

Everyone is looking at her. She taps her COR and queries 'proposal refusals' to see if anything useful comes up. She finds a letter by Charlotte Brontë. A bit old-fashioned, but at least some words to say. Heart in her mouth, her face flaming red as her hair, she begins to recite it.

"Tommy…Um…You are aware that I have many reasons to feel gratified to your family, and that I have peculiar reasons for affection towards…" *Poor choice. Too grand. Too late.* "…that I have peculiar reasons for affection towards…" *damn, he doesn't have a sister* "…towards your little brother…" *I mean, I did babysit him a few times* —"and also that I highly esteem yourself. Do not therefore accuse me of wrong motives when I say that my answer to your proposal must be…" *'decided negative' is way too strong* —"a regretful 'No.' In forming this decision, I trust I have listened to the dictates of conscience more than to those of inclination; I have no personal repugnance to the idea of a union with you — but I feel convinced that mine is not the sort of disposition calculated to form the happiness of a man like you. It has always been my habit to study the character of those amongst whom I chance to be thrown…" *Oh God, what does that even mean?* "…and I think I know yours and can imagine what description of woman would suit you for a wife. Her character should not be too marked, ardent, and original — her temper should be mild, her piety undoubted, her spirits even and cheerful, and her 'personal attractions' sufficient to please your eye and gratify your just pride. As for me, you do not… I am not this serious, grave, cool-headed individual you suppose — you would think me romantic and eccentric —" *Okay, this part is better* — "You would say I was satirical and severe. However, I scorn deceit and I will never, for the sake of attaining the distinction of matrimony and escaping the stigma of an old maid —" *Old Maid? Oh my God* — "take a worthy man whom I am conscious I cannot render happy." *Ugh.*

Lucinda takes a deep breath. A long silence slumps like a dead thing over the party. At last, her father says, "What on earth was that?"

She swallows and says, "What I feel. I'm sorry." She surveys the shocked faces staring at her like some sort of wild animal. Except for Tommy, who looks at the floor and gives the tiniest little snort of laughter. She wonders if he's identified the passage. If any of the others have, they give no sign. Her mother looks straight ahead, as if looking for some new daughter to manifest out of thin air in the middle of the room.

Lucinda can feel her father's anger through her back. But all he says is, "Roger, can I get you another drink?"

"What the hell was that, young lady?" They haven't moved since the Gilchrists left. A brief but awkward dribble of chitchat, and they excused themselves. Gilchrist walked past her like she was part of the wall. Tommy muttered "Cya" without looking up, but he had that smirk still ghosting his face. Lucinda figures he felt the same way about the matter as she did.

"I was trying to be nice."

"You were rude."

"Tommy Gilchrist? I barely know him. Now you want me to spend the rest of my life with him?"

"The Gilchrists are—"

"Very Important People. I know."

"They came to us. It's humiliating."

"I'm sorry, Dad. I am. But I just can't—"

"Birth rates are down sixteen percent from five years ago. And with the outbreak, the Enclave population is seven hundred and thirty-four below peak. Seven hundred and thirty-four, Lucinda. That means treatment facilities understaffed, maintenance crews falling behind, watchtowers unmanned."

"I know."

"Our Enclave is the last one within a hundred and twenty miles — maybe in the whole Northeast! The Nona warlords are getting stronger every day. We need you and your generation to step up, or our way of life will disappear."

"I know." She bows her head.

He finally sits, gesturing to her to sit beside him. She complies. "It's not *just* your duty, Lu," he says, his voice softer. It reminds her of when she was thirteen and failed to make the soccer team. Gentle, caring. Loving. *On the outside.* She waits for the hammer. "Not just your duty. It's your life. It's all our lives."

"I know." She can only manage a whisper.

"So, why?"

"I just…you surprised me. I wasn't ready."

"Well, get ready." *Here it comes.*

"Not with Tommy. Sorry. He's just…I just can't."

"Who then? If you have a better idea, we can explore it. But right now, Tommy is the only option on the table, and time is wasting."

Lucinda can feel her mother's eyes burning a hole through the top of her head. "I don't know…there's…it's just…" She trails off. How can she explain? She knew this was coming. Almost all of her friends were paired off by now. Dina and Rob, Heather and Jason, Jessica and Talbot. Claire, Elizabeth, and Emma already had babies. She hoped that accelerating her push to join Defense would distract her parents enough to put it off until… *Sebastien. No.* But something. She doesn't know.

Her mother's voice slices through her reverie. "Is there something you're not telling us, Lucinda?" She winces at the sharpness of her gaze. She feels naked, exposed, as if every instant of her liaisons with Sebastien were laid out across the coffee table to be dissected and judged.

"No, mom," she lies.

They look at her. "Go upstairs," her father says. "And think about what you've done, and what's going to change."

Lucinda nods and heads up the stairs, smothering the urge to run. Safe in her room, she escapes into the ecstasy of her COR, and waits for night to come.

"It's not fair," she whispers into Sebastien's shoulder. "I was tapping some books from the early 2000s, and people didn't get married till they were in their thirties."

She can't stay long. She told her mother she was going to the library to check out some data chips — older training knowledge that wasn't on the clouds. Not a total lie. The chips were in the library; she just didn't need them to pass the test. She only had an hour before she had to get back. But she had to see him. Touch him.

"I know," he says. "I mean, I didn't know *that*. I've never read an actual book. I know it's not fair. But…they're not wrong, either."

"Oh, thanks. That's great." Lucinda punches him gently on the arm.

"I mean, you have it *good* in here. All this stuff. Your COR thing. All the food. Beds, and houses, and streets. It took us twelve hours to get here from Concord Market. We got stuck at 128 because the bridge had collapsed — *again*, and then we had to go way out of our way to avoid Lady Fal's territory. It's rough out there."

"I know. But…"

"You have to make sacrifices. You can't have everything you want."

"Why not?"

"No one can."

"I just want you." She snuggles up against him, her head on his chest. "Do you?"

Lucinda doesn't answer. Can't. *What does she want?* A subterranean ocean of inchoate desire, lapping gently at the shores of her awareness, rises up, crashing over her, drowning her. She wants…everything. Anything.

"I have to go," she says. She unglues herself from his body and starts to dress. "I can't come tomorrow. I've got my practical."

"Okay. Are you coming to the show?"

"When is it?"

"I told you."

She grins. "I know. But I forgot."

He sighs, irritated but resigned. "Friday."

"Of course I'll be there. If I pass my practical, that is. If I don't, my dad won't let me go anywhere. Then I'll definitely be married off to some third-rank button-mule." She's feeling better. He has that effect — making her feel sexy, independent, powerful. She runs her finger up his side. He shivers.

"What is the practical, anyway? You never said."

"It's a mock-repair of one of the countermeasures."

"The what?"

"Countermeasures, dummy. You know, the defenses around the perimeter. You've never seen them?"

"No. Why should I?"

"I don't know. You live out there," she waves vaguely. "I thought maybe you'd seen a battle or a siege sometime."

"We've been lucky."

"Not as lucky as me." She kisses him. He smiles, and her heart lights up. "You know that green field out there that runs around the wall? It's a death trap for Nonalites. Spikes, flame jets, mines, nerve agents. Really nasty stuff. Defense is in charge of keeping it all running, and they test you by sending you out to 'repair' one. It's really hard. You have to tap your COR for the right information, and make incredibly subtle adjustments, or you, you know, 'die.' Not really. But you fail, and then you're out."

"Sounds fun. You shouldn't call us that, you know."

"What?"

"Nonalite. It's dismissive."

"I don't understand."

"You're *whelite*, right?"

"I guess."

"So, we're NON-whelite. Non."

"I never thought about it. What should I call them? I mean, you?"

"We call ourselves Niners."

"That's funny." Lucinda taps her COR but comes up empty. Not something the Enclavers thought was important. "What does it mean?"

Sebastien shrugs. "No idea. It used to be Ninety-niners when my dad was young, but it got shortened. It's the proper term for the people out there."

"Okay, Mr. Niner," she leans in and nuzzles his neck. He puts his arms around her. His deep-well eyes pour into hers.

"You'll be at the concert?"

"Of course I will."

"My dad is giving me a solo this time."

"I wish I could play an instrument." Lucinda's not sure whether she really does, but she knows he'll like that, so she says it anyway.

"It's not so great," says Sebastien.

"I think it is."

"It's just what I do." He's acting all modest, but she can tell he's pleased. "Can't you just load 'How to Play the Flute' into your COR, or whatever?"

"I could, I suppose, but that doesn't mean I could, you know, play it. I would know how it's supposed to be done — all the steps and positions and notes and things — but it's just knowledge. My muscles don't know what to do, just my brain."

"Just knowledge."

"Yeah. *Just* knowledge." She sighs. "I really need to go."

"Sure." As she starts to rise, he stops her. "Wait a second," he says, as he roots around under a pile of prop tabulae, knocking them over. He pulls out a small sheet of vellum. Lucinda can make out words shining blue on the transparent surface. Sebastien hands it to her. "I…wrote this for you."

She blushes, her heart suddenly up between her ears. She takes the vellum. As her fingers touch it, a quiet melody begins to play, delicate phrases sounded on a mandolin. "What is it?"

"Read it. It's something I wrote. It's not as good as Colery, or whatever, but still…"

She wishes she didn't have to pull her eyes away from the moon of his face, but she forces herself to focus on the words.

My nightingale will come at night
Her eyes like stars, her skin so white
Her mind like crystal shining bright
Her voice like gentle water flowing.

She sings to me of wondrous things
Of spinning nebulae and rings
Of fire and subatomic strings
And creatures in the oceans glowing.

And as I listen I can feel
My heart start spinning like a wheel
My soul imprinted with her seal
Her love the only thing worth knowing.

Lucinda can't speak for a long time. "Oh my God," she says at last.

Chapter 5

The Lady Fal's compound commands the top of a hill not far from the remains of one of the east-west roads. It must have been a densely populated area: Foundations and piles of debris fill the spaces between the trees, and they have to be careful as they make their way not to fall into a hidden hole or half-filled basement. Six ten-meter double-wides, parked end to end in a wide curve, form the outer perimeter, with a few rangers slotted in to fill the gaps and act as gates on wheels. The camp backs up against the side of an ancient water tower – a three-hundred-year-old edifice of local sandstone that now houses the Lady's offices, private quarters, storehouse, and armory. The open space in front is dotted with tents and makeshift huts for the militia and its hangers-on. Someone has hung an ancient sign on the side of one of the double-wides. Creek can't read letters, but Kimo spells it out for him: *Entering Arlington, Established 1635.*

Creek's heart thumps as one of the rangers backs up, creating a breach in the wall, and they pass between two of the caravans into the crowded camp. He glances at Kimo. *What have we got ourselves into?*

Tough-looking Niners and pale-faced whelite outcasts eye them as they make their way toward the curving facade of the building. The sun is out for a change, and everything looks bright and harsh and threatening.

They have decided that Creek should wear the Neural Ear for the meeting. Creek hates the Ear. It looks stupid, for one thing, like he's got a pot on his head — or a porcupine, the way the little probes dig into his scalp.

It's uncomfortable as all get out, and the unwelcome cacophony hurts his head. He doesn't know how it works. Kimo says it excites certain centers of the brain to translate sounds into meaning. He just knows it took forever to train it before its AI figured out his brain patterns (hours with the Duke or Candela — 'this is a rock, this is a tree, watch me jump, watch me lie down' — so stupid). He much prefers the clarity and simplicity of normal life. And he really hates that the Ear talks for him. He's jealous that Kimo doesn't need it to, since she could mouth-talk before she went deaf. But he never learned. How could he? Why should he? So, if he wants to communicate with any hearing people besides the gang, he has to let it do the talking for him. It's convenient, but to think that some robot voice is making words that supposedly match his thoughts really flares him. How can he know what it's really saying?

The Duke has been making Creek and Kimo practice with the Ear. He says they need to be ready to deal with 'normal' folk if they want to get ahead. *Normal, my eye…* Kimo doesn't mind it as much as he does, but she's like that. The Duke insisted that Creek might have to tell the Lady where and how they got the cube, so Creek has the damn thing strapped to his head, feeling like a foolie.

They arrive at the entrance to the tower. A tall Niner with a handsome brown face and a short goatee slouches in a canvas-backed chair, reading a book. A real antique book, made of paper. The Duke steps forward. Creek can tell that he's nervous, but he pretends to be cool and collected. "We've got a meeting with Lady Fal." The meaning buzzes in his head like a bee.

"Do you," says the man. It's not a question.

"Yes. We are here to negotiate a deal."

"Are you."

"Yes." There's a pause while the man looks them up and down. "May we go in, please?" says the Duke.

The man doesn't move. The kids look at each other. The Duke is just about to speak again when the man says, "Wait here." He takes his time getting up, and gives them another once-over before he disappears into the gloom of the building. The Duke turns to the others, a big smile breaking over his face. "Easy," he says.

The man comes back out almost immediately. "They'll come and get you in a minute," he says. He sits down and goes back to his book. Creek wonders what it is. It's pretty thick. The pages are yellow-brown and swollen from water damage.

They stand there for much longer than a minute. Time drags on. The Duke shifts from foot to foot, nervous as a garbage rat. The sun beats down on them. Creek eyes the shade where the man sits. Probably ten degrees cooler there. But he doesn't want to get too close, so he just sucks it up and takes it, raising his hand to shield his eyes.

The man keeps glancing up from his book to Creek's face. After about twenty minutes, he shuts it, holding his place with a finger.

"Do I know you?" he asks. Creek just looks at him. He does look familiar. His face is weathered, and his eyes are very, very sad, as if they've seen a million people die.

Another tall Niner appears in the shadows of the doorway. "Come with me." They file in, the Duke first, followed by Kimo and Creek.

The Niner leads them into the interior of the building. The ceiling vaults above them, thirty meters up. Long, horizontal windows just below the ceiling let in the bright afternoon sun, sending beams of light angling through the air, salted with dancing dust. The space has been divided into rooms by curtains of thick, red cloth on long horizontal poles about three meters above the ground, bound together by an assortment of ropes and cables. The Niner ushers them through one of these curtains into the presence of the Lady.

Lady Fal sits on a simple campstool with a tabula in her hand. The first thing that strikes Creek is the shimmer of her skin, dark and smooth like polished wood. Her hair is white and cut very short, accentuating the darkness of her face. Her cheekbones are high, her eyes large and slightly slanted. Her ruddy lips seem caught in a perpetual half-smile, like she's thinking about a joke she never shares. She wears a combat jacket over a knee-length dress patterned with small flowers, dusky canvas leggings, and worn leather boots that come up just above her ankles.

Lady Fal sets the tabula on a small three-legged table beside her chair and leans forward, clasping her hands together. "Hello again," she says, looking at Kimo. Creek briefly wishes he could hear the sound of her voice instead of the strange spikes of meaning that the Ear punches into his brain. He imagines it must be warm and full, delicious and comforting, like the soup Denissa used to serve at the shelter.

"I'm glad you came back. It's Kimo, right?" Her expression projects a kindly interest, but he can't shake the feeling that there is something else going on under the surface that he can't see.

Kimo nods and glances up at the Duke. He steps forward slightly. "We're here to negotiate the sale of a Maxwell TXM-3000 Recreate Mini that has come into our possession."

"Yes, Kimo told me. Where is it?"

"It's at our camp."

"And how do I know that?"

"We made this." The Duke jams his hand into his pocket. Man, is he nervous. The edges of his confidence are fraying badly. Creek hopes he doesn't muff it. The Lady watches him struggle, the bemused expression on her face unchanging. At last, he digs out the disk and hands it to her. "As you can see, it's custom. We made it from some uneaten food. You can see that we are in earnest."

Lady Fal takes the disk and turns it in her hands, holding it up so that the light from the high windows strikes it, sending sparks flashing along the wall.

"That's very thoughtful of you. My emblem, I see."

She places the ornament on top of the tabula and looks back at them. She focuses on Kimo, even though the conversation is with the Duke. Kimo's round face looks pale and worried, trapped in the Lady's gaze. "What do I need a Recreate for, now?"

"What don't you need it for?" asks the Duke, trying to regain his confidence. "You can make almost anything out of anything – you can replace electronic components, make medicine, anything you need. You know as well as I do that around here, every place has been pretty well cleaned out. Equipment is failing every day because nobody has the parts anymore. With a Recreate, you can make anything — below a certain size, of course." Creek looks at the Duke in surprise. Quite a speech. He must have rehearsed it.

"Where did you get this marvelous machine? As you say, the area *is* cleaned out. We haven't seen anything like it since the Counterstrike. How did a group of children come by such a treasure?"

The Duke bristles at the word 'children', but doesn't rise to the bait. He looks at Creek and nods. The Lady's attention sweeps them over, landing on Creek. He feels like he's been caught in a searchlight while sneaking around doing something he oughtn't. He looks away, then forces his gaze back to meet her eyes. He's got the story all prepared, so he takes a deep breath and begins. He shapes as the Ear speaks, so he can be sure it's saying what he wants to say.

"WHEN MY PARENTS DIED, I WAS RESCUED BY A SCIENTIST WHO WAS DOING FIELDWORK OVER BY THE SANDITON ENCLAVE. HE GOT ALLOWED TO BRING ME BACK INSIDE AND TOOK CARE OF ME FOR A WHILE. THE CUBE BELONGED TO HIM. YOU KNOW HOW SANDITON GOT WRECKED BY TC REGULARS WHEN THEY RETREATED LAST YEAR? WELL, HE GRABBED A BUNCH OF STUFF INCLUDING THE RECREATE AND WE SNUCK OUT THROUGH A CULVERT WHILE THE ATTACK WAS GOING ON. BUT DR. RUSH — THAT WAS THE SCIENTIST — HE CUT HIS

HAND ON A RUSTY GRATE WHILE WE WERE ESCAPING AND GOT SICK WITH THE TETANUS AND DIED. I TOOK THE RECREATE WITH ME AND HOOKED UP WITH THE DUKE AND KIMO AND THE OTHERS A COUPLE WEEKS AGO." He hopes the artificial voice can convince the Lady. There's enough truth in the story to sound plausible, and he has learned how to make his face appear sincere to grown-ups.

"Why didn't Dr. Rush make up a dose of multi-vax, or some other treatment for his condition? He had the machine, right?" The Lady smiles at him, innocent and threatening at the same time. Creek hadn't thought of that. His mind goes blank, a sick wave of fear sweeping up his face. *Pull yourself together.*

"HE NEVER HAD THE CHANCE. HE GOT FEVERISH AND COULDN'T DO IT HIMSELF. HE TRIED TO TELL ME HOW, BUT HE DIDN'T KNOW SHAPING AND HE WAS SO SICK I COULDN'T UNDERSTAND HIM." Part of that is true, too. Just not the part about the machine. The memory of the scientist staring up at him, his face a twisted mask of agony, suddenly fills his head, and he can feel his own face go all sad and scared. He hopes it's enough to convince the Lady.

He steps back, praying his part is done. His head is starting to hurt from using the Ear. It takes a lot of concentration to make it work, and he's not used to it. He wonders how Kimo can have it on so much of the day.

But Lady Fal keeps him in her knifing gaze. "Well," she says. "What do you want for it?"

The Duke intervenes. "We were hoping you'd make an offer first. We know what it's worth, but we'd like to hear what you think it's worth first."

The Lady smiles and looks at him for the first time. "Very smart. You know what you're doing." She sits up straight, placing her hands on her knees. Creek can tell that she's quite tall, at almost two meters.

"I'm very impressed with you, children," she says. "But here's the thing. Kimo, you're such a sweet young lady, but I had to check out your story, so I had you followed last night after you left here. I like to be thorough. When I heard you had arrived this morning, I sent a ranger over there with a couple of my men, and they found some friends of yours and invited them back here. I wanted to meet all of you. Such nice kids!" She calls "Sandoval?" and the Niner with the book pokes his head through the curtain.

"Lady?"

"I believe our other guests have arrived. Will you show them in?"

The man disappears, and a few seconds later, Lamarque and Candela are thrust through the curtain, looking very scared. Candela has Baby strapped to her chest. He's fast asleep. Lamarque holds the cube like a dead frog in his hands.

"Hello and welcome," says the Lady, spreading her arms. "What a pretty baby! What's its name?"

Candela stares at the Lady like a rabbit caught in a snare. "Just Baby," she whispers.

"I'm sure you'll come up with a name soon, honey. I'll take that, young man." She holds out her hands to Lamarque, and he passes her the Recreate, hypnotized with terror.

"Well, children. Thank you for this lovely gift. I will put it to good use." She sets the machine on the little table. Right in front of them, but it might as well be the moon. Gone forever.

"Now, what am I going to do about you? It's not safe for children to be wandering about in the woods on their own. What to do with you?"

Creek tenses up. He can feel the presence of Sandoval and the other man — tall, dark shadows — looming in the space behind them. He's sure that any second they're going to grab them all, take them out and shoot them. His heartbeat rises into his throat.

"You're very capable young people," says the Lady, after a long pause. "As I said, I'm impressed. It would be a shame to lose you. I'm sure I can find something for you to do. But you'll be staying with us now."

Chapter 6

You shot him."

Krauner stands in the doorway, digging his thumbnail into the side of his forefinger. The pain helps him focus. His commander sits obscured in the shadowed office, the red pinpoint of his robotic eye shining like Mars in the darkness.

"I had to, Doctor," Krauner answers. "He lost it. We couldn't just let him off. You know, make an example. It's one of your first instruc—"

"It never occurred to you to ask him who had taken it?" Krauner swallows. "Perhaps get a clue as to its present whereabouts? But that is beside the point, isn't it? Who cares if he had somehow lost it? He should never have had it in the first place. Should he?"

"No, sir."

"You had a simple job, Krauner. Transport my lab equipment from the forward position at Bedford Estates back here. A job you've done successfully, what? Six times? And yet, somehow you managed to get ambushed by a pack of Niners and lose everything."

"I'm sorry, sir. The transport cracked an axle, and—"

"Do you really think I care about your excuses?"

"No, sir."

The Doctor stands, still veiled in shadow. "Then, you find the Recreate in the hands of this junk man, but arrive too late to retrieve it."

"I'll find it, sir. Please, trust me. I'll find it." Krauner resists the urge to wipe the sweat from his brow. The tickling wants to drive him mad, but he holds on.

"No need. As usual, I have done your work for you. I know where it is."

"That's excellent news, sir."

"The same cannot be said for the rest of the equipment. And, as I'm sure you *don't* know, lieutenant, the Recreate is useless to me without the entire apparatus."

"Let me retrieve it for you, sir. I won't fail you."

The Doctor puts his hard, robotic hand on Krauner's shoulder. "My good man. You have been a hard-working, loyal soldier for me. But you can't expect me to give you chance upon chance upon chance." Krauner's stomach plummets into his heels. "Don't worry. I won't shoot you like you did that poor junk seller. No, no, no. I'll keep you in my employ. But in a different capacity. Durain!"

A slight officer in a trim uniform appears out of nowhere. Krauner's heart pounds. He thinks he might be sick. The Doctor turns to the newcomer. "Take this gentleman to the Pen."

Chapter 7

Lucinda's head aches as she comes out into the gray, rainy morning. Despite her magic time with Sebastien, she didn't sleep well. The reality of the morning's ordeal ambushed her as she lay in bed, and she found herself tapping every countermeasure she could think of, in the hopes that some of the information would remain in her meat mind. When she finally dozed off, she suffered through a long, unsettling dream in which she and Sebastien were trying to cross the greensward, and countermeasures were going off all around them. She had tried to warn him, but he kept getting hit by them. They didn't kill him, but he was repeatedly stabbed by spikes and burned by flame jets. They would almost make it across, and it would start again. She woke up exhausted.

Her mother is in the kitchen, of course, when she comes down. She doesn't speak to Lucinda, or even look at her. She moves around the stove with quiet efficiency, preparing eggs and toast. Lucinda brews herself some camomile tea, then sits at the counter. She's grateful for the silence. Her mother sets the plate in front of her, then heads to the sink to wash the skillet.

"You were back late," she says.

"I know. More studying."

"I thought the library closed at nine. It was after eleven when you came in."

Lucinda focuses on her meal. She had let her desire get the better of her, and they had made love a second time. She knows she should be more careful, but after the gift of the poem, she just couldn't help herself. "They let me stay late," she lies.

Her mother finishes up the washing, dries her hands, and removes her apron. "Do you want me to drive you to the barracks?"

"No thanks, I'll walk. I need to get my blood moving. I didn't sleep well."

She hopes this will prompt her mother to show some tender concern, but Marigold just gives her a robotic smile, says, "All right then," and goes out into the living room. Lucinda sits for a while, staring into her tea. After a few minutes, her dad bustles in.

"Ready?" he asks.

"As ready as I'll ever be." She looks up at him, trying to gauge his mood. He smiles at her, and she relaxes. "I'm ready."

"You're sure this is what you want?"

"Yes, Daddy."

"Well, give 'em hell."

"Yes, sir."

"Do you want me to drive you?"

"No thanks, I need to get my blood moving."

"Good luck, sweetheart." He puts his hand on her shoulder. It's the first time he has touched her in who knows how long. Even though she knows he's secretly hoping she will fail, and come round to marrying Tommy or somebody like him, the gesture moves her, and her eyes fill.

"Thanks, Daddy."

She didn't need to go by the Arts Center to get to the Defense building, and she couldn't sneak in and see Sebastien anyway, but she wanted to know he was in there, so she took a roundabout route. She taps her COR to check her messages. Mems from Charyse and Tina wishing her good luck, and a funny vidmeme from Jimmy Choate of a monkey with a bazooka — "Blow that test away!" Half a dozen others. She's still popular with the A-listers, even if she has defied the expected by going Defense.

Oh God. There's a whole letter from Sheena. *Can't that girl take a hint?* It's embarrassing. She sends a quick thumbs up to all the messages but Sheena's. If she keeps ghosting her, sooner or later, the girl has got to figure it out.

The flashing lights of a police cart bring her back to herself as she turns the corner. A small crowd has gathered across from the Arts Center. There's a medical van parked by the curb. Near the front of the crowd, she sees someone she knows: Tate Blanchard. She went to school with him. She doesn't know him well, but she knows he lives nearby.

"Hey, Tate, what's going on?"

His face is red with excitement. "You know those musicians? They came from outside and were going to play this weekend?"

"I know they're here," she says.

"Well, one of them has got it."

"Got what?" But she knows.

"*IT,* Lucinda. *Mindworm.* I guess the director went to check on them and let them out of quarantine when the guy went nuts and tried to break through the barrier."

Lucinda's heart starts to pound. "Which one?"

"Which one what?"

"Which one of the musicians?"

"No idea."

"They're a family. I think," she says, as if she didn't know them all intimately. "There's a father and a son and wife and a daughter. Was it the father or the son? Older or younger?" Blood pumps in her temples. As if in answer, her COR buzzes violently. She winces and grabs the side of her head. "Ow!"

"You okay?" asks Tate.

"I'm fine." She shakes it off. "So, do you know which one?"

"No. What difference does it make? Stupid Nonas. My dad says we never should let them in. I can't believe—"

"They're people, Tate." She hardly knows what she's saying.

"Barely," he says, snorting.

Three figures in pandemic gear climb out of the medical van. The crowd writhes, some people moving forward, some falling back. The three converse briefly, then head into the building.

"What's going to happen to them?" Lucinda asks, more to herself than to Tate.

"They'll throw them in the woods, I guess," he answers. "So much for the concert. Sucks to be them. Good thing nobody was in contact with them. At least we have the quarantine."

Lucinda walks away without answering. *It can't be him. Can it?* Her head throbs. Her skin is clammy and hot at the same time. She stops beneath an old sycamore, huddled alone, waiting to see who comes out of the building. One last look. But nobody comes out. Ten minutes go by. The crowd gets restless, and a few people move off. Twenty minutes. She can't wait anymore. She is already late. And she doesn't know if she even wants to see who comes out. With a violent shake of her head, she takes off down the street.

Thirteen minutes late, Lucinda arrives at a long, squat brick of a building jammed up against the wall. A wooden sign – white letters on a green background – juts up beside the walkway. It looks like it belongs in front of a garden center. Instead, it reads, "Hamilton Enclave Defense Corps – East Quadrant". She barely slows as she skips by, through the swishing door into the windowless barrack.

"You're late," Sorenson grunts from behind the front desk. He doesn't look up from his monitor. She's only known him for a few days, but already she doesn't like him. Or to be more accurate, he doesn't like her.

"I know, sorry."

"They're waiting in the conference room."

"Okay, thanks. How's…um…Mary?"

"Marie. She's fine. She's not fourteen minutes late. You'd better get in there."

Her head is pounding. Twice on the run over, the buzzing hit her head, almost knocking her to the ground. *Why did it have to start up again today, of all days?* "You have any prophen?" she asks. "I slept funny."

Sorenson, still not looking up, opens the desk drawer, grabs a white bottle, and tosses it to her. Lucinda slaps four capsules into her mouth as she heads down the dark corridor.

She turns the corner and pauses before the closed door. She smooths her hair, takes a breath, stretches her neck side to side, touches the panel, and enters.

"O-eight-hundred, Weston. O-eight-hundred," says Campbell, looking up at her through thick eyebrows as she bustles into the room. O'Brian sits beside him at the long table. A woman she doesn't know stands in the corner, arms crossed.

"I know, I know, I'm so sorry," says Lucinda. "Family emergency. It won't happen again."

"Not the start we're looking for. This isn't the fishery you know…"

"I know, sir, I know. I apologize. It won't happen again."

"Let's get on with it," says the woman. "Lucinda Weston, correct?" Lucinda nods. "I'm Lieutenant Chrysler from the Enclave Engineers. I'll be supervising your practical."

"You know how this works, Weston," says Campbell.

"Yes, sir."

Lieutenant Chrysler says, "Here is the scenario: One of the counter-measures in the outer ring got jammed during the last attack. We need you to replace the damaged component and calibrate one of the sensors." She picks up a cylinder about the size of a coffee cup from the desk and hands it to Lucinda. "There's a service tube to the outer ring. The workspace under the device is, shall we say, tight. That's why we picked it for you."

"Because I'm short."

"I thought you preferred petite," says Campbell.

"Not really."

Chrysler continues. "There's a gas mixture that has to be precisely balanced, and you'll need to do some tolerance calculations on the fly when you're in there. If you make a mistake, you flood the tube with nerve agent and 'die.' One chance. Pass/Fail. Sound good?"

"Sounds good."

"Very well. The car is outside."

They take a car to the gate. Lucinda looks out the window at the lush green lawns and the marching oaks, heavy with wet. The rain has stopped, but the sky is still dark as ash. She's grateful that their route takes them nowhere near the Arts Center. She breathes silently but deeply, trying to calm her swirling thoughts. *Was it him? Please God don't let it be him.* But even if it isn't, she'll never see him again. If he survives — and that's a big if — the Cantrells will never be permitted back in the Enclave. She can't think about it. She taps into her study files, but can't focus. Too late for that anyway. She taps her Friends Thread instead, hoping to lose herself in the dull but reassuring chatter about clothes, food, and sex.

They drive past the elementary school. A flock of uniformed seven-year-olds swoops around the playground, yelling and shrieking in some indefinable game. Lucinda remembers playing that game — something where the boys were soldiers (they were always soldiers) and the girls were horses and they would charge hither and yon, securing various little hills, protecting them from invading Nonalites. She's never seen an actual horse, but that never stopped anyone. A flick to your COR and you knew all about them. So innocent.

The car pulls up in front of a stately edifice of white marble and red brick just opposite the main gate. It was a bank before the wall went up, built in the 1920s. There are still white painted parking spaces along the curb, but since there are only about twenty cars in the whole Enclave, there's no shortage of room.

"Arrived at the Central Defense Building," chirps the car in a cheerful voice. "Have a great day."

They climb out and head inside. Chrysler leads her past the guard desk, the detector flashing green as it reads their CORs. Most Defense personnel are Second Class citizens, but they get special dispensation to receive the implant, with restrictions on the data they can access. They head downstairs, the first flight grand white marble, the second ancient linoleum with brown rubber treads. They enter what used to be the vault, the metal door still balancing on its massive hinges. Eight hatches line the back wall.

Another engineer waits for them in the room. She hands Lucinda a small satchel. "The sensor is in here, along with the tools you'll need. Make sure to put on the anti-static gloves before you touch the sensor." They head to the back of the room, and the engineer twists the handle on one of the hatches. It opens into a low, narrow duct of dull metal, disappearing into the darkness.

"The countermeasure has been deactivated for the exercise," says Campbell, "but don't touch anything you're not supposed to. There's a lot of dangerous equipment in there."

"It won't turn back on while I'm in there, will it?" She tries to make it sound like a joke.

"No, but there still are tanks of nerve agent in there, so don't screw around," says Chrysler. Apparently, the lieutenant has no sense of humor. "Put this on."

Lucinda pulls the headlamp onto her forehead. "It's commanded by your COR. Try it out." She feels the familiar ping, like a little bug in her head, when a new module opens in her brain. She thinks, *more light,* and the headlamp illuminates a patch of the wall. *Brighter,* and the spot gets brighter. *A little dimmer…dimmer…that's it.* "Seems to work fine," she says.

"You'll get an access request for chat when you get a ways in. Ready?"

Lucinda nods, and hoists herself in through the hatch. Her shoulders rub against the side walls, and she can barely raise her head enough to look forward. "Why did they make this so small?" she calls behind her.

"No idea. Do you fit?"

"Barely." She takes her time figuring out how to move forward, eventually landing on an awkward wormlike twitch, her elbows curled underneath her. "I got it! See you in a bit." She wriggles down the duct. She thanks her stars she's not claustrophobic.

About fifteen meters along, she hears another ping. She never enjoyed auditory chat. She can hear the sound, plain as day, as real as if someone held a bell to her ear, except the sound doesn't come from anywhere, it's just there, unlocalized, inside and outside at the same time.

Another little tickle, and Chrysler is talking in her head. "Can you hear me, trainee?"

"Yes, I can."

"Progress report."

"Good so far. I think I have about twenty more meters to go."

"Okay. Let me know when you get there."

"Roger that." The duct is stuffy, the heat increasing as she gets farther away from the entrance. Lucinda has to stop a couple of times to catch her breath. Finally, she reaches another access port. "I'm there," she says.

"Okay," says Chrysler. "Here comes the dump."

Despite her nerves, despite the traumas of the day, Lucinda can't help smiling. She loves this part. One second you know nothing, and the next second you're an expert on calculus, or Creole cooking, or computer repair. One second, you've never heard of Clarence Clegg, and the next, you can argue ad nauseam about the Forty Day Coup and the dissolution of the

United States. It doesn't stay, of course it doesn't stay, but the power that comes with the knowledge is like a drug. Suddenly, there it all is: The codes to open the hatch, the calibration techniques for the sensor, even the theoretical framework for the gas analogy of van Hoff's equation for osmotic pressure.

She taps the code into the panel beside the hatch and pulls it open with a touch of swagger. Here she is, about to join Defense, making a difference for the Enclave, but even more, for herself. Her declaration of independence. She flips onto her back and slides into the crawlspace.

The area under the countermeasure is, if anything, more cramped than the duct. Bulkheads and metal enclosures stick out into the space in exactly the right way to prevent a human body from lying comfortably. Lucinda thanks her dance teacher, Erin, as she twists her legs one way, her hips another, and her torso yet another, like a snake wriggling through the roots of a tree.

She finds the access panel for the sensor and flips it open. Her COR tells her the exact sequence of toggles to flip and how to pull and turn the unit at the same time so it pops out easily. She removes the new unit from the satchel. She's never seen one before, but she knows everything about it, even that it was designed by Sachiko Brown-Teshiga at Raytheon-Blackwater, a gray-haired woman with a smart bob and Old-World glasses. She slots it in and interfaces with the calibration program.

"How's it going, Weston?" asks Chrysler inside her mind.

"Peachy. Um, on schedule, no issues. Sorry." She starts to balance the gas ratios. The complexity of the process dizzies her, delights her. An ocean of numbers crashes through her mind. *Oh, the things she can do.*

And then a loud buzz hits her brain, like a zap from a tase-gun, and the knowledge vanishes. Halfway through entering an eleven-digit number. As if a blade has fallen and sliced off a finger of her mind. Lucinda stares at the panel before her in utter incomprehension. The knowledge never belonged to her in the first place, and now it has been taken away, and in its stead, terror. She shakes her head, trying to jiggle the knowledge back into place. Nothing. She shakes it harder. She strikes her head with one hand, then with both.

A sharp, uncomfortable buzz, and it's back. Just like that. The numbers coalesce from a meaningless jumble into an orderly arrangement of figures. Relief floods through her, followed immediately by thudding panic. *Did they notice?* Chrysler's voice speaks within her inner ear.

"Weston, are you there?"

"I'm here."

"We lost you for a second." *Damn.*

"It's no problem."

"What happened?"

"Not sure. It's fine. There's nothing to worry about. I'm still here and getting on with the procedure." She speeds up, entering the numbers, adjusting sliders at a feverish pace.

"Hold on there. Give us a second to trace the problem."

"It's fine. I'm fine," says Lucinda, over the insistent pounding of her heart.

"I'm sure you are, Weston, but we have to trace the problem. You know that. If it's a glitch in our system, then we'll fix it. If it's not…"

Sweat gathers on her upper lip. The skin tightens across her temples. She tries to breathe. There's a long silence on the other end of the line. She knows what's coming. *Why did it have to happen now?* She doesn't want to think about what it means. *It can't be. Just can't be.*

With a soft ping, Chrysler is back in her brain. "Um, okay. Lucinda." The voice is stiff and uncomfortable. "So, it's not on our end. It's definitely not on our end." There's another long pause. "So…um…I'm sorry. We've traced it to your COR."

She has a metal protrusion poking into the small of her back, but Lucinda hardly notices. The pit of Lucinda's stomach starts to whirl.

"Weston, have you been in contact with any infected persons?"

The tiny enclosure spins around her. Suddenly, her rebellious disregard for the quarantine around Sebastien and his family reveals itself in all its naked foolishness. *How could she have been so stupid?* But she can't tell them. Sure, a common symptom of Mindworm is COR malfunction, but it's not the only symptom, and CORs malfunction for other reasons, too. It doesn't have to be that. To even contemplate that she might have it is utterly impossible.

"No." Maybe true. She doesn't know for sure that Sebastien was infected. Maybe it was his father. Faulty reasoning, and craven, she knows, but she pushes it aside.

"You live with your parents, correct?" says Chrysler.

"Yes."

"Just a moment, please." There is a long pause. Lucinda watches the numbers on the device's calibration screen spin through their myriad combinations, her wild panic settling into blankness. Chrysler says something, but Lucinda has fallen into so deep a reverie that she doesn't process it. Then another voice activates her auditory nerve, startling her back to awareness.

"Lucinda? Lucinda?" The voice is so familiar, and sounds so close that she involuntarily looks back over her shoulder to see if her mother has somehow joined her in the tube.

"Mom?"

"Are you all right?" says another voice, right alongside — big, husky, confident but concerned.

"Daddy?"

"What happened, honey? They just said they needed to patch us in."

"It's nothing. Just a glitch."

Chrysler's voice cuts through, wrecking the normality. "Lucinda's COR malfunctioned, Mr. and Mrs. Weston. I'm sure you understand how serious that is."

"Oh my goodness," says Marigold. "Has it happened before, Lu?"

Lucinda groans inwardly. "It's nothing. It came right back. It's just a little glitch."

"Mr. and Mrs. Weston," says Chrysler, "we patched you in because we need to ask you — has anybody in your family been in contact with someone with the HNV-2209 virus?"

"Good heavens, no!" says Lucinda's dad, "How could we? You know as well as I do that there have been no new cases since July. And we've been observing the protocols rigidly. No contacts except those with blue clearance."

"Well, that's not entirely true," says Marigold, her voice calm as a fetid pool. "Is it, Lu?"

Oh no. "What do you mean, Mom?"

"I was afraid this would happen. All those trips to the library. You saw them, didn't you? You saw him. That boy."

For a moment, Lucinda can't speak. When she rallies, it's halting. She can't control her voice. It sounds shrill and distorted in her ears. "What do you mean, Mom? I don't—"

"Don't lie to us, Lu." Her mother's voice doesn't rise in pitch or volume, but the terrible coolness slides like ice down Lucinda's spine. "I know where you've been going. I found the poem. Lucinda — how could you?"

The poem. She'd hidden the vellum in her closet, under a box of old toys and a pile of clothes. How did she find it? *Unless she was looking for it.*

"You were going through my stuff? How dare you?" Lucinda finds something to hold onto in the anger.

"Don't 'how dare you' me, Lucinda!" For the first time, her mother's voice rises. "I knew where you were going. Do you think I'm stupid? You lied to us. You put us all in danger."

"What are you talking about?" says her Dad.

"You remember how she was spending so much time with that boy from the music troupe last year?"

There's a short pause as everyone takes this in. "Lucinda. Did you see that boy?" Her father's voice is hard and thick. She doesn't know what to say, so she doesn't say anything.

"She did," says her mother. "I caught her coming home after being with him."

"Mom…" Lucinda can barely choke out the word.

"Jesus, Weston…" It's Campbell. She remembers how he'd helped her with the enrollment form. He was gruff, but kind. "You realize you've put us all at risk. We'll all have to quarantine, and if you've got it, and spread it to any of us…Jesus, Lucinda."

She is utterly alone in a claustrophobic tube, out beyond the Enclave walls, deadly machines surrounding her. And yet their voices seem to crowd around her, pummeling her from every side.

"Mom…"

No one speaks. She pleads. "I'm fine. I'm really fine. I don't have any symptoms. Any other symptoms."

"I'm sorry," says Chrysler, not sounding sorry at all. "Lucinda Weston, in accordance with Hamilton Enclave Regulation 234–881, you are hereby expelled from the Enclave. The Enclave rescinds all rights of citizenship, harbor, and protection. The Enclave will provide you with a survival pack, to be left outside the front gates. Once you retrieve it, you are restricted from coming within two hundred meters of the Enclave barrier, and will be shot on sight if you violate said limit. May God protect you."

Chapter 8

Rain pours down Creek's face. Everything is wet – his hair, his shirt, his pants, especially his shoes, like his feet are encased in sponges. The dense, green foliage that hides him sags with damp, and little streams of water cascade off the bowing leaves, dripping down under his collar and making his neck itch something awful. He's been hiding here for almost an hour. The Steader he is supposed to rob shoulda oughta been gone — that was what Jojo at Intel had told him — and instead there he is, sitting on his porch with a rifle across his knees like he was waiting for them. What was supposed to be a normal crack-and-jack — slip into the mech room, tie into the panel, juice the blocks, and get out — has turned into a serious pain.

This is stupid! He's not leaving. This was Creek's third job as a power thief. The first two had been easy — he'd slipped through a fence to jack a wind turbine, and hooked up to a geothermal outside a small encampment of Steaders. In both cases, the supply had been a good distance away from the settlement, and he had seen no sign of other people. This was the first time he'd been sent to jack a house, and it wasn't going well.

Creek wonders if he should just slip away into the woods, leave it all behind. He's done it before. But Kimo is in the Icebox, and if he doesn't come back, she's gonna get it bad. *Never have friends. It always leaves you in the jam.*

He feels a haptic quiver behind his ear. The recall. Why Chekoba waited so long, who knows, but the trilling taps are like music to Creek. Hardly bothering to be quiet, what with the chattering of the rain, he rolls over to his left and crawls back out of the bushes, each move cascading down another splash of wet to drench his soaking body.

Chekoba waits in a little gully about thirty meters from the shack. He's a scrawny little man with a face like a turtle — a sour, angry turtle. Creek doesn't like him, but nobody cares whether Creek likes them or not, especially not Chekoba. Creek adjusts the Ear, which has slipped awkwardly to one side of his head. He hates it just as much as ever, but Ratalfa, the captain he reports to, insists he wear it. He flips it on and winces. He still can't get used to the whirring in his brain when it activates.

"The weezer's not moving," he says to Turtle-face. "He must know something's up."

"Did he see you?"

Creek shakes his head.

"Did he *hear* you?"

"No! I'm not an idiot!" Creek hadn't meant for that part to come out, but the Ear interpreted it all the same.

"Aren't you?"

"I don't even see the source. There's no turbine, no solars. Maybe he doesn't have juice after all."

Chekoba scratches his long, sad nose and frowns even deeper than before. "Jojo said he did, so he does. Maybe it's geothermal, or water-driven. I don't know. The guy's got power, and the Lady wants it. So we stay. Get back to your post. He can't sit there all day."

Can't he? Creek wants to say it, but he's tired of arguing with Turtle-face, so he hunkers down and crawls back through the soaking undergrowth. When he gets to his lookout, he can barely believe it — the Steader is gone. Did he go inside, or finally give up and go off to do whatever he was supposed to be doing in the first place? Creek counts to two hundred —

maybe he's on the toilet — but the rain drips down on the empty porch like it's been abandoned for years. He counts another hundred and then slips out from the bushes and tiptoes toward the door.

The moment he enters the shack, Creek knows that things just got a whole lot more complicated. It's obvious that there is no generator to jack. The guy has four enormous nuclear batteries — each one a meter tall and weighing more than Creek himself — lined up against the back wall, plugged into all manner of machines. Whatever this guy is doing, it isn't just homesteading.

Creek hesitates at the door. He knows he should go back to Turtle-face and report, but he's itching to find out what all the machines are for. Caution wins out, and he scurries back through the bushes to where Chekoba is waiting.

"What now?" Chekoba's voice buzzes in his brain.

Creek explains about the batteries. Chekoba stares off into space, his gloomy face getting gloomier by the second, as if his frown was being pulled down into a gravitational well. "You can't carry them out, can you?"

Creek shakes his head. *Of course not, dimmo.*

"Well, I'm not going to carry them, that's for sure." He broods. "We'll have to call for back-up, I suppose. There's nobody there now, right?"

Nod.

"Well, you'd better get things ready. Go back and disconnect everything you can, so we can get out as quick as possible."

Creek's heart, which had risen at the word 'back-up' *(maybe somebody else would handle this),* now drops back down around his knees. He silently curses Chekoba and dives back into the soaking brush. As he goes, he takes off the Ear and puts it in his tool bag. The hissing rush of the rain is giving him a headache, and he's better off using his eyes and his sixth sense anyhow. He's survived just fine that way for years. He doesn't need fancy contraptions to do his job.

He checks that the coast is clear and slips back into the shed. So many machines. There are a bunch of monitors with data streaming over them. Several devices have drawers or little doors on the front. He wonders what goes inside. One has a bunch of little vials in holders along the top.

He's just about to touch one of the vials when his nerves jump. He doesn't know what set off his alarms, but he has learned to trust them. Someone's coming. He figures he can't make it to the door, so he drops down behind one of the machines, cursing his crummy luck. He tries to make himself as small as he can. Why does he keep getting trapped in the soup?

Someone enters the room through a narrow door in the back of the shed. It's not the guy with the rifle. It's a woman. She's very pretty — soft golden hair and smooth whelite skin. She wears a dark green jumpsuit with the sleeves rolled up. She's got a pistol in her hand. She gives the room a once-over and lays the gun on a small desk near the batteries. Creek settles in for a long wait, but before he can take another breath, she has grabbed the gun again and is standing over him, looking down, the muzzle pointed at his head.

She mouths something. Creek stays still as a trapped mouse. In situations like this, he has learned that playing the scared child usually disarms adults. He huddles against the wall, trying to look as terrified as he can. Then he shapes, *DON'T HURT ME.* That should throw her off.

It works. Her suspicion dissolves into concern. She keeps mouthing, pointing at her ears. He just waits. She puts the gun down and gives him her open palms in the *I won't hurt you gesture.*

She starts acting things out, but Creek has no idea what she wants. He wants to laugh, but he stays in character. He recoils further. Then she puts her hand to her mouth and makes chewing movements. *Are you hungry?*

He nods. If he can get her distracted, he can make a break for the door. He is a little hungry, now that he thinks of it. They don't get fed well back in the enclosure. It wouldn't be the worst thing to enjoy a little grub before he beats it. He inches forward, and the woman stands up and backs away. She pulls a little chair forward from the small desk, and he crawls out from behind the machine and slips up into the chair, making himself as small and timid as he can.

She smiles at him and crosses to a cabinet near the back door. Now would be the time to make his move, but Creek hesitates. He is pretty hungry. He waits while she searches for something in the cupboard. She keeps stopping and miming various things. It finally clicks. She is trying to tell him about herself. She is a doctor — giving shots, taking temperatures, bandaging wounds. Maybe he'll be okay after all.

Thirty seconds later, he wishes he had bolted when he had the chance, because the man comes back through the main door, the rifle slung over his shoulder. He takes one look at Creek and starts shouting, unslings the rifle, and raises it. The woman jumps in front of him, waving her arms and shouting, too, but the man tries to aim around her. Creek leaps out of the chair and dashes for the door. He almost makes it, but the man reaches out a long arm and grabs him around the middle. There's a wild struggle, as Creek whips and squirms like an animal, while the man tries to put down the rifle. He manages to drop it, and suddenly Creek is wrapped in a suffocating bear hug. He goes limp. The man pushes the chair into the far corner with his feet, then slings Creek roughly into it. He leans in and starts shouting so fast that it's impossible to follow what he's saying. The woman stands over his shoulder, shouting too. He's glad he took out the Ear.

Finally, the man calms down enough to make some sense. He pushes his face into Creek's and starts mouthing deliberately. *What is he on about?* It must be an interrogation — *What are you doing here? Who sent you? Did you take anything?*

Creek waits it out.

The man raises his hand to strike. The woman grabs the man's arm, and they struggle briefly. They shout at each other some more. The woman lets go, raising her arms in a *go ahead, I'm not responsible* gesture. The man turns back to Creek and leans in. Creek flinches back into the chair and closes his eyes.

But instead of a slap, he feels a rush of wind and a whirl of dust across his face. He peeks through scrunched lids to see a billow of smoke swirling around the door, which hangs half-knocked off its hinges. A tall figure stands in the doorway, a short-barreled rifle in his hands. Sandoval, Lady Fal's personal guard. The book-lover.

A conversation ensues. Sandoval points at the row of batteries several times. The man keeps his mouth moving. Their eyes are locked, caught in the stand-off. The woman watches them.

Then, only for a second, Sandoval glances at Creek. The man sees his chance and takes it. He lunges for the pistol on the little desk and tries to take cover behind Creek's chair. Two bright flashes from Sandoval's gun — accompanied by a couple of dull thumps in Creek's mind — and the man and woman are lying on the ground at his feet. Sandoval lowers his weapon. He starts to curse, walking back and forth, jerking his head up and down. It goes on for a long time. He lays the gun on the floor and checks the man and the woman. The man lies on his back, his left eye blown out, along with the back of his head. The woman lies on her face, but Creek can see the huge circle of blood and flesh tangled in her golden hair. He's seen dead bodies before, of course, but not this close for a good long while. He can smell the gunpowder, and a sharp, ferrous odor rising from the bodies. He retreats into his silent world.

Sandoval touches his comm and starts talking with someone on the other end. *Probably Jojo,* Creek thinks, the thought skittering across his flattened mind like a water bug. Then he crosses the room and kneels down, taking Creek's head in his large, warm hands. He doesn't look him in the eye, instead scanning his skin and the surface of his body, looking for injuries. Satisfied, Sandoval rises again and checks out the contents of the room. Abruptly, he sweeps up his rifle and aims it at the entrance.

A woman comes in through the blown-out door. She is short and plump, with a round brown face. An open face. She reminds Creek of Nana Moja at the camp, who worked in the infirmary. She was nice.

This woman looks nice, too. Or she would, if she wasn't taking in the bodies on the ground and going all crazy. She runs and kneels beside the woman, then looks up and begins yelling at Sandoval. Sandoval yells back, the gun trained on the woman's head, but he doesn't fire. Creek feels strange and distant. He can't seem to care about what's happening between the two of them.

After a while, things calm down. The newcomer raises her hands over her head in a sarcastic, *don't shoot* gesture and sits in one of the chairs. Only now does she notice Creek sitting there. She says something to him, but he doesn't respond. He finds his gaze drawn to the pooling blood around the blond woman's head. His silence wraps him in its blanket of safety. Time stops. He barely notices when a troop of Niners bustles in and starts removing the batteries and machinery from the little house.

Suddenly, the Duke is there, too. He puts his hand on Creek's shoulder, a quick sign of care, then removes it.

YOU OKAY? he shapes. Creek nods. *LET'S GET OUT OF HERE, KID.*

Chapter 9

Her escape from the tube is a swirling nightmare: Chrysler's crisp voice guides her around the deadly machinery, but its cold precision only adds to the fever of panic and misery that overtakes her. She follows the directions because she has nothing else to hold onto. Her world is spinning away from her. No relief that her parents have fallen silent, not offering her a word of encouragement or forgiveness. She can feel their passive condemnation like an invisible weight. It takes hours.

Halfway through the process, her head buzzes shut again, and she is alone, her body impossibly wedged around a cylinder of nerve gas, the nozzle jammed against her cheek. If she moves, she dies; if she doesn't, she dies. She moans with relief when her COR kicks in again, and the chilly voice returns and guides her around the obstacle, over to one of the heat guns, and up through a hidden trapdoor, until she lies gasping on the grass in the gathering dark under a warm, light rain.

"We are reactivating the countermeasures," comes Chrysler's voice. "You must vacate the area." Lucinda gets to her feet and staggers for the ring of trees that surround the lush, green lawn. The moment she passes into the darkness beneath the branches, her mind goes silent — not the painful buzzing of disruption, but a surgical resection. Her COR goes dead.

The terrors of her escape are nothing compared to the void of despair that engulfs her when they cut her off. Through the entire ordeal, she still enjoyed that quiet hive in the back of her mind, buzzing just under the surface — her friends popping in and out, idle questions instantly answered, images, music, reveries, the gently bubbling cauldron of information and activity that has accompanied her through life. Suddenly gone. A terrible silence in her brain. Empty, and nothing to fill it.

She waits, hopeless and hoping, as night falls. The worst night she has ever known — worried by hunger, rankled by sticks and stones digging into her back, fighting off wave after wave of surging dread. Every hour or so, she crawls out to see if the gate has opened, to see if someone has left the survival pack, or if, impossibly, they have come to tell her there has been a mistake, she is reprieved, she belongs to them again. And through it all, the deadness in her mind, her COR cut off, useless.

Lucinda awakens drenched with dew under a pile of branches and leaves. The early morning cold drives little knives through her body. She feels like a chicken thigh buried in the back of the fridge. Gray mist hangs around the copse of maples and out over the broad lawn of mown grass in front of the gate.

Lucinda brushes off the wet leaves and peers across the grassy sward. The gate, flanked by watchtowers, stands mute and forbidding in the pale light. The road that once led to it is long gone, dug up when the troubles began. A wide flat lawn, carefully mown to golf course length, extends in a broad circle two hundred meters across along the perimeter of the wall. They could have just left it as dirt or gravel, but that wasn't the Enclave way. No place to hide, no cover for the attackers. A putting green of death. Elegance and murder, conjoined.

Ten meters in front of the gate, the ancient sign that marks the entrance to the Enclave rises from a low concrete base — at once a memory of kinder days and a taunting defiance to its enemies. Curlicued script, clean and white against a background of forest green, proclaims its bygone message: "Welcome to Hamilton Estates — Living Refined." The Nonas have destroyed it again and again, but always the Enclave restores it to its place. At the foot of the sign, Lucinda picks out a small dark hump. The survival pack.

She scrambles to her feet and starts to sprint out onto the lawn, then stops herself. *Is it a trap?* Will the countermeasures erupt around her — stabbing, burning, poisoning? Is that what they want? She waits. The blaring alarms that warn off intruders are silent. She remembers that when the Travises were exiled two years ago, they were allowed to depart in peace. She takes a deep breath and walks across the lawn, treading lightly, ready to run at the first sign of trouble.

She reaches the sign and kneels. Pops open the clasp that closes the backpack. She scans the walls, looking for a sign of life, a human being watching her from the ramparts. The walls stare back at her, silent and cold.

The backpack contains a tightly rolled rain shell, water bottle, decontamination tablets, a small knife, flashlight, igniter, first aid kit, pup tent, thin bed roll, energy bars, a solar-powered map, and a small black case. Lucinda chokes when she sees it — a frantic, guttural sob. Of all the objects in the pack, it offers the greatest hope.

Like a starving dog, she unlatches the case. Within, clipped into two neat rows, lie ten rectangles of black plastic. Tiny white lettering reveals the contents of each. *Wilderness Survival, Languages, Literature & Art, Entertainment...* Wafers of knowledge. Manna in the wilderness.

She grabs *Entertainment*, almost at random. Her fingers shaking with cold and desperation, she fumbles it up to the small slot behind her right ear and pushes it in.

Relief. The hole fills — though not completely. The chips are obsolete tech and contain a fraction of the knowledge she is used to. But enough. Stimulating her visual centers, the chip manifests an Old School jukebox. Tiny, but perfectly detailed, it floats in the space before her. With a swipe of her mind, it flies away, replaced by a video booth, a library, a concert hall. She flips back to the jukebox, selects a playlist of trag-pop, then dismisses the visual. The first tune fills her mind's ears — *My Dead Lovers* by Torla Howland. She likes the old things best, and this takes the prize — 150 years old if it's a day. The mournful strains, rising around her, fill the yawning need within her heart.

She hunches by the sign, eating two of the energy bars. They are dry and overly sweet, but she's starving. *No, you're not,* she reminds herself. *You're just hungry. Give it a few days and you'll be starving for real.* She puts half the second bar back in its wrapper and stows it in the bag. She stares at the Enclave wall. The rain stops, and the clouds thin. She can see the ghost of the sun rising above the trees behind. Time passes. After a couple of hours, a figure, helmeted, appears on the battlement. Lucinda waves. The figure waves back, a small, awkward gesture. Then it holds up its rifle, a cold reminder of her sentence and the injunction she faces. Ashamed, she retreats into the woods, turning her back on everything she has ever known.

She doesn't go far, about a quarter mile into the woods, down by the stream. When she was a kid, they used to let folks come out and picnic here every once in a while, but the recent increase in attacks has put a stop to that. No one from inside has been here in years. Still, there are signs of habitation — outcasts like her — energy bar wrappers and other bits of trash. She puts up her tent and arranges her things inside. She likes things orderly — even her mother had to admit she kept her room spotless. She starts to imagine her bedroom. *No.* No good down that road.

It is mid-afternoon when she finishes. She eats another bar — fifteen left (they don't expect her to last much longer than that) — and opens the little case again. She knows she should put in the one that says, "Wilderness Survival", but instead she leaves "Entertainment" in her access port and studies the contents more closely. The disks don't hold much, but there's an album of ten thousand songs, two thousand books, and two hundred vidis. As she flits through the catalog, a tinge of disappointment brings her down. It's hardly the most exciting material. She's seen a lot of the vidis, and there are only five immersives, none of which look that appealing. The music is better, but the books are almost a complete bust. It disheartens her that there can be so many choices, and so few real options.

Still, she's grateful to have *something*. She lies down in the tent, with the flap open. It has started to rain again, and the air is thick and muggy. Not much of a breeze. She chooses a film she's seen before. It's called *Port Hope,* and it's a real oldie, made in 2045, but she likes it because it's sweet and funny and the lead actor looks a little like Sebastien. It's not one of the immersives, of course, so she chooses theater mode, and the roof of the tent vanishes from her visual field, replaced by a large, dark room with a silver screen.

Lucinda hopes she can make it through the film without her COR buzzing out on her. She tries to focus on the story, but her restless thoughts flick here and there, and she soon loses track. Here she is, acting like she's in her room, just hanging out, lying on her bed watching a vidi on a lazy Saturday. Only she's not. She's in the woods in a tent, waiting to die. She's lying there pretending everything is fine when, in all likelihood, the worm is burrowing into her brain. *Is she feeling dizzy? Should her neck ache like that? Oh, it's gone. But is that a headache? Is she getting feverish?* After a half hour, she gives up and closes the vidi. She looks at the blue ceiling of the little tent and listens to the thrumming of the rain.

She finds it impossible to ration her food. She tries to resist, but the gurgling in her stomach drives her to distraction, and before she can stop herself, she's ripped open another package and devoured another energy bar. She's grown used to the sweet, oily grittiness of them, and her mind drifts to them again and again as she sits staring at the roof. She only has eight bars left, and it's still the first day. She puts them in the back of the tent, where they can't tempt her, takes the black case, removes the Wilderness Survival module, and slides it into the slot. She's avoided it up until now. The gesture has an air of finality to it, as if she's giving up on the hope that this is all a bad dream, or a terrible mistake, and that any moment Lieutenant Chrysler will stride through the bushes with a rueful smile on her lips and an apology on her tongue, and lead her back to her old life. To access the survival information feels like capitulation. *She's out here, she's not going back.* She had better figure out how to stay alive, at least until the Mindworm kills her.

As the chip clicks into place, the forest around her transforms from a charming but desolate backdrop into a tapestry full of story and meaning. Like a light snapping on, Lucinda knows the name of every plant, lichen, and moss around her. She can identify the slate and gneiss on the stream bed, and the tumble of rhyolite and basalt at the top of the glade. The sound of a cardinal, a woodpecker, and a chorus of titmice. She knows that the Spanish moss draping the trees has only recently moved in, marching north with the warming climate. She sees immediately that she has placed her tent in a poor spot, and that if the rain grows any heavier, she'll be sleeping in a puddle. She also realizes that she's been lucky — coyotes, feral dogs, and bears prowl these woods and have grown in number as the rolling disasters — civil war and political strife, disease and pandemic, the collapse of the food chain, migration, starvation, and death — have reduced the human population to next to nothing. She'd best take precautions. But first, she has to find something to eat. Besides the energy bars.

The plants around her don't look promising. It's almost October, and though leaves still cover the brush, they look pale and thick and tired. She spies some sorrel growing near the edge of the clearing and tries a leaf. She wants to spit it out – it's bitter and fibrous – but she forces herself to chew it and swallow. "Yuck," she says aloud. "Let's find some mushrooms." She grabs her pack and water bottle and heads out.

As she makes her way along the stream, the sun comes out above the trees and flickers through the leaves. Some have already begun to turn, though her COR tells her that fall has been arriving later and later as the climate continues to warm. Still, above her, the foliage glimmers red and yellow among the green. The air has a freshness she hasn't breathed in a long while. She can smell it. It's almost as if the Survival chip has augmented her sense of smell, though she knows that can't be true. But the scent of earth, of damp and rotting leaves, of bark and branch and mossy stump, fills her head. The living world with all its rich aroma, sweet stink, fulsome odor. It's almost more than she can bear.

She climbs the hill up out of the maple grove onto a flat open stretch covered with fir trees. Brown needles blanket the ground. Not the best place to look for fungi. She's about to turn back and head downhill again when she spots a flash of blue on the far side of the fir stand. She can make out the hood of a large, beat-up ranger. Her heart sings. She knows that car. It is their car. *Sebastien*!

Heedless of anything, she calls out, "Hello! Hello! Hey! It's me! It's Lucinda!" and takes off running across the downy ground. She barely notices as the buzzing zaps her brain and the knowledge vanishes from her consciousness. She staggers, but keeps running. She bursts into a small clearing where the car is parked. Two tents have been set up, with the remains of a small fire between them.

She pulls up short when she sees the dog. It lifts its head from a pile of clothes in the middle of the camp, but she doesn't comprehend what it's doing. It's lean and starved, a mongrel browny-gray, its eyes pale and wild. Her head buzzes again, and she shakes it violently, then freezes at the edge of the camp. The pile of clothes comes into focus. Ginnie, Sebastien's sister, stares up at her, her eyes blank and foggy, her dark hair stiff and filthy. The dog has chewed most of her nose off, so she barely looks human, but Lucinda can recognize her all the same. The smell of blood and feces assaults her nose.

Carlana, Sebastien's mother, lies a little behind the dog, face down in the dirt, her hands above her head as if she had thrown herself down in a fit of dramatic weeping. It reminds Lucinda of a character in one of the Shakespeare plays they acted out in high school — "Romeo and Juliet", or "Julius Caesar." Mindworm often causes hysterical delusions. She sees that one of the car windows is shattered, and the sides are stained and dented, as if it had been pelted with rocks and rotten food.

Then Lucinda catches sight of a pair of male feet sticking out from one of the tents. Her heart dies inside her. She knows those shoes. Just two nights ago, they lay beside her head on the dusty floor of the prop closet, in a world and a life that now lies beyond a chasm.

The dog continues to watch her, its eyes bright stones. Its tongue hangs out of the side of its mouth. Neither woman nor animal moves for a long time. Then a crazy rage grips Lucinda, and she screams, "Get! Get out of here! Get!" She stomps her feet. The dog flees about five meters into the woods, then turns and stops. She screams again. It retreats a bit further and stops again. She rushes at it, waving her arms, and it takes off, darting into the woods. But she can see that it has stopped again, not far from the camp. She starts to cry, then her gorge rises and she vomits into the soft, brown needles. "Go away," she moans. It watches her for a minute, then lies down, panting.

She knows she should bury them, or burn them, or something. But she can't. How could she? She knows she should go back and tend his body. *His body.* She can't do it. She makes a wide circle around the tents, trying not to look, and heads back down the hill.

Her COR buzzes back to life.

The vision of Ginnie's face, those sightless eyes, swallows her mind. She wishes she could cut it out, somehow load it onto the chip, and eject the memory with all the other knowledge. She shakes her head, again and again, trying to shake the thought away, but it's a part of her now.

Something stirs in her, and she stops. The wood has gone very quiet. The birds have ceased their chirping, except for an anxious call every now and then. Lucinda can't explain why, but something tells her to be careful. She creeps forward as silently as she can, knees bent, low to the ground. As she approaches the rocks at the edge of her campsite, she gets down and crawls, coming up to a large boulder that juts beside the stream. She peers over.

Six men with guns stand in the clearing, surrounding her tent.

Chapter 10

Kat Jemisen drives her van slowly over the rutted ground, pointedly ignoring the man with the gun sitting next to her. He had introduced himself as Sandoval, but since he was the guy who shot Trace and Jory, Kat doesn't feel he deserves her usual politeness. She doesn't care how much he protested that Jory had started it, and that he had only fired in self-defense. Or that he appears almost as upset as she is about the whole thing.

It took hours for Lady Fal's soldiers to arrive and load all her equipment into the van. *Back into the van.* They had only moved it into the shack a week ago. In retrospect, it would have been safer for them to keep working out of the vehicle — more mobility — but it was cramped and uncomfortable, and Trace had argued they were never going to complete the serum if they kept falling over each other. Now Trace was dead, and the shack was a smoking ruin, Kat was a prisoner, and her equipment belonged to Lady Fal. Not that it was really *her* equipment. She had stolen it, too. What a world.

"Slow down." She slows to a stop outside a long line of vehicles — heavy-duty trucks and rangers, mostly. Beyond, she can see a squat, round tower, about three stories high. Sandoval unrolls his window and gestures to someone she can't see. One of the trucks pulls out, creating a hole in the wall for her to drive through.

"Go in and park along the side of the tower, there." He points to the right. As she drives slowly through the encampment, she catches sight of the boy she saw in the shack. He has his head bowed, but she can see his closed, pinched face. *Who is he?* she wonders. A soldier leads him through the gate of a fenced enclosure on one side of the camp. More children sit on the ground. There are several tents, and a small square structure, no bigger than an outhouse, with corrugated metal siding and a vent at the top.

She parks as instructed beside the tower, and Sandoval leads her inside.

"Wait here," says the man. "Lady Fal will be with you shortly."

She looks around at the interior of the water tower. The curve of the wall calms her, impresses her. After a life spent in tents and shacks, it's nice to see a beautifully constructed building. She focuses on the hangings that separate the interior into chambers, trying to still the pulse beating in her temples. Whoever chose them has impeccable taste. Fabric like that was impossible to come by anymore. It must have come from some Enclave, looted and destroyed by this "warlord" *(or "warlady. Was that even a word?).*

Lady Fal. *It's got to be her,* Kat thinks. *It's just got to be.* But if it isn't, then she is in big, big trouble.

She hears the swish of a curtain behind her. "Katanja Jemisen, as I live and breathe." *That voice. It is her.* A thrill sweeps through her chest. She turns.

"Hello, Falernia. Been a long time."

Falernia Childress, a.k.a. Lady Fal, glides into the room. The two women look each other up and down. Lady is Fal is a good head taller, but Kat's sturdy presence exudes equal strength.

"It certainly has," says Fal. "What? Fifteen years?"

"Almost twenty. Not since Danbury."

"You went off with the medico and his family. What was his name?"

"Raymond Montarlo."

"How did that go?"

Kat spreads her arms. "See for yourself."

"You're a doctor now."

"And you're a war leader." Lady Fal nods. "I guess that's one way to make a living."

"In this world, it's the only way. It's good to see you, Kat." Lady Fal crosses the space between them and embraces her. Kat had planned to keep her distance, hold onto her righteous anger for Trace and Jory. But the warmth of the embrace surprises her, and the sweet smell of Fal's hair — so forgotten and so familiar — conjures sensations of the past that she cannot ignore. She finds herself returning the hug.

"Good to see you, too, Fal."

The two old friends regard each other, their eyes liquid.

"You hungry?" asks Lady Fal.

"I am, in fact."

"Come, let's have some food."

"I knew it was you. I *thought* it was you." Kat puts her glass down on the table. Real glass. With real wine in it. "When I heard they were taking me to 'Lady Fal.' You're the only Fal I've ever heard of, and if anyone was going to call herself 'Lady' it would be you."

Lady Fal laughs and sips her own wine. "Guilty as charged."

"So, you're a war leader? How's that working out for you? You enjoy terrorizing the local Steaders and looting their stuff? I gotta say it: I'm disappointed. I thought better of you." She levels her eyes at her old friend. Fal meets her gaze with quiet firmness.

"It's complicated, Kat. If it wasn't me, it would be someone else. Someone worse than me. I've tried reaching out to the Steaders, but the system we have is the system we have, if you can even call it a system, and they don't make it easy. They're used to fighting for their little bit of hell, and they don't tend to listen." She leans back and looks up at the dome high above them. "But I don't give up. I have plans."

"Plans."

"We've been, what? Forty years without a government? Almost as long as we've been alive. Oh, there's the odd attempt here and there. The Enclaves have trading agreements with each other, and there was that 'New Commonwealth' idea floating around when we were kids. But did it go anywhere?" Kat shakes her head. "No, it did not. If I can gather enough resources…"

"Whatever it takes."

"*Whatever it takes.* We can turn this camp into a community, that community into a town, that town into a city, that city into a new start for our people."

"Quite a vision. How's it going?"

Lady Fal laughs. "Slowly! But we're making progress. And I feel that you're showing up here today marks the beginning of a new chapter."

"How so?"

"Well, for one thing, we could use your help in the infirmary. I have a dozen soldiers down with malaria, and my nurse is learning his trade on the go."

"I'd be glad to help out."

"Good. Thank you." Lady Fall cocks her head. "Tell me about this equipment they found in your place. What's it for?"

Kat puts down her wine glass and folds her hands across her lap. "It's medical equipment. It's for synthesizing compounds for drugs."

"I thought so. And where'd you get it?"

"Well, Fal, I stole it."

Fal laughs again. "And you're lecturing *me*?"

"I know, I know. But I stole it from a bad guy. One of your lot. A warlord further south, in Old Connecticut. The Doctor."

"I've heard of him."

"He's a nasty customer, Fal."

"That's what they all think, until they run into me." She laughs. "Tell me more."

"Well, I was working with another woman, Dr. Tracy Langston — who is dead, by the way, thanks to your man Sandoval."

"I am so sorry about that, Kat." She places her hand on Kat's knee. "A terrible mistake. I understand it was self-defense, that your man drew first, but I know that doesn't help. Sandoval hates killing. He feels just awful, if that's any consolation."

"It's not. They were good people." She takes up her glass again and stares into the deep red liquid. She had liked Trace very much, and Jory, too. But death was the norm, not the exception, and Kat had to admit that she had kept herself from getting too close. "Well, what's done is done. Anyhow, in answer to your question. Trace and I were working down along the Hockanum River, helping Steaders — babies, bone-setting, water purification — the usual. Mindworm was particularly bad down there, so it was a lot of hygiene stuff and teaching people quarantine procedures.

"Then, we heard that this Doctor, as he calls himself, had a whole lab-full of sequencers, protein synthesizers, incubators, that sort of thing. Only it didn't seem like he was working on a cure. He was doing something else."

"What?"

"I'm still not sure. All we knew was that he was moving north, leaving a trail of burnt-out Enclaves and settlements in his wake, and this lab was moving with him. We hooked up with Jory — also dead now, thank you — who had a small militia, and we staged a little raid. We came up here and set up shop in that little shack in the woods, hoping nobody would notice us. Sadly, we were wrong."

"Not so sadly. I truly am sorry about your friends, Kat, but you know what this world is like. Don't you." It's not a question. Kat nods. "And now you're with me. You're safe."

"Am I?"

"Yes. How is the research going?"

"Slowly. Jory lost all his men but one in the raid, and that one proved to be no good. He stole a piece of our equipment and took off. Maybe the most important piece of all. We couldn't do much without it."

"What was it?" Lady Fal rises and moves toward the curtain to her bedchamber.

"It's called a Recreate Mini. It's the most advanced material synthesizer around. Top of the line technology before the Collapse."

Lady Fal disappears into her chamber. Kat can hear her opening a chest or closet. She reappears through the curtain, her hands behind her back.

"You mean this?" She brings out the cube. It twinkles gently in the candlelight. "I told you it was good luck, your ending up here."

Chapter 11

Creek comes out blinking into the gray light of a late afternoon. It's raining, as usual, and the clouds on the horizon threaten a downpour. He actually welcomed the time in the Icebox — living collateral while Kimo was out stealing power. It gave him a chance to get his head back. Seeing those people shot in front of him gave him the jingles. Especially the woman. Even though she was nothing like him — fair where he was dark, soft where he was taut as rope — her death had thrown him. As he lay in the blackness, listening to the drumming of the rain on the metal roof of the Box, he had bodysurfed on wave after wave of foggy memories of Her. Making him breakfast, dressing him, teaching him in the dim light of the bunker, her hands moving in slow, elegant spirals. He could never see her face, but the presence of her filled his mind. Somehow, this blonde, whelite woman — this doctor — whose ashes now lay at the bottom of the heap that had been the shed — reminded him of his mother.

He rarely tried actively to remember her, usually content to accept the random comings and goings of her memory. Now — locked in the blackness of the Icebox — he dug deep, trying to unearth what he could about that life, so distant that he could barely believe it belonged to him. He came up empty. A few fragments were all he had.

The yard is full when he emerges. Candela, the Duke, and Lamarque sit near the fence with Baby between them, watching his tiny limbs as they flail to and fro, and laughing. Rice, Sidecar, and Ketanya huddle in another corner, playing raquata. They are power thieves — like him and Kimo. Rice and Sidecar are kids his age, but Ketanya is older — maybe fifteen — but small and delicate. Creek has made no attempt to befriend them, and they have made no attempt, either. Civil but uninterested, which suits him fine.

Creek joins his friends in the circle. He tickles Baby's tummy, but Baby is too absorbed by something in the sky to notice.

HOW WAS THE ICEBOX? the Duke shapes.

GOOD. QUIET.

The Duke nods. *KIMO'S OKAY. I SAW HER COME BACK INTO CAMP. SHE'S GETTING DEBRIEFED NOW BY THE LADY. SHE SHOULD BE BACK SOON.* He looks up over Creek's shoulder and says something to somebody behind him. Creek turns. Rice is standing there. He's a scrawny kid with dirty blond hair and the pale face of a whelite.

IT'S HOW WE TALK, continues the Duke, shaping as he speaks.

Rice looks at Creek. He points at his ear. *You can't hear anything?* he's asking.

Creek shakes his head. It's the first interaction he's had with any of the other kids since Lady Fal decided they were staying. For the first couple days, Rice and Sidecar were out on assignment, and Ketanya just kept to herself. Creek didn't mind. They kept to themselves, too. Usually, it was better that way. The Duke and Candela had talked to them a bit early on, but Creek has just kept his distance, and nobody questioned him.

Rice makes meaningless gestures with his hands, flopping them around like a dimmo. Creek almost laughs, it's so stupid. He must be asking what the shaping means. The Duke says something to Rice, but Creek doesn't follow it. Doesn't really care. He looks out through the fence that separates them from the rest of the camp to see if Kimo is coming.

The Duke taps him on the shoulder. *WHAT?* asks Creek.

HE WANTS TO KNOW IF YOU'LL TEACH HIM.

TEACH HIM WHAT?

YOU KNOW. HOW TO SHAPE.

WHY DON'T YOU TEACH HIM?

HE WANTS YOU. YOU'RE BETTER THAN ME. YOU KNOW THAT.

Creek examines Rice. He has a nice enough face. Whelite pale, so clearly an outcast from some Enclave. He is scarcely taller than Creek. Thin and wiry. Probably a decent power thief, but who knows whether he would be any good in a fight. Creek considers. *Why not?* Something to do. He nods and taps the ground next to him.

Rice sits down, and Creek begins to show him some easy stuff. *MY NAME IS CREEK. YOUR NAME IS RICE. WHAT IS YOUR NAME?* He shows the kid how to make the shape that means his name. Rice doesn't get it at first, but after a few minutes, he starts to catch on. Ketanya and Sidecar drift over to watch. First one, then the other, kneels down to learn their names, too.

Creek has never cared that much about names. He usually just uses descriptors for people — Turtle-face, Slackjaw, Crazy Hair, One Eye. But they mean a lot to Kimo. She always makes a point of finding out people's names and sharing the shapes with him. Now, he feels important, like he's got privileged knowledge that nobody else has — showing them who they are.

They are just moving on to some new phrases when Kimo comes through the gate into the kids' enclosure, accompanied by Sandoval. She is wearing the Ear.

YOU OKAY? he asks her. She nods and sits by him.

YOU'RE FRIENDS NOW? she asks, looking at Rice and the others.

NO, JUST TEACHING THEM HOW TO TALK. HOW DID IT GO?

FINE. WE SUCKED A TURBINE NEAR THE BIG ENCLAVE OVER THAT WAY… She gestures vaguely behind her. *I THINK WE'RE GOING TO ATTACK IT. CHEKOBA SAID SOMETHING ABOUT USING THE TURBINE AS A CHARGING STATION FOR THE ASSAULT.*

OH BOY.

I KNOW. THOSE POOR PEOPLE.
THEY'RE JUST WHELITES. WHAT DO YOU CARE?
THEY'RE PEOPLE.
IT'S NOT LIKE WE CAN DO ANYTHING ABOUT IT.
NO.

Sandoval, who has been watching them, his eyes darting back and forth between their hands, kneels down. He has his book in his hand, one finger holding his place.

He mimes something like *What are you doing?*

Creek shrugs.

He, too, makes meaningless gestures with his hands, but it isn't as funny as when Rice did it. *Is that you talking?*

Creek nods.

The man glances up at Rice and the others and mimes some more. *Are you teaching them?* Creek nods again.

Sandoval studies him for a minute, his eyes narrowed into little slits. It makes Creek nervous. Then he opens his mouth to speak. But before he can get it out, something grabs his attention, and he stands up again, shading his eyes from the light rain with his hand. The hearing kids all perk up, too, craning their necks in the same direction, out past the enclosure to the circle of vehicles that form the outer barrier of the camp. Something is going on. Sandoval steps to the gate, undoes the chain, and strides away, leaving it open. The children hesitate for a moment, doubtful of their good fortune, then move as a body out into the yard.

Lady Fal stands outside the entrance to the water tower, her guards positioned around her. Sandoval joins her, and after a quick conference, steps forward, motioning to one of the Niners. The man runs out to the wall of vehicles, climbs into one, and backs it up, creating a breach in the barrier.

Two cars slide through the opening, coming to a stop about fifteen meters from the Lady. Creek's heart bumps as he sees them. The first car is most definitely the same car he saw at Junkman's place. The second is smaller, sleeker, more elegant. It looks out of place among the battered heaps that make up the camp's defensive ring. Its black hood is smooth and perfect, glinting in the stormy light.

Two men climb out of the front car. Creek recognizes them from the junk yard. They step to each side, heads slowly turning as they scan the crowd. Another man gets out of the front of the second car, scurries around it, and opens the door on the driver's side rear. A fourth man gets out, straightens slowly, and walks toward Lady Fal.

A chill runs down Creek's back as he watches the man advance. Something about him. He seems to emanate power and menace, moving slowly and deliberately. There is something odd about his gait. His right leg has the loose jerkiness of a normal step, but the left moves with an eerie smoothness that doesn't seem quite human. He looks up at the water tower as he walks, and around at the circle of vehicles that bound the camp. Creek can make out a jagged scar, forking like a lightning bolt, running down the left side of his face. The right side is all robot — made of plastic, dark gray, complete with an artificial eye that glows red under the darkening sky.

The man comes to a halt about three meters from Lady Fal. He says something. She answers. They talk for five minutes or so, the heavy air of the impending cloudburst pressing down on the camp.

Lady Fal makes a gesture that means, *What else can I say?* The man laughs, shakes his head, and turns away without another word. He climbs back into the car, which smoothly backs out of the circle, followed closely by its consort. Nobody moves. Rain starts to fall. At last, Sandoval breaks the spell, barking at the man who had opened the barrier. He jumps, as if awakened from a deep spell, hurries to his vehicle, and closes the circle up again. Lady Fal goes inside. The Niners break off into twos and threes, and drift back into the tents and buildings. The children head back to their enclosure. Nobody bothers to lock it, but it is the only home they have got, so where else can they go? Kimo is wearing the Ear. Creek gives her a nudge.

WHAT HAPPENED? asks Creek. She starts to answer, but the Duke intervenes.

DO YOU KNOW WHO THAT WAS? he shapes.

NO.

THE DOCTOR.

WHO IS THAT? Creek has some idea, but only vaguely.

The Duke snorts. *YOU DON'T KNOW ANYTHING, DO YOU?*

DO SO.

YOU KNOW HOW LADY FAL TOOK OUT TOP DAWG LAST YEAR?

NOT REALLY.

WELL, TOP DAWG CONTROLLED THE TERRITORY SOUTHWEST OF HERE, AND THEY WENT AT IT FOR A COUPLE OF YEARS UNTIL SHE HAD HIM ASSASSINATED AND BUSTED UP HIS OPERATION. The Duke doesn't know all the shapes, so Creek has to guess at some of what he's trying to say. Kimo helps some, too, filling in the gaps.

BUT SHE HADN'T EVEN STARTED TO MOVE IN DOWN THERE WHEN THIS NEW GUY SHOWED UP CALLING HIMSELF 'THE DOCTOR.' HE TOOK OUT THE GLOVER MEADOWS ENCLAVE, BEDFORD ESTATES, AND ONE OTHER. BURNED THEM TO THE GROUND. KILLED EVERYONE. THEY SAY HE HAS AN ARMY OF MONSTERS THAT CAN'T BE STOPPED.

MONSTERS?

THAT'S WHAT THEY SAY. Creek knows about monsters, mostly because of the Duke, who liked to tell stories at night to scare him and Kimo. He didn't really believe the boy, but he had the nightmares nonetheless.

WHAT KIND OF MONSTERS?

I DON'T KNOW. BAD ONES.

WHAT DOES HE WANT?

The Duke leans in, eyes wide. *THAT BOX YOU TOOK. HE SAYS IT BELONGS TO HIM. HE KNOWS YOU TOOK IT. HE WANTS IT BACK.*

Creek's stomach gets all cold.

HE ALSO ASKED ABOUT THOSE MEDICOS THAT GOT KILLED. HE SAID THEIR EQUIPMENT BELONGED TO HIM, TOO.

COME ON!

YEAH, YOU REALLY PUT YOUR FOOT IN IT.

DID NOT! I DIDN'T DO ANYTHING!

WELL, YOU TOOK THE BOX, AND YOU WERE THERE WHEN THEY KILLED THOSE MEDICOS…SO…

Creek looks around wildly, half expecting the Doctor's men to swoop in and carry him off in their black car. The Duke laughs. *I'M JUST KIDDING, YOU DIMMO! THE LADY WOULDN'T TELL HIM ANYTHING. SHE JUST SAID SHE COULDN'T HELP HIM, AND HE LEFT. HE MADE SOME THREATS, BUT HE WON'T DO ANYTHING. LADY FAL IS TOO TOUGH. DON'T WORRY.*

YOU'RE A JERK, DUKE.

The Duke laughs again. *AND YOU'RE A SUCKER.* He rises and heads out the gate toward the commissary, passing Sandoval. The man has been watching them for a while. He comes over to them, and drops down on his haunches, doing more miming — pointing at Creek, then at himself, then moving his hands, then pointing again. He wants something, clearly, but what it is, Creek has no idea.

Finally, he gives up and mouths something to Kimo.

WHAT? Creek asks her.

HE WANTS US TO TEACH HIM HOW TO TALK.

Sandoval leans his face right up in Creek's. He nods.

Chapter 12

Nonas *(No — Niners. Oh, Sebastien).* They wear a motley of gray and brown, bandoliers, black sighting helmets. When they speak, it sounds like when Sebastien would talk to his parents — the language of the Outside. Lucinda can't understand it, though every once and a while she can make out a word that sounds familiar. They don't seem to be in any hurry.

As quietly as she can, she eases the pack off her back, undoes the clasp, and gently pulls the teflon-coated zipper. The case of COR modules has a snap closure, and she winces as it clicks open, but the chatter of the stream drowns out the noise, and the soldiers continue their casual conversation. A couple of them sit on the big rock at the edge of the clearing, their backs to her.

She tears her eyes away from them and focuses on the case. She can't seem to read the tiny letters. But at last, she finds the one she's looking for. She thinks the eject command and the survival module pops out, leaving behind only a wisp of all she knew. Her trembling fingers fumble as she returns it to the case. She almost drops it into the stream, but at length succeeds in slipping it into its little clip and choosing another. She doesn't risk closing the case as she slides it back into her pack. She inserts the new chip behind her ear.

The language module doesn't give her instant fluency. At first, there is a slight delay as the bulk of her mind still operates in English, and each word or phrase is parsed and translated. The effort makes her lose some of the words. But it surprises Lucinda how quickly she can adapt her thoughts to the new language and follow most of the conversation. It reminds her of the time an embassy came from one of the Enclaves near Montreal, on the other side of the border wall. Her sixth-grade class had all uploaded French, and they'd spent a day talking with a group of children who had traveled with the diplomats. She met a girl named Marie Jeanette, and they had spent the afternoon chattering about food and dance music and their favorite vidis. They had promised to correspond. They never did.

The conversation proves much less interesting than she had hoped. The soldiers talk about someone named Rafeo who made a fool of himself at mess the night before. It's unclear what he did, but it seems to involve falling off a table. One of the soldiers defends him, but the others are casually merciless in their disdain. A small man asks if anybody has a ration cake, and one of the men sitting on the rock tosses him a small brown package and says, "That's three you owe me."

There's a silence, and the small one says, "We should keep moving. They're not coming back."

A tall soldier, thin with a short beard, says, "We wait."

"Yeah," says another man, a sweet-looking guy with a round face and a wisp of mustache —not more than eighteen, Lucinda guesses. "We don't want those *(something something)* Enclavers spying on us. We're supposed to be the spies."

"Do you know when the attack is?" asks the small one.

"Soon. This week. Next. When the big man says we're ready. That's why we're doing recon," says the thin soldier, who appears to be the leader. "Find out *(something something something)*. They got all kinds of little secrets. Don't fight with honor, like us."

Silence falls, and the platoon mills about. Lucinda's back starts to seize up. She has put herself in an uncomfortable twist so she can see them through a low bush *(she knew its genus and species five minutes ago)* without being seen. Her body yells at her to shift her position, but she doesn't dare. She has a wild desire to make a break for it, run back to the wall, and warn them. She imagines herself waving to the soldiers in the tower, shouting up to them, being let back in through the gate, welcomed with gratitude by the city leaders. Then she remembers the coldness of her mother's rebuke, and the fantasy disintegrates. What does she owe them? It's thanks to them that she's here in the first place. Rejected. Outcast. A pariah.

Without warning, Lucinda's COR buzzes out. A shiv of pain slices through the center of her head, and she twitches violently, unable to control herself. A taut gasp escapes her lips.

The soldiers turn in a body. She doesn't hesitate, but grabs her bag and scrambles away, her feet slipping out from under her on the loose gravel. For one horrifying moment, she's sure she's going to fall flat on her face, but her shoe finds purchase against a small rock and she pushes off, flying headlong down the hill on the side of the clearing.

The platoon hesitates for a stunned second, then a disjointed cacophony of shouts erupts as they take off after her. She can feel a searing in her back as she pelts through the brush, leaves, and branches whipping at her face and chest, but the burning doesn't slow her down. It drives her on, a white-hot whip of fire. Her feet pound the ground as she leaps over dead logs and mossy stones. She hears the crack of a rifle. She has no idea which way she's heading, taking the line of least resistance, sweeping through openings in the brush, following the invisible paths left by deer and other wildlife. She's fast, very fast, but she knows that they are following her, and they are fast, too.

As she approaches the bottom of the hill, a movement to her right grabs her attention. Two more soldiers stand beside the stream about thirty meters away, taking a reading with some kind of instrument. Her eyes meet those of an older woman, dark under her black helmet. Time slows down as they share a long look, curious and intent. She hears another shout from behind her. The woman yells in response, and she and her partner move to cut Lucinda off. Lucinda veers slightly left, but her way is blocked by a long outcropping of rock like a wall. She has no choice but to try to beat them to the intersect point. She puts her head down and opens up into a frantic sprint, heedless of the treacherous ground and the slicing branches. They are no more than five meters away when she blasts by them, leaping over a soggy depression in the forest floor and speeding away down the steepening grade. She barely notices when her COR sizzles back to life.

She reaches the bottom of the long slope. The stream turns here, blocking her path. She gathers herself and vaults across the water, landing gazelle-like, barely missing stride as she begins to sprint up the hill. She was always a good runner. But then, her luck deserts her. A hidden outcrop of rock, buried under the brown needles. Her foot hits half on, half off, and she stumbles, her ankle wrenching to the side. A fist of pain punches her, and she falls. Behind her, she hears cries from the approaching soldiers, and the sound of someone splashing through the stream.

With a moan of anguish, she pulls herself to her feet and struggles up the hill. She can hear them behind her. She hobbles as swiftly as she can up the slope, sometimes hopping when the ground is level enough. Her breath comes in whistles and gasps, but she keeps on, her lungs burning, her heart pounding out of her chest.

She reaches the top of the hill. The pine trees give way to an open meadow. Autumn flowers sparkle in the late afternoon sun, growing tall among high grasses around the ruined foundations of a house. She can see trees on the far side, a hundred meters or so away, banking around the crest of the hill in a wide circle. It might as well be the moon. She'll never make it across before her pursuers emerge and descend upon her.

Her COR buzzes out again. She grabs her head with a scream, the pain exponentially worse than any she has felt before. She staggers out into the meadow toward the ruins. Bolt after bolt of lightning pierce her head, but she keeps going. She hears a shout behind her.

She reaches the house, and, with a strangled sob, collapses onto the ground behind the remains of a low concrete wall. The long grass surrounds her, covering her from sight, but she knows that it's only a matter of moments before they come upon her. Clouds obscure the sun, turning the light gray and wan. She pulls the knife out of the backpack, then puts it away again. That will only make it worse.

It starts to rain. Her head buzzes again, but the pain brings a new sensation — a throbbing rage that almost blacks out her eyesight. Her mind goes blank, the chaotic anger of a beast. She rises from behind the wall. Barely two meters away stands the young soldier with the wispy mustache. He has slowed as he neared the wall, creeping forward with his gun held crossways in front. Two other soldiers flank him about ten meters behind. He raises his hand to her and says something, but she cannot understand him without her COR. The gesture is meant to placate, soothe the helpless girl into quiet submission, so he is unprepared when she leaps over the wall and barrels into him. He stumbles backward and they fall into the grass with Lucinda on top, trapping his gun between them. He screams as she buries her teeth in his face, ripping a hole in his baby-soft cheek. His scream mingles with hers. She bites again, the salt tang of his blood lighting up her frenzied mind like a bonfire. Then something flat and hard strikes the back of her head. A white flash explodes her world. Blackness.

Chapter 13

A hand gives Creek a gentle shove, pulling him up out of a dream in which his mother — faceless but distinct — showed Candela how to sew buttons. He opens his eyes. Kimo hunches over him, her face blending into the darkness like a misting ghost.

WE HAVE TO GO, she shapes. He can just make out her hands.

He shakes the sleep from his head and sits up. A tall silhouette blocks the doorway.

WHERE? he asks. She doesn't answer, just jerks her head toward the figure in the door. Creek can tell from his broad shoulders that it is Sandoval. Kimo motions for him to rise, so he pulls off the blanket and scrambles up. He slips on his shoes and follows her. Sandoval stands aside, and they pass into the yard.

They follow him out through the gate into the main camp. The weary light before dawn turns everything an ashy gray. It must be very early. All is silent around them. Creek can make out the snipes in their makeshift towers, but nobody else appears to be awake. Sandoval leads them around the water tower to the far side. A caravan is parked there. Square and clunky, not as large as a double-wide, but big enough for a small family. He nudges them up the little flight of steps and inside, then shuts the door.

The interior feels bigger than Creek thought from the outside. There's a small sitting area behind the driver's seat, and a little kitchen along one side. The space is divided by a wall, and he can make out a little bedroom through an open door at the back. The space is crowded with machines. He recognizes them as the ones that were taken from the shack. The exploded head of the man flashes through his brain, and the blonde woman, face down on the floor.

Two women sit at the little table, wedged in among the machines. The first is Lady Fal. She turns when they enter, and her sharp gaze immediately stabs him with irrational guilt for some unimagined infraction. The other is the woman from the shack — the one who had come in after Sandoval had killed the whelite woman and the man — the one with the sweet brown face and bright eyes. She stands when they come in, opening her arms in a gesture of welcome. She has a big smile on her face. It's hard not to like her. She keeps the smile going as she talks at them for a while, pointing this way and that. Kimo translates for him.

She tells him that the lady is called Katanja Jemisen, and that she is a doctor. He and Kimo are going to work for her now — cleaning up, holding things, helping out as needed, both here and in the infirmary. She asks if that sounds like fun. He nods. Dr. Jemisen gives him another big grin.

The grown-ups talk for a while, and then Lady Fal leaves. Dr. Jemisen takes them over to one of the machines — a squat box with a glass front. Inside are three rows of vials, each one marked with tiny writing. Creek wonders what they mean.

This one, the doctor mimes, *don't touch. Very bad. Don't eat.*

He looks to Kimo. *WHAT ARE THEY?*

BITS OF BRAIN AND BLOOD FROM PEOPLE WHO HAD MINDWORM.

Ugh. That's disgusting. Why would he want to eat that? What does she think he is, a toddler, or a dog? People are crazy.

She puts them to work. It's a heck of a lot better than power-jacking — no hiding in wet underbrush, no catching your clothes or skin on a jagged piece of chainlink, no constantly looking around to see if somebody is coming to shoot you or beat you up. Just cleaning, and stacking, and fetching. Boring, but Creek doesn't mind a bit of boring. Not one little bit. He can't really tell what Dr. Jemisen is doing, but who cares? She smiles a lot, and mimes *thank you* when he brings her something. It's different. Kimo has the Ear on, so the doctor talks to her when she has something complicated to explain. But hearing people usually focus on Kimo and pretty much ignore him. It's easier. Dr. Jemisen actually makes a real effort to include him. Creek doesn't know what to make of it. Nobody has been this nice to him before.

At lunchtime, Sandoval appears and escorts them to the mess. He sits with them while they eat. He keeps glancing up from his food to study Creek, as if taking his face apart with his eyes.

When they finish eating, Sandoval insists that they teach him some shaping. They give him the basic lessons. They haven't got very far when he shakes his head and mouths something to Kimo. She translates.

HE SAYS YOU LOOK FAMILIAR. HE WANTS TO KNOW IF YOU HAVE EVER BEEN TO EASTON OR LEEDSTOWN.

NO. Creek's pretty sure he's never seen the man before in his life. What a weirdy.

Sandoval shakes his head, frustrated by Creek's answer, and prompts them to start up teaching again. He proves to be a slow learner, but patient. *Again,* he'll gesture. *Again. Again. Again.* Lunch is long over by the time he releases them and returns them to Dr. Jemisen.

The afternoon turns out just like the morning. Fetching, holding, fetching, cleaning, fetching, rearranging. Creek's legs ache something terrible when finally Sandoval appears to take them back to their tent. Before they go, Dr. Jemisen asks them to show her how to shape a couple of phrases. What is going on? Are they running a school now? Creek has never had so many people wanting to learn how to talk. He's not used to the attention, but it's kind of nice.

THANK YOU, shapes Dr. Jemisen. *SEE YOU TOMORROW.*

When they get back to the enclosure, the Duke and Lamarque are sitting on the ground cleaning pieces of body armor. Candela sits nearby on a dirty cloak, with Baby beside her, batting at the air above him.

WHAT ARE YOU DOING? asks Creek.

CLEANING OUR ARMOR, shapes the Duke, proudly.

YOUR WHAT?

DON'T BE AN IDIOT. GUESS WHO GOT ASSIGNED TO RATALFA'S FIGHTING GROUP?

Creek shakes his head.

WE DID, DIMMO! WE'RE SOLDIERS NOW! Ratalfa was Lady Fal's second in command. *WHEN THE ASSAULT COMES, WE'LL BE IN THE THICK OF IT!*

WHAT ASSAULT? asks Creek.

WE'RE HITTING THAT ENCLAVE ANY DAY NOW. GONNA TAKE OUT THOSE STINKING WHELITES. Kind of strange for the Duke to be talking this way, considering he's a whelite himself. They kicked him out of his own enclave, of course, so it makes sense.

Chapter 14

The throbbing heat gradually resolves, like a lens slowly focused, into a circle of lights glaring down on her from an unfamiliar ceiling. Lucinda's head — indeed, her whole body — aches too much to move, but she blinks her eyes, trying to make the painful blobs of light go away.

"There you are," says a voice. "I wasn't sure we'd got you in time. It's always tricky when the disease has advanced so far. But we brought you back."

With an effort, Lucinda turns her head toward the speaker. A tall man, sixty-ish, stands beside the table where she lies. He wears a white lab coat over a dark shirt. His gray hair immaculately trimmed over a ruddy whelite face with a piercing blue eye.

One eye. One human eye. *Man?* Part man. The upper third of his face on the right side has been replaced by smooth robot-skin, a round robotic eye glowing dully red out of the gray plastic. A vicious-looking scar runs down the human side, ending below a thin-lipped mouth.

Lucinda feels too sick to be frightened. "Where am I?" she asks in a small voice. Her throat is dry, and it hurts to speak.

"You're alive, isn't that enough? What is your name, my dear?" The voice doesn't match the face. Rich, sonorous. Kind, even.

"Lucinda Weston," she answers. She tries to put her brain back together. She remembers the woods, the field with the ruined house, the soldiers, and then nothing but a white whiteness, followed by a black blackness.

"You're safe, Lucinda," he says. "And you're not going to die, thanks to me."

"Die?"

"You have Mindworm, my dear. It has infected your brain. But not to worry, my drugs are holding the virus at bay, so that it cannot kill you." She stares back at him, uncomprehending. "My soldiers brought you in. You killed one. Tore his face off with your teeth. They wanted to kill you, too, but they know my orders."

Lucinda tries to shake the bees out of her head. "I'm sorry. I didn't mean to…I don't remember."

"You finally succumbed, just as they came on you. You're not responsible. They've seen it before. They understand the risks."

"When…?"

"Two days ago. As I said, it was almost too late. I got you just in time."

"Thank you." He raises his left arm to brush back a stray hair, and she can see that his hand is artificial as well.

"Who are you?" she asks.

"My soldiers call me the Doctor. It's a bit grandiose, I know, but they seem to like it. And I *am* a doctor. You can call me Horace. Rest now. We'll talk more later."

Lucinda wants to ask him something, but her blurry thoughts won't mold into a question. She drifts into oblivion.

Time passes. Sometimes she is awake, sometimes asleep. He is always there — his voice calming, reassuring. He gives her injections that still the swirling agitations in her brain. After an unknown while, they begin to subside, until she spends more time conscious than not. His soldiers — mute and neutral — move her to a new place. A bedroom, with a little bed that must once have belonged to a young girl.

Her body feels like an empty glass — clean and clear, but inert. Hollowed out. She knows that she once felt passion — desire, and rage, and joy — but the person who felt these things seems to stand on a distant cliff, separated by a wide, gray sea. Small and indistinct. She idly wonders if the Doctor's medications are muting her mind, but the thought flickers away into the silent air. She rests.

The house is beautiful. Old. Rich. She can go where she pleases. She can't go far because she is still weak. But her mind is calm. And empty. There is a void in the place that sustained her as long as she can remember. Sometimes she rouses enough to become curious about a painting, or one of the statues that populate the mantels, or the many dark-bound books of real leather and paper. Forgetting herself, she taps her COR, and the emptiness crushes her into a small space, smaller than a mouse. She returns to bed and stares at the ceiling.

They sit in a small room, paneled in dark wood. The gray light of a rainy morning filters in through the window. At least a week has passed since she came to in the Doctor's surgery. She feels stronger, but strangely muted, as if all the color has washed out of her body. A young soldier brings in a china teapot and some biscuits on a tray. The Doctor pours them each a cup. "Well, Lucinda. I am pleased with your progress. Tell me: You're from Hamilton Estates, isn't that right?"

"Hamilton Estates, yes."

"I thought so. Isn't that my lucky day?"

"Why?"

"I'll tell you later." He raises his cup. "To have such a guest. The last Enclave on the Northeast corridor. A bastion of our civilization. How did you like it?"

Lucinda cannot read him at all. He is all politeness and detached concern, but she senses something underneath, like the rumble of a torquing fault line. "I loved it," she answers.

"And yet they drove you out. Didn't they?"

"Yes, they did."

"That must have hurt."

"Yes."

"They didn't even give you a chance, did they?"

How does he know that? "No."

"Of course not." He sips his tea. "Mindworm drives healthy people almost as crazy as the sick ones. Fear. They don't stop to think. It is unfortunate. The fact is, like everything, the disease is an opportunity, when viewed through the proper lens. But few people can appreciate that."

"And you can."

He smiles. "I can." The Doctor leans forward, extending his human hand toward her cheek. She recoils slightly. "May I?" he says, "examine your implant?" He pushes back her hair and cocks his head. The gesture is cool, professional, but also intimate. She feels a tingle on the back of her neck. "Fascinating. I read about these back in the day, but everything went to hell before I could try one out myself. It's a Datamyne COR module, yes?"

"Yes."

"Nice bit of hardware. I had an IQ-230 for years. Nowhere near the same capabilities. A glorified beeper."

"A what?"

The Doctor laughs. "Old tech they had before you were born. Anyhow, the IQ had only a rudimentary neuronal link. Doesn't matter. It got damaged when the—" he stops abruptly. "It was damaged. It was no great loss, though it did connect me to the world outside. This ocular prosthesis —" He points to the red robot eye "— doesn't have that capability. I'm cut off, at least for now. You're cut off, too, aren't you?"

Lucinda nods.

He draws back his hand. "That must hurt."

She feels a hot rush, as unexpected tears spring into her eyes. "Yes," she says.

"Let's see what we can do about that."

His full name is Horace Ashburn. "The Doctor" to his men, and to the frightened world. On more than one occasion, he asks her to call him Horace, but she resists. He tells her the house once belonged to a friend of his named Prendergast, a government muckety-muck before the Collapse who disappeared years ago. Ashburn moved in after…something. He won't tell her what happened, but Lucinda can sense the ghosts of a terrible ordeal. She guesses that his prosthetic face, his prosthetic hand, his prosthetic foot are recent additions, in place for less than a year. His brow darkens like a storm when he thinks of it.

She doesn't know what to make of him. He is so kind to her — gentle, understanding, patient. But once, while climbing the stairs from the kitchen to her bedroom, she heard him through the door of his study, screaming at one of his soldiers with such merciless cruelty that she feared for the man's life.

Nevertheless, this house — and his mastery of it — speaks to her. The order, the simplicity, the clarity of it resonates with something deep inside her. Warm wood, damask wallpaper. Thick drapes. It reminds her of her home.

No. NOT her home. She kills the thought. *Not anymore.* She looks around the bedroom he has given her. This is the only home she has now. It pleases her as best it can. It is generously silent, and though that silence is welcome after the seething maelstrom of her exile and her illness, it also reminds her of what she has lost. The empty space within her, that once swarmed with all the wonders of the world. She shakes away the gloom and rises. Perhaps she'll go for a walk in the little garden behind the house. Clear her head.

She has only taken a step when a lucent bell sounds in her mind, clear and light and cool. And then, impossibly, her COR snaps to life, like a drowning victim suddenly coughing out a liter of water and sitting up. Silenced for days, leaving her isolated and so, so lonely, it surges within her, almost knocking her down, so sudden and visceral is the sensation. Her mind's eye turns, and there — so real she can almost touch it — a door appears, floating in the space between reality and imagination. A massive door, flanked by columns of white and gold. Above, inscribed into the pale marble, it reads, *ALEXANDRIA.*

"Do you approve?" Ashburn stands at the real door to the bedroom, peering in with an expectant half-smile on his face. "It's not as extensive as the databases of the Enclave, but it's not bad. I designed the gateway myself."

Her mind's eye stares in wonder at the magnificent edifice. "It's amazing," she says.

"I wasn't sure if I had the coding right to tie into your device." He leans against the doorframe, crossing his arms and grinning. "I can't see it, of course. Does it look all right?" She nods. "Try it out."

"Thank you, Doctor!" She lunges at him without thinking what she's doing, and throws her arms around his neck. He accepts the gesture, though he does not hug her back. He seems surprised, uncertain how to react.

"I'm glad you like it," he says with half a laugh.

Lucinda backs away, suddenly embarrassed. She turns again to the gateway, resplendent and inviting.

"May I?"

"Of course. Go right ahead. I want to know what you think." He hesitates. The expression on his face changes — still indulgent, but layered with something hungry, calculating. *Wolfish.* "There is one thing. The cost of entry, if you will."

She swallows. "What is that?"

"You must call me Horace."

Lucinda hesitates. She does not know what it means, but she knows it is a step down a road, and she cannot see the end.

"Of course. If you like. Horace."

He smiles his twisted smile and gestures toward Alexandria. She opens the gateway with a thought, and steps into a new world.

Lucinda spins through the universe of knowledge. Sometimes familiar, but mostly new — he gives her access to subjects she has never considered: cybernetics, political science, eugenics, game theory, military history and strategy, but also music and literature that she thought had been lost to the Collapse. The Enclave maintained a vast catalogue of human learning. But now she understands that it held only a portion of the wisdom of the lost world. After the starvation of the last few weeks, she hurls herself into the world inside her head.

She only leaves her room to eat with him, and they talk, talk, talk about things she has never considered. Her existence in the Enclave feels so small, so limiting, so parochial. He tells her stories about his life — he won't say how old he is, but surely he has lived longer than anyone she has ever met. He speaks with such specificity about the magical world before the Collapse, about the cataclysms of the Fall, and the war for survival and renewal that even now is being waged around her. Somehow, this man — *part man* — was there. Saw it all.

Of his own past, he says little. He was a surgeon before the Collapse, who specialized in physical augmentation and life extension. How he became a warlord, he does not say. "Not important," he tells her. "It was necessary to the plan."

He speaks often of the plan. He tells her he can see the way forward. A beautiful future, the return of order, and plenty, and *knowledge*. Knowledge returned to the lost peoples of this ravaged continent. But only after a terrible struggle, where terrible things are done, and terrible losses are endured.

"The time is now, Lucinda," he says to her during dinner. He eats red meat and roasted potatoes. Since her recovery, she finds she has no appetite, and the smell sickens her. But she doesn't want to offend. He attacks the food like it is the future he wants to conquer. "With the tools I have, I must strike a hard, a fast blow. That blow will shatter the tenuous missteps of our current chaos and usher in a new dawn that will, in time, return us to the glory of past days. But the price is high."

He tosses down his knife and rises. "Lucinda. It's time you saw something. Come with me." He extends his robot hand to her. She takes it, cold and smooth, and follows him out of the room.

He leads her swiftly down the stairs, through the opulent living room with its white sofa and accents of crimson and glass. The guards at the door spring to attention as he passes between them.

A light rain is falling, as usual. Threads of mist snake around the buildings and trees. The air is thick and wet. The house stands in the ruins of an enclave called "Wallingford Gardens." The only building still intact. Ashburn's soldiers have used some of the nearby wrecks for shelter, setting up cots and bedrolls among the debris of caved-in roofs, collapsed walls, and shattered glass. Ashburn has the only proper house. It's a marvel — pristine and well-kept as if it were new. It stands like a fairy palace among the ruins. He hasn't told her how it survived, or how he acquired it. At dinner the night before, he had snorted, "Ole Prendie would have a laugh if he knew I'd taken up residence. Or a heart attack. Hard to say which."

Lucinda follows him up the muddy street, cleared of grass and weeds by the regular passage of vehicles, but rutted and heaved. He leads her to the left, down a small hill. A tall fence, razor wire spiraling along its top, blocks their path. Four soldiers, two on their side and two on the other, keep watch over a wide gate. Ashburn waves his fob over the lock, and one of the soldiers swings it open to let them pass. Lucinda's nose picks up a light stench drifting on the breeze. As they enter the yard, it grows stronger.

At the back of the yard rises another fence, taller and stronger, forming an enclosure within the enclosure. Inside, she can see human shapes huddling in small clumps, or lying on the ground, or hanging off the steel palings. The smell emanates from them, and she crinkles her nose and puts her hand to her face as they come to a stop before a second gate, this one solid steel.

"Who are they?" she asks. "Prisoners of war?"

"No," he answers. "They are my army. My elite force."

They certainly don't look elite. Nor do they look like soldiers. They wear a hodgepodge of clothes, many dressed in filthy rags. Their faces and hands are filthy, too. But it is their expressions that strike her most. Some slack-jawed, some with darting eyes, whispering and shaking. Some swatting haphazardly at invisible insects. Some staring catatonically into a distance so far away that she cannot imagine what they see.

"They are my Afflicted," Ashburn continues. "Like you. Victims of Mindworm, kept alive by my medicines. But unlike you, they don't receive the full protocol. When I need them, I release them, and their unleashed madness breaks all resistance to my forces. They are my Athena's spear, my Thor's hammer, my thunderbolt of Zeus."

He turns toward her. "What do you think? Are you appalled?"

She swallows. "I don't know," she says. "Do they suffer?"

"Of course," he says. "Don't we all? At least they live. And they have me to thank for it. I need you to see this—" he leans into her until his face almost touches hers "—and understand. These are the steps we must take to see the New Dawn."

Lucinda looks up at him, her heart and body strangely still. She has not lied to him. She does not know what she feels. She should be outraged, she supposes. But her soul remains muted, unmoved by what she sees. *Is he right?* She can't say.

"They look so placid. Don't they attack each other?"

"Rarely. The virus has found an ingenious way to make sure it doesn't waste itself on an already infected body. Perhaps you have noticed a particular augmentation of your senses — perhaps one, in particular?"

She thinks. "I guess…smell? I have been way more aware of how things smell recently."

"Good girl. Yes. Hyperosmia, it is called. I've muted it as best I can for you. For them, it's overpowering. Humans don't normally use their scent receptors to their full capability. They don't need to. Mindworm realizes their potential for its own purposes. They become like dogs, or badgers. But that's just the start of it. Truly ingenious, this virus. Almost as if it had a plan. I noticed that you didn't touch your food at dinner. A shame. You're too thin already."

Lucinda blushes. "I'm sorry. I haven't been hungry since…"

"It's all right. Another symptom of your condition. You've more or less stopped producing a certain chemical in your stomach — butyrate, if you're interested. Go ahead. Check it out."

She nods obediently and taps her COR. She learns that butyrate is a four-carbon short-chain fatty acid produced by microbial fermentation of dietary fiber in her lower intestine. It is associated with intestinal health and energy metabolism, and has anti-inflammatory properties that enhance intestinal barrier function. "I see," she says.

"Mindworm gives you a bad stomach. Isn't that thoughtful of it? But butyrate also happens to be one of the more prominent volatile organic compounds released by our bodies. The Afflicted can smell it at a great distance, and can you imagine what it does to them?"

"It drives them crazy?"

"Exactly. Here, let me show you. Soldier!" He calls to one of the men guarding the fence. "What's your name?"

The man comes over. "Catalho, sir."

"Guarding the cage is lousy work. How would you like a promotion?"

"I'd like that very much, sir."

"Show our guest your M-pack."

The soldier, a dark-skinned man of about thirty, reaches for his belt and pulls off a small case about the size of a pair of binoculars. He extends it to Lucinda.

"It's functioning properly, I assume," says Ashburn.

"Yes, sir."

"Let's find out. Enter the cage, please."

Catalho looks at him, his eyes widening, then nods. "Yes, sir." He unlocks the gate and steps inside. His fellow soldier closes the gate behind him.

Ashburn watches him as he stands uncertainly at the edge of the crowd of Afflicted. "The M-pack conceals the butyrate signal we give off through our breath and skin. To them, he's just another sick person, and the virus has no interest in him, so neither do they. Walk among them."

Catalho obeys. Sure enough, as the soldier gingerly steps around the hunkered bodies, not one of them pays him the slightest attention. They continue to loll and mutter and groan to themselves, trapped in their own private misery. Caltalho finishes a circuit of the enclosure and stops again by the gate.

"Now, turn off your M-pack."

The man turns sharply to him. "I'm sorry, sir?"

"Turn off your M-pack."

"But—"

"My good man, you want that promotion, don't you?"

"Yes, sir, but—"

"Then you have two choices. Turn off your M-pack and get promoted, or come out. I'll order your comrades here to confiscate it, and we'll throw you back in there and see how my Afflicted like you then. Your choice."

Lucinda feels a chill like a cold hand up her back. Catalho stares at her, pleading silently for her to intervene, but she remains silent. He exhales, puts his back to the fence, about fifteen meters from the nearest Afflicted, draws his pistol, and switches off the pack.

At first, nothing happens. The Afflicted continue to jerk and quiver, oblivious to his presence. After thirty seconds, one of them — a woman of about fifty — raises her head. Another, then another, does the same thing. The muted chattering rises in pitch, punctuated by barks and cries. More and more rise to their feet, their mouths working, their hands spasmodically clenching. They cast about for the scent, testing the air like dogs. Then, almost in a body, they zero in on Catalho, pressed up against the chain links, the gun shaking in his hand. They move in on him like a pack of hyenas. He raises the gun. "Please, sir!"

Ashburn raises his hand. "All right, soldier. Activate your M-pack." The Afflicted are almost upon him. He switches on the pack. The diseased woman knocks the arm with the pistol to one side and grabs him by the neck, teeth bared, head shaking. He fires into the ground, struggling to escape her grasp. The mob falls on him, a tangle of flailing limbs. Then, all at once, they lose interest. They roll off him, eyes dull, mouths slack. They wander away, or crawl into a ball on the ground. The quiet moaning and muttering resume, as if they had never stopped.

"Well done, my boy," says Ashburn. "Did they bite you?"

"No, sir."

Ashburn gestures to the other soldier, who has been watching with horrified fascination, to unlock the cage. Catalho stumbles out, breathing heavily, sweat shining on his brow. "Go see Amall. Tell him that I want you reassigned to my personal staff. Tell him you are relieved for today. Go to the commissary. Get drunk." He grins like a wolf. "That's an order. I will see you bright and early tomorrow morning. You are dismissed."

Catalho can only nod. He turns and trudges up the path, silent as a ghost. Ashburn looks at her. "I ask much, but I keep my word. You see?"

Lucinda turns to watch the Afflicted in their cage. At last, she speaks. "Why am I not in there with them?"

Ashburn grins, a crooked slash of a smile, and puts his human hand on the side of her face. She doesn't flinch. "When they brought you in, they wanted to throw you in the cage immediately, because of what you did to their comrade. But as soon as I saw you, I knew that you…are special," he says.

"Because of my COR?"

"For many reasons." He withdraws his hand. "But yes, I have a need for that particular attribute of yours. You won't like it, but it must be done. Now, you must rest."

When they return to the house, Durain — Ashburn's adjutant — is waiting for them in the hall.

"Dr. Ashburn?"

"Yes?"

"Everything is ready for the morning."

"Good. I'll meet the captains in my study in thirty minutes."

Durain nods and withdraws. Ashburn takes Lucinda's hand in his, holding it as gently as a baby bird.

"Lucinda Weston, what happens next will change everything. A terrible cost, especially for you. But it must be done."

Chapter 15

Katanja Jemisen sips chamomile tea as she writes up her notes from the day's work on a pink-cased tabula. She doesn't look up as Lady Fal slips through the door and takes a seat beside her.

"How is it going?" asks the Lady.

"Not bad. Thank you for the kids. They are a tremendous help."

"Kimo is very smart. I'm not sure about the other one. He's hard to read."

"Creek is smart, too. Just guarded. I wonder what he's been through. Kids like that. What he's seen. I can't imagine."

"Sure you can. Probably not much different from what you've seen. Or me. What have you learned?"

"A little. I've spent most of my time making sure everything survived the trip. Your fighters weren't exactly careful with the equipment. Luckily, everything seems to be working. Tomorrow I can get back to work, pick up where we left off."

"And where is that?"

"Not very far, I'm afraid. We had just started looking into what the Doctor was doing when your man shot my friends."

"I've apologized for that three times already, but I'll keep on apologizing if that will help."

"It won't. Dr. Langston wasn't just a good person whom I had grown to like quite a lot; she was the microbiologist. I was a glorified lab assistant."

"I'm sorry. Again. But you're no dimwit, Kat. I know you can do this."

"Thank you for the vote of confidence." Kat pours more tea for the two of them. They sit silent, each lost in her own world.

"So," says Fal, "where are we?"

"We identified three totally different lines of inquiry in the Doctor's work."

"Go on."

"Well, they were fabricating a number of compounds that suppress certain systems, as if they were trying to control symptoms."

"That doesn't sound like a cure."

"No. But the machines produce several compounds that inhibit the progress of the virus, and control some of the more extreme expressions. I don't fully understand it, but that's what they do. But then, there's also a set that seems to *promote* some of the disease's effects — adrenaline enhancers, drugs to increase blood flow, things like that."

"Accelerating the disease."

"Intensifying its expression, anyway. Sort of. I'm not sure."

"Would accelerating it somehow cure it?"

"I can't see how." Kat sighs and rubs her eyes.

"What's the third line?"

"The what?"

"You said there were three lines of inquiry."

"Right. Sorry. It's been a long day. That's the one that appears to head toward a cure. But it's *so* rudimentary. Like they had barely started the actual work. I can't tell if any of it leads anywhere."

"You've only just begun. You'll figure it out." Fal stares into her tea. Kat has the impression she was only half listening to the conversation.

"That's what I've got. Now, what's going on? Something, obviously."

Fal draws her hand across her forehead. "Sorry, Kat. I'm just worried. We're so exposed. No cases in camp right now, but if we get even one, we're screwed. And now there's this Doctor showing up and talking tough."

"He is tough."

"I can handle him. If those machines *did* belong to him, which I doubt, well, they don't belong to him anymore. They're ours. But — and I know you're doing everything you can, and I know you're exhausted — we have to figure out if there's anything real about this 'curing Mindworm' talk. And we have to do it fast. The assault is in three days."

Kat shakes her head. "You still plan to take out Hamilton Estates?"

"I know you don't like it."

"You're right. I don't."

"Well, we don't have any choice. We're low on supplies. The farm at Wilson's Corner failed — some kind of fungus. Plus, the fighters are getting itchy. We've been sitting too long. With the resources of that enclave, we can make a move to a more permanent settlement."

"They have countermeasures. Good ones. You're going to lose a lot of people."

"I know. So do they. They can handle it."

"What about the people who live there?"

"What about them?"

Kat leans in. "You can't build anything if all you do is kill and burn and destroy. I'm a doctor. I don't like killing. And the Falernia I knew didn't like it either."

"I know what I'm doing. We'll keep it orderly. Trust me."

A quiet throat-clearing from outside the van breaks the intimacy. "Yes?" says Fal.

Toroniyo, her adjutant, slides in. "I'm sorry to bother you, my Lady."

"What is it?"

"Our scouts have returned from Hamilton Estates. I'm afraid—" He stops, his eyes darting nervously about.

"Afraid of what?"

"It appears that the, uh, the Doctor has beaten us to the punch. Hamilton Estates is overrun."

Lady Fal doesn't speak for a long time. Then she says, "Thank you." The man exits hurriedly, glad to be gone. The silence falls again.

"Well," says Kat, "So much for that."

"Yes."

"Is it a problem?"

"It's not great."

Kat leans in. "I told you he's dangerous."

"He thinks he is. I've dealt with his type before. I'll deal with him."

Chapter 16

Lucinda stands in the ruins of her past life. Smoke swirls thick in the air, from the burning Hamilton Bank, the burning Hamilton Library, the burning Hamilton Town Hall. A fat smell hovers in her nostrils. She does her best not to recognize it as the odor of charred flesh.

They have cleared away the bodies — at least those of the Enclavers. The soldiers are still dealing with the corpses of the Afflicted, tossing them into the backs of half a dozen trucks, but many of them still sprawl here and there along the street where they fell, overcome at last by the fevered rage that ripped through their brains without the protection of the Doctor's medications.

She didn't watch the battle. She sat in Ashburn's car some distance away, the green lawn obscured by a thick wall of trees. But she could hear the sound of the assault — the deep booms of heavy ordinance, punctuated by the staccato clatter of small arms; the sharp clap of the NNEMP that had knocked out the countermeasures; the serried whoosh of shoulder-launched missiles. Where Ashburn had acquired these high-grade weapons she didn't know — no petty warlord had ever brought such force to bear. She figured his old friend Prendergast had something to do with it. When the grisly chattering of the horde of Afflicted rose on the wind, as they swarmed across the green into the breaches in the wall, Lucinda slipped a chip into her COR and filled her mind with a Schubert string quintet. She did a crossword. Time slipped by her muted mind. Then Ashburn returned and led her into the wreckage.

She wonders that she does not feel more. She expected to be shocked, horrified, maybe even burst into tears at the sight of all she once held dear broken and defeated. She doesn't. It appears small and far away to her — a make-believe town, no more real than the paint and canvas villages in the musicals they used to put on at the Arts Center. She once played Fiona in *Brigadoon.* She half tries to remember the story, but the details escape her. It was a fantasy, like her past.

Perhaps it is the absence in her COR. When she lived here, her brain would hum with whisperings from friends, idle news, rabbit-holes of curiosity, an ever-present cadence of life and information. Now her mind is as silent as the ash-strewn streets around her. The life of the place, its constant thrumming in her brain, has gone. It is not even a tomb. It is nothing — barren, devoid of interest, of spark.

"Lucinda." She turns to look into his face. His robot eye gleams like an ember in the smoldering dark.

"Yes."

"This must be very disturbing."

"I'm all right."

"You understand it was necessary. They were hoarding everything for themselves. Technology and resources that we need if we are ever to—"

"It's all right." She does not ask him who survived. If her parents or her friends still live, if she can see them. She doesn't want to know.

He searches her face, looking for a hidden clue. "You are a wonder," he says, with a tiny shake of disbelief. Then he smiles. "You must come with me, my dear. I need you for a task that only you can do. I think it will please you."

They head down the broken street, picking their way between the detonation craters. They pass the high school. A group of Enclavers mills about in a pathetic mass, soldiers prodding them into a line as they shuffle into the building. She spots someone in the crowd. *Sheena.* The girl doesn't see her. Lucinda keeps walking, looking straight ahead.

"We need to replenish the Afflicted," says Ashburn. "We lost more than I'd like, but since my lab equipment was stolen, I've had to ration their medications." He stops for a moment and takes her face in his hands. "But not yours, my dear, not yours. You are too important."

They mount the hill and come out into the square in front of the Arts Center. It still stands, but everything around it has been destroyed. Houses lie in rubble, smoke stinging the air, small fires burning everywhere. Seeing the building sends a flutter through Lucinda's heart. *He is gone,* she reminds herself.

On the steps of the Center stands a towering man of metal. Three meters high, its body sleek, gun-gray. Its shoulders broad, its arms reaching out, two meters long, the ends bristling with heat weapons and missile tubes. Its head looks human, or human-like, the face an idealized vision of perfection — straight, symmetrical features, evenly proportioned; large, deep-seeing eyes; a full, confident mouth; stern brows that bespeak a platonic virtue. It stands without moving, a beautiful, terrible statue. A platoon of soldiers encircles it, weapons at the ready, their faces pinched and nervous.

"Here we are, my dear," says Horace. "Do you recognize it?"

"Of course," she answers. "It's our soldier."

"It killed thirty-three of my men, and twice as many of the Afflicted."

"It's not moving."

"No. Its controller perished." He smiles. "Our luck. It almost turned the tide against us. Almost. You see, my girl, people fear machines. They want their power, but that power terrifies them, and they fear to give them too much leash, lest they be destroyed by their creations. So they hold them in check, even if it leads to their own destruction. Your soldier, as you call him, is not autonomous. Did you know that?"

"No."

"He has a consciousness, of sorts, but cannot act independently. He must link to a human who controls him from a remote location. If the human is killed, then the robot ceases to function. In the past, when this thing was created — during Civil War Two, I reckon — the human remained far behind the front lines, safely barricaded behind walls and troops. But here…We stumbled upon that human when we were storming the Defense Building. The Afflicted broke through and killed everyone inside. We don't know who controlled the soldier, but when they died, it froze."

"I see." Lucinda cannot take her eyes off the soldier. He is beautiful, cold. His eyes stare off into a space beyond human thought. He doesn't seem dead, just impossibly distant. Rapt.

Ashburn turns to her. "I need you to link with it, Lucinda. You are an Enclaver. You have the implant. You can speak to the soldier. I need it to restore what was taken from me. You will be my vessel."

She tries to read his human eye. *Who is this man? What has he done? What will he do with her?* She knows she cannot trust him, but he offers her life when everyone else offered only death and madness. The muting of her heart — so like despair, but not despair — holds her at a vast distance from all this destruction. *What, then, does it matter?*

"Of course," she says.

He takes her to the Defense Building. The top story has been blown off. Three hundred years the building stood, and now it is just a shell. The lower levels are still intact, though the glass around the front desk lies like a glittering carpet across the sidewalk. She remembers the last time she entered this building — Sorenson, Campbell, Chrysler. They must be dead, somewhere. She doesn't feel anything about them.

Ashburn leads her to a room on the second floor. They have to step around a hole where a piece of the roof fell through and shattered the balcony that rings the large, open lobby. The room contains a stack of servers and a terminal, sitting on a credenza that must be four hundred years old. Ashburn sits at the terminal, engages the device, swiping and typing with the confidence of the brilliant. "We should only have to do this once," he says as he works. "Once you're linked to the machine, you won't require the system, as long as you are in range."

He finishes what he is doing and turns to her, his robot eye flaring. "I put my trust in you, Lucinda Weston. Not something I do easily. Just remember that without me, you will die." His voice has never held that note before. Not to her. He has been so gentle. She has seen the violence that bubbles just beneath the surface, that makes him a destroyer of cities and a master of men. But always aimed at others. Not her. Her blankness protects her, and she nods.

"I understand." Sensing that she should, she adds, "Horace."

He cocks his head. "Good. All right," he says. "Here goes."

The ping sounds within her like a beautiful little bell. She accepts, and suddenly a voice hovers in her mind, distinct from her, separated not by space, but by thought.

Captain Talbot? it asks.

No, she answers. *Talbot is dead. I am Lucinda Weston.*

Do you wish to establish control link?

Yes.

Done.

And suddenly he is there. A partition of her mind holds his essential identity. He is called Artaxerxes, and he is a Controll H-51 CyberWarrior, build-date June 24, 2128. He saw action in the war against the Texas Confederacy, was deactivated at the time of the Collapse, then commandeered by the Enclave in 2201. An old machine, but no older than most of the tech they've got.

Hello, Artaxerxes.

Hello, Lucinda Weston.

Come to me, Artaxerxes.

On my way.

"Well?" asks Ashburn. Without answering, Lucinda rises and heads downstairs. She feels powerful. Her COR thrums in a new and joyful way. More than messages or bits of information. Another entity, part of her, joined to her. She feels complete. Unlonely. The aching longing that has cried within her all her life silenced by the presence inside her.

They wait in front of the building. Soon, the clang of his feet on the pavement echoes off the ruined facades. Artaxerxes comes around the corner, moving with the beautiful efficiency of a giant cat. Soldiers stop and stare as he strides by. He towers over them, his perfect features serene and deadly. He comes to a stop in front of them. Ashburn looks up at the mighty figure, his eyes flashing. "Well done," he says. He turns to a fighter who stands gawking nearby. "Fetch Durain." The man backs away, transfixed by the dark machine, and turns tail into the Defense building. After a minute or so, Durain appears. If the hulking form of Artaxerxes unnerves him, he doesn't show it.

"There you are," says Ashburn. "We are ready. We strike tomorrow."

"Sir, tomorrow? The men are exhausted from the attack."

"It must be tomorrow. She will know of our conquest here by nightfall. We can't give her time to prepare."

"We lost most of the Afflicted. We need at least a week to renew the ranks."

"How many do we have?"

"Not sure, sir. Twenty-five, thirty maybe."

"That will have to do. And with this" — he points to Artaxerxes — "we cannot be stopped."

Chapter 17

Creek and Kimo go to Dr. Jemisen's caravan every day. The work never varies — clean, fetch, fetch, clean — but Kat's warm smile and earnest, if awkward, attempts to communicate, confront Creek with an unfamiliar sensation — safety. As he sprays down the interior of a small machine like an oven, he muses on all the places he has called home in his short, busy life. The camp under the bridge, the garbage pile behind the burnt-out 7-11, the car with Dr. Rush, John Chaico's School, the vagral caravan by the river, the freezing culvert under the highway, too many ditches to count, and way back, almost lost in the mist, the house with the bed and the windows and the woman he thinks must be his mother. Nowhere — even in that last, tender memory — did he feel as safe as he does right now. Not at all what he expected when Lady Fal took them prisoner. The enclosure, the Icebox, the wall of vehicles, the snipers and warriors that surround him, should scare him whiter than a sheep. They only reinforce the feeling of safety.

He can't trust it. *How long can it last?*

Sandoval brings them back to the enclosure at the end of the day, as usual. As they pass through the gate, Sandoval puts his book under his arm and carefully shapes to Kimo, *DO YOU WANT IT?* He holds up the book.

DON'T YOU? she asks, surprised.

He shakes his head. *I'M OVER,* he shapes. Must mean he's done.

Kimo's eyes light up. *YES PLEASE!* Creek wonders how Sandoval knew she would like it. *He* knows that Kimo loves stories and reading and all that sort of thing, but how could he? When they were at John Chaico's school, she always had her nose in a book. She hasn't seen one since then, and she grabs it like it were something precious — like a peach, or something — and presses it to her chest, her face glowing with pleasure.

Sandoval points at Creek, then at himself. *Teach me.* Creek glances at Kimo, hoping that maybe she will offer to teach him instead, since he was so nice to her, but she is already reading the first page of her new treasure, and beelines for their tent, disappearing inside without looking up. Creek shrugs. *OKAY.*

They head toward a corner of the enclosure with an old maple tree. Sandoval likes to lean against it when they have their little classes. They pass the Duke, sitting in his usual spot, cleaning his battle-visor. Creek can instantly read the tension in him. It reminds Creek of the time he stumbled on a rattlesnake near the culvert, its tail whirring, almost invisible with threat.

WHAT'S UP? he shapes.

The Duke waves him off, not looking up as he rubs at the interior of the helmet as if he wants to wear it away. Baby lies on the ground, arms and legs sweeping like a waterbug.

WHERE'S CANDELA? asks Creek.

The Duke shrugs and polishes harder.

Creek looks to Lamarque, who watches from the side, his big eyes anxious and concerned. *WHAT'S GOING ON?*

THEY ARE FIGHTING, shapes Lamarque. Of course. What else? They were always going at each other, bickering and snarking, until inevitably Candela would storm off, leaving the Duke holding Baby, a stupid expression blanking his face.

WHAT HAPPENED?

The Duke gives him the eye. He puts down the helmet and points at it. *SHE'S MAD ABOUT THIS. SHE SAYS IT'S TOO DANGEROUS. HER, BABY, HER, BABY. BLAH BLAH BLAH. IT'S NOT FAIR.*

SHE'LL BE BACK.

The Duke shrugs. *Whatever.* He looks to Lamarque for support. Lamarque just stares back, looking miserable. Clearly, something else is going on. Creek waits. He knows the Duke, knows he can't keep anything to himself. The Duke fights it for a minute, then caves. He mouths something while he waves his arm, like he's saying *I didn't do anything!*

WHAT HAPPENED?

The Duke's mouth keeps working, as if he's having an argument with himself. Finally, he calms down enough to start shaping. *I WAS TALKING TO KETANYA. SHE WAS ADMIRING MY GEAR AND TELLING ME HOW BRAVE I AM. AND THEN SHE KISSED ME. I WASN'T EXPECTING IT.*

DID YOU KISS HER BACK?

A red flush washes down the Duke's face to his neck. Again, he waves his arms and shouts. *I don't know! Maybe.*

WHERE IS CANDELA?

The Duke shakes his head. *NO IDEA.* He points at the water tower and makes a stitching gesture. There was a group of people who did sewing and mending for the camp. Candela was good at it, and had made a friend there. Then, his face turns sour. He gestures toward Ratalfa's tent. *OR MAYBE AT RATALFA'S. I DON'T KNOW.*

Oh. That was it — why the Duke was so upset. Ratalfa was one of Fal's lieutenants, and their immediate superior. Creek had seen him hanging around the enclosure, talking up Candela. He would prance in without a shirt on, posing like a twelve-point stag. Candela would laugh and shake her head and smile. Creek hadn't thought much of it — Ratalfa was kind of lame, if anything. But clearly, the Duke was jealous.

SHE'LL BE BACK.

WHATEVER. The Duke buries his head in his work, attacking his battle helmet with ferocious intensity.

Creek gives up. Those two. He and Sandoval continue toward their corner. As they reach it, Sandoval taps him on the shoulder. He points at the Duke. *What's wrong with him?* Creek shrugs. None of his damn business.

They sit at the base of the tree. It provides some shelter from the light, misting rain that has started to fall.

WHAT DO YOU WANT TO LEARN? asks Creek.

I DON'T KNOW. YOU — WHAT ARE YOU?

Creek shows him the shape for *TEACHER.* He shows him the shape for *STUDENT.* They go through *LEARN, TEACH, READ, BOOK, TABULA.* Not sure what else to do, he looks around. A squirrel perches in the high branches of the tree. Creek points up at it and shows Sandoval the shape for *SQUIRREL.*

It becomes a game— Creek thinking of animals, showing the shape, and forcing the man to guess what it means. *DOG, WOLF, BIRD, CAT, COW…* It's pretty funny to see the man flounder trying to figure out what they are, though he surprises Creek several times by guessing correctly.

Creek shows him *BEAR* — arms crossed over the chest and clawing. Sandoval likes that one, and repeats it several times. He laughs. He does it again, growling and baring his teeth, ripping at his chest with mock ferocity. His clawing hand catches the opening of his shirt and pulls it down, revealing his collarbone and shoulder. Creeks sees a small tattoo on the man's skin — a skull with a flaming cross behind it. His heart stops.

Show me another one, Sandoval mimes, but Creek can't take his eyes off the mark, which still peeks from under the dun fabric of the man's shirt. He feels sick. His head swirls with unbidden memories — fire and smoke, people running, pleading, falling. Men with skulls instead of faces — bare-chested and striped with red — striking indiscriminately with spears and clubs. They ride shaggy ponies with manes and tails also stained red, and bamboo poles that jut up from the saddle holding dirty flags, hand-painted — a gray-white skull on a background of red flames, with a black cross behind it. He lay on the ground, his head half under a bush, pretending to be dead, watching a rivulet of blood trace its way through the dust.

Sandoval, still smiling, gives him a gentle nudge. *Hey, what's next?* But Creek can't focus on anything but the half-hidden tattoo. That vagral caravan — another place he had almost felt safe. He had only stayed because of that boy — what was his name? Silvio. Deaf like him. He had his own shaping language, and it took a while for them to really communicate, but they figured it out. Turned out there was a lot in common between how Silvio talked and what Creek had learned from his mother.

Then, Creek had watched Silvio's brains spill from his head, cracked open by a tall man with a huge club and a skull tattooed on his chest. Sandoval follows Creek's gaze to his own left shoulder. The smile vanishes. They lock eyes, the man's face a clouded mask. Never trust anyone.

Creek takes off, blasting past the Duke and Lamarque, out through the open gate, into the main yard. He doesn't know where he is going. Where can he go? Anywhere. Away. Not here. He turns to look behind him. Sandoval is chasing him, shouting something. The man is fast. Creek redoubles his effort. He swerves toward the ring of vehicles, then back again toward the tower. His feet are thinking for him. He turns again. Sandoval is gaining. Why is he so fast?

Creek slams into something — someone — knocking the wind out of him. The person, a young woman, reaches down to help him up, but he pushes her away as he scrambles to his feet. Too late. Sandoval catches up to him and grabs him by the arm, whipping him around.

The man shouts in his face. He starts talking, fast, like somehow that's going to help. Creek wriggles and writhes, trying to get free, but Sandoval's grip is like a bear's jaws. Creek's brain goes white.

Without warning, an enormous *boom* shakes his skull, and a crater appears in the earth not five meters from them, sending them flying like cornhusk dolls in a whirlwind.

Chapter 18

Creek's head floats near the ground, pulsing gently. Everything has slowed, and the air hangs like a thick blanket, insulating him from the chaos around him. The silence of the outer world, so familiar, mirrors the silence in his thoughts — a flat, dull blankness. He perceives the space around him, but cannot parse it into any kind of sense. He sees shapes moving to and fro, flying through the air, splitting apart in graceful arcs of red, bursts of orange and yellow, fountains of brown and gray, billows of black. None of it means anything to him, except that he finds a muted beauty in it all, a ballet of twisting shapes and colors.

Something grabs his head. It hurts. His eyes drift back to the captivating mosaic, but a painful wrench pulls them back. The fog lifts a little, and he finds himself looking into the burning eyes of Sandoval, inches from his face. The man is shouting at him, and Creek grins vaguely at the absurdity of it. Then the man shakes him again. The last of the blanketing calm falls away, and he returns. He is lying on the ground, dirt in his face and in his throat. He coughs and wretches. He looks around. A battle rages on every side.

Fal's men, taken by surprise, are running this way and that, wildly shooting, loose and disorganized. They remind him, incongruously, of a day last summer, when he had run through a field on a rare, sunny day, and dozens of grasshoppers had leaped out of his way in graceful arcs.

Fal's captains, including a shirtless Ratalfa, stand in a loose pack near the entrance to the water tower, yelling and waving their arms in a futile attempt to bring order to the panic.

A surprise attack. Enemy fighters have taken up positions in front of the truck-wall, and are laying down a covering fire. He can see a fleet of trucks and rangers, some bristling with weapons, others stacked with fighters, circling the camp. An orange-bright explosion sends one of the cars that form the defensive perimeter tossing into the air in a shining burst of fire and steel.

Through the break, a mob of people rushes like a torrent. They have no weapons, no body armor. They wear a motley of civilian clothes — some of the women in dresses, some of the men in ragged slacks, even shorts. They make no sense on the battlefield. But any idea that they are harmless dissolves as they stream into the yard. Their mouths are twisted in hideous contortions, their eyes wild and bloodshot. Even in his silent world, Creek can feel their anguish pulsing off them like an exposed heart. They move at an incredible speed, falling on the defenders before they can process the strangeness, ripping at their clothes, tearing at their faces, burying their teeth into necks and cheeks. Some are gunned down but rise again, charging at their attackers in a foaming rage that freezes Fal's men with fear and surprise. A group of ten throw themselves headlong at the captains in front of the tower. Ratalfa goes down, along with several of the others. A frenzied melee blocks the entrance.

Sandoval scoops Creek up like a sack of tubies, swerves to the right, and begins to run along the curving side of the tower. Before he has gone ten steps, Candela appears at the tower door, staring at the seething mass of fighting before her, her face blanched and frightened. Sandoval reverses course and darts toward her, leaping over one of the mad humans who is ripping at the ears of a young captain. He grabs Candela's hand and pulls her after him. They scramble over to a row of water barrels lined up against the tower wall. There, he pauses to scan the field.

A group of Fal's fighters has pulled one of the trucks into position against the tower, where a mounted gun swings to and fro, mowing down the screaming berserkers. But the attackers have established themselves all along the perimeter, and have them pinned down. No chance of a counterattack.

WE GO, shapes Sandoval. He looks around, seeking an escape, sees the doctor's van parked a dozen meters away. Sandoval turns to Creek. He mimes, *You walk?*

Creek's legs have returned to his body. He nods.

They move around the outskirts of the building, the defender's truck blocking them from the worst of the fighting. They reach the van. The space around it is empty, almost quiet, as if the battle were far away.

Sandoval leads Creek and Candela to the van door. It is locked. He bangs on the metal frame, shouting. After a moment, it opens, and they quickly tumble inside. Dr. Jemisen stands there, her face gray and frightened. She holds an ancient pistol in her hand.

He pushes her into the driver's seat, his mouth moving in a blur. She nods and presses buttons on the dashboard. Creek can feel the engine come to life beneath him. Sandoval looks back and sees that there are no seats in the interior, only a couple of freestanding chairs. He points to the bedroom in the rear. Creek heads back, but as he passes the door, which hangs open, he glances through it, wheels around, grabs Sandoval by the sleeve, and tugs him to the entrance.

Candela stands outside the door, her head ricocheting between the van and the battle beyond. Her feet are dancing nervously, first toward the door, and then toward the fighting. Sandoval reaches for her. She backs away.

She mouths something, pointing. The man shakes his head. She looks at Creek. *BABY? WHAT ABOUT BABY?*

Sandoval leaps out. They begin to argue violently, shouting and gesticulating. Creek watches, hating his impotence, wishing he could help.

At last, the man puts his arm around her. She briefly resists, then submits, and they scurry up into the van.

Sandoval yells at Dr. Jemisen. She nods and the van jerks forward, throwing Creek's legs out from under him. He scrambles up and peers out through the windshield. They pull around the water tower. The fighting has reached a fever pitch. Most of the berserkers are dead, though a few still tear at the corpses on the ground. The remaining defenders have organized, and now three vehicles form a wall along the front of the tower. The air between the opposing forces shimmers with bullets tracing yellow lines through the dim light. A missile shimmers across the open space, and one of the trucks explodes in a nova of flame. Dr. Jemisen jolts to a stop. She yells at Sandoval, looking for a way across and not finding one.

The door to the tower opens. Lady Fal, fully clad in battle armor, strides out, firing a hail of bullets that shine like a thousand fireflies. Behind her, a dozen soldiers stream out, each carrying a warshield bristling with munitions. They push forward to the middle of the field, unleashing a storm upon the attackers, who dive for cover.

Sandoval pounds the dashboard. Dr. Jemisen leans on the accelerator, and the van lurches forward, racing across the open area behind the Lady and her forces. The van leans dangerously to one side as she puts it into a sharp turn, and comes to a stop before the gate of the enclosure. Before Sandoval can stop her, Candela rushes to the door and out into the field. Creek can see her through the glass. She looks wildly around her, calling and crying. Sandoval curses and follows her to the door.

The door to the Icebox opens, and Larmarque appears, a swaddled bundle pulled tight to his chest. Candela throws her arms around him, and the two just stand there, as if they are alone in a quiet meadow, only flowers and a gentle breeze around them. Sandoval leaps out of the van. Candela takes Baby in her arms as the man comes to their side. She shakes off his efforts to corral her, and speaks fervently to Lamarque. Before he can respond, Sandoval grabs them both and throws them up the short stairs.

A bomb lands not far away, knocking him to the ground. He rises quickly, shouting something into the wind.

Kimo appears from the tent, clutching her book to her chest. Sandoval waves her past him, scanning the enclosure for the rest of the children. Creek knows that Rice and Sidecar are on assignment. He has no idea where Ketanya is. Once he has confirmed the enclosure is empty, Sandoval dives for the van, covering his head with his hands as a stream of bullets sweeps over him. He stumbles up the steps and yells at Dr. Jemisen. *Go!* He slams the door. *Go!* he screams again. The van leaps forward.

Candela is up in Lamarque's face, her mouth moving a mile a minute. He shakes his head and turns away, miserable. Creek catches his eye and asks, *WHAT?*

DUKE, shapes Lamarque. *I DON'T KNOW WHERE DUKE IS.*

Dr. Jemisen steers the van toward a hole in the perimeter. Through the window, Creek can see the remaining defenders gathered around Lady Fal, laying down a blistering rain of fire on the attackers. Maybe they can turn the tide.

A white inferno incandesces on the left flank. A dozen fighters vanish — vaporized. A stillness falls on the battlefield.

A black car has pulled into the breach in the wall. Beside it stands a figure, tall and gaunt, his robot eye sparking darkly in the gloom and smoke. To his left towers a hulking mass of gleaming metal. Three meters high, its massive face looking down on the battlefield with the implacable gaze of a god. It raises its long left arm, and another third of Lady Fal's line vanishes in a ball of blinding silver, as if a miniature sun has flared into existence, then winked out, carrying them all into another universe.

But Creek only dimly registers the horrible, beautiful destruction. He is caught out of time, his eyes fixed on another figure, standing beside the Doctor. A woman — a young woman — with red hair and skin pale as a seashell. She appears to him like a creature out of myth — a naiad, or dryad, or selkie. How he knows about these creatures, he can't recall, though the thought conjures dim visions of that other woman — unlike her, yet somehow alike — and murmurs of stories in the sleepy night, washing against the margins of his memory.

Then the van has passed through the perimeter. It bounces violently this way and that, swerving as Dr. Jemisen fights to control their flight, avoiding the ruts, holes, and bare foundations of the ruined houses that surround the camp. Another flash of white illuminates the darkness behind them. The van finds the remains of a road, and they speed away into the gathering night.

PART TWO

Chapter 19

They camp under the bridge. Kat maneuvers the van off the road — if you can call the overgrown track they have been bumping over a road — and they hide it behind a vast tangle of knotweed. They cut branches using Sandoval's field knife to protect the vehicle from any eyes that might pass their way.

The boy named Lamarque leads them down the embankment. The sight of the little camp fills Kat with a mixture of wonder and pity for the children who called this place home until a few weeks ago. Pity for their desperate poverty, and wonder at their resourcefulness and grit. Candela takes Baby into the little chamber and puts him down, while Sandoval lights a fire.

"We should be all right," he says. "They haven't followed us."

After a bit, Candela comes back out. She carries two packages of dried noodles.

"Is that all?" he asks her. She nods. Her eyes are red and swollen with weeping. Sandoval takes them from her without a word.

They sit in a circle around the fire, staring at the little licking tongues of orange and yellow. No one speaks, each lost in thought. They are all exhausted. The terrible bouncing over the rutted road, the nervous moments when they were forced to stop while Kat employed the lifters to get the van over a rock or fallen tree. Every moment sure to bring the whine of an engine or the blast of a rocket that would blow them to dust.

Now, sitting around the fire, the full force of what has happened descends on them. In her mind's eye, Kat sees the tall, fine figure of Lady Fal, her friend, leading the sortie, and the final white explosion as they drove out of the camp.

"Do you think anybody…" Lamarque starts to say. Sandoval shakes his head, stifling the question. Candela begins to cry again, the storm rising until she is sobbing. Kimo crawls over and wraps her arms around her.

"We had to go," says Sandoval. "We would all be dead."

At length, Candela's weeping subsides, and Kimo sits beside her, their knees and thighs touching. "We don't know what happened," she tells her. Her voice is breathy and sweet, with a light accent that charms Kat no end. "Maybe he got away, too. If he did, you know he'll look for you and Baby. We'll see him again. Trust me." Candela listens to her with a starving look and nods, wiping away the tears.

Sandoval stands and begins to speak. He tries to make some signs, to include Creek, but he can't keep it up and looks helplessly to Kimo. She nods gravely and translates for the boy.

"We have to decide what to do," Sandoval says. "We can't stay here, or anywhere nearby. The Doctor controls this territory. The van is a good thing for us, but he'll want it."

"He'll want the equipment, too," says Kat. "Remember his first visit?"

Sandoval nods. "That may be why he attacked. Though obviously he knew he would win. He had us seriously outgunned. Military-grade ordinance — I mean, a battle robot? No idea where he got it. And those… those people."

"Who were they?" asks Lamarque.

"I don't know."

"Civilians," says Kat. "Infected. At the final stage of the disease. You know it causes madness and uncontrolled aggression. Like rabies on steroids."

Sandoval shakes his head. "How?"

"I've been trying to figure out what this equipment was for. I think I'm starting to understand." She leans forward. "I think this Doctor used these machines to make drugs that can control people with Mindworm. He doesn't have a cure, but he has medicines that can keep them alive, and then others that enhance aggression."

"Jesus," says Sandoval. "How can he control them? Most victims I've seen can't control who they attack."

"I have no idea. Somehow, he can direct their fury. But that's not the worst. It's unsustainable. Before long, the damage to the brain gets too much, and they die, probably in more pain than they would have if he had just let the disease run its course. It's incredibly cruel."

"And he did all that with the machines in the van?"

"I think so. I haven't figured out the control part, but the other stuff, yeah."

"No wonder he wants it back. If he doesn't get it—" He waves up the hill toward the hidden van. "—he's out of drugs and loses his army."

"Yes. I mean, who knows how much he has stockpiled — but yes."

"All the more reason for us to get out of here. As soon as he discovers the equipment isn't in the camp, he'll come after us." He reaches across and picks up the noodle packages at Candela's feet. "But first things first. Lamarque — do you have a pot? Is there water nearby?"

The boy nods. "Inside."

Sandoval turns to Creek. *GET WATER?* Creek disappears into the pump room.

"We're going to eat, then sleep. I'll figure out where we go. We'll leave before it gets light."

Candela stands. "Wait! What about the Duke? We have to go back for him!"

Sandoval shakes his head. "He's gone."

"No! He's not gone. He's alive. I know it. He needs us! He needs Baby! He needs me. We're not coming. We're going back to find him. You can go, but we are staying!"

The whole evening has been unsettling for Creek. Candela's misery makes him feel sick and scared. He envies Kimo for the ease with which she can give Candela comfort. He wouldn't know where to start. He looks from face to face and sees desolation everywhere. He tries to understand it, but he can't. He himself doesn't feel much. He never has. He didn't really care about anyone at the camp, except maybe the Duke, a little. The people he cares about — Kimo and Candela — are alive. Lamarque is okay, and Dr. Jemisen has been nice to him. Sandoval scares him, especially now. That tattoo. But he didn't act like a murderous cultist when he saved them.

He sees the loss in their eyes and wonders if there is something wrong with him. Some piece missing that would allow him to share their misery.

And then there are those Mindworm people. The way they swarmed over the camp like an army of roaches. *Monsters*, the Duke had called them. Creek has seen a few people with Mindworm, but these people acted like they had *Super-Mindworm*. They moved like lightning. He felt sick to his stomach just thinking about them.

He is glad when Sandoval orders him to get water. He gets up and goes into the little chamber under the road. Baby is fast asleep on the bed. Creek finds the pot — an ancient rectangular aluminum piece, badly dented.

As he comes back out, Sandoval and Candela are screaming at each other. Fighting about something, probably whether to go back and search for the Duke. Creek can't bear to look at Candela, the tears shining on her cheeks, her face a canvas of agony and determination. — and steals out past the others toward the spring. As he goes, he can see them all standing now, arguing, with Kimo in the middle, looking wretched.

The night is almost black, but a bit of moon makes a gray splotch on the cloudy sky, and Creek knows the way to the spring without light. He feels the squish of the bank before he tumbles in. He knows where to find the little pool where the water is cleanest. He fills the pot, then sits on the bank for a while, swaddled in the silence.

His mind wallows in a comforting blankness. Sometimes it's good not to think. Then, the moon breaks through a ragged hole in the sky, and the little clearing glows with its cold radiance. It wraps him in comforting solitude. A place he knows well. People are crazy.

Chapter 20

Kimo stands between Sandoval and Candela. The jumbled echoes of their fight squawk and rumble in her ears, while the Ear tries to keep up with their flying words. She hopes she can act as a bulwark between them, diffusing the anger that crackles and breaks the air. It's a trick she learned long ago, when her parents would fight about the future. They loved each other with a rare passion, but they held equally passionate opinions, and both knew they were right. She found her quiet presence could drain the rage from the fight, and eventually they would start to listen instead of yell, and work out a compromise.

Kimo believes in magic. In spite of all that has happened to her — the illness that rendered her deaf, the loss of her home and her family, the long and painful journey that brought her to this place — she knows that there is beauty in the world, wondrous and strange. She carries that certainty within her, but she knows that other people don't — can't — possess it, and she has learned, even at such an early age, that her power in this world is to create bridges, and open doors.

Her tactic succeeds, at last, and Sandoval and Candela calm down enough to come to an agreement. Lamarque goes in to check on Baby, and Dr. Jemisen falls asleep, exhausted with the strain of driving them to safety. Creek disappeared a while ago into the woods, ostensibly to get water from the stream. He has been gone too long.

She goes inside. Lamarque gives her a big grin that makes her insides quiver a little. He has such a nice face. She removes the Ear and connects it to its little solar charger, so it will be ready for the next day's adventure. It's bound to be a busy one. It feels good to take it off. It requires a lot of concentration to use, and it itches. She's used to it, and it helps her fulfill her role in the group. It is also the only thing she has that connects her to her parents. But she feels relieved by the gentle, shapeless murmurs of the real world after a long day of Earing.

She goes to look for Creek, and finds him sitting by the water, staring at the surface, which shines a dim silver in the moonlight, as small clumps of algae drift with the sullen current.

He nods when he sees her. *HOW'S IT GOING?* he asks.

GOOD, she shapes.

ARE THEY STILL FIGHTING?

NO. THEY FIGURED IT OUT.

WHAT HAPPENED?

CANDELA WON.

WON WHAT?

WE'RE GOING BACK. NOT ALL THE WAY TO THE CAMP, BUT CLOSER, TO SEE IF WE CAN FIND THE DUKE. SHE'S AGREED TO STAY WITH US, SO LONG AS WE GO BACK.

WOW. OKAY. THAT SOUNDS DANGEROUS.

SANDOVAL HAS A PLAN. HE TOLD HER NOT TO WORRY ABOUT IT. HE'D TAKE CARE OF IT.

Creek frowns into the water. *WHAT ABOUT THE GIANT DEATH MACHINE?* he asks.

THE WHAT?

THAT ROBOT THAT KILLED EVERYBODY.

Kimo shrugs.

I HATE ROBOTS, Creek continues.

THEY'RE NOT ALL BAD.

He snorts. *I'VE SEEN THREE IN MY LIFE, AND THEY WERE ALL BAD. AND THAT ONE WAS THE WORST. I DON'T WANT TO GO BACK.* Creek shivers despite himself.

Kimo believes in magic. She knows that the world has beauty tucked into unexpected corners, and nothing is really as bad as fear makes it. She knows that there are mystical creatures that appear out of the darkness to restore faith in this fallen world. She knows because she has seen them. Here, in this place.

THEY'RE NOT ALL BAD, she shapes again. *I KNOW. I'VE SEEN IT.*

It happened a year ago, last spring. She was on her own, then, before she met the Millers (god rest them) who took her to John Chaico's, where she met Creek and the others. She was living in the little pump room under the bridge. She had just found it. A dead man was there, but he had died a long time ago, and his bones were dry and picked, so it wasn't hard to move them out. It was just after the big hurricane, she remembered, and she found a crate of dried potatoes stuck on a branch in the swollen stream. She almost drowned fishing it out, but succeeded in the end. She went to the stream to fill the water jugs. The moon had been out then, too, and she'd watched it for a while, flashing in and out of the broken clouds.

And then it happened — through the trees, she saw a pale white light bouncing and bobbing like a wayward fairy. Moving with silent care, Kimo crept around the spring toward the light. She came before long to the edge of an old road — little more than a track — choked with chunks of concrete heaved this way and that by roots, weather, and time.

Peering through the bushes, she saw a figure working its way gingerly down the uneven path. It appeared to be a whelite man in his fifties. He wore a white coat, like a doctor might wear, though it was soiled and filthy with mud. Kimo could just make out his smooth gray hair and a long but well-proportioned face. But this was no man, that was clear, because the face was eclipsed by light beams shooting from his eyes. They shone like little flashlights, illuminating the path before him. Kimo had never seen anything like it and could only watch, frozen in wonder and fear.

The man, or whatever it was, carried something in his arms. It was large and long, wrapped in what looked like a sheet. As he came even with Kimo's hiding place, he stumbled on a jagged bit of roadway, and the sheet fell away. Kimo stifled a gasp. It was a woman. A girl. Her eyes were closed. The man stopped, raised his right knee to support the girl's body, and awkwardly, but with immense care, re-adjusted the sheet. While he was busy with his task, his eye-beams fell full on the girl's face. Kimo almost gasped again.

It was the most beautiful face that Kimo had ever seen. Her features preternaturally symmetrical, perfectly balanced, delicate but full. Her skin shimmered like the moon coming out from behind a cloud.

The man completed his task, gently settled her again in his arms, and proceeded on his way. They vanished into the night.

Kimo tells the story to Creek, simply but clearly, leaving nothing out.

IT WAS A ROBOT? he asks.

I THINK SO. AND IT WAS GOOD.

HOW DO YOU KNOW?

IT LOVED HER. IT LOVED THE GIRL.

CAN ROBOTS LOVE?

THIS ONE COULD. YOU READY TO GET BACK? I'M HUNGRY.

Creek nods. He carefully lifts the pot of water, and they trudge silently back to camp.

Rain falls in sheets as the van bumps along the rutted track. No one speaks. Kimo sits with Lamarque and Creek on the floor, their backs against the door.

They had passed a restless night and a dull, anxious day. Sandoval has not shared his plan, only saying that they had to wait for evening before they attempted the Duke's rescue. They spent the day packing the few items of use from the camp into the van — four blankets, the cooking ware, and some makeshift weapons the children had crafted out of sticks and rusted nails. At last, Sandoval gave the nod, and they boarded the van, their weariness battling against a growing dread. He asked her how to shape *TRUST ME* for Creek. Creek didn't look impressed.

Only Candela seems pleased with the idea of going back. She stands just behind Sandoval, who is driving, peering out through the windshield. Dr. Jemisen has retreated to the bedroom at the back of the van. Kimo's knees brush up against Lamarque's as they hunker on the floor. It feels good, comforting.

WHAT'S GOING TO HAPPEN? he asks her. He's been practicing so he can join in their conversations. Another nice thing about him.

WHO KNOWS? Creek answers.

ARE WE GOING TO DIE?

PROBABLY.

HE HAS A PLAN, shapes Kimo, nodding at Sandoval.

WHAT KIND OF PLAN? Creek is all jitters, his eyes darting again and again to the rain-drenched windows. *HOW CAN WE POSSIBLY FIND THE DUKE, IF HE'S EVEN STILL ALIVE? WE'RE JUST GOING TO GET CAPTURED BY THAT DOCTOR GUY AND KILLED.*

WHY WOULD HE KILL US? WE'RE JUST KIDS.

HE'LL PROBABLY GIVE US MINDWORM AND MAKE US INTO CRAZY SOLDIERS, Creek argues. *I WISH I'D RUN AWAY THIS MORNING BEFORE WE LEFT.*

IT'S GOING TO BE OKAY, shapes Kimo, projecting all her certainty onto her friend.

With a violent wrench, the van veers sharply to the right, throwing the kids against the wall. Next thing they know, they are thundering down a steep incline, bouncing wildly out of control. Kimo smashes her head against the side of a machine. The pain sends sparks flying behind her eyes, the Ear cutting into her scalp, as they are thrown like dolls around the inside of the vehicle.

With a last, awful shock, they level out. Suddenly, they are speeding along a smooth road, flat and straight. The three kids struggle to their knees to look out the front of the van. They are flying down a four-lane highway made of perfect Hard-Tru, impervious to the ravages of time and change, the last great work of the days before the Collapse. The rain has stopped, and Kimo can make out the ghost of the sun above the horizon. They are headed west, not east.

Candela begins to scream. The van swerves in a drawn-out ess as she grabs Sandoval by the shoulders, trying to pull him from the driver's seat. "You promised! Turn around! Go back! You promised…" Sandoval throws her off him with a violent shove, and she tumbles down the center of the van, landing in a heap. He turns. "I lied!" he shouts. Dr. Jemisen appears from the sleeping area and wraps her arms around Candela, cradling her and subduing her in the same gesture. She struggles for a minute, but the woman is too strong, too firm, and at last her frenzied wildness subsides, only her heaving shoulders testifying to her misery. "Duke…" she says quietly, over and over.

The sun breaks through the lowest bank of clouds and hangs over the road like a bleeding hole.

Chapter 21

Ashburn stands over her, holding her arm as he gives her the injection. He smells like smoke. Lucinda's mind is still, nothing to link with her COR, except for the reassuring presence of Artaxerxes in a quiet corner of her brain. They are still at Lady Fal's camp, far from Alexandria and the massive servers at the Doctor's headquarters that can sate her mind with the drug of connection. She winces as the needle slides in.

The Afflicted who survived the attack, and those prisoners destined for infection, are locked up in the gated enclosure. Lucinda is different. Ashburn has commandeered Lady Fal's chamber in the tower for his own, and she receives her treatment there. She sits on a fine wooden chair, four hundred years old if it is a day. *Lady Fal liked beautiful things,* she thinks.

"What was it like?" he asks her.

"What?"

"Controlling the soldier."

"Artaxerxes. His name is Artaxerxes."

"Whatever you please. Was it, well, fun?"

"It was exhilarating. But—" How can she explain to him the complexity of her feelings? Yes, it was thrilling to control him — not control him, it's not as if she tells him what to do. It's more like thinking a thing, a wish or a want, and it is done. She looked at the line of opposing soldiers and wanted them gone. And then they were gone. A swell of energy filled her as 'Xerxes charged his weapon. His power coursed through her body, along with a surging euphoria. And then they were gone — limbs flying, bodies twisting, burning, toppling.

But that exhilaration was stained with a deep discomfort. Not that she had never seen carnage like that. When she was eleven, a minor warlord attacked the Enclave. Her teacher took her class up to the viewing chamber in the north wall to watch. Stupid Nonas, totally unprepared for the countermeasures. Bobby Aldridge used the word "decimated" to describe the slaughter, and Lucinda primly reminded him that the word literally meant "to kill one out of ten." This had been its opposite. Barely one in ten survived. The children cheered, and giggled, and had ice cream, and then went back to class.

This was different. It sullied the placid pool of detachment that had bathed her since her rescue. What had she done? Her father would say it didn't matter. They were Nonas. Savages. Barely human. But she remembers the face of the woman whose quarters they now inhabited, as she rallied her soldiers against the onslaught. A face like Athena. Or a lioness. She wasn't sure which. She taps her COR to find a fitting parallel, forgetting that she is not connected. The emptiness depresses her. How can she process the complexity of this moment on her own? Her mind is flat, her thoughts barren, no defense against the naked image of Lady Fal's face. The woman's eyes. Like…what? Her COR would have supplied a metaphor, a context.

Lady Fal had not been afraid, that was for sure. Facing down the death that Artaxerxes brought down on her, she had never wavered. Lucinda searched for words. Strong. Fearless. Without fear. Something Lucinda could never comprehend. She had always been afraid.

"Did it upset you?" Ashburn leans down, studying her closely.

"A little," she confesses.

He touches her face, as though she were a precious vase, a crystal chalice. "I'm glad. I find your innocence rejuvenating." Then he shrugs. "But it must be done."

"Of course."

"There is no joy in killing." She nods, but knows he lies. When the robot blasted the enemy soldiers into piles of twisted ash, his human eye was shining, his mouth a slash of savage joy.

He gazes hungrily into her eyes, trying to read her. She can feel his power. It throbs around him. But she feels her own, too. He needs her. It pleases her despite herself. Who has ever needed her before? Maybe Sebastien, but he was just a boy.

Ashburn says, "Still, you found it exhilarating, you say? How so?"

"I mean Artaxerxes. He's an extension of me. I feel what he does."

"How erotic."

"It's not like that at all," she says, looking away and frowning. She can feel his eyes cutting into her. Probing for a secret place within her that even she has never seen. She bathes in the electricity of his attention, but he unsettles her. There is a coldness behind the warmth. An icy core wrapped in a blanket of kindness.

"It's not like that," she says again. "It's like a fulfillment, the realization of a…a promise. Oh, I can't explain." She looks away. "It's not…sexual…" She hesitates to say the word, to bring it into the air between them. "It's not even like he's separate from me. Except he is."

"Is he always there?"

"In a way, yes."

"What's he doing now?"

"Waiting."

"Thinking?"

"Just waiting."

He shakes his head, chuckling, as he puts her medicines into their special case. "Good. He's a powerful weapon, and I don't want him turning on me one day."

A sudden boldness, and she says, "Does it bother you that you need me to control him? I mean, that you can't do it yourself?"

Now he laughs out loud. "Of course!"

"Don't you trust me?" she asks. It's important that she knows.

He smiles again. "I do, my dear. Not wisely, but too well. But I don't trust robots."

"We're the same thing. He is me. You can trust him."

"I hope so, Lucinda. I hope so."

Durain appears at the doorway. "Sir?"

Ashburn turns, all business. "Yes, Durain."

"The camp is secure."

"How many survivors?"

"Sixty-one. We've put thirty in that caged-in area, along with the Afflicted."

"Who've been sedated?"

"Yes, sir."

"Why only thirty?"

"It's what we can manage with the supply we have. Even so, we're going to run out in two months. Maybe sooner."

Ashburn begins to pace. Lucinda catches the little drag in his gait as he pulls his artificial leg along. "And the equipment?"

Durain shifts uncomfortably. "No sign, sir. We're still looking."

"Where is it?"

"Not sure. Three vehicles managed to break out during the attack. We've located one about half a kilometer from here. We're still looking for the other two."

In one step, Ashburn is on him, all gentleness vanished in an instant. "Find them. Do you understand? Find them."

"Yes, sir."

"Everything depends on it. Everything."

"Yes, Doctor."

Ashburn leans in. He is a full head taller than Durain. "You've already failed me once. Your orders were very clear. Nobody gets out. Hold the perimeter. Three vehicles?"

"They had—"

"I don't need your excuses. Find my equipment, Durain, or you know where you'll end up."

"Yes, sir."

"Where will you end up, Durain?"

"In the cage with the Afflicted, sir."

Ashburn stares the man down. "Get out."

Durain flees, leaving them alone. Ashburn stares into the space the man had occupied, as if he could spy through it to find where his stolen equipment hides. Lucinda rises and goes to him. She touches him on the arm.

"Hey," she says.

It breaks the spell. He turns to her. A curious surprise crosses his face.

"Hello," he says. "Sorry."

"They'll find it."

"They'd better. For your sake."

"I know. They will." His eye softens. He touches her face again with his cold, robot hand. "I'm glad I found you. I want you around."

A buried thrill catches in her chest.

"Tell me," he says. "Can your…can Artaxerxes help? Does he have any capabilities that could assist us?"

"Let me see." She clicks into the space where Artaxerxes lives inside her mind.

It's like coming home. It reminds her of when she was eight years old. They were visiting her mother's parents, who lived up on the hill. They went every Sunday, and usually Lucinda had to sit inside, dressed like a doll, answering her grandmother's empty questions about school and craft projects and whatnot. This time, there were other guests, and the grown-ups had business to discuss. She was sent out into the garden to fend for herself. At the back of the property, she discovered a large forsythia she had never noticed before, perhaps because this was the first time she had seen it in bloom. It was a rare, sunny day. The thousands of blossoms burned like mirrors of the sun, glorious yellow in the brightness. Lucinda found that she could crawl underneath it, and that hidden within was a little cave, a private place, canopied with green leaves and yellow blossoms. She sat there for a long time, forgetful of the time. Perfectly at peace in her secret world, until she heard her mother calling. She didn't want to leave. The space where Artaxerxes dwells feels like that. She asks her question. He answers.

"Yes," she says. "He thinks he can help."

Chapter 22

Kat and Sandoval sit in the front of the van, stopped beside the road some eighty kilometers from the camp. Night has fallen. They made good progress at first, rolling along the flawless and immortal Hard-Tru surface of the highway, but a collapsed bridge halted their advance, and they had pulled over to consider their options. Candela and the children lie sleeping in a wayward pile on the bed.

"Now what?" she asks him.

"I don't know."

"You don't have a plan?"

Sandoval shakes his head. "My only plan was to get us away. After that…"

"You lied to her."

"I had to. She wouldn't listen. I liked the boy. But you know as well as I do that we couldn't go back. For anyone."

They sit in silence for a while. Kat sighs. "I shouldn't have left. I shouldn't have left her."

He starts to put his hand on her shoulder, but then stops himself. "You know you did the right thing. There was no chance. His firepower… Unbelievable."

"She wasn't expecting it."

"She underestimated him. She was used to idiots like Top Dawg, Slash, and that other guy…I forget his name. This Doctor…he's in another class." He stares out the window. "It's crazy. Where did he come from? Six months ago, nobody had ever heard of him. Now he's running everything."

"Who knows? There's always someone new, causing trouble."

Sandoval shifts in his seat to look directly at her. "How did you meet her?"

"Oh, I've known Fal for years. We were kids together in a little Steader community down near Old Danbury. She was always the tough one. There was another kid who was bullying me, and she beat him up, even though she was about half his size. What she lacked in stature, she made up for in ferocity. He didn't know what hit him." She smiles at the memory. "Then the camp got overrun, and we got separated. I ended up with the medico and his family. He was a good man. Taught me everything I know. Gave me this van."

"Woman with a mission, eh?"

"Something like that. He taught me to want to help. I was on the road for twenty years, scavenging medical supplies where I could find them, bringing them to Steaders all around the northeast. I even made it into Canada for a little. That was an eyeful."

"You're lucky you didn't get killed."

She gives him the stink-eye. "Lucky, or smart?" He laughs. "Anyhow, yeah, Fal and me go way back. We're old friends. *Were* old friends." Kat shakes her head. "Of course, when I found out she was a *warlord*, and you all were just preying on the poor Steaders trying to survive up here, she got an earful from me, let me tell you."

"You loved her."

"Yes, I did. You see, Sandoval, she may have been just another warlord, but she wasn't content with that. She told me she had plans — big plans — to make a town, an enclave, but not one only for whelites, but for everyone. The beginning of a new society. She was going to call it Hope."

"Hope, huh? She never told me that."

"I don't know if she really meant it. She said the time wasn't right, she needed to shore up her position, subdue this warlord or that, get enough resources, soldiers, vehicles. And with Mindworm still a threat…blah, blah, blah. That's the problem we have. Always an excuse. And always the little guys, the Steaders, who have to pay. Now this Doctor shows up."

"And so much for Hope."

"Yeah." They fall silent, listening to the screams of a million frogs pulsing in the night. Kat leans back, eyeing him. "Your turn. You strike me as a man with a past, Sandoval. What's your story?"

"Long and uninteresting."

"I doubt that. How did you meet Fal?"

"She saved my life."

"And?"

"I owed her."

She waits for more. It doesn't come.

"That's it? That's your story? You can do better than that."

He just looks at her.

"Okay," Kat says, grinning despite herself. The grin fades quickly. "…But you didn't go back. To stand with her at the end."

Sandoval stares at the dashboard. "No, I did not." He looks back at the bedroom and the sleeping children. "I felt I was needed elsewhere."

Kat snorts. "A sentimentalist, for all your toughness."

"Practical. These kids are survivors." Silence again. Then he says, "So what are we going to do, Kat Jemisen?"

"You don't think we're safe?"

"I do not."

"You really think he'll bother with us, this Doctor? We're just a bunch of nobodies."

"With a top-notch vehicle and a bunch of priceless medical machines, that I'm guessing he wants. No, needs. Yeah, I think he'll bother."

"Then we have to hide. Get off the highway."

Lamarque appears behind the driver's seat, rubbing sleep from his eyes. "I have to pee," he says.

"So?" says Sandoval.

"The bathroom is backed up. It stinks in there."

Sandoval looks out through the windshield, into the darkness. "Okay. Be quick, and get off the road as far as you can."

The boy nods sleepily and slumps down the stairs into the night.

"Maybe we just drive," says Sandoval. "Head for California, or Texas, or hell, Canada. Maybe they'll let us in." Kat senses a hunger, like a muted trumpet, in his voice.

"I wouldn't count on it."

"Why not?"

"The rise of these warlords," says Kat. "When they let me in, everything was still collapsed. Just handfuls of Steaders trying to stay alive, and a few enclaves with their gates shut. Now, people are rising again, only not in a way that's going to please the authorities up in Canada."

"What about the west? California."

She gives him a side eye. "I am not taking these children across the desert. Have you ever seen it?"

"No."

"Neither have I. And I don't want to. They say it hasn't rained on the other side of the Alleghenies for fifty years. And who knows what the leftovers from the Texas Confederacy have been up to out there? Or the First Nations. I don't want to run afoul of either, and I don't want this van to break down in the middle of nowhere so we can all die of thirst together. No thank you."

"We have to get away from the Doctor. We aren't safe here."

"I know. But how far? It's a big country. My guess is he'll check along the highways — this westerly one, and the one that runs down the coast. If we can get far enough off the road, he'll never find us. Never."

"How do you know?"

"He's a doctor, not a god."

"What if there are trackers on these machines?"

"There aren't."

"How do you know?"

"I know."

He looks at her, unconvinced.

"All right, Mr. Cynical," she says. "Here is what we are going to do. We are going to head north and west."

"Why?"

"There's a place I know. Head west until we reach the next exit ramp. It's pretty wrecked, but I think we can get through. Then we work our way upcountry. We'll have to travel by day because I won't know which way to go without certain landmarks."

"That's crazy."

"That's the way it has to be. We'll be fine. I don't think our Doctor friend has aircraft, or he would have used them."

"I don't think anybody has aircraft."

"The First Nations do."

"Not in these parts."

Kat nods reluctantly. "True. The western tribes do, though, and it's only a matter of time before they come east. Still, the Doctor doesn't, so I think we'll be okay traveling by day. We should reach our destination in three days or so, depending on the terrain."

"And then?" asks Sandoval.

"Then we see."

Chapter 23

Lucinda watches Artaxerxes as he slowly stalks the muddy ground at the edge of the compound. He doesn't look down, searching for signs like a human would, but she knows he is examining every rut and flattened blade of grass. He begins at the entrance, making a slow circle around the vehicles that form the perimeter of the encampment. Several times he stops, and she follows in her mind the measurements and calculations he makes of the perturbations and deformations in the dirt, looking to distinguish and recreate the paths of tires back and forth across the muddy field. He takes samples of air and dirt, logging infinitesimal quantities of polycarbons shed by vehicles as they passed. Their long lattices spin within her like tiny ships.

He comes at last to a break in the wall. During the battle, several trucks had pulled back to form a barricade — the Lady Fal's last stand in front of the tower. He finds a thin line, invisible to her human eye but clear as a ski track through virgin snow to his analytic toolset (Lucinda has never seen real snow, but her COR has shown her pictures). It heads at a right angle to the line of trucks, down the hill into the tangle of trees and ancient foundations. Examining the ground under a variety of spectra, he pulls the faintest trace of a tire tread out of the mud. He takes a sample, separating out a few droplets of synthetic lubricant and other chemicals, and stores them as unique identifiers of the vehicle. He picks up the infinitesimal residue of radioactive decay from a nuclear battery.

His voice sings in her head. "A vehicle exited the area on this path within seventy-six hours. Shall I pursue?"

"Yes," she commands.

Chapter 24

Creek starts awake as the van comes to a jolting halt. He had finally managed to fall asleep, though the hunger pangs and the never-ending bouncing up and down made it almost impossible. He closes his eyes again, willing himself to drop off, but when the van does not start moving, curiosity gets the better of him and he scrambles over the bed toward the front compartment.

They've been on the road for three days. Not that you could really call what they were traveling on 'roads.' Muddy tracks, yes, treacherous meadows zig-zagged with old foundations, yes. Their progress had been slow, arduous, and uncomfortable. Dr. Jemisen had some provisions stocked away, but they were mainly snack bars and crackers — old and mealy — and they ran out in the middle of the second day, even though they were being careful. So, they hadn't eaten since yesterday afternoon. It was now approaching evening, gray and rainy. Like always.

Coming out into the workroom, Creek sees that the door hangs open, and the others have already left the van. He slips on his shoes and follows them down onto the ground. Autumn is well underway, but the air is thick and damp, and pillows of mist drape the slopes of a rolling land.

The van has come up a path through a fir wood, and out into a meadow along the top of a hill that slopes down toward a line of gnarled trees and brush that mark the passage of a stream. The land on the far side of the stream rises again — another meadow that mirrors the one where they now stand. At the top of the hill, nestled against the trees, stands a house.

Dr. Jemisen and Sandoval stand a little apart from the others. The doctor is pointing across the stream and back at the van. She looks distressed, like she didn't expect to be on this side of the water. Sandoval shrugs and nods, and makes placating gestures with his hands. Creek has avoided him throughout the journey, and Sandoval seems content to let him be, but he has been busy with Kimo. During the hours they weren't driving, both he and Dr. Jemisen have dived into shaping lessons with a vengeance. Creek, in spite of himself, is impressed with their progress.

He looks at the house. It's hard to make out in the gray light, but it appears to be a good-sized dwelling made of dark materials, all on one floor, with a sloping roof and a long wooden porch across the front. There's another building — maybe a barn — on the right. He hasn't been in a house since mama, and he can barely remember it, though images of red brick and white trim flash into his mind.

He glances over at Candela. She's got Baby pulled up close to her breast, and she's rocking gently back and forth, whispering to him. She stayed in the back for the whole first day, and she still hasn't said a word to Sandoval. But yesterday, when the man was having a lesson with Kimo, she had appeared at the doorway and watched for a good hour.

She must have felt his gaze, because she turns and smiles. It makes his insides twist and his face go red, but he smiles back as best he can. She turns her attention back to Baby.

Dr. Jemisen crosses back to the children. She mimes as she mouths. *We're going to drive the van down to the stream. Then we're going to cross over to the house.* She waves her hands and does a little dance, like she's trying to say *It'll be fun.* Creek can't see how. She claps her hands and heads back to the van. The children follow her. She holds up her hand.

DON'T GET IN, she shapes. *TOO MUCH WEIGHT.* She mimes driving down the hill and crashing. *YOU RUN!*

Creek checks with Kimo and Lamarque. Candela watches at a little distance, Baby slung at her side. They all look down the hill. The grass is damp and tall, with autumn wildflowers growing in thick patches. But it seems pretty smooth and level, not so steep as to be frightening. They begin to work their way forward, slowly at first, then picking up speed. Lamarque breaks into a run, galloping headlong down the slope. Kimo follows him a second later. Creek hesitates for a moment, then begins to jog faster and faster. The breeze whips his hair back, little flicks of rain striking his face. He can't help it when a huge grin breaks over his lips, the wind billowing into his open mouth. Up ahead, Lamarque falls, half on purpose, and begins to roll, but the tall grass slows his progress too much, and he spins back up onto his feet. Kimo races past him, her head thrown back, and Lamarque dives for her legs, trying to trip her. She dodges his hands and continues on her way. He leaps up again, giving chase. Creek watches the two of them careening down in front of him. They reach the bottom and fall into a heap of arms and legs just in front of the line of bushes that mark the edge of the stream. Creek speeds up and tumbles on top of them, and they roll about in a frenzy of laughs and tickles. They subside at last, lying breathless and companionable in the long grass. Creek feels itchy and wet, and happy. He looks up as Candela saunters down the hill to them, taking care. The sweet look on her face makes Creek feel warm. They roll onto their sides and watch the van make its slow, cautious way down the meadow.

It takes almost two hours for them to get to the house. First, they unload what they will carry in their first trip — blankets, the cookware, the first aid kit, and some other odds and ends. Sandoval decides that he, Lamarque, and Dr. Jemisen will come back later for the mattress. He insists that they camouflage the van, even when Dr. Jemisen points out that they will have to pull most of it off to get the mattress out. He takes his knife and cuts large branches of witch hazel and chokeberry. He threads some through the roof rack and pinches others in the windows and doors to provide a frame. They hang, weave, and balance others until the van is mostly covered. Creek thinks that nobody walking along the stream would be fooled, but Kimo runs to the top of the hill and back down.

UNLESS YOU'RE LOOKING FOR IT, YOU'D NEVER SEE IT, she shapes.

OKAY, he answers. He doesn't believe it.

Then there is the matter of getting across the stream. They push through the dense shrubs by the van only to discover that the water runs deep and fast. After a short but awkward hike upstream — in which more than one shoe gets submerged in the icy water — they reach the ruins of a bridge. The stream bubbles around the tumbled rocks, foaming white here are there, but careful steps from stone to stone should allow them to cross relatively dry.

Sandoval appears angry at himself that they hid the van before finding the ford. He keeps mouthing like he's swearing at himself. Now it's Dr. Jemisen's turn to calm *him* down. She gathers Creek and the others and points at the other side. *Be careful.* As if they wouldn't.

One by one, they make their way across the water, Sandoval standing in the middle to help the others over a particularly wide gap between stones. Lamarque slips near the far bank, soaking his right leg up to the thigh, but otherwise they cross in safety. They begin the climb up the slope toward the house. It's not as steep as the hill on the other side, but quite a bit longer, and they are all winded when they reach the top. As they approach the house, Creek's stomach starts in swirling. It broods above them, dark and mysterious. He wonders if it is occupied, half-expecting some hooded figure to burst out at them, gun blazing. Or maybe animals have made it their home — wolves or bears or coyotes.

They reach the top of the hill and stand before the wooden porch. Creek's heart sinks, and he can tell that the others have plunging hearts, too. The house is half a ruin. Dirt and debris litter the porch. The front door has come off its hinges, bringing with it part of the wall, and they can look through into the wreckage of the interior. Broken furniture lies chaotically here and there. A beam has fallen, smashing a long table into pieces beneath it. A portion of the roof has come down, and the remnants of the rainstorm drip down onto the battered floorboards. Filth and leaves and branches cover every surface, as if some black elf decided to return the house to the woodland, then gave up halfway through. Neither an interior space, nor an exterior space, but some sort of rotten hybrid.

Dr. Jemisen takes a few steps forward. I THOUGHT THEY MIGHT STILL BE HERE, she shapes. She shakes her head, then walks through the hole in the wall into the space that would be the living room. She turns to the others, her expression resigned but hopeful, and raises her arms in a wide gesture, as if to say *Welcome home.*

Chapter 25

Lucinda finds Horace in the study. It is a beautiful room, and reminds her of her father's den in that other enclave — half a lifetime ago, it seems. Dark wood moldings, the walls painted a deep red, like drying blood, globes and rods of brass and glass reflecting the warm light of the antique lamp on the desk.

He slumps in an armchair of rich leather, a cut crystal tumbler balanced on the arm, winking with a golden radiance of scotch. The bottle sits on the floor, three-quarters empty. He holds a tabula in his robot hand.

"Lucinda, my dear," he slurs. *He's drunk,* she thinks.

They have returned to the house, leaving Durain in charge at Lady Fal's camp.

She is glad to be here. Everything is clean and beautiful, and reminds her of home. Her room once belonged to a girl, younger than her — early teens, she guessed — a girl who loved frills and lace and patterned silk. All old — some a little moth-eaten — but as good as one could find in this fallen world, and they warm her blankness with their faded charm.

Better than lace is Alexandria. Her COR came alive the minute they entered the compound, and she quickly excused herself to spend the afternoon lazing in warm oceans of data. Astronomy, Greek Tragedy, the migration patterns of birds, the history of vidis from silent cinema to immersive AllSense. Whatever strikes her fancy.

"Good evening, my dear," Ashburn gurgles from his chair.

"Good evening, Horace." She says his name because she needs something from him.

His eye droops, heavy with drink. It scans her body. He hasn't tried anything. Ever the gentleman. But she reads the hunger in his gaze and wonders if it is coming soon.

"Are you all right?" she asks.

"I'm fine. Who wants to know?"

"I do. You seem a little down, is all." He takes another long sip of whiskey, fumbles for the bottle, and refills his glass.

"Not down. Well, maybe a little. There's always a bit of a letdown after a big operation. What next, one wonders? What next, Lucinda?"

"I don't know."

"I suppose you don't."

She looks away, and a silence falls. She hesitates to tell him, but she must. "I need my treatment, Horace. I'm overdue."

"Are you now?"

"Yes."

"Well, that could prove difficult. We're running a bit low, aren't we, Lucinda?"

"I don't know. I suppose so. But you said—"

He waves his hand at her, and for a second, she thinks she's made him angry. But he says, "I know, I know." He rises, swaying. "We won't need to worry about it when we get my equipment back. Any word?"

"Artaxerxes has tracked down the first vehicle."

"There were two unaccounted for, yes?"

"Yes. This one went north, toward Salem. But it's not the one. He found it. It's a small roadster."

"Did he find the people who took it?"

"Person — yes."

"And…"

"He took care of them."

"He didn't interrogate them?"

"That's not really his specialty. I'll send him after the second trail tomorrow."

"How long before the trail goes dead?"

"Hard to say. A few weeks, at least. The cars leave behind very small amounts of various elements, but they are distinctive, and Artaxerxes can identify signatures of a few parts per billion. He'll find them."

Ashburn shakes his head. "It stings me that I'm forced to rely on a robot to do my dirty work. But such is our modern world."

"Why?" she asks.

"Why what?"

"Why do you hate them so?" Her own connection with Artaxerxes is so much deeper than love.

He looks away, staring deep into that place where she cannot reach him. She fully expects him to put her off, but he surprises her. "I knew another, not like him, but like him all the same," he says, quietly, more to himself than her. "I found him here, in this house. I thought I had been granted a miracle. He was my lodestone, my gateway to eternity. But he betrayed me. He buried me in fire and ash and left me to die. But I didn't. Shattered, burned, barely alive — but *alive* — I crawled out of the tomb he made for me. I fell into dark water, cooled my scorching skin. I crawled like a primeval thing. I dragged myself along a road of agony. But I would not succumb." He takes a sip. "My destiny drove me on. At last, at long last, after unimaginable torment, I made it here, the only place that remained for me, where I could rebuild myself, renew my soul, and rise, phoenix-like, to claim my destiny." He laughs, a mirthless bark. "They cannot be trusted. But then, neither can men. They are the tools we have, so we use them, but must always be ready to strike them down should they seek to disobey us." He cocks his head, looking deep into her eyes. "Are you talking to him now?"

"Who?" she asks, suddenly nervous.

"Don't — you know. Artaxerxes."

"…yes…"

"I should have known. It sickens me." His eye drops to her breast. He draws a deep breath. "My, my, my."

Her heart sinks. Is this the moment? She can't fight him off, she knows that. Her head is cloudy, the tendrils of her disease beginning to wrap around her thoughts. "But you told me to. I'm doing what you—"

He grabs her, his metal fingers digging into her arm. "It sickens me." His robot eye burns, but not half so bright as his human one. Abruptly, his intensity dissolves. He doesn't release her, but his grip relaxes. "I'm sorry, Lucinda. I am a jealous old man. I envy the link you share. One day, I hope, you and I will find a way to connect like that."

He releases her. "Sit with me," he says, "Let's talk."

"My treatment?"

"Oh yes, yes." He rises, swaying, and crosses to the Chippendale secretary where he keeps her medications. He gives her the treatment — three shots. She can smell the scotch on his breath, and the foggy cloud of lust that surrounds him, and she braces herself to resist should he make a move. But he doesn't. He tosses the syringe onto the secretary and collapses back into his chair.

"Now. Sit with me. Let's talk."

Her mind clear again, she sits as requested. But they don't talk. He stares into space, lost in thought, sipping now and then from the crystal glass. Five minutes pass, then ten. He seems to have forgotten her. His eyelids droop. He falls asleep.

Lucinda is almost out the door when she notices the tabula on the side table by his chair. The screen faces upward. It is open and unlocked. She hesitates. His breathing is slow and regular, his hands drooping over the arms of the chair. She steps back into the room, as quietly as she can, and looks down at the screen. Journal entries. She picks up the tabula and opens the command window, moves up the hierarchy. Entries going back more than a year.

He snorts and shifts, almost colliding with her hand. She pulls it back just in time. He settles again, oblivious to the world. She opens the command window again and initiates the upload function. The tabula finds the memory module in her COR — it's small, but sufficient for a simple file like this. She starts the upload. It only takes a few seconds. She is just about to close it and replace the tabula when another folder catches her eye. It is titled "Rolfus-Mindworm-res." On an impulse, she copies that one, too. She closes the window and returns the screen to the entry he was working on, puts the tabula back on the table, and slips out of the room.

Chapter 26

Creek sits on the front porch, watching Sandoval, Lamarque, and Dr. Jemisen drag the carcass of a feral cow up the hill. The trouble they are having makes him almost glad he broke his collarbone falling off the roof. It's a hot and muggy day, though at least the rain has stopped for now. He can see that they are arguing, no doubt all in terrible moods after the struggle of hauling the animal from its pasture, almost a kilometer away. They thought they'd hit a gold mine when they found the cows the day before yesterday, but they've been unable to budge the animals off their preferred grazing ground, and everybody was hungry enough now that it seemed like a good idea just to slaughter one there and drag it back here.

They have been at the house for a week. Sandoval keeps saying, "Once we get everything sorted out, things will be a lot easier," but so far, they haven't got much of anything sorted, and everybody is exhausted, sore, and hungry. Luckily, the stream is full of fish — mostly small and muddy-tasting, but they caught a trout, too. Everyone but Dr. Jemisen has lived off the land for at least part of their existence, so they can forage enough to survive. But nobody has felt the pleasure of a full belly since Lady Fal's.

Creek doesn't know why he is still here. It isn't like this house is great. It's a disaster. A ruin. And *Sandoval.* That first night, he told Kimo about the mark he had seen on Sandoval's chest. She just shrugged and told him not to worry about it. She said, *SANDOVAL IS GOOD.* She thought everybody was good. Every day, he told himself, *I'll leave tomorrow.* And every day, he would find an excuse to stay. And now that he had hurt himself, it is more than an excuse. It's a necessity.

Candela comes out of the house and squats down beside him. *HOW ARE YOU FEELING?* she asks.

OKAY.

DOES IT HURT?

A BIT.

She strokes his hair, a concerned look in her eyes. His heart flutters, and the blood rushes to his face. He hopes she doesn't notice. *HOW'S BABY?* he asks.

SLEEPING — FINALLY. She looks down the hill at the other three. The cow lies on a sledge they concocted out of broken boards from the collapsed roof, held together with bits of rope and a few scavenged nails hammered in with a brick. The front has come off, and now it is jammed into a small hillock hidden under the long grass, threatening to completely come apart under the carcass. Creek can see that the argument has intensified, with Sandoval and Dr. Jemisen waving their arms and pointing this way and that, and Lamarque stuck in the middle.

I SHOULD HELP THEM, shapes Candela. She ruffles his hair again, stands up, brushing the front of her dress, and heads down the hill. Creek watches her go. He feels small and helpless. He wishes he could be the one to go down there and figure out how to get the sledge moving again, or at least lend a hand with pulling.

His accident was so stupid. He thought he would impress Candela and the others when he scrambled up the corner post like a monkey from a fairy tale and swung himself up onto the roof. And at first, he did. He felt like a king when Sandoval threw the tarp up to him, and he banged it into place with the brick and some spare nails. He was doing what none of the others could do: protecting the interior from the rain and wind. Then he put his hand down on what he thought was roof, but was actually just the stretched tarp, lost his balance, and came tumbling down through the hole, bringing the tarp with him. He was so mad at himself that he didn't even notice the pain in his shoulder for a minute. He twisted his ankle, too. Not as bad as the collarbone, but he was still hobbling around.

Eventually, Sandoval had hoisted Lamarque up on his shoulders, high enough to get him onto the roof, and he had redone the job properly. Humiliating.

Instead of being useful, Creek had to watch as everybody else did everything. They had been busy — clearing out the debris, lugging more essentials from the van. Under Sandoval's guidance, they had carted stones and wood from the house down to the stream and constructed a makeshift crossing — not a bridge, exactly, it was too uneven for that — but a safe passage that ensured dry feet so long as you moved with deliberation. Most of the medical equipment was still in the van, but they brought over the mattress, the refrigerator and specimen freezer, and the precious single battery pack. It wouldn't run forever, but it would give them power for a couple of weeks, at least.

The others have decided to roll the dead cow off the sledge so they can repair it. It takes all four of them hauling on the two ropes they found in the van to get it to move. Creek has to swallow a laugh when it jerks forward and Lamarque goes tumbling. He gets up and hobbles down to the others, wincing as he goes, but determined not to be left out. They are arguing again when he gets down there.

WHAT'S GOING ON? he asks Candela.

LAMARQUE ASKED IF THEY COULD CUT IT UP HERE, BUT SANDOVAL SAYS NO. HE SAYS WE HAVE TO BRING IT INTO THE HOUSE AND HANG IT UP FIRST. She makes a disgusted face.

So does Dr. Jemisen, who gives him a quick *HI, CREEK.* She says something to Sandoval, shaping as she speaks.

WE'RE NOT BRINGING THIS DEAD ANIMAL INTO THE HOUSE.

Sandoval notices Creek, too, and tries to shape as well. *YES WE ARE. ANIMALS WILL EAT IT OUT HERE.* He tries to say something else, but runs out of shapes.

WHAT IS HE SAYING NOW? Creek asks Candela.

HE SAYS WHEN WE FIX THE BARN, WE CAN HANG THINGS IN THERE, BUT FOR NOW, IT'S THE HOUSE. HE SAYS WE HAVE TO HANG IT OR THE MEAT WILL BE BAD. She makes another face.

Sandoval and Larmarque reinforce the sledge while Dr. Jemisen and Candela flatten the grass on the slope and clear the path of any stones or debris that might stop their progress. Then they must roll the carcass in the other direction to get it back on the sledge. It's almost dark when they finally pull it up to the porch. They are all covered in sweat, grime, and blood. Dr. Jemisen looks ready to fall over.

More arguing about how best to get it up the two steps to the doorway. While they are fighting, Kimo comes back from foraging. She's got some hen-of-the-woods mushrooms, acorns, and late-season greens.

AND LOOK AT THIS, she shapes.

WHAT?

She unwraps a bundle to reveal about fifteen apples. Spotty and misshapen, most of them, but big and delicious-looking.

WHERE DID YOU FIND THOSE? Creek asks.

I FOUND THE FOUNDATIONS OF AN OLD FARMHOUSE OVER THAT WAY — she gestures vaguely behind the house — *THERE'S A BUNCH OF TREES THERE. WE'LL HAVE TO GO BACK. I THINK THERE MIGHT BE POTATOES, BUT I WANTED TO CHECK WITH YOU BECAUSE YOU'RE THE REAL FORAGER.*

It was true. Of all of them, Creek had spent the longest on his own and knew the most about what you could live on in the woods. Which made it all the more frustrating that he was stuck at the house.

They ultimately decide to pull the hanging door off its ruined hinges and lay it down on the steps like a ramp. Even with all of them (except Creek, who has to watch) pulling and pushing, they almost despair of getting the animal up into the house. At last, with a scream of rage from Sandoval that Creek can feel through his whole chest, the meat-toboggan slides up onto the porch and through the door. They all collapse onto the floor, panting like dogs.

Sandoval doesn't let them rest for long. He orders Kimo and Lamarque to take two storage bins and fill them with cold water from the stream. He and Dr. Jemisen put together a hoist with the ropes and an iron from the fireplace. Candela helps them at first, but Baby wakes, and she disappears into the back bedroom to feed him. Creek wants to go with her, but he is too embarrassed and stays to watch the others work.

When Kimo and Lamarque return, the four of them succeed in hauling the cow into the air. Candela returns in time to secure the rope to the central post of the house. They wash the carcass with cold water, heedless of the mess they are leaving on the floor. Sandoval takes the small quantity of ice they have from the freezer, wraps it in a spare shirt, and positions it in the chest cavity. He then wraps the torso with a blanket to hold the ice in place. They step back to admire their work.

But only for a moment. Sandoval looks at the filth covering him from head to foot and points toward the stream. As a body, they troop down and splash into the chilly water. Creek watches them from the house, feeling useless and sad. When they return, they are laughing and smiling. They collapse onto the porch, unable to move another step.

Sandoval begins to talk, though his communication is still more pointing and miming than actual shaping. *TOMORROW... I will cut up the meat. We will freeze what we can. WE NEED...* He asks Kimo for a word, then addresses Creek. *SALT. HOW DO WE GET IT?*

Kimo, less exhausted than the others, rises and disappears into the house. She returns a few moments later. She places the Recreate Mini on the floor before them. *WE CAN USE THIS. IT CAN EXTRACT MATERIALS AS WELL AS REMAKE THEM. WE CAN USE PLANTS.*

PLANTS? asks Dr Jemisen.

SOME PLANTS HOLD SALT IN THEIR ROOTS AND STEMS. WHAT IS BEST, CREEK?

Creek blushes, glad to be useful. *COLTSFOOT AND HICKORY ROOT ARE GOOD. AND WE SHOULD FOLLOW ANY DEER PATHS WE FIND, TO LOOK FOR SALT LICKS. I'M SURE THERE ARE DEPOSITS AROUND HERE.*

Kimo translates for the grown-ups. Everyone falls silent, too tired to talk anymore. They watch the gray light fade over the valley. Tendrils of mist begin to slither among the trees and shrubs by the stream, like long, curling vines. It reminds Creek of a story they were told at John Chaico's school, about a girl who fell asleep for a hundred years, and a wall of vines and thorns that grew up around her as she slept, protecting her from all who would find her. He wishes that the mist would grow up like that, too, and shield them from the rest of the world.

At last, it becomes too dark to see, and they troop inside. They barricade the gap in the wall with the fallen door and more loose beams and boards. Lamarque builds a fire in the fireplace, and after a quick meal of sorrel and apples, they all collapse into slumber, winding up their day of toil with a night of sleep.a

Creek awakens in the dark. He doesn't know why, but his heart is pounding before he even rises into consciousness. He looks about him. The fire has fallen into ash, and there is no moon, so he can make out nothing but vague shapes. One shape in particular appears to be inching through the blackness toward the slightly less black patch that marks the barricaded doorway. Too frightened to be still, he follows the shape. The movement sends a knife of pain through his shoulders, and he gasps.

The shape makes a sharp gesture. It is Sandoval. He has probably said "Hush!" or some such thing. In any event, the gesture clearly means *be quiet!* Creek can barely make him out in the gloom. Sandoval puts his finger to his lips and gestures for him to wait where he is. He nods and dutifully stops. The man continues his careful pace toward the doorway.

At first, Creek can see nothing. Then, he catches a movement on the far side of the barricade — a blacker blackness moving in the black. The man freezes. There is a brief pause, and then a white burst flashes in the dark. A dull pop echoes in Creek's head. Two more flashes, like little stars, pop into the night and vanish. In an instant, Lamarque, Candela, and Dr. Jemisen are tumbling into the room beside him. They all gesture madly. Creek is glad he can't hear all the shouting. The dark blotch that is Sandoval rises, as though he has come out of a crouch. There is some kind of hustle and bustle that Creek can't follow. A light illuminates the cabin. Candela has found the electric lantern. Sandoval stands at the barricade. There is a wide hole in the boards at chest level. Dr. Jemisen's pistol hangs from his hand.

They all crowd forward. Looking through the holes in the barricade, Creek can make out a huge, dark shape lying on the porch. Thick, hairy, and black. A bear.

POOR THING, says Kimo. Sandoval looks at her in disbelief. *IT'S JUST TRYING TO LIVE,* she continues.

They look at the silent mass for a while. Then Sandoval hands the gun to Dr. Jemisen and takes out his knife. He gestures to the others. Everyone go to bed. I'll deal with this.

Everyone nods and drifts off toward the bedrooms. Sandoval holds his hand out to Creek. *CREEK, YOU STAY AND HELP.*

Creek doesn't want to, but he is too afraid to refuse. The others disappear, and he is alone with the man. They stare at one another.

HERE IT IS, shapes the man. *OUR BEAR.* He claws his chest with his hands.

Creek nods. He can't tell if the man is acting friendly or threatening.

Sandoval pulls his shirt collar down to reveal the tattooed skull. *DO YOU KNOW WHAT THIS SYMBOL MEANS?*

Creek nods. *YOU'RE A FOURTH HORSEMAN.* It scares him to make the signs.

Sandoval copies the shapes, then mimes riding a horse. *FOURTH HORSEMEN?*

Creek nods.

I WAS, YES, says the man. His eyes are black in the glare of the lantern. *NOT NOW.* He points over his shoulder as if to say *a long time ago. YOU KNOW FOURTH HORSEMEN?*

Creek shrugs, his heart like ice. He knows enough. Religious fanatics. A Death Cult. One of many that rose up after the Collapse. By all accounts, the worst. They thought killing and burning would bring on the end of the sorry world.

Sandoval takes a step forward. Creek takes a step back. *LISTEN, CREEK. WHEN I AM LIKE YOU* (your age?), *I ALMOST DIE. YOU UNDERSTAND? I AM VERY SAD, VERY ANGRY. VERY DARK. FOURTH HORSEMEN TAKE ME. I AM…* he mimes being lost. *YOU UNDERSTAND? NOT NOW. NOT ANYMORE. DID I…* he mimes stabbing… *YOU? SOMEONE YOU KNOW?* It's the longest speech the man has ever made.

Creek shrugs again. He doesn't want to upset him

I'M SORRY, shapes Sandoval. *I'M NOT THAT ANYMORE.*

Creek just looks at him.

He mimes pulling things together. *I WANT TO FIX IT. BUT I CAN'T. IT IS PAST. BUT NOW…* He leans in. *I WILL PROTECT THEM. I WILL PROTECT YOU. YOU CAN TRUST ME. I WILL SHOW YOU. YOU WILL SEE.* He smiles — a sad, sad smile. *NOW, WILL YOU HELP*

ME? He crawls through the hole in the barricade and sets to, field dressing the fallen bear. Creek watches him work.

Chapter 27

Lucinda lies on her bed, staring at the ceiling. The sky outside her window is black. Dawn won't come for several hours, but she hasn't slept. A light rain streaks the glass.

She misses Artaxerxes. He has been out of range for two days now. He has strict instructions to return, she knows, but she wishes he were there to calm the fluttering in her heart. The file sits unopened in her COR. She knows she must read it if she wants to understand Ashburn, but she hesitates. She doubts that he will figure out she stole it, but worries that the information will change her, and that she will be unable to hide the change. But she must know. She gulps in air and taps the file. The entries are undated, but each has a number.

#1

Made it to Prendergast's. Now stabilized enough to start this up again. Need parts — I thought Prendie had a valetbot, but I can't find it. Probably took it with him. Only searched the first and second floors, though.

#2

Found it! It was in the garage. Looks like he was already scavenging it before he took off — missing one arm and half its head — but lucky for me, the pieces I need are still there. Now I just need someone to do the work. I miss Letitia. She was a pain in the ass, but a genius with a scalpel. I can do the foot myself, but not the face plate. Have to see if I can track down Rolfus. Last fall, he was in Mystic. Maybe he's still there.

Lucinda scans through the next few entries. Most are just a line or two — nothing to record, fixed the water purifier, here's a list of edible foodstuffs. The eighth entry is a detailed record of the procedure for attaching the robotic foot to his stump. The complexity of the procedure astounds her.

#18

Time to go surgeon hunting.

#19

Well, that was an ordeal, but successful, so that's something. Found Rolfus where I thought he'd be. He's got a nice little workshop in the basement of the aquarium. Drawing power from a geothermal unit. He's useful to the local hoodlums — they have an ion lance or two which he keeps up and running — so they let him be. He even has a car. He wasn't happy to see me. Still steamed about Old Saybrook. I talked him down. He was resistant to helping me, but I told him about my set-up at Ole Prendie's and that got him interested. I talked about old times, flattered his ego, and blabbed about what we could do there together. He bought it. He did the procedure. I still didn't trust him, so I refused the anesthesia (who knows where it came from). The pain was purifying. He did beautiful work, I must admit. The eye functions perfectly, and the face plate is less uncomfortable than I anticipated.

The best part of the whole thing was his stuff. He's amassed a lot of fine old tech — gene splicers, centrifuges, homogenizers. Could be useful when I get back to working on the Project, but first things first. The best thing is a Recreate Mini. Amazing little machine. I convinced him to move his operation back to Wallingford. I can keep my eye on him here, and I have no doubt he will prove useful. It will take several trips to get everything back, but it will be nice to have a proper lab again.

The next dozen or so entries don't tell much — more about setting up the lab, complaints about Rolfus, and a number of philosophic diatribes that remind her of things he has said to her over dinner. An entry catches her attention:

#34

Interesting discovery today. I've been poking around in Ole Prendie's files from his days as Director of Advanced Weaponry for the New States. It's taken a while to break through his encryption, but I managed it in the end. Bunch of stuff about the various countermeasures around the Enclave (fat lot of good they did!) but some juicy bits about weapon systems they were working on when everything went to hell: Missile tech, improved ion cannons, and most interesting of all, a folder on biological warfare. He mentions attempts to create bioweapons for use against the Texas Confeds — several targeted to take out their leadership and break down their command structure. One of the tests involved a virus that sounds a lot like this Mindworm that Rolfus has been talking about. In particular, its efficacy at disrupting the operation of neural implants. Apparently, it's been wreaking havoc among the survivors all up the coast. Could it be the same?

#35

Rolfus agrees that this Mindworm sounds similar to the tech Adv. Weap. was working on. Some Nonas probably broke into a secret weapons cache and leaked it. Fools. God, Rolfus is tiring. Now he's all outraged at the terrible things we did during the war. Bleeding Heart. Sounds like a very clever idea to me.

There's a noise outside. Be right back.

Well, that was fun. A bunch of raiders attacked the house. It's been a while since I've been in a firefight. The countermeasures took care of most of them, but I went out with my trusty heat gun and killed their leader. The rest surrendered. I was about to torch them, too, when I had a thought — I've spent decades battling these idiots. Fat lot of good it's done me. What if I used them? It wouldn't be bad to have my own fighting force. Immortality will wait. In fact, much easier to fire up the Project again if I can gather more resources — take down an Enclave or two. That's where all the good stuff is. So I said I would spare them if they swore loyalty to me. They all did, on the spot. Eight of them, and five more from their camp. Thirteen apostles.

#36

Saw my first Mindworm victim today. One of my new soldiers manifested symptoms and attacked three of the others. They shot him before he could infect them, but it was thrilling to watch. The violence, the power, it's impressive. If I could harness that power, I'd have something, that's for sure.

I had Rolfus collect a sample from the corpse. I told him we should work on a cure. He swallowed the idea whole. I have other plans, but he doesn't need to know them. If I can get him to show me how to use his equipment, I can pursue my own line of research while he fiddles around with "saving lives."

Over the next several weeks, the entries are short and matter-of-fact. Ashburn appears busy attracting more fighters to his camp and taking a crash course on virology. One reads:

#44

I need more data on the virus. There's only so much we can do in the lab. I ordered my men to bring me some victims. Rolfus balked (of course!) at the idea of confining them for study, but I reminded him they were dead anyway, and running trials on a few could save thousands. He wanted to ask for consent. I told him, "of course." We didn't, of course.

Then:

#57

I have identified two areas of pursuit. The first is to amp up the aggressiveness, so that the afflicted can't be stopped by bullets or anything. Normal Mindworm victims don't often kill their prey — the virus wants to survive and spread, so generally it's a bad bite followed by collapse. I want them to tear people to pieces. But then, how to control them? I don't want them attacking my soldiers, or — god forbid! — me. I need them to pursue my enemies like hellhounds, but leave my men alone. I think a good solution could lie in Rolfus' observation that many of the afflicted express hyperosmia. If I can augment this symptom, and link the aggression to a unique signature that only non-infected subjects present, one that I can effectively mask in myself and my soldiers, I think we might have something.

Finally:

#82

I've done it. I think. Rolfus has been doing good work, and though he (thankfully) hasn't found a vaccine, his treatments are keeping the afflicted alive for days, if not weeks. He's done his job, and I can't stand another minute of his whining. I infected him with my augmented virus while he slept. Now to test the whole regime.

#83

No response yet. My little virus bomb is still gestating.

#84

Nothing.

#85

Nothing.

#86

Success! Rolfus started showing signs of infection when his aural implant malfunctioned and sent him to the floor, screaming in pain. I had him sedated and isolated. Now we try his medicines.

#93

My virus appears to respond to his treatment regimen. Not as well as the endemic variety does. A week, and he continues to survive, though he is distracted and morose, muttering to himself and hardly eating. Tomorrow we amp up his aggression and see what happens.

#94

I gave one of my soldiers a butyrate masking agent and had him bring Lenora, one of our camp followers, into the pen with Rolfus. He ignored them both, whispering to himself in his private little hell. Then the soldier exited the pen, leaving the girl inside. She was alarmed, but what did she have to fear from this strange little man? Five minutes later, he pretty much tore her head off.

Lucinda closes the file, breathing in gasps. *What now?* What can she do? The thought of looking him in the eye makes her physically sick. What has he done? To her? To all of them?

Trembling, she watches the raindrops sliding down her window, as if she could follow their slippery path out of this den of death. She reaches for Artaxerxes, but he is still out of touch, and the lack of him lashes her soul. She wishes she could run away with him, into the wild blue yonder. But she can't. The Mindworm would kill her before they got far, and even before that, it would fry her COR and she would lose him. She hates to admit it, but she needs Ashburn, for better or worse. She needs the medicine he gives her.

And to make the medicine, he needs his machines back. She curses the people who stole them. No doubt a few of Lady Fal's thugs who ran from the battle at the first sign of trouble, and who plan to sell her salvation to anyone who can trade them a few rounds of ammo or a case of rotgut.

If she could get the machines back, if she could be the one, she might have something she has never had: Control. She has never been in control of her life. Not at home, not in the wild, not here. Always at someone else's mercy. She has a giant death machine at her beck and call, and still, she has no control. She knows what he wants, the way he looks at her. It will take more than 'Xerxes to keep that from happening, no matter how much it sickens her. If she did this, if she got the machines back for Ashburn, maybe she would have some control. Maybe she could make a deal.

Chapter 28

D iary of Kat Jemisen: No date.

I haven't had a chance to write in a while, but I want to make sure I get it down before I lose it.

How strange it is to be back here! Every time I come into the kitchen, I expect to see Leila cleaning carrots or working on her battle stances; every time I go out onto the porch, I expect to see Leonard fussing with that wood-splitting contraption he devised. And every morning I wake to the aching absence of Talia's gleeful shrieks. These children are wonderful, but it's strange for me that they are so silent. Not for them, of course. It's not like I've been around children all that much. But whenever I have — and especially here, in this house — I've been treated to the chaotic, wild, and NOISY energy of childhood. These kids experience the world in such a different way. I mean, we do have little Baby's clockwork cries to mark the passing of the hours, but that's different.

Lamarque is too old for play, of course. Or at least wants to think he is. He follows Sandoval around like a hopeful puppy, ready to hold a beam, hand him a tool, or just watch him work — anything 'manly'. Sandoval doesn't stop him, but doesn't exactly encourage him, either, offering the boy neither praise nor blame. I shouldn't call him a boy. He's trapped in that awful chasm between boy and man. Anyhow, Sandoval doesn't have much experience with children, you can tell. They make him uncomfortable, but he does his best. I hope he's glad for the help. There are so many repairs to be done, and he's really the only one qualified to do them. I can't hammer a nail to save my life. Thank heavens he got the roof repaired, so the living room doesn't get rained on anymore, and he made the front door secure again, which was a relief after the bear (btw —bear meat is nasty. We eat it anyway, but I can't wait until we're done with it and can move onto the cow) — but I digress.

As for Kimo and Creek, they are such quiet, thoughtful children. Kimo, I get, at least a bit. She likes to help me in the lab (we finally dragged the equipment up the hill after we got the roof repaired). We've set everything up in the far bedroom, where Leonard and Leila used to sleep. It's separated from the main part of the house by a long corridor, so I have some privacy to work. I think that part of the house was added later. But once again, I digress. So yes, she helps me when I need her. I sometimes come upon her and Creek sitting on the floor by the fireplace, talking to each other with their beautiful, mysterious hands. I have pushed them to teach me, and they are willing (especially Kimo), so every day I understand a little bit more. But there is still so much I can't follow.

She and Creek have that connection, but Kimo spends most of her time alone. She has a book she got from Sandoval before the attack. She loves it more than anything. It's an old book, with pictures that don't move, and no sound or special effects. It's called Tales of Ahl-Sa-Heira by Tasha Chee-young. Kimo's always got it. I think she's read it three times already.

As for Creek, I can't figure him out. He's been hurt, of course — he fell through the roof when we were trying to fix it the first time, snapped his collarbone. But I've never met a kid who has such deep silence around him. It's like he's wrapped in an invisible bubble, or force shield, or something. I can't explain it. He's no trouble, and helpful when he can be. But I can't ever tell what he's thinking. He never laughs, or at least I've never seen him laugh. He watches. He watches Sandoval work. He'll watch Kimo read for hours (I don't think he can read, himself. I offered to teach him, but he pretended not to notice. I didn't push it. I don't want to embarrass him). Often, he'll watch Candela when she's busy with Baby, or working in the kitchen (she's a good cook. I wish she'd do it more. Nobody else really knows much about it). Candela will notice he's watching her, and give him a big smile, and he'll leave the room. I wonder what's going on there...

Speaking of Candela, I think she's better. She's still very quiet and only talks to Sandoval when she has to. But she's not crying anymore. I haven't talked to her about the Duke. It's all still too raw. But she seems to be coming to terms with our reality.

I should get back to work. Kimo and I spent the morning reorganizing the samples. Basically, all the work we did at the camp was lost when we fled. Actually, not so much when we fled as when we suddenly had to make room for a bunch of bear and cow meat. We've used half the sample bags to wrap it, and most of the space in both the refrigerator and the freezer. Luckily, there weren't all that many samples to begin with. Storing infected blood and brain tissue alongside a side of beef violates pretty much every safe science protocol I can think of, but desperate times, and all that. As long as everything is kept separate, we should be fine. Who knows, maybe it will lead to a breakthrough (ha ha).

Chapter 29

READY? *s*hapes Sandoval. They are at the stream, all of them. Kimo and Candela wait on the far side with Dr. Jemisen. Lamarque stands knee deep in the freezing water, shaking his hands after pushing a stone into place beneath the surface.

They have been working for two days straight with hardly a pause, rebuilding the bridge to allow the van to cross. Lamarque and Sandoval have done most of the hard labor. Creek's shoulder has almost healed — thanks to Dr. Jemisen's bone-knitter — but it still aches like the dickie at night, waking him despite how tired he is after each day's struggle. He has helped where he can, alongside Kimo, shoring up the construction with stacked sticks and twigs, running errands up to the house for tools and refreshments. Dr. Jemisen has slipped naturally into the role of overseer, directing everything like an engineer. Candela has mostly just watched, sometimes with Baby slung at her hip, sometimes from the porch above.

They have collected stones from the old bridge and bricks from a second chimney that had fallen into ruin at the back of the house. They dragged several dead tree trunks down from the top of the hill. One broke free and almost rolled over Lamarque. He jumped over it just in time, landing in a heap. That boy sure is accident-prone. But Creek would never tease him about it. He was the one who actually got injured, after all.

With the last stones in place, they now have a passable roadway across the stream. It consists of two parallel tracks of stone, at just the width for the van's wheels, supported by logs, with culverts built in for the stream to run through. It doesn't look very sturdy, and Creek questions whether it will hold the weight of the van, but nobody asks him for his opinion, and Dr. Jemisen and Sandoval seem satisfied that it will work.

Sandoval and the kids have pulled the camouflaging branches from the vehicle. Now he climbs into the driver's seat. Lamarque tries to follow him, but Sandoval shoos him off. Something about too much weight.

Dr. Jemisen appears around the side of the vehicle. Clearly, she wants to drive. He ignores her and starts to back up. She swings up onto the stairs. Creek can see them arguing. Sandoval tries to put her off, but Dr. Jemisen won't take no for an answer. After a minute or so, Sandoval gets out of the seat and thrusts roughly past Dr. Jemisen, annoyed. She shakes her head and climbs into the driver's seat. Creek smiles to himself. He likes it when adults behave like children.

The boys move to the bank. Dr. Jemisen maneuvers the van to the edge of the bridge, bouncing over the hillocks of grass and weeds. Sandoval places himself midway across the bridge and begins to direct the van into position. *Right, more right, too far, straighten it out.*

Everyone stands in anxious silence as she begins the slow traverse across the stream. The tracks they have laid are fairly flat, but there are still several uneven places that make the van jump alarmingly. Sandoval backs up, directing the doctor as she negotiates the bridge.

Creek spots it well before it happens. The front left tire rises and falls over a rounded stone that somehow was chosen for the top layer, even though it didn't lie flush with its neighbors. The wheel comes down hard, right on the seam between the stone and the edging of the track. The edging stone slips and begins to slide away, into the water. Dr. Jemisen tries to adjust, twisting the wheels back to center.

Sandoval starts shouting and waving his arms — *No, no, no!* — but it is too late. The move pushes the edge-stone further to the side, and it falls into the stream. The van seems to balance for a moment. Then, with comic slowness, it teeters over, further and further. The left track gives way completely, like a chute has opened. Rocks, sticks, and logs tumble down into the babbling water. Sandoval leaps for the van and throws his weight against the side, as if he can somehow stop eight thousand kilos of metal. He can do nothing, of course, and as the vehicle topples over, he jumps back into the water to avoid getting crushed.

The van crashes down onto its side in the stream, sending up jets of water. The sight is beautiful and terrible, the violence of destruction turned balletic in the silence of his world. It only takes a few seconds, but it seems to him that it moves in slow motion, stretched out into timelessness. He knows that this is a calamity for them that will not be remedied, but the magic holds him spellbound.

The van comes to rest on its side, mostly in the stream, its front partially resting against the bank. Sandoval, soaked to the skin, wades in and climbs up the front axle to what is now the top. Everyone else watches, frozen by the tragedy. After a minute, Creek can see the window open, and the man helps Dr. Jemisen clamber out. She looks shocked but unharmed. The two make their way down the front onto dry land. Sandoval gestures for them all to come close. It breaks the spell that has held them, and they all cluster around the two adults.

WE HAVE TO GO, shapes Sandoval. *THE VAN IS BROKEN…* He runs out of words and turns to Kimo for help. Creek feels sorry for her. With the two grown-ups still so sketchy on shaping, she has to wear the Ear way more than she used to when it was just the kids. But she doesn't seem to mind. She likes to be in the middle of things. It seems to Creek like a lot of trouble just to keep him in the loop, but if that's what they want, it works for him.

She translates what Sandoval has to say. *THE CASING FOR THE BATTERY IS CRACKED. HE DOESN'T THINK THERE IS*

DANGEROUS RADIATION, BUT WE DON'T WANT TO TAKE THE CHANCE. HE WANTS EVERYBODY TO GO BACK TO THE HOUSE WHILE HE AND DR. JEMISEN FIGURE OUT WHAT TO DO.

The doctor is making the same mouth shape over and over. Creek has seen it enough that he can recognize it. *I'm sorry. I'm sorry, I'm sorry…*

Sandoval takes her by the shoulder and shakes his head. He ushers everybody away from the van. They troop up the hill. No one looks at anyone else.

Come out onto the porch, signals Dr. Jemisen to Creek and Kimo. They're sitting by the fireplace in the back room. Kimo is reading her book, while Creek watches her, sometimes turning his attention to a small bit of wood he's whittling into nothing in particular.

They've spent the day apart, everybody staying away from everybody else, all processing the disaster at the stream. Sandoval disappeared somewhere for most of the afternoon, while Dr. Jemisen busied herself in the lab. Lamarque offered to help Candela with Baby, but she told him she didn't need him, so he wandered off somewhere, too. Everybody was on edge, but didn't want to cross that edge into open conflict.

Creek and Kimo follow Dr. Jemisen out onto the porch. Creek sees the others gathered. Lamarque and Candela stand on one side, while Sandoval sits with his back against one of the posts on the other. Kimo slips down beside him, so Creek follows suit.

Dr. Jemisen heads down the steps into the yard, then turns and faces them. She's got something in her hand — a piece of old wooden siding about half a meter long. She puts it down and begins to shape while she speaks. He guesses she has practiced with Kimo, because every now and then she looks to her for reinforcement.

"*OKAY,*" she shapes. *I KNOW EVERYBODY IS FEELING SCARED — AND FRUSTRATED —* she looks at Sandoval — *ABOUT WHAT HAPPENED TODAY. THE VAN WAS OUR ESCAPE, IF THE DOCTOR*

FINDS US. I APOLOGIZE. I MESSED UP. I TRIED, BUT NO GOOD. THAT'S OVER.

SO. WE ARE HERE. WE HAVE THIS PLACE. IT IS ROUGH, BUT WE FIX THINGS SO FAST. WE MAKE A HOME. TOGETHER. THAT IS BIG. WE HAVE EACH OTHER. IT IS A DANGEROUS WORLD OUT THERE, BUT WE HAVE EACH OTHER, AND WE CAN PROTECT EACH OTHER IN THIS PLACE.

I WON'T FORCE YOU TO STAY — she gives Sandoval another pointed look. *BUT WE ARE FAR AWAY FROM THE TROUBLE BY THE COAST. I BELIEVE WE ARE SAFER HERE THAN ANYWHERE ELSE. SO, I HOPE YOU WILL STAY.*

I LIVED HERE MORE THAN TEN YEARS AGO, WITH A LITTLE FAMILY. I DON'T KNOW WHERE THEY WENT, OR WHAT HAPPENED TO THEM. I WISH I DID. BUT NOW WE HAVE THE CHANCE TO START A NEW FAMILY, IN THIS PLACE. FOR ME, THAT'S A BIG THING. TO MAKE SOMETHING IN THIS RUINED WORLD? TO BUILD SOMETHING? THAT'S BIG. AND BEAUTIFUL.

She speaks to Lamarque. The boy comes over and picks up the piece of siding from the ground, glancing at it as he does. She stops him and signals Wait. She continues. *I WANT EVERYBODY TO SEE IT TOGETHER. I BURNED IT WITH THIS.* She holds up a medical device like a little wand. Creek recognizes it as a device for cauterizing wounds. *IT'S NOT GOOD,* she continues, *BUT IT SAYS WHAT I'M THINKING. IT'S A NAME. FOR OUR NEW HOME. A SIGN.*

Lamarque flips the piece of wood over and reads it. His eyes widen briefly, and he nods. He lifts it in front of him so the others can read it. Dr. Jemisen shapes it out for Creek:

HOPE FARM

She turns to Sandoval. He regards her for a moment, then rises in one smooth motion. He goes inside, returning soon with a nail and a brick.

He gestures for Creek to join him. Creek hesitates. He doesn't know if he believes in the promise of the sign. But everyone is watching him, and he doesn't want to make a scene. Eyes on the ground, he joins Sandoval.

They cross to the post beside the steps. Creek holds the sign against the post while Sandoval hammers in the nail with a few sure blows. They step back to admire their work. Lamarque, Kimo, and Candela join them, and they all stand side by side, looking at the sign.

Chapter 30

He runs the road alone. The servos in his limbs roll with easy precision. Out of range of his mother, he pursues his singular mission, deviating neither right nor left from his simple goal: Find vehicular signature tracings.

His communication range from mother is minimal. Five hundred meters. If she had a COR amplifier, like his last mother, he could travel up to three thousand meters while still maintaining direct contact. She has no amplifier, but has permitted him to maintain active status beyond her communication threshold in the pursuit of his objective. She has placed no limits on him beyond a temporal one — he must return within 360000 seconds. He constantly updates how long he has before he must turn around, calculating the increasing distance and his travel time over various terrains.

He picked up the first signal at the edge of the encampment, logging the vehicle as a Stellcom/LG Traveller Van, Model 24CT53890B. Following the signal, he arrived at a small camp beneath a fallen bridge that showed signs of recent habitation, including the remains of a fire and food particles on the ground nearby. The trail then angled back toward the water tower, before veering suddenly down an embankment onto the western highway. The van's passage down the hill left one clear wheel rut in the mud and significant disruption of foliage. He knew he was on the right track. When he came onto the Hard-Tru surface of the highway, he found a skid mark turning toward the west. He broke into a run.

His top cruising speed is twelve meters per second. He evaluates the growth along the side of the road, looking for any indication that the van might have left the highway and moved cross-country. He has the schematics of the van model in his lattice, and knows it has lifters — not heavy-duty, but enough to get it through rough terrain.

A spike in radiation levels — so small as to be almost undetectable — pulls him up short. He walks to the side of the road. Before he even sees the tire track in the mud, he catches traces of ammonia, urea, potassium, and chloride. Human urine. Then comes the tell-tale alpha emitters, zipping past his sensors. He runs again.

It doesn't take him long to reach the ruined exit, to find the track through the brush. He begins to climb into the hills above the road, his quarry's path clear at last. He moves swiftly, surely, leaping over fallen trees, thrusting aside the branches and tendrils that have already begun to reclaim the land.

But he doesn't get far. Before he has gone half a kilometer, his chronometrics inform him that he must return to mother. He has reached the limit of his tether. Without pausing, he swings around and heads for home. Every step has been catalogued in his memory. He will return. They will not escape him.

Chapter 31

WE NEED POWER, says Sandoval. *THE BATTERY IS ALMOST DEAD. WE HAVE TWO DAYS, MAYBE LESS. AFTER THAT, THE COW GOES BAD.* Creek watches the flames from the fireplace flickering across the faces of the family, red and orange in the dark, throwing up large, wild shadows on the walls. They've just finished dinner — the last of the bear meat, some apples, and some wild cress Creek found down by the water.

Two days have passed since the disaster at the stream. The van lies on its side in the water, a useless hulk of metal and plastic. Sandoval made a careful examination of the underside of the vehicle, and although he found a long crack, he doubted the radiation levels would be dangerous to them. But they can't be sure. He ordered them to only collect water and fish upstream of the crash, just to be on the safe side.

WHERE CAN WE GET POWER? asks Lamarque.

Sandoval turns to Kimo.

I SAW A PLACE, I THINK, she shapes. *WHEN I WAS FORAGING, I FOUND AN OLD FARM. THERE'S NOT MUCH LEFT, BUT THERE ARE SOME OLD FIELDS. I WAS IN ONE OF THE FIELDS, LOOKING FOR TUBIES, OR CARROTS, OR WHATEVER. I DIDN'T FIND ANY, BUT I THOUGHT I SAW A WIND TURBINE ON A HILL TO THE*

WEST. IT WAS HARD TO BE SURE. IT WAS STICKING OUT FROM BEHIND SOME TALL TREES.

DID YOU INVESTIGATE? asks Dr. Jemisen.

Kimo shakes her head. *IT WAS TOO LATE. IT WAS FAR AWAY, AND UP A BIG HILL. I COULDN'T GET THERE AND BACK BEFORE DARK.*

THE HARD THING WILL BE GETTING THE BATTERY UP THERE TO CHARGE IT, says Sandoval.

SO, YOU PLAN TO STEAL POWER? WHY NOT JUST ASK FOR IT? asks Dr. Jemisen.

The man looks at her as if she has a hole in her head. *ARE YOU NUTS? THAT'S NOT HOW THE WORLD WORKS. EVERYONE GUARDS THEIR POWER WITH FORCE, WITH GUNS. YOU TAKE, OR YOU GET NOTHING.* Sandoval has gotten much better at shaping, that's for sure.

Kat shakes her head, but drops the fight. Before the crash, thinks Creek, she would have argued the point, but now…

Creek can't help but notice that they could have easily had this conversation without including him. Just tell him what to do when they decided. He can't understand all the effort the grown-ups are making to keep him engaged. It's nice, he supposes, but weird. Unlike any grown-ups he has ever known.

In the end, they decide to send Sandoval, Creek, and Kimo. Sandoval braves the wrecked van and removes several of the seatbelts. Candela shapes them into a kind of mesh sling for the battery, with shoulder straps and a support belt at his waist. They detach the battery from the refrigerator and freezer, and he hauls it onto his back.

He curses roundly as he staggers under the weight, but finds his balance after a minute and trudges around the cabin, testing the harness. He nods, satisfied. *IT WON'T KILL ME,* he says. They don't have connectors, but Kimo assures them that most power stations have spare cables, or stuff that you can jury rig. She still has her toolset from Fal's camp. Creek left his behind when they escaped. He feels stupid about it now, but there's nothing he can do. Kimo is always thinking ahead like that.

They make good progress toward the farm, following a trail that was once a country road. Now it's little wider than a deer path, but animals (or maybe people?) have kept it open enough to allow them to move along at a good pace.

The rain holds off for most of the morning, though the sky is white-gray. The leaves are turning, and Creek gets lost in the flickering wonder of a million splashes of color — green, yellow, brown, and fiery red. He has always liked fall, even though it means the days are growing shorter and harder. For one thing, it doesn't rain as much. And the skeeters aren't as bad. The air acquires a fresh snap, which brightens his mind and makes him look at things more closely than at any other time of year. When they were at John Chaico's refugee camp, he would sneak away on autumn afternoons — sometimes with Kimo or one of the Breslove brothers, but usually by himself. There was a trail (not unlike this one) that led up a little hill to an old scenic overlook (There was even a sign, barely legible — Kimo told him that's what it said). You could look out over the valley at the endless procession of trees in every direction, shimmering into the distance in a thousand thousand hues. He felt a hunger to see what was under all those trees. Probably nothing — just more hardship and danger, the occasional wolf or madman with a rifle — but he hungered nonetheless.

He comes back to himself and finds that he's fallen behind. Kimo's little back is disappearing around a curve up ahead. He shakes his head and scurries forward to catch up.

They reach the ruined farm a little before noon. The farmhouse has collapsed in on itself — nothing more than a heap of damp, rotting wood, its rust-red paint fading into sullen brown. The barn is nothing more than a weedy foundation. Still, the fields have held off the encroaching wood. You can still make out what used to be rows of crops — long, thin hillocks running parallel to one another, covered in dying grasses and the occasional leafy plant. Creek knows wild edibles pretty well. He's less confident about cultivated crops, but he thinks there might be some turnips, beets, and a potato plant or two still fighting for life among the weeds.

WE STOP FOR FOOD, shapes Sandoval. They find a spot to sit on a huge fallen tree that must have once shaded the front yard. They unpack their lunch — three apples and some dried strips of beef. The beef is tough and tasteless (they've made some salt with the cube, but only a very little). Creek finishes quicker than the other two and goes to investigate the furrows. After a few minutes, he pulls up some beets — wizened and long, but edible. He shows them to Sandoval, feeling useful for a change. The man nods, grim but approving.

Kimo finishes her lunch and walks to the edge of the field near the house, searching the nearby hills. She signals for them to join her.

She points up toward the top of one of the hills that ring the little farm. Creek follows her finger with his eyes. There it is, poking out from behind an enormous fir at the edge of an outcrop of pale gray stone. The white blade almost disappears into the white-gray sky, but he just makes it out, sticking out toward the horizon.

Sandoval sees it, too. *LET'S GO*, he says. He heads back to the fallen tree and hoists the battery back up onto his shoulders, making awful faces as he does so. Then, without looking at either of them, he tramps to the edge of the rising hill. It takes a minute to find a way through the undergrowth, but they discover the bed of a little stream.

The journey up the hill takes as long as the trip to the farm. The streambed grows boggy in places, and thorny tangles grab at their legs as they seek a passage forward. Sandoval requires frequent stops to rest — the incline is steep, and the weight of the battery on his back threatens to topple him at any moment.

At last, they reach the top. The hill flattens out into a gentle slope dotted with fir trees widely spaced, the ground brown and soft with pine needles. Sandoval only just manages to stop the children from rushing out of the scratchy, stuffy underbrush. They can see the base of the turbine rising out of a square tech shed about thirty meters away. There's no fence.

They sit and watch for a good ten minutes. Creek can hardly stand it. At last, Sandoval appears satisfied that nobody is around. He signals, and they cross the distance to the shed. The thick bed of needles feels delightful under Creek's feet, and the light breeze delights his sweaty face. It's a good five degrees cooler up here, compared to the farm below.

The turbine towers over them, reaching up above the tallest trees like a white mast. Sandoval, his face drenched and red, lowers the battery onto the ground. They circle the building, constantly checking the area. From the back of the tech shed, they see a long conduit running down the far side of the hill. Sandoval gestures to Creek. He nods and creeps down the incline, following the conduit. The ground is cleared around it, so it's easier to cover distance. He sticks close to the edge of the brush, ready to dive in at the first sign of trouble.

Creek goes about four hundred meters before he sees the track opening out into a clearing. He takes to cover in the brush, silently cursing the thorny tendrils that grab at his clothes. He slips through the underbrush, slipping like a mountain cat between the grasping vines, and comes to the edge of the clearing. He counts slowly to one hundred, then turns around and heads back the way he came.

IT'S A CAMP, he tells the others when he returns. *SOME SHEDS AND TENTS. I DIDN'T SEE ANY PEOPLE. MAYBE THEY ARE INSIDE, OR THEY'RE OUT HUNTING AND FORAGING. I WATCHED FOR A LONG TIME.*

IT'S SAFE THEN? asks Sandoval.

Creek has no idea. *YES. WE NEED TO BE QUICK, THOUGH.*

The man nods and leads them back to the door of the tech shed. He signals for them to be quiet. What does he think? They're going to start yelling? Sandoval draws his pistol. Then, in a swift movement, he pushes open the door and leans in, gun first. He looks this way and that, then nods and enters the room. They follow.

The room resembles every turbine tech room they've ever seen, and Creek has seen a few. The rising cylinder of the turbine base makes a curving wall at the back, with a rounded door providing access to the internal mechanism. A broad control panel extends from the front of the wall, with controls for angle and blade speed and readouts on temperature, wind, and rotation velocity.

Sandoval turns to them. *I WILL STAY OUTSIDE AND STAND GUARD, YOU—*

WE KNOW WHAT TO DO, shapes Kimo. Creek nods. The output has been rigged to an enormous storage plate along the left wall. This, in turn, is linked to an empty charging bay that can hold six batteries, though it is empty at the moment. No surprise, the charging bay holds a different make of battery, and theirs won't plug in.

Kimo looks it over. *WE'LL HAVE TO JURY RIG A HOOK-UP TO THE PANEL.* She turns to Sandoval. *CAN YOU PUT THE BATTERY OVER HERE?* She points at a spot well inside the room, just to the left of the charging station. He gives her a look but obeys, dragging the device across the floor by the harness. Without a word, he disappears into the yard.

Creek and Kimo cross to a small locker in the corner of the room. Inside, they find what they are looking for — an assortment of cables and adapters of various sizes and shapes. None of them matches their battery, of course, but they can modify one for their purposes.

I'LL WORK ON THE ENDLINE CONNECTION, says Kimo. *YOU DO THE TIE-IN.* Creek heads over to the large battery panel. The charging station is hardwired in, so he'll have to cut in a branch at the panel. The generator has a shut-off, of course, but it's often linked to an alarm, and he doesn't want to risk alerting whoever lives below. Sometimes they even install a booby trap. That means cutting in while the system is hot. It's a dangerous business, but Creek has done it before and hardly considers the risk.

He never thought he'd say it, but he likes this work. Sure, he never had a say — the grown-ups told him he was a power thief, so he was a power thief. But it's one of the few things he's really good at. He never had a chance to be useful to anyone but himself. It gives him a boost to contribute.

He disappears into the work. It takes all his concentration, cutting in at the right point, keeping everything separate so he doesn't electrocute himself. He works as quickly as he can, but carefully. Step by step. At one point, he senses a faint vibration, as if something knocked against the side of the shed, but he's so focused on his work that he barely registers it. All he knows are his hands, the metal, rubber, and plastic, the reassuring peace of his silent world.

He is completely unprepared when a large pair of arms wrap around him and drag him backwards. Before he can begin to struggle, a dark sack is thrown over his head, and everything goes black.

Chapter 32

When Lucinda was eleven years old, she almost died of influenza. She'd been sick for days — weeks, even — her whole body shaking with fever, wracked by spasmodic coughs, her joints throbbing, her mind a frenzy of ugly dreams. In her memory, a night came at last when she slept — a good sixteen hours — and when she awoke, it was like she had become new. The shattered fragment she used to be had been replaced by a new Lucinda — a whole Lucinda — calm, exhausted but refreshed, emptied only to be filled by something purer, better, more whole than she had ever known.

The return of Artaxerxes makes her feel like that. A quiet vibrancy fills her soul. She doesn't need to see him. She knows him. He is part of her. He enters the camp, parks himself on the back patio, and waits.

She dresses carefully, taking her time. He must not see her as a patient. As a girl. For all of her life, she has been dismissed because of her age and sex. In the face of collapse, the Enclave had retreated into the past, and the easy assumptions of the patriarchy. Her decision to join Defense was a slap in the face to those assumptions, and she had faced resistance from everyone she knew. Now, within the cloaked desire in Ashburn's eye, she has marked his easy dismissal of her as something to be taken seriously. She knows she has powers she can exert over him, but she prefers to face him on her terms. She goes over what she will say to him, whispering at herself in the mirror, as she used to do before a particularly delicate negotiation with her father.

She finds him in the laboratory. It is full of machines. Some are used to maintain his robotic systems, while others baffle her. She considers tapping her COR to identify them, but she has other business. As she enters the lab, she catches him looking at a schematic of some complex piece of technology. It looks vaguely familiar. She almost asks what he is working on, but chooses not to press him.

"He's back," she says, standing in the door. He doesn't look up at first, lost in his work. But when she doesn't enter, he glances over and stops, momentarily frozen by her loveliness. Her heart quickens.

"Look at you," he says. "What have I done to deserve you?"

She doesn't answer. "He's back," she says again.

"Yes. And what's the news?"

"He's found them." She holds her ground, standing tall, projecting quiet confidence. "They headed west down the highway and pulled off the road about fifty kilometers from Fal's camp."

"Did he pursue?"

"He reached the end of his allotted time before he could," she says.

Ashburn shakes his head. "Useless," he mutters.

"Not really. He can easily find it again."

"I'm not sending an expedition into the wilderness half-cocked. He has to do better."

"I agree." Lucinda bows her head slightly. She hesitates. *Go for it.* "Let me go with him. We can track them and report back. Then you can send your expedition."

He studies her face for a minute, his expression dark, unreadable. "Can't you just send him out with a longer leash? Give him more time to find them, wherever they are?"

"I think it would be better for me to be there, to give real-time commands as we assess the situation. I'm limited in what I can program him to do."

"You won't run off?"

She laughs and tosses her head. It strikes a false note. The gesture reminds her of how she used to tease Sebastien. Then, it had been natural, easy, all fun. Now she feels like an actress. A bad actress. She bears down. "Of course not. I need that equipment returned just as much as you do. More. Don't I?"

"Do you?"

"Obviously! Who knows? Maybe we can get it back, just the two of us, and you won't need to send anybody else. Artaxerxes is an expeditionary force all to himself." Her heart pounds.

Ashburn's human eye probes her. It seems colder than the robotic one, though it flickers with a thirst that grows ever more pronounced. It gives her chills. Then he says, "No. I need to keep you close. Durain will put together a team. You can instruct Artaxerxes to stay with him through the completion of the mission."

Damn. Not what she wants. "I could," she says. "But it would be better if I went along, to make adjustments if they're needed."

"No. I need to take a few more scans of your COR. Just order him to protect Durain and his team. They can do the rest."

Lucinda can feel her fantasy collapsing. She steps into the room, keeping her head high and shoulders firm. "Horace," she says, knowing the power it gives her. "If we want to succeed in our goals, we have to use our resources to the best advantage. You need the equipment back. *I* need the equipment back. Artaxerxes is the only tool we have to make that happen. His capacities are limited without me in range. Do you really trust Durain to get this done?"

Ashburn stands, his face severe, but she detects a flash of surprise in his eye. She presses on. "I will take care of it, Horace. 'Xerxes and I will find them. We will deal with them. You can trust us." She steels herself and places her hand on his arm.

He stares into her eyes for what seems like an eternity. "What are you, Lucinda Weston?" He smiles his razor smile and shakes his head. "Very well. I still need to finish those scans. You can leave in a few days. We can wait that long. And take Durain." *Durain.* She doesn't like Durain. *Little snake.* Her impulse is to argue, negotiate, but she bites her tongue. This is good enough. She can handle Durain. "Of course."

"Don't try anything. Just scout the situation and return."

She nods.

"You will return, yes?"

"Of course. I have to, don't I?"

"Yes, but will you?"

"Trust me."

Chapter 33

D iary of Kat Jemisen.:

October 27th.

Made a breakthrough today. My lab notes have all the technical stuff, but I wanted to get it down here, too.

I went back to the beginning and figured out everything they were already doing. The entire apparatus produces a kind of drug cocktail. Most of the compounds that the equipment manufactures aim to suppress various symptoms of the disease, and to slow its attack on the central nervous system. I can't tell how long they could do so, probably not more than a few days before you'd need another dose. A couple of them also seem to be related to behavior modifiers manufactured by the Army in the last stages of the Civil War. I've come across them before. I've treated a few surviving vets in my time who had experience with them, and still manifested residual effects — they were designed primarily for TC prisoners to make them more compliant and suggestible, to get them to spill information.

Then there's a group of compounds that go against the very idea of control — agitators, I call them, meant to exacerbate the rabies-like fury that mindworm creates. Whoever developed this cocktail is a nasty, nasty person.

The interesting thing is that while most of the machines are programmed to make this series of treatments, there's one that was doing something I just couldn't figure out. But this morning I isolated a compound that — at least temporarily — seems to bind up the virus and, as it were, expose its delicate underbelly. The thing about Mindworm is that its viral envelope is extremely hard for our immune cells to attack. This compound is like a burly guard who holds the virus's arms behind its back so you can give it the once-over. It's unstable at the moment; environmental factors degrade it after a few hours, but it's the beginning of something. I think if I can get it to survive a bit longer in the bloodstream, I can pair it with a targeted covalent inhibitor that could actually work as an effective antiviral treatment. Not a vaccine, but something that actually kills the damned virus, doesn't just mitigate its effects. It would help to have more live cultures of the virus to study.

Sandoval and the children are overdue. They were supposed to be back with the charged battery before sunset. It's well after dark now. I'm worried.

October 28.
Still no sign of them. I fear something terrible has happened. Lamarque wanted to go after them, but I told him no. Baby's got a cold. I've spent most of the day helping Candela take care of him. I'm exhausted. It's almost midnight. I'm going to bed. I hope tomorrow brings better news.

October 29.
They are back. Thank God. They returned just before noon. I should say that they WERE returned — they were in custody. Two soldiers brought them to the house. They didn't give their names. They just identified themselves as warriors of the Nipmuc Tribe, which has recently joined the Federation of the First Nations — what my parents called 'Native Americans', banding together to stake out their claim to the country now that the governments have all gone away. Anyhow, a tall woman with long black hair was in charge, with a shorter man minding the prisoners while we talked. They both carried ion spears, and I could see she had at least one pistol, too. My, my, she was beautiful.

She spoke excellent English, which made me glad because, though I've come across a few native people in my travels, I've never had to speak a word of their language (Algonquian?) She explained that they'd caught Sandoval and the kids stealing power from their wind turbine. I told that man not to just steal it. Try and find out who owns it, I said, but would he listen?

Apparently, the Nipmuc have a camp on the other side of the ridge, and they took them there and held them for questioning all day yesterday. I checked in with Kimo to make sure they were all right. She signed back that they were treated well. Fed and given a comfortable place to sleep. The woman was interested in our exchange. They don't have any deaf people in their community, and nobody was able to talk to the children (Kimo had the Ear, but she played dumb — smart girl). That meant Sandoval got all their attention. From the look of him, he wasn't badly treated, either, but damn was he mad at himself for getting caught. He practically had steam coming out of his ears.

The woman (I wanted to ask her name, but I got all shy and she didn't offer) said that they had determined our band of thieves posed no threat, so they were returning them to us. She said this part of the country was now under First Nations control. I asked her if we could stay in the house. She looked at me as if I were crazy. "Of course," she said. "Why shouldn't you?"

Perhaps the most interesting thing — they had charged our battery. Good thing, too, because the freezer was starting to thaw. I didn't want a hundred kilos of meat going rotten. Or my specimens to die. I thanked her assiduously and asked her if there was anything we could do for them. She said she didn't think so. Then I told her I was a doctor. That got her interest. Their medicine woman was recently killed (she didn't say how). I offered to come to the camp and see if there was anything I could do. She thanked me. I said it was the least I could do after our behavior toward them. She smiled just a little and said, "The wind is for all — just ask first."

Chapter 34

Creek sits in the doorway of the quonset, watching the quiet industry of the Nipmuc camp. It's warm for this time of year, and he'd much rather be sitting out here than inside the stuffy building. He's supposed to be helping Dr. Jemisen, but she doesn't have anything for him to do, and when he slipped away, she didn't stop him.

The camp is small. Creek counts fifteen buildings, most of them weatherworn metal huts like this one, wrapping a central clearing like two round arms. Several tents. A larger structure, maybe a meeting hall, rises where the two arms meet. There are a few smaller sheds scattered around, but that's about it.

It's a poor-looking place. It reminds him of the outskirts of John Chaico's refugee camp — much smaller, of course — there were at least two hundred people there before the massacre — but with the same attempt at permanence that only underscores the impermanence.

Still, the Firsters don't mind. Creek watches them go about their business as if they have everything they want. A group of six — men and women both — are sitting in folding chairs outside the building opposite him, doing something with long strips of dried grass or leaves. They are smiling and laughing. People pass by them now and again, and they greet each other with cheerful faces and words that Creek can't make out. They glance his way now and again, but don't say anything, just look. Behind another building, he can see a group of warriors drilling with ion lances. He watches two others shore up one corner of a hut. It looks like the dirt got washed away during the last rainstorm, and they are trying to support it with stones they've shaped with a kind of circular saw thing.

In his pocket of silence, Creek wonders at all these lives. Amazing to think that they all existed, doing the same things they are doing now, before he knew about them, and that they will go on existing when he leaves. His life has been so solitary, it's hard to fully comprehend the reality of others. The world appears so empty most of the time, but there are people everywhere, hidden in little corners of the wilderness like this one. Not so many as there used to be, according to the stories he heard at the school — not by a long shot — but millions of people still spread across the vast and ancient landscape. He is not sure whether he likes that thought. Most of them are desperate or cruel, fighting for survival or dominance. At least these Nipmuc seem more interested in their own lives than in messing with his.

A young face thrusts itself into his, breaking his reverie. Three Nipmuc kids, a little younger than him, have appeared out of nowhere and are crowding around him, talking. He shrugs, shakes his head, points at his ear. It doesn't stop them. They keep talking, making signs to each other that he can't understand, determined to break him down by just repeating themselves over and over until he gets it. He'll never get it. He stands, shaking his head again, and goes inside. They don't follow him.

Dr. Jemisen is talking to a young woman who is sitting on a broad table at the back of the room. There are a couple more smaller tables in the space, along with some shelving units with various supplies on them. The Nipmuc told them it was the infirmary, but it is doing double duty as a storeroom. Creek sees boxes of food — rice, cereals, and other stuff presumably liberated from an abandoned warehouse or shopping center. Creek is impressed — hardly any of that stuff left anymore. He wonders where they got it.

The young woman listens to Dr. Jemisen, nodding every once in a while, then says something to her and hops off the table. The doctor reaches into her bag and gives her a small bottle of pills, and she goes, giving him a brief, embarrassed smile as she slips past him.

Dr. Jemisen mimes a round stomach. She's pregnant. *HOW DO YOU SHAPE…?* She acts out being sick and throwing up. He shows her. *SHE IS THROWING UP. I GAVE HER SOMETHING TO HELP.*

DO YOU NEED ME? he asks.

MAYBE LATER. She mimes cutting and sewing. *An operation. ONE OF THE WARRIORS CUT HIS LEG VERY BADLY. I'LL NEED YOU FOR THAT. SORRY. I HOPE YOU ARE ENJOYING YOUR TIME HERE. IT IS GOOD, ISN'T IT?*

SURE, he answers, noncommittal. She peers at him, and he looks away. It makes him uncomfortable. She's always trying to get inside, figure him out, like he's a puzzle. He's not a puzzle. He just doesn't have an answer for her.

HAVE YOU MET PEOPLE?

NOT REALLY. JUST SOME KIDS.

ARE THEY NICE?

He shrugs. *WE CAN'T TALK.*

One of the workmen who was shoring up the hut appears in the doorway, holding his wrist. He speaks to Dr. Jemisen. She replies and leads him to the table. Forgotten, Creek slips back outside.

Chapter 35

Candela holds Baby to her breast. He suckles. It hurts some, but not too badly. Dr. Jemisen said she has mastitis on one side, but it is getting better. Still, this side doesn't hurt nearly as much. It feels weird, but okay.

She still can't wrap her head around being a mother. She's seventeen. Maybe eighteen. She's not sure. She never knew her own mother, and though she helped some of the women at the refugee camp, she never thought of herself as mother material. But here she is. She looks down at his little head. She does love him — of course she does — but he confuses her. He's a little alien, and when he looks up into her eyes, she sees secrets he'll never tell her.

She watches him eat, and her mind settles into that comfortable blankness where she spends much of her day. But she doesn't get to linger there, as she would prefer. Sandoval comes in and pulls her out of her quiet place. Every time she sees him, anger like a black coal smokes in her heart. She doesn't let on — she won't give him the satisfaction of a showdown. She knows her silence drives him crazy, and she likes that just fine. After what he's done, he deserves it.

She can still remember the Duke's hands on her body, running through her hair, holding her face as he kissed her. She misses him so much. She misses his bony elbows and his shock of dirty blond hair that could never agree on which direction to go. She misses his narrow hips and his long, delicate fingers. She never had someone take care of her like that. He always looked out for her. Made her feel safe.

And now he is probably dead, and she blames Sandoval. Deep down, she knows that isn't fair. She knows he was right not to go back — safer for the younger ones, and for Baby, and even for her — but that doesn't make it hurt less. She's not going to help him out by forgiving him, or talking it out, or anything like that.

Sandoval isn't one to start a confrontation, either. Oh, he'll happily wade in if someone else goes on the offensive — he loves being attacked — turning the tables, bossing people around, and getting all indignant. But he won't start the scrapping.

He sees her and frowns, like he usually does. She turns her body slightly so that he doesn't have a full view of her breast. He says, "Sorry, looking for something." He doesn't tell her what it is, but gets all busy turning things over, moving the few bits of furniture this way and that.

"Must be outside," he mutters. He says it to himself, but Candela knows it's for her benefit. She keeps her eyes on Baby and doesn't let him know she heard him.

She does like his broad chest and the stern but strong set of his chin. If they weren't at war, she'd be the first to admit that he was a honey. But he'll never hear it from her.

He finishes pretending to search and heads outside, pushing the barricade with a clatter. *Good. Let him suffer.*

Baby has fallen asleep, his mouth still loosely attached to her nipple. She watches him sleep for a while. She can see the Duke in the curve of his eyebrows and the shape of his lip. It hurts more than the pain in her breast. How is it that this mysterious creature, so small, so round, can conjure the Duke so vividly, so keenly remind her that he is lost to her, probably forever? They are almost nothing alike, and yet the ghost of his father hovers around Baby, silently tormenting her. When they first arrived here, Kimo had tried to console her by saying that Baby meant the Duke would always be with her, and Candela can see that is true. But it wounds her, it doesn't bring comfort. What good is it, being constantly reminded of him? It just brings home the fact that he is gone, and this little, helpless creature has taken his place.

She rises slowly and carries Baby into the back bedroom. Sandoval has created a crib of sorts out of wood from the ruined shed, tacked together with spare nails, and strapped with bits of cloth from the seats of the van. She recognizes the appeasement in the gesture, but it's not enough. Her Duke is gone, and it's Sandoval's fault.

Creek comes in. Candela gives him a smile. He's a sweet, funny kid. He doesn't say anything, just watches her as she lays Baby in the crib, and covers him with his new blanket. The Nipmuc gave it to her, just this morning, along with other gifts for the cabin, including salt and a bag of Manitoban flour — an exquisite delicacy. Candela has eaten bread made from wheat flour before — once when she was a girl, when the Clarks were taking care of her (before Amos Clark got a bit too interested in her and his wife kicked her out). She still remembers the magical sensation of it in her mouth — airy but chewy, filling but delicate. Bluebird, one of the Nipmuc, has promised to teach her how to make bread, and Candela wonders if it will be the same. She assumes that Kat and Sandoval have had bread before, but she doesn't think any of the youngsters have, and it pleases her to think she can give them such a wonderful new experience. She doesn't often get a chance to contribute. Everyone just assumes she has to look after Baby all the time, so they rarely ask her to do anything. For the most part, that's just fine. She's happy to stretch out on the mattress and watch the spiders in the rafters, or sit in the chair on the porch (another Sandoval creation) and watch the rain. But it feels good to help when she can.

The blanket is one of the most beautiful things she's ever seen, with rich stripes of brown, red, and black. It's a bit coarse, but so much better than Lamarque's jacket, which is what she was using before. She tucks it in around Baby's tiny body, and pauses in still wonder at his seashell eyelids, pearly blue and blush. He is beautiful, but strange.

All of a sudden, Sandoval is at the door. Is this it? *Is he actually going to have it out with her? Let him try.* She glances at Creek, who watches the man with veiled eyes.

"They've found us," Sandoval says, his face like a storm cloud. "Stay in here. Don't come out for any reason. Do you understand?"

He disappears before she can say a word. Baby starts to cry.

Chapter 36

Lucinda squints down the hill at the van wreckage in the stream. It looks so out of place. The meadow spills down before her, the grass mostly blond and brown now, and the line of trees shimmer with bright red and yellow, even in the dingy gray of the late afternoon. Alien it lies, metallic blue and black, with happy water babbling around it as if it were just another rock or fallen trunk. Across from her, she can see a low house, and a trickle of smoke rising through a hole in the roof. Artaxerxes stands at her side, towering above her and enveloping her in the impenetrable shield of his commitment. They have found them.

"Well," says Durain, coming up behind her right shoulder. "You think that's them?"

She points to the van lying on its side in the rushing water. The little man curses. "Suppose they wrecked the equipment. That'd suck."

"We'll just have to find out," she says.

"We should head back."

"No. We're here. Let's get the stuff."

"He told us to investigate and report—"

She turns on him. "Do you really think he'll be happy to expend time and resources on an expedition if we could just resolve the situation ourselves? No. He won't be happy. We have 'Xerxes. We can do it on our own."

He gives her a shifty look. She hates his rat face. "We really should…" He trails off, waiting for her to finish his sentence.

She completes it for him. "…do our job," she says.

Durain frowns. She can tell he's nervous, not so much about what Ashburn will think, as about the safety of his own skin. He's not a fighter. He got where he is because he knows how to butter up the chief. Lucinda has watched him do it. And he's got organizational skills well beyond most of the fighters. She wonders where he came from, how he met Ashburn. She has never asked either of them for the story. The less she has to do with Durain, the better.

"Xerxes and I will cross over to the other side and see what's going on," she continues. "You stay in the woods by the stream while we approach the house."

Durain shrugs. He may not like the plan, but if it means he can stay back, he'll go for it. *Coward.*

As they descend the meadow to the stream, they keep a sharp eye out for any movement in the house. Lucinda asks Artaxerxes to search for heat signatures in the high grass. Nothing. They all must be inside. They pass through the trees along the bank. The van lies on its side, rising like a weird stage from the bubbling water. They have been cannibalizing it for parts. The wheels have been removed, as has the side mirror, the bumper, and the front fender.

The stream flows swift and dark here, rushing downhill from the rising land to the right. Someone has built a makeshift bridge across it out of logs and stones. Half of it has collapsed, but the other side looks sturdy enough, as long as they watch their step. Durain sways uncertainly in several places, fighting for balance, and Lucinda half-wishes he would fall in. Artaxerxes doesn't bother with the bridge, slashing through the water on his enormous legs.

Creek watches Candela. She stares at the door where Sandoval had stood, her dark eyes smoldering.

WHAT DID HE SAY? he asks.

HE SAID TO STAY IN HERE, she answers.

WHY?

THEY'RE COMING.

His heart sets in pounding. He knew it. He knew they wouldn't be safe. Why did he stay? The answer stands in front of him. A million emotions play across her face. He wishes he could do something — give her comfort, offer advice, take control — anything. All he can do is wait in silence.

Baby is crying. His face is swollen and red, and he rocks back and forth in the crib, pushing off his blanket and waving his tiny fists. Candela gives a frustrated sigh and picks him up again. She walks back and forth, whispering fiercely. Creek's secret heart aches in ways he can't understand. He longs, deep down, to exchange places with the child, to lose himself in the soft folds of her, but he cannot acknowledge the need in any conscious way.

She looks at him and gives him a smile, and it is like the sun comes out. Then she goes back to her pacing. What can he do? He wants to run away; he wants to stay.

Candela jumps at a noise he cannot hear. Something is happening. She is talking to herself, her mouth moving rapidly in a breathless monologue. She jumps again. Baby is frantic in her arms, squirming so much that she can barely hold him. She starts a third time. Candela lets out a scream, the violence of her emotion thundering even into his silent world. Then she is moving for the door.

STAY HERE, she shapes, moving swiftly, and she is through the door and gone.

Creek stands in the middle of the room, lost.

Lucinda gazes up at the house on the top of the hill. Not exactly what she expected. She imagined the men who stole the machines having tents or lean-tos gathered around a fire pit, roasting game over an open flame.

Like bandits from an old story. This place looks downright homey. She gestures to Durain. "Wait here." He nods, crouching down beside a large hemlock.

"You should stay here, too," whispers Durain.

"No."

"You can control him from this distance, can't you?"

She hadn't thought of that. "I suppose," she mutters.

"Dr. Ashburn told me to keep you safe. You should stay here and let the robot take them out. Then we secure the equipment."

He's right, and she hates him more for it. She wants to stride beside her giant warrior. The power he gives her is like nothing she has ever felt.

"I'll be fine. I can talk to them."

"About what? We should let him eliminate them, and then we can take our time."

"They're people, Durain."

"People who stole from us."

"Let me handle this. It'll be fine."

Before he can argue any further, she heads out onto the hill, Artaxerxes at her side. The gradient is long but not steep, but she feels the effort in her legs, more so as her heart starts thumping of its own accord. Someone has cut a path through the grass from the bridge up to the house. The grass has been cleared immediately in front of the house, as well, defining a semicircle of yard about forty meters wide. The yard is surrounded by a low stone wall that arcs from the woods above it on either side. Some of the wall has fallen in places, shrubs and long grasses filling the gaps. The ruins of a good-sized barn stand against the forest on the right.

The path passes through a break where an iron gate once hung. She can see the old hinges and latch rusting on either side, but the gate itself has fallen apart or been scavenged for another use. She passes through the breach. Artaxerxes steps easily over the wall. They enter the yard.

About ten meters from the porch, a shot cracks the silence of the valley. A male voice calls, "Stop right there." They stop. "If you come any closer, I'll shoot, and I won't miss."

"We don't want trouble," says Lucinda. Looking into the gloom of the porch, she sees that the front of the building has partially fallen in, and the door has been replaced by a barricade of boards, blocks, and other detritus. She can just make out the figure of a large man hunkered down behind a barrel.

"Sure you don't," says the man. "You've brought that thing here to *not* make trouble. Sure."

"You have our equipment. We just need it back and nobody gets hurt."

"That's not going to happen. Now, please leave our property."

Before Lucinda can speak again, another *bang* cracks the air, and a narrow rush of air blows past her cheek. "I missed on purpose," says the man. I can't hurt the robot, but I can kill you."

She steps behind the giant soldier. "If you do, he'll destroy you."

"I'll take that chance."

Lucinda feels sick inside. This is not how she wanted things to go. Maybe she was naive, thinking that thieves could be reasoned with. She taps her COR and instructs Artaxerxes to power up his weaponry. A rising hum emanates from his chest, while his missile launches rotate into place with a loud click. She hopes the effect is suitably intimidating.

"Look," she says. "It doesn't have to go like this. You can't win. You know that. Just give me the stuff, and we'll leave you in peace." Her COR gives Artaxerxes his targeting instructions.

"I don't believe that for a second, lady. I was at Lady Fal's. I saw what you people do."

Artaxerxes alerts her that he is ready.

"I don't want to do this."

"I'll bet." Another *bang!* Another breeze whistles past her ear. *Enough of this nonsense!* But still she hesitates. It was easy to order him to fire in the heat of the battle at Lady Fal's. Not so here.

Suddenly, another shape flits through the darkness of the entrance. It runs low and fast to the man, disappearing behind the barrel. A little, elfin figure. Maybe a girl, maybe a boy. Lucinda's heart stops. *What?*

The man grunts fiercely, "Kimo! I told you to stay back." She can't hear the child's answer, but the man says, "Just stay down." The snap of a cartridge into place. Lucinda tells Artaxerxes to power down his weaponry. *Children?* She searches his system for an alternative.

Before she can react, another figure barrels out of the darkness. A young woman. Holding a baby. Lucinda's mind reels. *Who are these people?*

The man shouts, "Candela! Get out of here!" Heedless, the young woman with the baby runs forward a few steps. "Go away!" she screams. "Go away!" Tears flood her eyes. "Killer! Killer killer killer killer killer!" Her shriek strikes Lucinda like an axe.

Another *bang!* from behind the barrel. Lucinda's left hand explodes in white fire. She whips it up, her brain numb with shock. In the palm, near the thumb, a neat red hole spreads like a tiny rose. She turns it over. The back of the hand is ragged and torn. Blood begins to flow, and with it, pain.

Lucinda wavers. *What is going on here?* This was supposed to be a band of rough fighting men, fleeing the battle with the equipment, hiding out in the old cabin till they could sell it, probably planning a counterattack against Ashburn's people at Fal's camp. But a kid? A mother? A baby? *What the hell is she supposed to do now?*

She knows what Ashburn would do in this situation. No mercy. Take them down. Take back what is his. *But how can she…?*

Artaxerxes shuttles new information into her COR. He shows her another way. Cruel, but not murderous. She orders him to activate the system.

"I'm sorry," she says to the baby.

When the sound wave strikes them, Creek is still at the back of the house, in the bedroom. Something held him back when Candela rushed out of the room, though he wanted to follow her. He stands in the doorway, trying to see what is going on. The burst hits him full on. He can't hear the shrieking blare that knocks the others to the ground, but he can feel it — a sickening throb that makes his stomach churn, his eyesight tremble, his hands and legs start to shake.

Creek flattens himself up against the thin cabin wall. It provides minimal protection from the shuddering pulse, but enough to let him move. Nauseous and confused, he stumbles to the window. They've thrown some plastic sheeting over it to provide some protection from the oncoming chill. He pushes through it and tumbles out onto the ground at the rear of the house.

Almost at once, the nausea vanishes. The sonic beam must be narrow. He scrambles to his feet and sprints around the exterior, stopping at the front corner. He peeks around.

The giant mechanical soldier stands on the porch, its sleek and shining arms at its sides, its huge, beautiful head slightly bent forward. The magnificent monster that destroyed Lady Fal's camp. Beside it stands the woman with the red hair, pale and glorious as a forest goddess. Her head is thrown back, as if she channels a divine ecstasy from some higher plane. The sight takes his breath away.

As quickly as he can, Creek slips behind the low wall that rims the yard and runs, bent over, to the front gate. He can see Sandoval writhing on the ground, holding his head. Kimo's legs stick out from behind the barrel, unmoving. He can't make out Candela or Baby.

Keeping low, he creeps up behind the goddess. The robot gives no sign that it clocks his approach. Thank mama, he went foraging earlier in the day, and still has his knife in his pocket. It's small, but sharp.

He doesn't stop to consider where to strike. Low as he is, he goes straight for her right leg, driving the blade deep into the back of her knee. She falls forward. She's a good foot taller than him, so he doesn't wait for her to react. He keeps his forward momentum and barrels on top of her, pulling out the knife and twisting her around as he straddles her torso. Her eyes bug wide in terror and surprise. Before she can start to fight, he thrusts the knife blade under her chin, hard enough that it draws blood. She freezes.

Creek has only tried to speak once before. At John Chaico's school, some of the hearing kids convinced him to talk at a birthday party for one of the boys. Fedoneo. They promised him their ration of sweets if he would say 'happy birthday' with his voice. He had played around with it some on his own, trying to mimic what he could of other children. He understood it in theory. So, he tried. The other kids almost lost their minds with laughing. He could see them aping the sound he had made, setting each other off into fits of hysterics. At least he couldn't hear how ridiculous it must have sounded. He never got the sweets.

Now, taking a deep breath, he yells the words "Stop it!" with as much force as he can muster. He doesn't know if she can understand. He hopes she can read it in his eyes.

PART THREE

...sed carmina tantum
nostra valent, Lycida, tela inter Martia, quantum
Chaonias dicunt aquila veniente columbas.

...but our songs
Have no more strength, here among weapons of war,
Than the doves of Chaon when the eagle comes.

— Vergil, Eclogues 9, 11-13

Chapter 37

A proper soldier would have ordered Artaxerxes to tear her assailant's head off, but Lucinda just stares up at the feral boy straddling her, unable to process the strangeness of him. He yells again. "Stop it!" His voice is wild and guttural. He pushes the knife point further into the skin below her chin. She orders the soldier to cancel the sonic weapon. A moment later, the man is kneeling beside her, his rifle pointed at her head.

"Tell the robot to lie down on the ground," the man says through clenched teeth. She obeys. It is surreal to see the towering machine spread out like a junk pile in the dirt. It hurts her to see him so vulnerable, but her knee hurts more, and the knife and the gun speak loud and clear.

The man orders her to rise. She tries, but the pain in her hand and leg explodes in a white fire. She blacks out. The next few hours are a fevered blur. She comes to inside, in a room full of medical equipment. Probably the stuff they stole from Ashburn. A dark-skinned woman with an apple-round face examines her, then patches up her wounds with the skill of an experienced medico. The warm, dry gentleness of her hands — expert hands — makes Lucinda feel safe despite herself. The woman says, "I'm going to give you something to make you sleep while we figure out what to do with you." Her voice is so quiet and cheerful that it doesn't sound threatening. Lucinda doesn't resist. She sleeps better than she has in months.

When she wakes, a teenage boy with skin so black it is almost blue sits beside her, holding a pistol and looking nervous. She considers calling Artaxerxes, gambling that the boy will be too scared to shoot her. Something holds her back. The boy leads her to the outhouse (an experience so novel, so unpleasant, that if she weren't already disoriented, it would have sent her into a fit of outrage), then brings her into the main room of the house. A strange group awaits her, watching her silent entrance. Her enemies. She supposes. Hardly the band of rugged thieves she had imagined.

First, there is the man who had shot at her. He alone fits the description of a brigand — tall, dark, and handsome — emphasis on the dark. He scowls at her. Behind him stands the girl with the baby, who had run out and screamed at her. She is soft and round and pretty. Then the medico. Then two smaller kids. The girl who brought ammo to the man, who has a wide face with bright black eyes. And the boy, younger even than her. The boy who had stabbed her in the knee and howled at her like a coyote.

They are so different from anyone she has known. In the Enclave, everyone was white, most people were blond or sandy-haired (except for a few redheads, like her). So many years of genetic isolation, everybody pretty much looked the same, or related. Many were. These people are new. Rough, to her eyes, but beautiful.

The interrogation is long, but civil. The medico does most of the talking. She says her name is Kat. Why did you come? What do you want? Tell us about the Doctor. Does he know where we are? Lucinda answers her questions calmly, but doesn't mention Durain. She wonders where he is. He certainly made no effort to save her. Probably took off at the first sign of trouble.

The woman then asks about Artaxerxes — how he works, what he can do, whether he is a danger to them. It almost makes Lucinda laugh. Of course, he is a danger, but only if they treat her badly. She doesn't say this, just thinks it. It seems so obvious. He is hers, she tells them, and only obeys her.

"And you control it with the chip in your brain, the one with the port behind your right ear?"

Lucinda nods.

Kat looks up at the brigand, as if asking him whether he believes her. He nods. Lucinda reckons him for a soldier of some kind, who would know something about battle robots like hers.

Then Kat turns the conversation to Lucinda herself. Her story. Somewhat to her surprise, Lucinda finds herself telling them everything. How she lived in the Hamilton Enclave, was studying to join Defense, her secret relationship with Sebastien. How they had expelled her. Her perilous escape through the countermeasures. She can't explain the flood coming out of her. And she can't stop it. She has been silent for so long. Ashburn never asked her anything about her past life, except for a few technical questions about the Enclave's defenses. Now here she sits, spilling everything to a roomful of strangers.

"Why did they kick you out?"

"Sebastien's family came down with it. Mindworm," she says. "When they found I'd been exposed, and exposed others, they made me leave."

"And do you…Do you have it?"

Lucinda hesitates. Swallows. "Yes," she says.

The boy with the pistol and the young mother both take a step back. The medico raises her hand. "It's okay. The virus is transmitted by fluids. That's why it causes a frenzy in people. It drives them to scream or bite or spit."

"What about Creek?" asks the man. Lucinda doesn't know what this means.

"I'll test him," said Kat. "I'll test everybody. But I think it's unlikely. Just keep your distance from her."

The interrogation ends abruptly. The teenage boy takes her away and locks her back in the medical room. In the corner stands a little bed, a dresser, a small table, and a chair. They bring her food — dried meat and some kind of root vegetable. She wonders if she should do something defiant. She is their prisoner, after all. Yell, or go on a hunger strike or something. But she *is* hungry. And for whatever reason, she isn't angry with these people. She doesn't know what she feels.

The cart comes to a halt in a field about a kilometer from the house. It's an awkward conveyance, not meant for carrying people, so every time it hits a root or a rut, it jars Lucinda's whole body, jamming knives of pain through her wounded knee. At first, she held onto a defiant stoicism, but it hurt too much, and now she doesn't let pride stand in the way of a good groan or yell.

"I think this is far enough," says the man, Sandoval. "Tell it to stand over there, under that tree." Lucinda considers telling Artaxerxes to rip him in half — the soldier could do it in a heartbeat. But the teenage boy has the pistol trained on her, and no doubt she'd die as quickly as the man. Besides, she agreed to do this. She orders 'Xerxes to walk to the tree, and he complies, the top of his head rising past the lowest branches.

"Tell him to wait."

"I don't need to tell him," she says. "He'll do that on his own until I give him further commands."

"Do it anyway."

Lucinda takes in a deep breath, trying to calm the bubbles in her chest — exasperation or fear, she's not sure which. She tells Artaxerxes to wait. "Okay," she says.

"How long will he do it?" asks the man.

"Until he receives another command."

"So, days?"

"Days, weeks, years." She feels tired all of a sudden. "His battery will keep him going for centuries. Is that long enough?"

"Not really." The man scowls at her. He always seems to be scowling. "He's not going to run off somewhere, back to the Doctor or anything?"

"No. I told you already. He's mine. He only does what I say. Until I die or reassign him to someone else."

"I'm going to keep checking. Every day. So, if he's gone…"

"Can we go back now? Your wife, or whatever, said she'd give me my meds."

The cart starts rocking and bouncing as the man swings it around and heads back toward the house. Lucinda pushes away the rising panic as she watches Artaxerxes, standing motionless beneath the tree, growing smaller and smaller. She winces when he disappears behind the roll of the hill. She still holds him in her mind, dreading the moment when he will go out of range and his solid presence will flicker out like a candle snuffed in a distant window. She has felt it before, but she always knew he would return. She had ordered him to do so. Why hadn't she done that? Why hadn't she ordered him to wait until nightfall, then return, weapons blazing, to eliminate her captors in a blaze of white energy? They could not have stopped her. She had not done it.

"Lucinda?" The man's voice brings her back. "That's your name, right?"

"Yes."

"Mine is Sandoval. And the boy is Lamarque." She turns and looks at him. His back is to her as he drags the wagon, so she can't see his face.

"Okay."

"Kat will treat you when we return." He sounds embarrassed, uncomfortable. It pleases her a little. "She's looking for a cure, too. With those machines you came after. A better use for them than what your Doctor wants them for, no?"

She doesn't oblige him with an answer. They come over another low rise, and the house appears in the distance, nestled between the trees. She almost cries out as Artaxerxes goes out of range, leaving a hole in her mind.

Chapter 38

Durain curses himself again as he waits outside the door of Ashburn's study. *How did he get himself into this position? How did he let himself get suckered by that impulsive girl?* And then, more basic questions. *How did he end up here, adjutant to a madman who was less than half human to begin with?* He had always been good at survival — talking down those bandits who wanted to kill him, worming his way into Big Billy's good graces, finagling the position of commissar in camp so he could get all the best supplies, switching sides at the perfect moment when Ashburn moved in. He had always looked out for himself, always succeeded at keeping one step ahead. And now, here he stands, no doubt about to have his throat ripped out by the robot hand of a lunatic. All because of that girl.

"Come," sounds the voice of doom, muffled behind the solid oak door. Durain runs his hands through his hair, takes a deep breath — probably his last — and turns the knob.

Ashburn sits in shadow at the end of a long worktable strewn with circuits and gadgets. Durain, who never had a head for tech stuff, has no idea what any of it does. Ashburn holds a delicate circuit board in his human hand and strokes it gently with a probe of some kind. He doesn't acknowledge Durain's presence, but says softly, "You're back."

"Yes, sir."

"Alone."

"Yes, sir."

"Why?"

Durain swallows. Nothing for it. He tells Ashburn the straight truth — no excuses — how they found the cabin, how Lucinda insisted on approaching with the battle robot, how he had stayed behind, how she had been captured, and the robot disarmed. How he had returned to report. As he speaks, Ashburn never looks up from his work, but grows terribly still, potential energy building around him like an electric storm, waiting for the slightest spark to set it off. Durain wants to shout, to scream, "I told her not to do it! I begged her! It's not my fault." But he's smart. He knows Ashburn hates a toady. He knows that is the quickest way to get a metal hand shoved through his ribs. He tells it like it is and waits for punishment.

He finishes, and a long silence falls. So long, Durain begins to wonder if Ashburn is trying to force him to speak, to make the excuse, to open the door to his own destruction. He resists the compulsion to stand up for himself. He hasn't got this far by walking into traps.

"So, they have her?" Ashburn says quietly.

"Yes, sir."

"And the soldier?"

"Yes, sir."

Ashburn sighs, a deep, slow sigh. "She makes me do things I would never do for anyone else. I can't explain it." He looks at Durain. "I've had so many companions, so many women, and they always fell short in my mind. I controlled them, not the other way round. Lucinda…? I can't say. She reminds me of… Never mind. You can find this place again?"

Durain did not expect this. His heart rises. Maybe he won't be killed after all. "Yes, sir. It's about eighty kilometers west, down old 90."

Ashburn rises. "How many men, do you think? Ten? Twenty?"

"Ten should be sufficient, sir. They aren't well armed. It was, if you'll excuse my saying so, Lucinda's tactical errors that allowed them to capture her. She tried to negotiate, allowed them time to encircle her, overpower her. Sorry."

"Don't be. I agree. Ten men, then. Bring her back alive, if you can. If we act quickly, her medications will still be effective. We can expect her help, and the soldier's. Let's be done with this inconvenience."

Durain almost laughs with relief. "I will leave first thing, sir. We should have the equipment, and the girl, and the soldier, back in our control within three days."

"All right." Ashburn returns to his seat and takes up his work again. "Bring me good news, Durain."

Durain all but skips out of the room.

Chapter 39

reek hunches on the edge of the examination table in Dr. Jemisen's lab. It's made from the side of the ruined shed, and he can feel the roughness of the wood through his pant leg. He detects a faint mustiness in the air, as if the wood is whispering its age to him. But mostly he feels his heart beating hard against his chest. He's nervous. He rubs his left forefinger and thumb together. The spot where Dr. Jemisen snapped out a blood sample with her little poker.

She has her back to him as she works at one of the machines, but glances over at him and smiles as she waits for the test result. She said five minutes, but it feels more like twenty. Ever since Lucinda revealed to them that she had Mindworm, a low-grade panic has murmured in his gut. Dr. Jemisen assured him that the chance he got infected when he attacked her is vanishingly small, but that doesn't do much for the fear. He needs to know, but doesn't want to find out.

She made him promise not to worry, that they would do the test first thing in the morning, and to get some rest. But he couldn't sleep, so he sneaked off before she got up — to go foraging, he told Kimo, and himself. But really, he went out to avoid the moment that is about to come, even as he hungers for the diagnosis. For a ten-year-old boy, Creek has had too many moments like this, that will determine whether he lives or dies.

The screen on the machine changes. He can't tell what it says, but it goes from one line of text to many. A whole paragraph. That must mean bad news. Why would there be so many words if it wasn't bad news? He swallows. His head spins. She turns back to him.

NO, signs Dr Jemisen.

NO WHAT?

YOU DON'T HAVE MINDWORM, CREEK. I DIDN'T EXPECT YOU TO, AND YOU DON'T. She laughs. He just stares back at her. *THAT'S GOOD, ISN'T IT?* He nods. He can't believe it. He was so sure. He almost feels disappointed. Not that he wants to die a screaming, frothing lunatic — no way — but it seemed so inevitable that he would succumb at last to the terror that has been stalking them all since before he can remember. He shakes his head. That's just stupid.

I WANT TO DO…HOW DO YOU SHAPE? — she takes a vial and mimes fiddling with it — *test?* He shows her. *I WANT TO DO MORE TESTS ON LUCINDA, BUT I THINK HER MEDICINE MAKES HER NOT GIVE PEOPLE MINDWORM EASILY. I THINK SHE IS SAFE TO BE WITH US.*

Creek nods again. Now that it's over, he needs to get out. A creeping elation is rising inside him, and he needs to be alone when it explodes. He doesn't want to embarrass himself by laughing or smiling in front of her. He needs to run down to the stream, or up the mountain, or somewhere. His heart still pounds, but not with fear. A fierce joy threatens to overcome him, and he needs to let it out in private.

CAN I GO NOW? he asks.

Dr. Jemisen cocks her head as she studies him. He waits, smothering his excitement. She chuckles and shapes, *YES, OF COURSE. YOU'RE FINE.*

Creek jumps off the table and heads for the door. He puts on his coat slowly and carefully. He waits until he is halfway down the path before he breaks into a run.

Chapter 40

Lucinda sits on the little table in Kat's med-room. The machines blink and whir around her. *These are what I came for,* she thinks.

"You look tired," Kat says, as she fiddles with a hypoderm. "Can't sleep?"

"I'm fine," answers Lucinda. It is a lie. She can't sleep. The yawning silence in her head makes her giddy, as if the bed she lies on hangs upside down over a swirling void that wants to suck her into non-existence. She has had periods without her COR before, but she was too ill at the beginning of her stay with Ashburn, and too distracted on the journey to destroy the Enclave, to sit in the emptiness. And then she linked with 'Xerxes, and even though no data streamed across her mind, he filled the gap.

Now she has nothing — no friends, no content, no Artaxerxes. The terror of solitude floods through her. On top of that, she can feel the effects of her last treatment fading. Spikes of wild panic, sudden anger, and disorientation jab at her sanity. Nothing she can't handle, at least for now. But she is past due, and can feel the incipient madness poking at the curtains of her brain.

"Now, just to confirm," continues the medico. "You were receiving three injections when you were with the Doctor. Is that right?"

"Yes."

"You don't happen to know what they were, do you?"

"No. Sorry."

"That's okay. I can guess based on the notes I have and the way the machines were set up. I think I can give you what you need to keep you going. At least for a little while."

Lucinda feels the thrum of her heart quicken. "How long?"

"Hard to say. We have a decent stockpile of materials, but it won't last forever." She places her hand on Lucinda's knee. "Now, don't worry. I'm sure we can trade with the Nipmuc for what we need. Besides, I'm holding out for a cure. If I ever get the time to focus, I believe we'll get there. I'm not too far away, Lucinda. Just need some time."

"Can I help? I can help."

Kat shines her wide smile. "If you want to, honey. Though honestly, the best thing you could do is keep those kids busy. They tried to help for a while, but it was almost more work keeping them on task. And with all the ruckus with you (no offense), and the house and the tribe, it's hard to find a moment of quiet. But we'll get there. We'll get there. Now, fold up your sleeve so I can get at your arm."

Lucinda complies, and the medico administers the shots with brisk efficiency. Ashburn tended to linger, and she sometimes caught him smelling her hair, which chilled her spirit. A few seconds, and the procedure is done.

"I'll wait with you for ten minutes or so, just to make sure everything is okay. Are you comfortable enough in here?"

The lab is Lucinda's treatment center, but it is also her prison. She has her little cot in the corner so she doesn't have to sleep on the table, but that's it. They lock the door, even when the medico is here working, and she has to knock and ask them to escort her to the outhouse.

"I'm fine." She is feeling better. Her heart has ceased its insistent thumping, and she can feel her tattered consciousness sew itself back together. But the emptiness remains. The catacombs of her mind, echoing with loss. "Doctor?" she says.

"Call me Kat, please. What do you need, honey?"

"Kat. Did you happen to find a small case when you, um, captured me, or whatever? I had it on me when I arrived, but when I woke up, it was gone."

Kat crosses to a small cabinet and pulls out the little black case. Lucinda's heart starts jumping again. "You mean this?"

"Yes." She tries to hide her almost desperate eagerness at the sight of the case. Kat clicks it open and studies the small black wafers.

"These are for your…your implant, no?"

"Yes. They're emergency data modules. May I have them back, please?"

The medico eyes her, her normally placid features pursed with suspicion. "They won't let you communicate with the Doctor, or anything like that?"

"Oh no, no! They come from before, from the Enclave. It's just some survival data, some music, books, vidis, that sort of thing. Nothing harmful, I swear. Just…" She can't put it into words. She feels nervous, almost dirty, like she is asking for pornography.

Kat considers for a moment. Without speaking, she hands Lucinda the case, pats her on the knee again, and leaves the room, locking the door behind her.

Lucinda waits as long as she can, a few seconds only, then grabs a chip at random from the case. She pushes it into the slot. Like a tropical flower, the menu opens in her mind. *History*. She selects a file and gorges herself.

Chapter 41

"Hold it right there. Good." Sandoval checks his balance on the rickety ladder, leans a bit more, and hammers in the nail. The last hole in the roof. "That's it," he calls. A thud on the board from inside confirms that Dancing Willow, who was holding it in place within, has heard him. He tucks the hammer into his belt and descends the ladder.

Dancing Willow and her partner Peter Chukela have been coming every day to help secure the house. No more banging in rusty nails with old bricks or rocks — they brought proper tools and supplies — hammers, saws, levels, measuring equipment, hardware. Even lumber and shingles — rare treasures from across the border wall. The Nipmuc have set up trading with the Western Tribes. Sandoval was at the village when the first transport flew over the mountain and landed in a blast of wind and dust. It took his breath away. He'd never seen anything like it.

As he comes around onto the porch to grab the crate of shingles, he pauses to look over the house. How different it looks, compared to when they first arrived. The rotting railing fresh and bright with smooth new balusters. The doorway rebuilt, with a strong casing of shaped oak. Even the barn has been refurbished, with a new facade and a bolt on the door. The windows still need work — most are boarded up, though the Firsters say they expect to receive some plexi soon, scavenged from an abandoned factory somewhere in the Northwest. And now, the new roof. It looks like a home. *Like Hope,* he thinks, then pushes away the thought. He must not indulge in idealistic fantasies.

Dancing Willow comes out of the house, holding a box of nails. "This is all we have, so use them sparingly," she says. Sandoval takes the box and sticks it in his pocket, hoists the shingles onto his hip, and heads back to the ladder. As he passes the front door, Candela comes out. "What a beautiful day!"

Sandoval looks up. It's true. He hadn't noticed. Buoyant white clouds roll across a rare blue sky. The air has a nip in it, but it's hardly cold, the sun glowing on his bare forearms. "Yes," he says. He doesn't know what else to say. Candela makes him uncomfortable, to say the least. Like he should do something, but he has no idea what. "Baby's asleep," she says, "FINALLY." She throws him a face-cracking smile and skips down the hill to the stream.

Her behavior toward him has changed since they fought Lucinda and the robot. She ended her silent treatment and has been spending time just sitting with him while he works, chattering away about nothing in particular. He can't account for it. She can't possibly have a crush on him. He knows how fiercely she misses the Duke. But she is being so nice to him. He wonders if he is expected to reciprocate. She is pretty — warm like toasted bread — but so young. He doesn't know how old he is, exactly — maybe thirty-five, maybe older — but that's more than twice her age. And yet she's a mother — the mother in their strange little family. And what is he?

He pauses his work and watches her. *Is that what they are? A family?* Sandoval can't remember his mother and father. He was raised in Zaquero's war band, down near old Providence. They never told him where he came from. He pressed Zaquero on it one night. The old warrior — his face a weathered cliff, his blind right eye like a dead fish — said, "It doesn't matter. Only today matters. Only this moment. You belong to us." But the belonging didn't feel like a family. No women or children besides him, for one thing, and no sharing that wasn't dictated by the Rules of Division — He got a twentieth share, Toko and the other men each got a twelfth, Zaquero took the rest. They were a war band, bound by the laws of killing and looting. Survival. When they left him to die after the skirmish against the Truro militiamen, it didn't surprise him. He meant nothing to them, and they meant nothing to him.

The Fourth Horsemen had found him and brought him into their dark fold. Those years — he can almost say he can't remember them. Almost. There had been so much indoctrination, such frenzy, so many drugs. Much of that time was a fever dream. He wishes he could cut it out of his mind. That he could rest in the knowledge that those days were lost. But too many images — slaughtered children, women with skulls cracked open, dirt and blood and death — haunt his mind in the night. The best thing that ever happened to him was that ambush by the river, when that raging Steader — deranged by the loss of his family — had knocked him from his saddle, leaving him to bleed out in a ditch for the second time in his life.

When Lady Fal found him in that ditch — alone and terrified, trying to die with bravery, and failing — when she brought him back to her camp, that was something deep. But not a family. She was his god, his savior; she gave him a purpose, and he owed her everything, down to the last drop of blood in his veins. But she was so far above him. She would never be family. She was his leader.

And yet, when the moment came, when he should have stood by her side, thrown his body in front of her when the final blast came, had he done it? No. He had run. Not to save himself. But to save these children. *Why? What were they to him?* It had not been a selfish act. But, still, it was a betrayal. He couldn't understand it.

And now, what have they become? They gather around the table he made at the end of the day, the fire warming their faces with its flickering glow. They talk about what they have done, sharing the food they have gathered freely and without conditions. The children joke and chatter, hands flying.

As he watches them gobble up their meal, their simple pleasure fills him with spinning emotions that he can't articulate.

So, is that what they have become? A family? *What does that make him?*

Kat comes out of the house, leading Lucinda to the outhouse. Lucinda throws him a sidelong glance as she walks past him into the yard. She moves carefully, limping badly on her injured leg, but the awkwardness of her movement somehow accentuates her beauty. Sandoval buries his attention in the box of shingles, rifling through it in pointless busywork, but she draws his eyes to her like a star. If Candela makes him uncomfortable, Lucinda completely befuddles him. Her lithe, athletic frame, her skin, pale as a seashell, her hair burning like a maple in autumn. She's scarcely older than Candela, but she *feels* older. She carries an ancient sadness he can't describe. It makes his skin shimmer.

"Do you need help?" shouts Peter Chukela from inside.

Get it together, you idiot. Sandoval slaps himself on the cheek, then calls back, "Just getting organized! Heading up now." He balances the shingle box on his hip and works his way up the ladder with his free hand.

Creek sits on the porch, the rare sunlight warming his legs and shoulders, whittling a stick into something that is supposed to be a spoon, but looks more like a tiny club for an elf. He briefly looks up when Kat leads the red-haired lady to the outhouse, then returns to his work. He is so intent that he jumps a little when Lamarque taps him on the shoulder. The boy sits down next to him and watches him for a while, his dark face blank, his lips pursed.

IT SHOULD BE THINNER, Lamarque shapes.

Creek gives him a look that says, *I know, dummy.* These things take time, and he's never been very good at whittling. Sandoval has given him some pointers, though, and he thought he'd give it another try.

Lamarque sits there for a few minutes more. Creek wishes he would go away. He radiates tension, like he has something on his mind, and Creek doesn't want to know what it is. But clearly, he is going to find out whether he wants to or not, so he puts down the spoon and looks at Lamarque. *WHAT'S UP?*

Lamarque just stares at the floor for a minute, then asks, *DO YOU LIKE KIMO?*

OF COURSE.

ME TOO.

I KNOW. SO?

I MEAN, DO YOU LIKE HER?

I SAID YES. What the hell?

LIKE HER LIKE HER?

THAT MAKES NO SENSE. Creek's heart starts to bounce.

Lamarque raises his eyes to look right at him. *I LIKE HER. AS A GIRL, YOU KNOW?*

Creek waits.

I THINK MAYBE SHE LIKES ME, TOO. BUT I'M NOT SURE. YOU TWO HAVE BEEN TOGETHER FOR A WHILE NOW, AND I WASN'T SURE IF YOU, YOU KNOW, HAD A THING.

A THING?

YOU KNOW, A THING. YOU GUYS EVER KISS?

NO!

NO?

NO! WE'RE FRIENDS, THAT'S ALL.

WOULD YOU MIND IF I DID?

DID WHAT?

KISS HER!

WHY SHOULD I? Creek throws the words at him. His hands don't feel like they belong to him.

*I DON'T KNOW. I JUST WANT TO MAKE SURE IT'S OKAY IF I SEE IF SHE'S INTERESTED. IF WE…*he hesitates…*GET TOGETHER.*

I DON'T CARE.

Lamarque leans in. *YOU'RE SURE YOU DON'T MIND?*

NO! He grabs the misshapen spoon and goes back to carving.

OKAY. THANKS, MAN. Lamarque touches him on the shoulder, like he is made of glass. Creek carves harder and faster. After another minute, Lamarque nods, gets up, and heads inside.

Does he mind? Yes. No. Kind of. He doesn't know. He and Kimo have been friends for so long, a third of his life. They first met at the Steader camp by the lake when he was with Dr. Rush. It was like a miracle. He had never met anybody who was like him. They were thick as thieves. She taught him so many new ideas. They expanded the language his mother had taught him — almost doubled it, he reckoned. He hated to admit it, but without her, he never would have been able to navigate the hearing world. Then they got separated when the TC Regulars busted up the camp. When she showed up again at John Chaico's, more than a year later, he could hardly believe it. Another miracle. His own, private miracle.

She belonged to him. He never thought about her romantically. Of course not. Those feelings were reserved for Candela, impossible as that was. Kimo was more like a sister to him. And Lamarque was a good guy. No reason they shouldn't hook up, if that's what she wanted. He had picked up the vibe between them days ago, but hadn't given it much thought. But now that it was out in the open, Creek wasn't sure he liked it. Maybe he *was* supposed to be with Kimo. He didn't know. Not like he really wanted to kiss her. It just made him uncomfortable to think about *them* kissing.

After a minute, he tosses the spoon onto the porch, pockets his knife, and runs down to the stream. Clouds are rolling in, shrouding the sun, the sky returning to its usual dull, mottled gray.

He stares at the water rushing by. *What was he doing here? What was it doing to him?* People around all the time, probing him, expecting things of him, needing things from him. That wasn't his way. He traveled the silent world alone. Every time he tried to hook up with people, everything went into the grinder. He had almost died at John Chaico's, he had almost died at Lady Fal's, and now they were on the run from a madman with an army of berserk zombies. Only they weren't on the run. They were playing house. It was stupid. It was dangerous. It was going to get him killed.

He has to leave. They don't need him. Kimo has Lamarque. Candela has Baby. He should just leave. Now, before it gets hard. He has his knife. He has his jacket. What more does he need? If he heads back to the house for food or whatever, he might never get away. He can forage for what he needs. He's done it plenty of times before.

Creek gets up. He eyes the van wreck, trying to decide if he should take anything from it before he goes. As he crosses the bridge, he tells himself not to look back, but something pricks at his mind, and before he can help it, he has turned toward the house.

Candela is walking down the hill. The sight of her makes his head go all funny. Too late to run away. She'll see him going up the hill, and chase him, and then he'll never get away. He dives into the bushes by the water's edge.

She doesn't see him. It's too chilly to wade in, so she starts throwing little stones into the stream. They vanish without a ripple in the froth. Creek watches her through the thicket, his heart as turbulent as the water. He wishes she would go away and leave him in peace. He wishes she would find him and take him in her arms. His feelings swirl in agitated circles.

Candela grows tired of pebbles. Creek hopes (and doesn't) that maybe she'll go back up the hill. Instead, she sits on the ground with her back against a tree. He watches her face as she gazes into the bubbling water. She begins singing to herself, her mouth moving in beautifully rhythmic shapes. Then she starts to cry. Creek's heart leaps into his mouth. *What is happening?* He thought she had been happier — smiling at everyone, laughing at Lamarque's stupid jokes, helping out in the kitchen, and with the chores. Tears pour down her cheeks, unchecked, as she sings an unknown song that rises from a depth of misery he can't comprehend.

He can't take it. All this craziness with other people is just too much. He turns away.

From the corner of his eye, he catches a movement at the top of the hill. At the same time, something changes in the atmosphere. A strange tickle in his nose, like ozone, or some chemical he can't identify. He crawls a little way up from the stream, careful not to disturb the branches around him and arouse Candela's attention. He peers up at the crest of the hill.

What he sees sends him scrambling down the bank, crashing headlong across the stream, waving his arms in panic.

Chapter 42

Lucinda comes out of the outhouse. It's a new experience for her, and she still finds it disgusting, but the rare freshness of the day quickly overwrites the sensations of the stuffy, smelly box. She looks out over the little valley, then back at Kat, who waits for her. "Can I just stand out here for a minute?" she asks.

"Of course." Kat gives her space.

The sun shines in Lucinda's eyes, low above the hills on the far side of the stream. The glare sparks a low glow of something inside her. Is she…happy? Such a rare occurrence, a day like this. She came out without her jacket, and the air is crisp and cold, but the heat on her face and shoulders vanquishes the chill, at least for now. She feels good. Almost safe. She has the *Survival* chip slotted, so the natural world is fat with meaning. Each tree and shrub and grass a familiar friend. She misses Artaxerxes, but at least she knows he is not far away. She briefly contemplates making a run for him, but why? *These people are not her enemies.* Like the brightness of the day, her mind is clearer than it has been in months.

Sandoval and his Firster friends are busy behind her, banging and shouting from the roof. She wishes they would stop — such a lovely morning, how much nicer it would be if there were quiet! — but there is something cheerful in the bustle of activity. Almost hopeful.

A vigorous gust of wind rolls up the hill, and even the cheerful sun can no longer stop her from shivering. She starts to head back inside when a commotion below draws her attention back down the hill. The young woman who screamed at her *(Candela?)* is laboring up the slope, shouting and waving her arms. The boy who attacked her *(Creek is his name)* runs beside her, soon outpacing her.

"Sandoval! Sandoval!" Candela is shouting. Lucinda turns to see the man stop his work, perched at the top of the ladder set against the house. The boy reaches the yard first, his hands moving in quick, wild patterns, then pointing to the tree line at the top of the hill opposite them. Candela soon follows, gasping for breath, and points in the same direction. "They're coming. They're coming."

As if waiting for its cue, a large Rover bursts through the trees, followed quickly by another. They halt for a moment, then start working their way down the hill to the stream.

"Inside! Everybody inside!" shouts Sandoval. He scrambles down the ladder, leaping off two meters from the ground, and gathers them all with a gesture, pushing them to the door and into the house. As they pass through into the dark interior, he whirls on Lucinda. "I thought you said they didn't follow you."

"I...I...I'm sorry," says Lucinda. She tells him about Durain, her eyes on the ground. "I didn't know what to do. I'm sorry."

He glares, but doesn't press it. "Can everybody come in here? Now!" he shouts. Then, turning to the Firsters. "I'm sorry about this. There's a window in the back that opens onto a trail behind the house. You can get out that way, but you have to leave now."

The Nipmuc woman says, "We're here. We'll help." The Nipmuc man nods in agreement and crosses to the corner, where their packs are lying. He removes two objects, like sticks, and hands one to the woman. Within seconds — twisting, unfolding, snapping into place — the sticks transform into weapons. The woman holds a small steel crossbow, an explosive dart already loaded in the channel. The man has an ion spear — not full size, but deadly, with a triple-pronged head like a trident. "Never leave home without a weapon," he says, a wide smile dimpling his face.

"Thank you."

The teenage boy, Lamarque, appears with the small girl — Lucinda can't remember her name *(K-something)* — from one of the bedrooms. Their eyes are wide and scared. "What is it?" he asks.

"She lied to us," says Sandoval, not even looking at her. "There was someone else with her when we captured her. He's brought them back."

"How many?"

"Don't know." He turns to Creek. "Did you see how many?"

The boy makes a gesture with his hands. The man nods. "If it's only two, then probably eight to twelve. Not good, but it could be worse." He crosses to the door and peers through the narrow lookout. "I don't see them, so no frontal assault. My guess is they are going to flank us from the woods on either side. Dancing Willow and I will take the window in the kids' room. Kat and Chukela take the lab. Lamarque, get yourself a weapon and go with them, in case it comes to hand-to-hand. Candela and the kids, you're safest here in the living room." He gestures at the tables and chairs. "Barricade the door."

"I need to get Baby," says Candela. Sandoval nods, and she hurries into the back bedroom. Creek follows her. They reemerge, almost immediately, Candela holding the baby and the boy dragging a makeshift crib behind him.

"What about me?" asks Lucinda.

"What about you?"

"How can I help?"

"Them, or us?"

She swallows. "You, of course."

He eyes her. "Stay here with the kids. Help with the door. Everybody move."

Sandoval strides off, the Nipmuc woman at his shoulder. The boy Lamarque goes to the fireplace and grabs an iron poker. He looks scared, but hoists it onto his shoulder and follows the medico down the hall to the lab. Candela and the children immediately set to work pulling the furniture toward the front door. Lucinda moves to help them, but Candela gives her such a scathing look that she backs off. She stands there, watching, unsure of what to do.

Lamarque follows the medico into the lab, his heart in his mouth. Peter Chukela takes a quick look around, then comes back to him and pats his shoulder. "You and Kat move these machines to the edges of the room. We'll use them as cover if we have to."

"We need to keep them safe," says Dr. Jemisen. "It's what they're after. If they get destroyed, we're as good as dead."

"We're as good as dead if we don't stop them. I don't think they're here to have a conversation." Dr. Jemisen nods and starts rolling a machine to one side of the room. The action unfreezes Lamarque, and he rushes over to help her, almost tripping over his own feet. She gives him a reassuring smile. He feels one step behind. Everything is happening too fast.

Peter Chukela crosses to the boarded-up window. "Be right back." He disappears back into the main hall, returning quickly with his work bag. He sets it on the floor by the door and takes out a laser drill. He fiddles with the controls, then proceeds to put a two-centimeter hole through the side of the house. Peering through, he says. "Yes. They're out there. I see three — no, four — no five." He spits out something in his own language. Lamarque wonders if he just swore. Peter Chukela looks around at the walls. He nods.

"Okay," he continues. "They'll make a play for the window. That's the weak point. Crouch down here. One on either side. Doctor, take this, and give me the pistol." He holds out his ion spear. She takes it. "You know how to use it?" She shakes her head. "Okay. Put your finger here. Press this button when they start to break through. Then squeeze here when you strike. Try to keep the point low, I don't want fried feet." He grins. "What's your name, kid?"

"Lamarque."

"Okay, Lamarque. If anybody breaks through, let them have it. I'll be up here." Lamarque nods. His head is underwater, and he can barely hear what the man says. Peter Chukela gives him a wink. "It's going to be okay, kid. Don't worry." Lamarque feels the rising panic subside a little bit. He grits his teeth and nods.

Peter Chukela climbs up onto the doctor's stool, and, with a quick jump, grabs one of the rafters. He swings himself up onto it with an easy motion. He points to the angle where the wall meets the ceiling. "We need to fix this when they're gone. Letting in the cold. But for now, it's good." Lamarque notices a small square of light, illuminating part of the ceiling. There must be a hole in the wall, just below the eaves. The Nipmuc man's calm demeanor amazes Lamarque. He acts like they are just starting another day's work, not like there are enemy soldiers about to break in and kill them all. It's hard to believe, but it works. Lamarque can feel his heart rate slow.

Peter Chukela balances himself between two rafters, placing his face up against the little hole, the pistol right by his cheek. "I see them. They're moving slow. Lamarque, reach in my bag. There should be a little box of earplugs in the side pocket." Lamarque scurries over to the bag, finds the box, and tosses it up to the man, who catches it and quickly slides a plug into his ear. He wonders at the grace of the little man, perched like a spider in the rafters, his movements efficient, his balance almost superhuman.

A silence falls, marked by the rapid rhythm of blood pounding in his ears. A muted *bang* from the far side of the house makes him jump. Sandoval's rifle. It has started. A second later, Peter Chukela fires. "Got one!" he says. He fires again. "Got another!" He learns forward, trying to aim down closer to the side of the house. Then he swears again, pulling back and reaching for the rafter. Too late. A frightening blast, and the top of the wall explodes beside him, sending him flying. He grasps at air and tumbles to the floor. He tries to swerve in midair, but the ground comes up too fast. His head strikes the floorboards with a sickening crack.

A cacophony of gunfire batters the boarded window. Splinters fly in every direction. Lamarque and Dr. Jemisen cover their ears. The remains of the window fall violently in, knocking Dr. Jemisen in the head. An instant later, a dark figure bursts through the breach into the room. It sees the inert figure of Peter Chukela on the floor and raises its weapon. Dr. Jemisen lunges out with the spear. An arc of white energy crackles across the room, rippling around the figure, which shakes with a wild spasm and falls to the ground.

Another figure is already pushing through the open window. With all his might, Lamarque strikes it with the poker. The iron bar thwacks it full in the forehead, and it falls backward through the window onto another enemy pushing in behind.

"Go!" screams Dr. Jemisen. She grabs Peter Chukela with one arm and starts dragging him toward the door. Lamarque stares at her, his mind blank, uncomprehending. She shouts again. "Lamarque!" His mind returns, and he grabs the fallen man by the other hand. Dr. Jemisen discharges the ion spear wildly at the window, sending sparks flying and setting fire to the frame. The branching lightning burns his cheek. Lamarque can just make out the shadowy figures of their assailants diving for cover at the blast. Then they are through the door. Dr. Jemisen slams it shut and turns the ancient key in the lock. "Won't hold them long," she says. They pull Peter Chukela down the hall.

Kimo, Creek, and Candela huddle up against the long table, which they have flipped on its edge and pushed up against the front door.

"Look out, they're coming!" screams Dr. Jemisen. They maneuver Peter Chukela around the corner in front of the fireplace, and the doctor kneels to examine him. A moment later, Sandoval and Dancing Willow burst into the room.

"Status!" shouts Sandoval.

"We got two," says the doctor. "But they hit Peter and pushed us out. Door's locked, but won't hold them long."

"We got two as well, then the third backed off. Not sure where to. They used a shock grenade, so we had to pull out. We saw three. How about you?"

"Five."

"That means at least four left, maybe more."

"They've got the equipment," says Dr. Jemisen. "Won't they leave now?"

"They'll be vulnerable moving it out of here. They'll take care of us first."

Lamarque looks across at Kimo. The terror in her eyes mirrors his own. He swallows his fear and forces a smile. Dancing Willow cries out, "Get down!" Lamarque ducks, and a whistle of air streaks past his ear. He whips his head around to her. She stands in the center of the room, her crossbow in her hands, her eyes flaming. He turns back down the hall and sees a man sprawled at the entrance to the lab. She fires again.

With a loud crash, a portion of the roof collapses above her. She leaps back, just avoiding the clattering of boards and shingles. Two masked figures drop through the hole. At the same time, a blast shatters the lock of the side bedroom, and a hooded soldier busts through.

"Go! Go! Go!" shouts Sandoval, hurling himself at one of the figures. There is a wild scuffle, a dizzying moment of confusion. Someone pushes Lamarque into the clump of bodies that rush toward the back of the house. Somehow, they find their way through the door. At the last second, Sandoval appears out of nowhere and slips through the crack. He slams the door closed.

"Peter," says Dr. Jemisen. Sandoval shakes his head. Lamarque looks around. Impossibly, the rest of them made it through.

A threatening silence falls. They stretch their ears to hear what's going on outside the door. They catch sounds of shifting, the occasional footstep. Someone says softly, "Where is he?" But the blast they all expect does not come.

Sandoval whispers, "What have we got? I lost the rifle in the scuffle." Dancing Willow raises her crossbow. "Anybody else?" He looks at Dr. Jemisen.

She shakes her head. "Out there," she says. "I was checking on Peter."

The silence lengthens. After a minute, Sandoval says, "Where's Lucinda?"

Everyone looks around. Lucinda is not among them.

Chapter 43

Lucinda runs up the hill toward the high meadow. She had watched Candela and the two children barricade the door, at a loss for what to do herself, then followed an impulse she couldn't articulate, slipped into the back room, and climbed out the window. If she had known, she took the same route Creek had used to stop her own attack. She hid by the side of the house until she saw the soldiers move in, and while they were occupied with the window, she skirted past them, keeping low in the high grass at the edge of the woods.

Was she escaping? Was she helping? She didn't know. It feels good to run. It has been too long. As she crests the hill, Artaxerxes pops into her COR. Like warm bread and butter on an empty stomach. Like Christmas morning. Like coming home.

He stands where she left him, his magnificent head tucked between the branches of the tree. She stops in front of him, and his deep, quiet eyes turn down to look at her, sending a thrill down her back. She has a brief, wild impulse to throw her arms around him, but stops herself. Instead, she gives him a command, and he leans down to pick her up. His hands and arms are hard but smooth. There is something so simple about the way he lifts her. Easy. He shifts her so she can sit on his forearm, her hand on his shoulder. Then he begins to run. Her heart sings as he lopes across the meadow, his gait surprisingly smooth, hardly jarring her at all. Like flying.

Her hair whips behind her like a comet. She can scarcely breathe. But it only lasts a minute. They are back at the house in no time, and at her will, he slows to a stop.

She can hear short pops of gunfire from inside the house and watches, unsure what to do. Her only thought had been to get to Artaxerxes. What to do with him, she has no idea. Whose side is she even on? Does she have one? She had come here for Ashburn. She imagines the curl of his lip when she returns, triumphant, with the stolen equipment, a gift no one but she can bestow. The power she would have over him.

On the other hand, these people fed her, treated her, and if they haven't all welcomed her, they have taken her in. But for what? To prevent her from doing her job — the first real job she has ever had. She was their prisoner, wasn't she?

She thought of dinner the night before. They had let her out of the lab, and invited her to join them for the evening meal. Sandoval glowered at her, as usual, but Kat was kind and welcoming. The dancing light from the fireplace, bowls of food passed back and forth, laughter and joking, the flickering of the children's hands, like butterflies. She had not participated, but she watched every move. So different from her meals with Ashburn, where she sat silent as he monologued about deep and powerful things, dazzling her mind but subduing her spirit. Different from dinner with her parents, half a lifetime ago, it seemed. Those stilted, halting affairs, where conversation meant interrogation about her and her day, punctuating long stretches where everyone tried not to chew too audibly.

Several figures appear on the roof, snapping her out of her reverie. She recognizes the leader by his reedy frame, even though his face is covered. . Just the sight of him makes her stomach turn. Lucinda can't say why she despises him so. His thin voice, his empty eyes, his ever-present hollow smile. He is a cipher, a facade, a non-man. She would never find a real person there. Only a presentation of one.

She and Artaxerxes begin to move even as Durain fires the charge that blows a hole in the roof, as Ashburn's soldiers drop onto the people below.

"I lost track of her when the shooting started," says Candela. "We were so busy with the barricade."

Sandoval curses. "Of course. Great." He listens through the door, trying to divine the movements of the enemy. The children crowd around him. He can smell their fear.

There is a rap on the door. He leans his weight against it.

A voice calls from outside. "There's no way out," it says. A woman's voice. "Come out, and you live. We just want the equipment."

"Yeah, right," says Sandoval.

"There's nothing you can do. Just come out. If you don't…" Another pause. "Well, don't say I didn't warn you."

"We have children in here."

"Just come out."

He looks back at Dancing Willow. She shakes her head, then glances down at the heads of Kimo and Creek. He curses silently. "Okay! Okay." He turns the doorknob.

A thundering crash shakes the house, followed by a staccato series of metallic pulses.

Silence. Ten Seconds. Twenty.

Lucinda's voice sounds through the door. "You can come out now."

Sandoval turns to Dr. Jemisen. She shrugs. He opens the door.

The front of the house has been torn off, all the work of the last weeks undone. Artaxerxes towers at the threshold, his cannons still pulsing with an eerie, blue light. Lucinda stands at his side, her hair blazing like flame in the sunlight. A tangle of bodies lies in a heap in the center of the room, smoking to the rafters. The air reeks of charred flesh.

"Sorry about the door," says Lucinda.

They are staring at her like she's a creature from another planet. If she had imagined a euphoric welcome, this wasn't it.

At last, Sandoval speaks. "You came back," he says.

"Yeah."

"Why?" Lucinda stares back at the huddled group, suddenly self-conscious.

"I…I…"

Kat presses forward. "Let the girl alone, Sandoval," she says. "She saved us. That's what matters. Thank you."

Lucinda nods stiffly. The Nipmuc Woman, ignoring the awkwardness, pushes past her to kneel beside the still form of the Nipmuc Man. The medico follows.

"He's breathing," says Kat. "Peter? Peter!" She strokes his face. He groans. "We need to get him back to the village," she continues. "I don't have the equipment to deal with a head injury like this. Can you send for Keisha Two Crows?" The woman nods and moves to her satchel, pulling out a comm set. She steps around the pile of bodies out onto the porch.

"Take the kids outside," Sandoval tells Candela. She nods and shepherds the children through the gaping breach in the facade. Lucinda is alone with Sandoval. He just looks at her.

"What?"

"Thank you," he says at last.

"You're welcome."

"It must have been hard."

"Not really."

He shakes his head. "You're a strange…aren't these your people?" He gestures at the bodies.

"I don't have people. I didn't know them. Just the one guy, and I couldn't stand him." She steps forward, scanning the corpses. "Where is he?"

"Who?"

"Durain."

"Who's Durain?"

"He's the Doctor's…I don't know the term." In the old days, she could just tap her COR, and the word would appear. It irritates her. "His… helper…his…"

"Adjutant?"

"Something like that. The one I told you about — who came with us the first time. I saw him on the roof. He was just about to drop down. He should be here."

"That's not him?" Sandoval points to one of the bodies.

"No." Lucinda swears as she skirts the corpses and runs out through the gaping hole that used to be the front door. Sandoval follows her. It has started to rain. An obscuring mist blankets the hills on the opposite bank, but they can make out the hulking shape of a personnel carrier like a dark smudge at the top of the clearing beyond.

"Weren't there two of them?" says Sandoval.

"Yes. Dammit. I could have sworn he jumped through the hole."

"Did you see him?"

Lucinda thinks. "No. We were already moving for the door."

"How long to the Doctor's camp?"

"Two days or so. Maybe less if he pushes it. Which he will."

"So, we have four days, maybe five. Okay."

"Will you run?"

"What do you care? No. Run where?" He turns to face her, very close. It makes her heart race. "I need to know where you stand. When I first saw you, you were standing next to the Doctor like his…I don't know. His personal witch, or something. You killed my Lady Fal."

"I know. I'm sorry."

"And you think that's good enough?"

Lucinda shakes her head.

"You're here now. I didn't want you here, but Dr. Jemisen insisted. Now you do this—" he waves toward the house. "I don't know what to… can we trust you? When your Doctor shows up, are you just going to turn the battle robot against us and wipe us out? Whose side are you on?"

Lucinda stares up into his dark eyes. She can feel rents in the cloak of numbness that surrounds her — eddies and little bursts of grief flickering in her soul — but she is not ready for it to fall away. She pushes them closed again. "I'm here. I'm not going back."

Kimo comes tearing around the side of the house with Lamarque in hot pursuit. She is laughing. Lucinda watches them in awe. Ten minutes ago, they were in fear for their lives, and now they are laughing, playing. How can one be a child, stay a child, in a world like this?

"Can I trust you?" Sandoval cocks his head toward the children. "Can they?"

Lucinda nods. She didn't realize she had made a decision, but she has. "Yes. They can."

Chapter 44

Horace Ashburn sits in the dark, staring at his hand. Not his hand. His robot appendage. A non-part of him. Almost an enemy.

"And how did you escape?" The beads of perspiration on Durain's forehead catch the light like little planets.

"The robot attacked just as I was about to drop down. There was nothing I could do."

"You lost your entire unit. Nine soldiers. And a transport."

"She betrayed you. I had to warn you." The stench of him tickles Ashburn's nostrils — the left side robotically identifying the Staphylococcus, Corynebacterium, and Cutibacterium feasting on the man's sweat. He scowls.

"Twice now, Durain. Twice now, you have failed me. Failed to keep her safe. Failed to keep her under control. Now she is gone. My battle soldier is gone. My men and women are gone. My transport is gone. My equipment is gone, which was the whole purpose of this disastrous venture. How many more mistakes should I condone, Durain? How many?"

Durain's face goes white. He swallows. "I don't know, sir. I returned to you so you could know what happened. I could have died there, I suppose. Instead of knowing, we'd just be gone, and you'd have no way to find her. If you want to kill me for that, sir, go ahead. I can't stop you."

Ashburn almost laughs out loud. *The gall of this little man!* He's got guts, that's for sure. Even if he had turned and run at the first sign of trouble. Ashburn must admit he has a point.

He holds the silence for a long time. Make the man sweat even more. Then he says, "Very well. What's our supply of meds for the Afflicted?"

Durain can't speak for a moment. He stutters, "Four days at the outside, I'd say, sir."

"Then there's not a moment to spare. Sedate them, load them on their transports, and muster fifty fighters. That should be more than enough. Have everything ready to move out at dawn. Yes?"

The man visibly relaxes. "Yes, sir. Who will lead the expedition, sir?" He clearly thinks it will be himself.

"I will," says Ashburn. "And now that I think of it, Durain—" His robot hand strikes like a mantis at the man's throat. The metal fingers push easily into the flesh and encircle the trachea. "I think I'll take care of everything myself." Durain barely has an instant to register surprise before the hand rips his windpipe out. He topples like a marionette.

The blood has coagulated into a thick, fetid pool when Ashburn's third in command, Tommaso, appears at the door of the lab. Ashburn ignores him for a good ten minutes as he puts the finishing touches on a circuit board. The soldier watches, gray-faced, wishing he were anywhere else. Ashburn slots it into a small device, snaps on the lid, and places it on the table before him.

"Congratulations on your promotion," says the Doctor, at long last. "Please clean this up and bring the unit leaders to the briefing room in thirty minutes." He holds up the device he has been working on. "We can end this farce once and for all."

Chapter 45

I 'm sorry we can't do more." The chief raises his hands in a gesture of regret. Lucinda can see the muscles in Sandoval's jaw working double time.

"How long will it take?" he asks.

Tom Pegan-Soaring Hawk shrugs. "Hard to say. I will send the message today. The Tribes are meeting near Oneida Lake. But listen to me, friend: I do not think they will come." *He has beautiful hands,* she thinks, watching his long fingers dance in the air, as if he were painting the convocation of the First Nations in the air.

They are seated beside the fire circle in the center of the Nipmuc village — Sandoval, Lucinda, and Kimo. Several other tribal leaders sit with the chief, but Lucinda doesn't know their names. She also doesn't know why Sandoval wanted her to come. *To keep an eye on her, no doubt.*

"Why not?"

"We only recently signed the Treaty. We have received two shipments from the First Nations. The relationship is new. They are moving east, but it will take time. We are a very small mouse in a very large field. They have bigger game to hunt."

"Okay. How about you?" asks Sandoval.

The chief gives a rueful smile. "As I say. We are just a tiny mouse. We can give you some small arms — a few rifles, an ion spear or two. But our weapons are few, and we must protect ourselves." He places his hand on Sandoval's arm. "We are pleased to know you, Rej Sandoval, but our acquaintance is brief, and this is not our fight."

"They almost killed Peter Chukela."

"That is exactly my point. I must think of the safety of my people."

Sandoval drops his head and grimaces, as if he were in pain. "The Doctor isn't your average petty warlord, Pegan. He's not content with a little patch of ground and a few turbines. He wants it all. How do you know he won't come after you next?"

"I don't. But look around —what could he want from us?" He gestures to the simple quonsets and shacks, then leans in."You must understand, my friend, this is all there is of my nation. Out there in the world, I know, there is great loss. One in fifty left from the old days. Think what that means here. Over the years since the Collapse, we have gathered all those who identify as part of the Nipmuc People to this little village. To protect ourselves and our heritage. There are no more. I must think of that above all else."

One of the elders says something to Tom Pegan-Soaring Hawk in their language. The two speak back and forth for a minute, then the chief turns back to Sandoval.

"I will post scouts along the western road and in the woods above your homestead. With luck, they can give you advance warning should this Doctor send a force. I'm sorry, but that's the best I can do, Sandoval. Speak to Dancing Willow about the rifles." He rises, signaling the end to the meeting.

Sandoval frowns. Lucinda can feel the tornado of violence spinning in his head, but he keeps his cool.

"Thank you, Soaring Hawk," he says. He starts to go, then turns back, not quite ready to drop it. "You'll contact the First Nations?"

Tom Pegan-Soaring Hawk nods.

"Tell them this: the Doctor won't stop with us. Especially when he gets his drug factory back. He'll grow his army of infected souls with me, and this woman, and this child—" he points to Kimo "—

and hundreds like us. Remember that. Now is the time to strike him. I'm not just being self-interested here. He's coming, but he's vulnerable. Wait too long, allow him to build his forces, and you won't just have a skirmish on your hands — you'll have an all-out war. Tell them that."

The chief nods, his small, kind eyes bright as pebbles in a stream. "I will tell them."

Sandoval swings away, muttering under his breath. Lucinda and Kimo follow. Dancing Willow catches up with them. "That went better than I expected, actually," she says. "Tom is a cautious leader. But he heard you, and he will reach out to the Tribes."

"What good will that do?" says Sandoval, spitting the words out as if he doesn't like the taste.

"The First Nations have consolidated territory from the Pacific to the Great Lakes. They are ready to bring the East into the fold. They just need something to fight for."

The man laughs bitterly. "A little house in the middle of nowhere. Why should they care? Tom Pegan obviously doesn't."

"You know that's not true. You said it yourself. Strike the doctor before he's ready. It makes sense."

"I was talking through my hat."

"Your what?"

Sandoval shakes his head. "It's an old expression. Zaquero used to say it. My old war band leader. It means making stuff up."

"I thought you made a lot of sense. Now come on, let's get us some weapons." She strides away without waiting for him. He follows her with his eyes for a moment, looks at Lucinda, shakes his head again, and goes after her.

Inside the weapons locker, it's clear that Tom Pegan-Soaring Hawk was not downplaying the strength of the village. A few rifles, three ion spears, and half a dozen crossbows are all they have.

"Let's leave the crossbows," says Dancing Willow. "The learning curve is too high. Two rifles, the ion spears, and a couple of these—" she picks up a rectangular black case.

"What's that?"

"Grenades. Messy, inaccurate, but easy to use, and handy if things go south."

"Which they will."

Dancing Willow laughs. "Aren't you a pessimist."

"I prefer realist."

"Grab those boxes of ammo," she says to Lucinda. "Leave one and take the rest." She pulls an ion spear off the rack, leans down, and places it gently in Kimo's hands. "Ever used one before?"

Kimo shakes her head. Her eyes are wide and serious.

"Don't worry," says the soldier, putting her hand on Kimo's head. "I'll show you how. And I'll be beside you when the time comes."

Sandoval gives her a sharp look. "You will?"

"Of course. You said it yourself. They hurt Peter. I can't stand for that. Besides—" she grabs another ion spear and tosses it to Sandoval. "You won't last ten minutes without me."

Creek carries the last bundle of branches up from the stream. They are long and straight, longer than he is tall — two meters or more — and he finds it difficult to keep them all together. They constantly threaten to see-saw into confusion in his small arms. Lamarque sits on the ground by the makeshift barricade — nothing more than firewood, branches, and pieces of the ruined shed stacked up alongside the two carts. He uses a laser blade to sharpen the tips of the long branches and then pushes them through the barricade at an angle, setting their feet into the ground, to form a loose spear wall. It doesn't look very threatening to Creek, but it is better than nothing. He drops the sticks at Lamarque's feet and begins to sharpen the end of one with his knife.

A tingling on the back of his neck makes him turn. Candela has come out of the house with Baby on her hip. He always knows when she is coming; he doesn't know how. He watches her loose, easy motion as she strolls down the hill. She says something to Lamarque, but he doesn't catch it.

She is the only reason he is still here. In the night, he actually crept out of bed and stood at the ruined doorway for a quarter of an hour, willing himself to go. Just go. They were all going to die. Or worse. The Doctor would arrive with his army of monsters, and they would run rampant over them. He would take them to his cages and infect them, and Creek would drool and scream and rave and eventually fall, maybe after attacking the Nipmuc village and ripping out the throats of the children he had met there.

And the same would happen to all of them. To Lamarque, to Kimo, to Kat (probably not to Sandoval. Sandoval would die in the battle, Creek was pretty sure of that). And Candela. He imagined her face twisted and split by the disease. Then he pictured himself on the road, alone again, safe and alive, but crying in the night, carrying the knowledge that he had left her to that horrible fate. So, he went back to bed. He stayed.

She doesn't see him watching her. If she did, he would dart his eyes away quicker than she could notice. But she doesn't notice. She passes right by without seeing him, down toward the stream.

Lucinda winces as Kat gives her the third shot. With treatments every few days, it's hard to find a spot that isn't tender.

"I know this one is a little early," says Kat, "but I don't want anything to go wrong for you when the fighting starts. We need you. How are you feeling?"

Lucinda rubs her arm. She feels cold. "I'm all right."

"Let me run a quick diagnostic." The medico hooks her up to one of the machines and presses a few buttons. Readings start streaming across the little screen. Kat shakes her head. "I don't like this. We're not getting the same response that we had, even two or three treatments ago."

"Do you mean it's not working anymore?" It's true that her mind has not been as easy and clear the last few days. She put it down to anxiety over her — *their* — situation.

"It's not a cure, unfortunately. We're holding the virus at bay, but there's no telling how long it will last. Did the Doctor ever talk about that?"

"No. But he never told me much. He said I needed to put myself in his hands. But I know he never expected the Afflicted to last very long. He just needed them to live long enough to win whatever battle he had in mind."

"What about you?"

She shrugs. "I was different. But he never told me how, or why. I'm guessing he only gave them the bare minimum, but I got the full dose." She looks at the floor. "He made them, you know."

"What do you mean?"

"The Afflicted. He designed them." She tells Kat about the file, about the virus designed by Advanced Weaponry, about Ashburn's re-engineering of it to make his army of berserkers.

Kat lets out a horrified grunt. "Those men. God! Sick, sick, sick. So, he never had any intention of finding a cure. I've been trying to figure out if the data we have was leading in that direction, but I've come up empty. No wonder. He never did any work to that end. I'm sorry, my dear."

Lucinda smacks her head with her hand. "Oh my gosh! I totally forgot! I'm so stupid!"

"What?" Kat leans in.

"There was another file. I downloaded it, too, but then I was so freaked out by the journal that I totally forgot to look at it. I'm so stupid!"

"What was in it?"

"Ashburn, the Doctor, had an accomplice. A guy named — I forget — Rolfus! That's it. He had scruples. The Doctor couldn't stand him, used him as the first test of his new virus. But he was working on a cure. I think he was getting close, and Ashburn didn't like that, so he took him out. Which one of these machines is your data manager?"

Kat points at a small terminal in the corner of the room.

"Can you set it up for file transfer?"

"Sure." Kat gives a few commands. Lucinda reaches out with her COR and finds the interface. She copies the files from her memory to the machine. It takes seconds.

"There," she says. "See if that helps."

Chapter 46

The family sits in a circle in the main room. Creek watches the light from the fireplace jumping and flaring across their worried faces. Dancing Willow has joined them and sits beside Kat near the fire, oiling her crossbow. Her sister, Bright Swallow, has come as well. She is younger than her sister, but taller — a solid, strong warrior.

Sandoval stands before them, holding an ion spear in his hands. He places it on the table.

LISTEN AND LOOK. WE DON'T KNOW WHEN THEY WILL COME. MAYBE TONIGHT, MAYBE TOMORROW. WE ARE IN GREAT DANGER. I KNOW. AN ARMY IS COMING FOR US. BUT WE'RE NOT DONE YET. WE ARE DEFENDING. THAT'S AN ADVANTAGE. WE HAVE THE HIGH GROUND. THAT'S AN ADVANTAGE. WE KNOW THEY WANT THE MACHINES SO THEY WON'T JUST BLOW US UP. THAT'S AN ADVANTAGE. He looks at Lucinda. *WE HAVE THE SOLDIER. THAT'S A HUGE ADVANTAGE. HERE IS THE PLAN. KIMO, I NEED YOU FOR THIS PART, SO COME HERE WITH ME.*

Kimo stands and joins him. She translates for him as he lays out the plan. He and Dancing Willow will hide in the brush by the river. When the army arrives, they will snipe as many as they can and then retreat up the hill to the barricade. The robot soldier will cover their retreat.

Next to him, Lucinda raises a finger and corrects him. Sandoval responds, but Creek can't follow. He looks to Kimo. *WHAT WAS THAT?*

THE ROBOT'S NAME, she answers. *ARTAXERXES.*

The robot has a name? Creek had no idea.

Sandoval continues, pointing at Bright Swallow. She will also cover them as they fall back. He hopes that maybe the robot's attack will discourage them enough that they will give up. *I DON'T THINK IT WILL, BUT WE CAN HOPE,* he shapes.

If they succeed in crossing the stream, the robot will join them at the barricade, and they will make their final stand there.

Lamarque raises his hand. "Yes?" says Sandoval.

ME TOO. I WANT TO COME, TOO.

The man looks at the boy as if seeing him for the first time. Weighing. *DANCING WILLOW, LAMARQUE, AND I WILL BE HIDDEN BY THE STREAM.* Lamarque smiles and looks over at Kimo. She frowns, and his smile falls away.

WHAT ABOUT US? asks Kimo.

YOU, CREEK, KAT, AND CANDELA WILL STAY IN THE HOUSE. KAT HAS HER PISTOL, AND WE'LL LEAVE ONE OF THESE — he holds up the ion spear. *WE WANT YOU SAFE.*

WE CAN RUN AMMUNITION TO YOU AT THE BARRICADE, she shapes.

Sandoval frowns and shakes his head. *TOO DANGEROUS.*

YOU HAVE TO LET US HELP. Kimo's face is set. Creek has seen that look before. Kimo acts all compliant, but when she makes up her mind about something, watch out.

Sandoval frowns. *WE'LL SEE.* Creek knows that means they won't.

Kat leans in. *THESE KIDS HAVE SEEN AS MUCH TROUBLE AS YOU. LET THEM HELP.*

He drops his hands and says something to her. Creek looks at Kimo. *HE SAYS WE ARE JUST KIDS.*

AND THIS IS OUR WORLD, SANDOVAL, Kat shapes, her gestures strong and defiant. *YOU KNOW THEY CAN HANDLE IT. THEY ARE BETTER AT SURVIVING THAN WE ARE.*

The man shakes his head again. *I just think—*

WE NEED THEM. WE NEED EVERYBODY.

The adults continue arguing. Dancing Willow gets involved. The conversation goes on for a while. After a while, Creek looks to Kimo. *THEY ARE DISCUSSING WHETHER THE AMMUNITION WILL BE IN THE HOUSE OR AT THE BARRICADE. SANDOVAL WANTS IT OUTSIDE, AND THE OTHERS WANT IT IN THE HOUSE.* Creek thinks both places sound risky.

Eventually, Sandoval gives up. *All right, all right,* he motions. Creek can see that he wants to be in charge, military style, and that this democratic process gets under his skin. But he nods brusquely and moves on. *WE STACK THE AMMO HERE BY THE DOOR. I WANT EVERYONE TO GET SOME REST. THEY COULD ARRIVE ANY TIME, AND WE HAVE TO BE PREPARED.*

And with that, he ends the meeting.

Kimo looks from face to face as Sandoval goes into the side bedroom to consult with Dancing Willow and Bright Swallow. Dr. Jemisen watches them go, her eyes veiled and thoughtful. Candela fusses with Baby, but Kimo can read the anxiety in her movements — too busy, too energetic, almost like she is performing the role of mother. Lamarque catches Kimo's eye, the eagerness in his expression jacked into desperation. He has told her he wanted to tell her something. She thinks she can guess what it is. Now is not the time.

Creek commands most of her attention. He has that veiled look, as if there were a storm breaking inside him, but so deeply that no one can read the infinitesimal whispers of it on the surface. No one but her. She fears he will do something desperate. Maybe even leave them. He has been keeping it secret, but she knows him so well. She can read his discomfort around all these people, his fear that they are leading him to his destruction. She sees alarms of self-preservation blinking all around him, telling him to go, run, hide.

She doesn't want him to go. Even in their desperate situation, she believes in the promise of this place, aptly named by Dr. Jemisen. For all of them, but especially for Creek. He needs this. He needs them. He just doesn't know it yet.

She knows she must do something. That she is the only one who can do something. For all of them.

The room is very dark, just the light from the fire warming the faces of Candela, Baby, and Kat, who sit with Lucinda, silent and withdrawn. Lucinda has the entertainment chip slotted in behind her ear. For much of the day, she had used the medical module, searching the archive for any insights that might help Kat complete the vaccine. Now, she absentmindedly flicks through the collection of books and vidis, not landing on anything specific, the inane busy-ness of it calming her jangling nerves. The quiet presence of Artaxerxes calms her, too — placid and powerful, he stands guard in his corner of her mind.

Kimo comes out of the back room, Lamarque and Creek in tow. She holds an old book with a yellow cover in front of her like a plate. Her wide-spaced eyes focused laser-like on Lucinda. Kimo holds the book out to Lucinda, and she takes it without thinking.

"Will you read to us?" the girl asks.

"Oh, I don't think I..." Lucinda extends the book back to Kimo, but she refuses it.

"Please."

"What about Creek?" She knows that the strange contraption the girl wears on her head gives her a kind of hearing, though she doesn't know how much the girl understands. But it seems like reading a story would only exclude the boy, and that doesn't seem like a good idea at this time.

Lamarque interjects. "She knows that book by heart. She's read it like a hundred times. She will translate for Creek. Please?"

"Maybe someone else? Candela?" She looks for help from the young woman at her side.

"Can't read," says Candela in her lazy voice. She lays Baby on his blanket on the floor, where he lies on his back, swiping at unseen motes and gurgling quietly to himself. "I'd like to hear a story."

"Kat?"

The medico cocks her head and smiles. "They want you, dear." She rises. "I'm going to get a few things stowed, and then I'm going to bed." She heads down the hall and disappears into the lab.

Lucinda feels suddenly nervous. She once told a story to a group of Third Class kids on COR-day, and she'd done a few plays at school, but this feels different — these kids all looking at her, expectation and — was it? — trust in their eyes. Hell, they would probably be dead or enslaved by this time tomorrow. It was a lot of responsibility.

She looks down at the book. It is called *Tales of Ahl-Sa-Heira* by Tasha Chee-young. She is unfamiliar with it, though she has heard of Chee-young — a prizewinning author from the late 21st century. They rarely used actual books in the Enclave, though they all learned to read as a matter of course. "The pillar of civilization," one of her teachers had called it. Books were art pieces, signs of status. Her dad had fourteen, proudly displayed beside their fireplace, though Lucinda doubted he had ever opened any of them. Of course, Prendergast's house was full of books, most like this one — more than 100 years old, with cloth or leather bindings, and no active media.

"All right," she says. "I'll try." She opens the book. "How about this one?" Lucinda looks through the table of contents and picks a story at random. "The Tale of Arda Twelve-Sired." She begins to read.

Chapter 47

This is the tale of Arda Kole-Soweio-Tal-Prenta-Rhys-Chiraga-Mies-Radaman-Toque-Zalia-Smith-Weku, the greatest of the Innovants. Listen how she was born—"

Kimo stands beside Lucinda, shaping. They get into trouble almost immediately with the long list of names, and Kimo starts laughing as she tries to spell them out to Creek. They have to go over it a couple of times before she is satisfied. It doesn't get much better after that. The book is written in an elaborate style, full of strange terms from an imaginary world created long ago. Kimo stops her frequently to explain things to Creek. In another context, Lucinda might have become annoyed at the constant interruptions and repetitions, but she understands the importance of this moment to the children — an escape from the deadly reality they face.

"In the days before the Omnipote, twelve Mendicants petitioned the Registrat to have a child. They were the purest of the pure, and the poorest of the poor. Their lives were hard, my Little One, harder than yours even, and they dreamed of a daughter to bring sunshine to the dark corridors of the District. But the Registrat refused their plea, saying, 'How can you, beggars that you are, bring value to the people with such a child?' The twelve Mendicants went back to their hovel, weary and sad.

"The next day, they could hardly raise their voices to ask for alms. 'This is no use,' said Kole to the others, and they picked up their bowls and prepared to return home. Just then, a tall man approached them. He wore a cloak of shimmercloth and a hat lined in yatik fur. He had one leg. The other was a rod of purest lucifite. 'What is your grief, my Mendicants?' he asked. They told him of their grief, and he listened, an expression of deep sympathy on his face.

"'Hear me, friends,' he said. 'I am a Teleomancer from north of the Borderline. I can help you. In exchange, I ask one little thing. The smallest thing. Nothing of importance.'

"The Mendicants gathered around him, eyes bright as zircons. 'What thing? What thing?' they cried.

"'A sole,' he said. Or that is what they heard. They looked at his one foot, and saw that for all his finery, his shoe was old and worn. They agreed, and thanked him for his generosity.

"Then the Teleomancer removed the lucifite rod from his stump, and balanced on one leg. He pointed the rod at each, and spoke words in the tongue of the Sirenoids, and pulled from each their essence. Then he spun three times on his heel, and, like the conductor of a hymnorche, twirled his rod this way and that way, and before their eyes appeared a wondrous crystal creche. Then he replaced the rod on his stump and said, "In three quarters, the creche will open, and you will have your wish."

Lamarque stands up. "Read that part again."

Lucinda complies. Lamarque takes a narrow log from the pile by the fire and pretends it is a peg-leg, hopping around on it for a bit before raising it up and waving it around. He spins three times, loses his balance, and falls on top of Creek. Creek pushes him off with a huff, but Lucinda catches a glint of pleasure in the boy's quiet eyes.

"The Twelve expectant parents watched and waited. Just as the Teleomancer had promised, in three quarters the creche burst open like a firelily, and out came the most beautiful little girl they ever had seen. They named her Arda, which means 'dawn' in the dialect of the lower peoples. She made—"

Before she can finish, Lamarque runs across and grabs Candela's hand. He pulls her up to stand by him. "Arda," he says. She giggles, and then strikes a pose like one of the glamor girls Lucinda used to goggle over in the Montreal fashion zines.

Lucinda starts up again. "She made their lives happy and prosperous, and after not many years, the twelve left off being Mendicants, and purchased a small villa above the Falling Waters.

"When Arda came to the celebration of her sixteenth spin, her parents planned a joyful celebration for her, and all their neighbors and their children came to make merry. At the height of the party — just as Arda was beginning the Dance of Maturation — a black cloud boiled up from the ground, there was a crack of thunder, and the Teleomancer appeared among them. How they jumped!

"'I have come for my soul!' he cried. And then the twelve parents of Arda realized their terrible mistake. They thought he meant a sole for his shoe. They had known the price was low as dust, but in their great desire, they had failed to read the print. Their pure hearts had only seen the generosity, and not the calculation of the Teleomancer. And now Arda was lost. They begged and implored with all the skill of their years as Mendicants, but to no avail. The Teleomancer grabbed Arda, twirled thrice, and vanished."

Lamarque has fully embraced his role, strutting and swooping around the room, making grand gestures and wild, fierce expressions. Lucinda can barely keep her eyes on the page. She wonders if the performance is more for Creek or for Kimo. She has her suspicions.

"He carried her back to his Spire in the North, a dark and twisted fortress at the edge of the Chasm of Tran-too-tral.

"'What will you do with me?' asked Arda, terrified." ("What will you do with me," echoes Candela in a high-pitched voice).

"'You are made of the essence of twelve pure beings,' he replied. 'I will disintegrate you and discover the key to your essential code. It will give me the power I need to rule the Northern Provinces, and eventually, the whole Conglomerate!' He laughed a laugh as dark as the Folds of Despair.

"The Teleomancer then put Arda into a dungeon at the bottom of the Spire, below the deepest cages of his tormented servants. How wretched was she!

"Now, the Teleomancer had a child, named Kaliste, a young person of sixteen spins, who still searched for his purpose in the Plentitude. Kaliste had a soft heart, and it grieved him that Arda was captive in the abysses of the Spire. He asked his father if he could bring food to the prisoner as she waited for her doom."

Candela notices that Kat has crept back into the room. She leans against the wall of the long hallway, an expression of benign indulgence on her face. Candela drags her into the playing space before the fire. "You are Kaliste. You are Kaliste."

Lamarque has other ideas. When he hears that there is a romantic hero in the story, he waves his arms, saying, "I want to be Kaliste! Let me be Kaliste! Dr. Jemisen, you be the Teleomancer," and thrusts the log into the medico's hands. Kat looks around her in mock trepidation, but accepts the log and the role. It takes a minute to explain the cast change to Creek, who has watched with a look of confusion on his narrow face. At last, all is settled, and Lucinda continues.

"Kaliste gathered food and descended the five hundred circles of the Spire, past dungeons and prisons and abattoirs and torturezones and rendering mills and brutalizers, to bring the nourishment to Arda. And when he came to her — Oh, my Little One, didn't he fall in love with her in an instant?

Kaliste said, 'Arda, my Arda, I cannot stand by and watch your disintegration, and see your essence used to further the ambitions of my parent. I love you."

Lamarque makes a gesture — arms in an 'X' over his chest, hands closed, rocking slightly back and forth — Lucinda sees a hug in the gesture. He gives it first to Candela, who acts out a swoon in high dramatic fashion. Then he turns and makes the same gesture, much smaller and more tentative, in Kimo's direction. The girl takes it in with a cock of her head and a screwed-up mouth — perhaps a smile, but perhaps not — then gives Lucinda a little nod as if to say, *let's keep going.*

"Kaliste made a promise to Arda that he would help her escape. And Arda thanked the Equimote for seeing her plight in the fog of travail.

"Kaliste prepared a sleeping draft for the Teleomancer and slipped the drugged posset to his father after dinner. The sorcerer always removed his magic leg when he ate, and Kaliste stole it while he slept. With its power, he froze the minions of his father, and rescued Arda from her dungeon, and hand in hand they fled for the Borderline."

Kat begins a bit uncertainly, but the confidence of Candela and Lamarque quickly frees her from her shyness, and soon the three of them are hamming it up like the best traveling players Lucinda ever saw. She thinks of Sebastien, almost forgotten in the months since her exile, and a stab of guilt makes her wince.

Lucinda lifts her eyes now and again to watch Creek, who observes the mad proceedings with a frown on his face, as if he is watching a building fall, or a storm race in. But intent, and fascinated. She wonders if he is alarmed, or amazed, bothered, or pleased by the performance. He is a mystery to her.

"Now, the Teleomancer had lost his magic rod, but he had more tricks up his sleeve. He had three Cards of Power, given him by the Thieves' Cartel. Without hesitation, he played the first Card and summoned the Malevolent Eye, whose gaze will rot the heart of any that meet it. 'Find my child and Arda the Twelve-Sired before they escape my land!' And the Eye rose into the air on a cloud of poison, and sped South."

Lamarque darts over and picks up Baby and begins waving him around at arm's length, "The Eye!" Candela gasps and reaches out instinctively, but Baby shows no signs of distress, his eyes and mouth open in infant wonder.

"As dawn arrived, Arda and Kaliste were toiling through the Mires of Traal, still far from the Borderline. Arda looked back and said, 'I see an evil green cloud following on the horizon.' And Kaliste said, 'That is the Malevolent Eye, sent by my father to capture us. We are lost!'

"But Arda said, 'Do not despair, Kaliste. Take your father's magic rod, and turn me into a golden statue, and yourself into a deep pond. But instead of water, let the pond be filled with Spirit of Venenum, and place me at the bottom.'

"Kaliste spun three times on one leg, and instantly he became a placid fishing-pond, with alder trees growing along its bank. At the bottom, glowing softly, lay a golden statue of Shebet-Inann.

"The Malevolent Eye came roaring up on its cloud of poison, its red and green iris flicking back and forth, searching for the lovers. And everywhere it looked, the plants withered and the grass died. It swooped past the little pond, and its gaze caught a glint of gold at the bottom.

"Now the Eye was very greedy, and its lair was filled with shiny and expensive things that it could gloat over. 'What is this?' it said to itself.

'A golden statue of Shebet-Inann? Why that must be worth a trillion rindi at least.' And the Eye forgot about its prey and hovered over the pool."

Lamarque waves Baby back and forth over the imaginary pond. Candela holds her breath, delighted but fearful, while Kimo begins to laugh, interrupting her shaping. This only makes Lamarque play harder.

"Lower and lower it floated, until with a gluttonous rush it dove into the pool, orb and axon. And the Spirit of Venenum, so toxic to its mucilage, seared and burned and crackled around it like a frothing cup of crema.

"The Eye shrieked in pain. It wrenched itself from the pool, spinning and dancing as it tried to shake the Spirit from its skin. But the damage was done. Whimpering and blind, it turned and limped North, guided only by the hissing of the wind around the turrets of the Spire."

The performance has become so elaborate — with people grabbing blankets for capes, and acting out every moment of the story — that Lucinda begins to feel her own role as narrator is hardly necessary. But Kimo continues to shape away, so she reads on. The laughing and joy of the little family amazes her. It is hard to believe that they are awaiting the arrival of an army that will more than likely destroy them all. But the story suits the moment. A pair of lovers fleeing a powerful villain, using improvisation and guile to escape his clutches. When at last the Teleomancer, in a fit of rage, transforms himself into a terrible metal monster, an Olethrot, Lucinda closes the book with her finger in the page.

"Wait a moment," she says. She gives a mental command. The room falls silent. A clanking drifts in from outside, growing steadily louder.

Through the opening in the front of the house, Artaxerxes appears. He has to bow his head and bend almost double to work his way through the shattered wall, but he does no further damage to the house, smooth and careful as a cat. He comes to stop beside Lucinda. He cannot stand fully upright, his head tucked between the rafters. The firelight shimmers across his sleek, chromed body. The hush continues, everyone caught in a moment of awe. Then everyone cheers.

Creek gestures with his hands.

"Go on," Lamarque interprets. Lucinda bends back to the page. A warm feeling flushes her face. She feels good, welcome, as if she had performed a magic trick.

The house is quiet. The children are sleeping, heartened by the triumph of Arda and Kaliste over the evil Teleomancer — even if it is just a fairy tale. Lucinda sits on the porch, looking out over the hill. The sky is cloudy, but the specter of the moon paints the dark with white. She can just make out the platform of the van in the stream, and the shadowed form of Sandoval sitting on the low stone wall, rifle in hand, keeping watch.

Footsteps behind her, and Candela comes out of the house. She sees Lucinda and starts to withdraw, but Lucinda rises and stops her. "No. Please." Candela nods, and the two women stand in awkward silence. They have said very little to each other since her arrival — Candela nursing a silent anger, and Lucinda unable to appease her.

"Thank you for reading," Candela says, after a minute or two. Her voice is softer, kinder than expected.

"Thank you for your acting. I think the kids really enjoyed it."

"It's a beautiful story."

The silence falls again. A misting rain starts to fall, and they can see Sandoval pull his hood up over his head.

"Love," says Candela, suddenly. Her gaze is far away. What does she mean? Lucinda longs to ask her about Baby's father. The Duke. She knows he was lost when they destroyed Lady Fal's camp. And she knows Candela holds her responsible. She doesn't dare ask. Then, Candela turns to her and says, "Have you ever been in love, Lucinda?"

The question surprises her, unsettles her. She thinks of Sebastien — of his deep eyes, his kind face, his laugh, his beautiful music. Certainly, she felt more for him than she had for anyone else in her life. But was it love?

"No," she answers.

"Not this Doctor? He's coming for you, isn't he?" Candela has challenge in her eyes.

"No! No, no, no. God no."

"Then, when he comes, you won't change sides, or run away?"

"No," Lucinda says. She wasn't completely sure what she would do before this moment, but she knows now. "What is the shaping for 'Trust me?'"

Candela shows her. She copies the shaping back.

Candela nods. "Good." They stand in silence for another minute. Then Candela says, "Not that it really matters. We're going to die either way."

"Don't say that."

"It doesn't matter."

"Of course it does. Think of Baby."

Candela lets out a bark of exasperation. "Why him? Why does everyone think I only belong to him now? I love him, of course, but my life does not belong to him. It belongs to me." She stares defiantly at Lucinda.

"I don't know. You brought him into this world."

"So my life is no longer mine? And what a world."

"I'm sorry. I don't know anything."

"You really don't."

"I'm sorry."

Another silence. The rain subsides, and the moon peers out through a rent in the clouds.

"I'm sorry, too," says Candela. "I don't know what anything is anymore." She shakes her head, then squints into the darkness. "What's that?" She points across the stream to the opposite slope.

Something has come out of the forest. A small shape, low and glinting a dull silver. It moves down the hill with surprising swiftness. Sandoval stands, rifle at the ready, but does not fire. The thing crosses the stream and barrels up the rise toward them. Lucinda can see that it is a beautiful robotic horse, its pistoned legs rolling with almost supernatural grace. A dark figure sits upon it, hunched low. She can just make out the long hair flowing from its head. They come to a halt in front of Sandoval, and the two exchange a few hushed words.

The figure dismounts, and they walk the rest of the way up to Lucinda and Candela.

"…and have something to eat and drink," Sandoval is saying.

The mysterious figure resolves into a young Nipmuc warrior, short and trim, with a pleasant, round face.

"Forgive my intrusion," she says. "I have ridden from the western road. I came as fast as I could. A large force is moving across country in this direction. They will be here by dawn."

Chapter 48

"This isn't going to work, is it," says Sandoval to Dancing Willow, a little distance away from him in the brush on the near side of the stream.

"You never know."

"I'm sorry I got you into this."

She shoots him a rueful grin. "You didn't. I'm tired of seeing people get pushed around by thugs like this. Who knows? We might make it out alive."

They look back up at the top of the meadow on the far side as vehicle after vehicle rolls in through the woods. "How many, do you reckon?"

Sandoval counts in his head. "I'd say thirty. They have five trucks and three rangers, plus that one big transport. That's old New States Army. Wonder where he got that."

"And what are those boxes? Look like horse trailers."

"They are."

"What's in them?"

"Not sure. Nothing good, you can count on that."

Dancing Willow brings her rifle sight to her eye. "Shall we get this party started?"

"Might as well. Lamarque?"

Sandoval turns to his right, where the boy hides. His rifle looks too big for his thin body. His eyes pop out of his dark face, his lips pursed tight. But he nods and levels his weapon. Sandoval turns back to Dancing Willow. "After you."

Dancing Willow scans the soldiers milling here and there among the vehicles, easy and relaxed with the confidence of impending victory. "You look like an officer." She squeezes the trigger.

Sandoval sees a figure drop to the ground like an empty sock puppet, and instantly, the top of the hill dissolves into chaos. Some soldiers hit the dirt while others dive for weapons stacked against the wheels of the trucks. He starts firing — not too fast. Choose a target. Aim. Fire. He feels a momentary sympathy for the hapless soldiers, gunned down by an unseen foe, but he thinks of Lady Fal, and sympathy morphs into cold rage. To his left, Dancing Willow shoots at a consistent, measured pace. Lamarque has not yet fired a shot. Sandoval gets it. He wonders if he made the right decision to bring him along.

A small group tries to move down the hill, weaving and avoiding as best they can. But the dead grass is high, and the footing is bad, and their progress is slow. Willow and Sandoval pick off a couple before they get a quarter of the way down, and the others dive for cover. One soldier, however, takes off toward them down the hill at a breakneck run, spilling and rising several times. It reminds Sandoval of the day they arrived, and the kids tumbling down the hill with giddy laughter. Only this guy has a gun.

Willow fires and misses. "Reloading!" she yells. Sandoval takes aim and fires. Or doesn't. His rifle jams.

"Dammit!!" He slaps the magazine and snaps the bolt. Nothing.

"Gimme a second," says Dancing Willow. *What's taking so long?* Sandoval tries to keep his cool, but his heart thunders as he tries to clear the jam. The rifle doesn't cooperate. The enemy soldier trips about twenty meters from the stream bed, but rises quickly and begins firing into the bushes as he runs forward. Sandoval flattens himself behind a tree, frantically banging on his rifle, not sure what he's doing anymore.

A *crack!* from his right. Then another. Then another. Sandoval peeks out from behind the tree. The soldier lies face down in the tall grass, his gun still in his hand, thrown out over his head. He turns to look at Lamarque. The boy sits behind a tangle of hawthorn, holding the rifle as if it were a live snake. His eyes are as big as plates.

"We gotta move!" yells Dancing Willow, joining him behind the base of the tree. Sandoval looks back up the hill. Several trucks have begun descending, moving slowly but inexorably closer. One has a large machine gun fixed to its bed. Another has some sort of antenna rising two meters into the air. Soldiers crowd the backs of the others, weapons at the ready.

"Lamarque!" The boy turns his blank face toward him. "Wait for my signal, then run as fast as you can for the barricade. Stay low, don't move in a straight line. Don't look back." Sandoval turns and shouts up the hill to the house. "Lucinda! Now!"

The trucks roll down the hill. The machine gun starts sweeping the stream bed, sending up a thousand geysers in the water, leaves and branches spinning in chaos all around them. They press themselves tightly against the tree.

From behind the barn, Artaxerxes comes striding like Ares on the fields of Troy. He raises his right arm, and from below his massive hand, a missile swings down and screams across the meadow, hissing and sparking like an airborne viper. It strikes the machine gun truck in the middle of the hood, and the vehicle explodes in a nova of orange and red, the gunner sent flying high into the air.

"Go! Go! Go!"

Lamarque hesitates for just a second, then takes off up the slope, weaving and ducking, his rifle clutched to his chest. Dancing Willow follows, turning now again to fire at the approaching forces. Sandoval finally succeeds in clearing his rifle. He slaps in a new magazine and follows her, also swinging round now and then to shoot. From behind the barricade, Bright Swallow stands and lays down a covering fire.

It hardly matters, though. Artaxerxes continues his terrifying progress down the hill. Two more missiles whistle across the stream, two more vehicles burst into holocausts of flame and death. Then, he deploys his machine gun and sends a sheet of withering fire across the field. Windshields shatter and tires burst. Scattered gunshots ricochet off his armor plating, but he continues his advance.

They reach the barricade and tumble behind it. Kimo is there with a water flask, which she hands to Lamarque. He grabs it as if it were the most precious thing in the world, and glugs down half the flask before surrendering it back to her.

Lucinda is there, too. She looks calm, her expression slightly distant, as if she were recalling some pleasant memory from long ago. "Isn't he beautiful?" she says, almost to herself. "I'm spinning up the proton cannon."

Artaxerxes stands magnificent at the base of the hill, a mountain of strength holding the enemy at bay. He extends his arms, and his hands reform into wheels of silver. They begin to spin, faster and faster, until they are nothing but a blur. The blur glows blue, brighter and brighter, and the air around him starts to crackle.

Then, without warning, Lucinda lets out a cry of pain. She grabs her head and falls to the ground, writhing and clawing at the dirt. The wheels spin down, the blue fades, and Artaxerxes drops his arms to his sides, standing as still and lifeless as a wall of stone.

Chapter 49

Lucinda drives her head into the damp earth, trying to press the riving pain out of her brain. White shapes fluoresce before her tight-closed eyes. She is dimly aware of Sandoval kneeling beside her, holding her shoulders, speaking words she cannot comprehend.

The agony is unbearable, far worse than any pain she has experienced so far. She can barely breathe. *How is this possible?* Dr. Jemisen gave her a treatment only last night. She hasn't had a single episode up to now while the drugs were in her system. Unless something has gone horribly wrong and the drugs are only making it worse. Or…if Dr. Jemisen has deliberately…*that makes no sense.* The medico has shown nothing but kindness and fealty to her oath as a caregiver. Besides, their survival depends on Lucinda wielding Artaxerxes against their enemies. *But what is going on?* Nails of pain drive through her skull, sending molten pulses down her neck.

And then the pain is gone, as quickly as it appeared, only a residual ache behind her eyes. The entertainment chip — she had been listening to an old Katya Preecher album to calm herself down — boots up again, and the melancholy strumming of an acoustic guitar caresses her inner ear. More comforting, still, Artaxerxes occupies his sheltered corner of her mind. He has cancelled all functions and waits for new instructions, but he is there.

And something else. She hears, or rather feels, a series of clicks in her brain, like someone turning the dial on an ancient vidi screen. They had one — a television, it was called — in the Enclave museum. Then a clear *Ping!* A voice sounds inside her head.

Hello Lucinda. Can you hear me?

Ashburn. A wave of dread rolls through her body, from her head to the pit of her stomach. *How did he...?*

"How did you...?" she says aloud.

I started working on it the moment you came into my care. It has taken some time. Upgrading my facial prosthesis, decoding the access protocols to your COR. Boosting the signal proved to be the hardest part, but once I had adapted one of the cell transmitters from your Enclave, it all came together. If only I had finished before you left me, we wouldn't be in this position. Ah, well.

Lucinda pushes herself up onto one hip. She looks down the hill. Artaxerxes stands about twenty meters from the stream bed, silent and inert. Soldiers are fording the stream in twos and threes, taking up positions in the trees and brakes. A truck is parked on the makeshift bridge beside the drowned van. She recognizes the antenna-like apparatus rising from its bed. One of many that used to line the walls of Hamilton Estates.

On the far side, they have moved the horse trailers into a line along the top of the opposing slope. In front of them, chilling her heart even at this distance, stands Ashburn. She can make out the dark plate that covers half his face, and almost imagines she can see the red glow of his robot eye.

"What happened?" Sandoval leans in, gripping her arm. "Are you all right?"

She swats him off. "I'm fine," she lies.

"What's going on? What's wrong with the battle robot?" She doesn't answer, trying to clear her mind. "Lucinda!"

"He's in my brain!"

"What? Who?"

"Him!" She flings her arm out in a wild gesture toward the Doctor. "Just be quiet. I'm figuring it out." She isn't, but she needs him to stop talking.

It's beautiful, isn't it, Lucinda? To be this close. I suppose you used to do this all the time, with your boyish lovers, didn't you? But now, the connection we had, back home, now we can go deeper. Deeper than we ever thought possible.

Lucinda wants to vomit. She feels violated, naked, powerless. "I don't want this," she says to the void.

I AM disappointed in you, Lucinda. I thought when I arrived, you would fight on my side. You promised to return to me, to bring back my equipment. The equipment I need to bring order to the fallen world. You kept it for yourself. Very selfish of you, my dear. My poor Afflicted.

"Leave me alone." Her voice is barely a whisper.

I can't do that. You know that. Don't worry. I've ordered my fighters to hold the stream. They won't fire unless they have to. But I must have my equipment back.

Above, Ashburn's men open the horse trailers. The Afflicted pour out. Fifty or more. The soldiers begin to drive them down the hill toward the water. Some grab their heads, some stumble forward in spasmodic jerks, but they advance with terrifying swiftness. A grisly chattering rises from the mob.

You know you have nothing to fear from them, my dear. They won't harm you. I'm sorry about your new friends, though. But it's the only way I can get back what belongs to me. And you.

Sandoval scans the field beside her. He curses, then turns to Lamarque and the others. "Get inside. Get inside. Now!" The Afflicted begin to wade across the stream.

Lucinda clenches her fists. "Please. Call them back. We'll surrender."

It's too late, Lucinda. I am sorry. I am confident you will come to understand.

"No. I won't." She takes a breath, trying to still the thundering of her heart. She pushes Ashburn's voice to the side and focuses on Artaxerxes. She begins to power up his proton cannons again. The blue wheels spin.

What are you doing, Lucinda?

She watches the Afflicted as they stagger through the water, falling and flailing, making their inexorable way toward them. *It's not their fault,* she thinks. *They are victims just like me. Unluckier even than me.* She can't do it. She powers down the proton cannons. She asks Artaxerxes to fire up the sonic wave weapon. At least it will buy them time.

Don't do that, Lucinda. Don't do that.

"Keep them back, 'Xerxes, keep them back!" Artaxerxes sends a blast out in front of him. The Afflicted topple to the ground, some writhing, some still as corpses. He turns to the left, to the right, mowing them down like a scythe through winter grass. It is a strange sight. Outside the cone of effect, no sound reaches their ears. It is like watching a vidi with the volume off, or one of those ancient silent films Lucinda saw at school in her History of Culture class. The Afflicted, and many of the soldiers along the bank, fall over like someone has flicked a switch. It's almost comical.

A group of ten or so evades the beam and begins to lope up the hill toward them. Artaxerxes swings around, but he can't bring them down without striking Sandoval and the others, so he holds his fire.

Lucinda hears a *crack!* beside her, and one of the Afflicted falls. A second *crack!* and another goes down. She glances to her right and sees Sandoval, his rifle at the ready, taking them down one by one. "Don't," she says, but so quietly he cannot hear her. To her left, Dancing Willow runs toward the Afflicted, waving her arms. Several see her and begin to pursue her. Fast as a leaping deer, she races between them, down and to the left, toward Artaxerxes. They turn and follow her.

"Fire! Fire!" she calls. "Don't worry about me." Lucinda gives the okay, and Artaxerxes lets loose a sonic blast across the field. Willow and the Afflicted fall senseless to the ground.

Bright Swallow gives a cry and leaps over the barricade, fires twice, and sprints toward her sister. An Afflicted veers off and charges shrieking like a wild bird. She swerves and fires, but misses. The Afflicted descends on her, but falls at the crack of Sandoval's rifle. Bright Swallow kneels beside her sister and takes her head in her hands.

Sandoval takes aim and pulls the trigger. His rifle jams. "Dammit!" He drops the gun and runs a little way along the barricade. He stops, kneels down, and opens the case of grenades. Quickly but carefully, he removes one.

Lucinda looks behind her. Lamarque and Kimo are at the door. Candela is ushering them past her into the safety of the house. They exchange a glance. Then Candela looks past her and steps out onto the porch, her face a mask of surprise at what she sees. Lucinda turns back.

One of the Afflicted still comes on, approaching them fast in an awkward lope. He appears to be a boy of sixteen or seventeen. Tall and lanky, with a pale, whelite face beneath a tangled nest of straw-colored hair. His eyes are big and blue, or would be if his bloodshot whites didn't dim them to a soggy purple. His mouth works wildly, as if he were trying to eat his own lips. Sandoval grabs the pin of the grenade and prepares to pull it out. Then he pauses.

"Duke?" he says. At the same moment, Candela cries, "Duke!" from the porch. Sandoval swings around to look at her.

A mistake. The Afflicted boy covers the remaining ground in a flash, leaps over the barricade, and smashes into him, knocking him to the ground. The grenade goes flying over the barricade, landing in the shorn grass of the path. Sandoval tries to fight him off, but the boy has gone into a frenzy, his Mindworm-induced strength too much even for the larger, heavier man. The boy beats on his face until the blood flows, then tears into Sandoval's cheek and neck with his teeth. The man lies still — dead or unconscious, Lucinda can't tell.

"Duke! Dukie!" screams Candela again from the porch. The boy looks up from the mangled face of the man. Lucinda can see the children in the shadowed doorway behind her. Lamarque stands with Kimo, his arm around her shoulder. Creek peers out from the doorframe, his face the same neutral mask, his eyes glinting like chromium in the darkness.

The Duke rises from the motionless Sandoval. He looks at her, takes a step, then backs off as if he smells something unpleasant. He sidles toward Candela, his head cocked to one side, his face slicked with blood and spittle.

"Duke. Baby. What did they do to you?" says Candela, her cheeks soaked with tears. She holds her hands out to him. He slows, scrunching up his eyes like he is looking into the sun. Then, he shakes his head violently, lets out a strangled roar, and attacks. They fall to the ground in a tangled heap, arms and legs flailing. She holds him by the neck, fending off his snapping jaws and kneeing him repeatedly in the side. He strikes her, hard, a stunning blow, and she lets go. He goes for her throat.

Out through the door, Kat Jemisen hurtles in a dead run, the pistol in her hand. She reaches them as the Duke's teeth slide into the angle beneath Candela's chin. She grabs him by the hair and places the gun to his temple. "I'm sorry, sweet boy," she says, and pulls the trigger. The blast knocks him off the girl, and he tumbles into a jagged heap, his limbs every which way, his bloodshot eyes staring blankly at the crushed, brown grass.

Candela rolls onto her side, her body shaking with violent sobs. Her hand, guided by her heart, reaches across and comes to rest on his knee. Kat kneels beside her, wrapping her arms around the shuddering girl. "I'm so sorry, honey. I'm so sorry. I'm so sorry."

Chapter 50

Lucinda is utterly unprepared for the shattering grief that erupts at the Duke's appearance among the Afflicted, and the sudden ending of his life. The children surge forward from the door and clump around Candela and Kat, heedless of the danger. Kimo bursts into tears and buries her head in Lamarque's chest — an expression of emotion so out of character that Lucinda doesn't know what to make of it. Lamarque weeps, too, holding Kimo tightly, sniffling and gulping air. Creek stands a little part, looking anywhere but at the body of the Duke. His little face is taut and dark, and what he is thinking no one knows, but inchoate emotion throbs around him in a cloud.

A groan from Sandoval grabs her attention. He rolls on his side, probing the wounds on his face with his hand. She goes to him, kneels down.

"Are you all right?"

He winces. "What does it look like? No. Where's the Duke?"

"We need to get you inside." She puts her arm under his shoulders and tries to help him rise, but a stab of pain runs through her brain again, and she lets him fall, her mind's ear clicking like a safe opening.

Lucinda.

"No."

I didn't want to do this. I know how much it will hurt you. I hoped you would understand. I still hope so. I believe you will come to see that I am right, that I am your true friend, and your salvation. If you survive. But I can't wait any longer. This farce must end. Run. Run toward the stream, or into the forest. I have ordered my soldiers to spare you, if they can.

"Leave us alone!" She shouts into the wind, as if the wind could help her. She orders Artaxerxes to spin up his proton cannons again. He begins to stride with purpose toward the bridge.

No, my dear. I didn't want to do this. You leave me no choice.

Like fingers digging into her brain, she feels his thoughts burrow down through axons and synapses, down into her COR, where he wraps his mind around the haven where Artaxerxes lives within her, and begins to pull. She fights him as best she can, holding on for dear life, but his surgical attacks overwhelm her every attempt. Briefly, they struggle. Then, with a snap, Artaxerxes is gone. The hole left behind swallows her, and she falls to the ground. She reaches out for him, trying to catch the threads of his presence, but he flies away from her like a ghost on the wind.

Creek stands with the others, close to them, but miles apart. His blood pulses in his ears, but he wraps his silence around him like a blanket. Candela lies at his feet, her arms around the body of the Duke. His heart twists into an agonizing knot. He wants to reach down, to hold her, to bury his face in her silken black hair, to comfort her, or be comforted. Or both. He doesn't know how. He just stands there, like a crooked stick, as his world comes apart.

Just below, he sees Lucinda trying to pull Sandoval up from the ground. She pauses, lets him drop, and spins, holding her head. She shouts something to no one in particular, then falls again to the ground, reaching out like she's trying to catch a dandelion wisp, or something.

In the middle of the bridge, Artaxerxes halts. He stands still for a moment, then turns and moves up the hill towards them. Once again, his hands become wheels which start to spin, blue and white. As he passes, soldiers rise and regroup, recovering from the sonic blast, and fall in behind him. Some of the Afflicted, too, pull themselves up, shaking their dazed heads and walking in little circles before they catch the scent of blood and zero in on the little group standing at the top of the hill.

Dr. Jemisen rises and starts yelling down at Lucinda. Lucinda turns and screams something up at them, shaking her head in a frenzy. The robot continues its approach, moving slowly but with deadly purpose up the slope, the soldiers and the Afflicted forming into a loose line behind it. Dr. Jemisen takes Kimo and Lamarque by the shoulders and pushes them toward the house. She reaches for Candela and tries to pull her off the Duke's body. Candela shoves her away, screaming into her face.

Creek sees Bright Swallow, who has been tending to her sister, raise her head and take in the advancing robot. She sprints to the center of the field, where the grenade lies in the brown grass. She dives for it as the ground around her explodes with enemy gunfire. Her hand wraps around it, just as a bullet finds its target. With a shuddering jerk, she flips over and lies still. Artaxerxes comes on, an army at his back.

Each moment that follows sears itself into Creek's memory, bright as an arc-weld. Candela rises in a single, swift motion. She leaps over the barricade, runs forward, scoops up the grenade from Bright Swallow's hand, and races down the hill toward the robot. In the deep quiet of his world, time slows down. She trips on a tussock of grass and falls. The fall is beautiful, graceful as a swan landing on water. One of her shoes falls off as she scrambles to her feet, no pause in her forward motion. Her hair flies behind her. She pulls the pin from the grenade without slowing her pace. Several of the soldiers fire at her, though most are as caught as Creek is by the mystical beauty of her flight. A bullet strikes her in the shoulder, and she spins without losing her balance. The rest miss.

The robot's proton cannons fully charge, white and blue, crackling with power. Artaxerxes raises his arms and takes aim. Candela charges into his embrace, slamming the grenade against the smooth grey metal of his chest. A star explodes where they stood, blinding and bright, illuminating the heavy clouds that hang low over the field. Soldiers and Afflicted spin through the air. Creek seems to be looking at the birth of the universe, though it is the end of his hope. The shockwave almost knocks him down, but he keeps his feet. Around him, the others cover their ears. He hangs in silence. The world stops.

The light fades quickly, though to him it takes an age. When it is gone, a shallow crater is all that remains. That, and a small pink shoe.

Lucinda's head throbs, the stabbing pain now a constant thrum with every beat of her heart. But she knows silence, too. The blast has knocked out the COR transmitter, and Ashburn no longer whispers in her mind. Her release does nothing to still the aching loneliness that yawns within her. She stares at the crater, the spot that once held Artaxerxes. He was no longer hers. He had never really been hers, but he belonged to her, nonetheless.

The others lie around her, knocked flat by the shockwave. Who knew those grenades were so powerful? Near her, she sees Sandoval roll onto his side, breathe deeply, and drag himself to a sitting position. Looking down the hill, she sees Dancing Willow rise shakily to her feet and head toward her sister, skirting the center of the field where the enemy soldiers lie scattered like rushes. They, too, are pulling themselves together. Even the Afflicted, who at first just stagger in wayward circles, catch their scent on the rifling wind and turn their haggard faces toward the barricade. The soldiers move into formation, captains on either side marshaling them into position. Far away, on the top of the hill, Lucinda sees the tall, gray figure of Ashburn, hands in the pockets of his long coat, staring down on the carnage.

A rod of pain shoots through her head. She hears a loud *bang!* and at first thinks her skull has cracked open, but recognizes it as the report of a gun nearby. Sandoval, his head drooping over the stock of his rifle, fires at the approaching enemy. They return fire, and she can see and feel the bullets whistling over their heads, or burying into the heavy wood of the barricade. Lamarque bends down and runs to the barricade beside Sandoval, leveling his weapon and taking aim. Kimo squirrels up beside him, laying a stuffed bag of ammunition between them, an ion lance in her free hand. Another crash of pain, and Lucinda falls to her knees. Dancing Willow appears at her side, dragging her sister behind the barricade, where Kat is waiting with her kit.

Lucinda's vision goes dark for a moment, and somehow she finds herself lying on the ground. Kat is now leaning over her, holding the side of her face and speaking, but Lucinda can't hear what she is saying. A roar like the distant oceans fills her head, alongside a thousand little explosions of pain, like fireworks going off inside her brain. She turns on her side, blinking at the pain, looking up at the house. Bullets strike the walls, sending dust and splinters flying. One hits the little sign by the door, and it slips, not falling, but swinging askew, its message sliding down toward the ground: Hope Farm.

And beside it, heedless of the onslaught, as if his aura of silence were a suit of armor, stands little Creek. He looks out over the field, his mouth open, his dark face a fierce painting of undefined emotion. His eyes a mirror of the lost world. His hands fly in a series of shapes, pointing and pounding his chest, repeated over and over, as if through sheer force of will he could spin the world and rewind time. *I love you. I love you. I love you.*

Then something catches his attention, up to his left, toward the north pasture. His hands stop their agitated flutter. He points. A bomb goes off in her head, and her vision blurs and blackens. As she loses consciousness, she hears a voice beside her *(Is it Dancing Willow?)* shouting, "The Eagle is coming! The Eagle is coming!"

Darkness overwhelms her.

Chapter 51

Lucinda awakens in the medical lab. The machines hum and blink around her. She is alone. Her head still pulses with a low-pitched ache, but otherwise she feels okay. She rolls off the cot and finds her shoes, neatly placed near the door. She slips them on and heads down the hall.

Coming out onto the porch, she is surprised to see the field full of people. Thirty or more soldiers stand in small groups, or move through the grass, kneeling now and then beside the many corpses that strew the field, mostly Afflicted, but a number of the bodies wear the dark blue and black of the Doctor's forces. These new soldiers wear close-fitting jackets and trousers in greens and browns, decorated with beads and feathers, some with leather fringe along the seams. Their heads are bare, and their long black hair bathes their backs or hangs in braids. Along the edge of the field stands a row of robotic horses, their pistoned legs gleaming dull silver in the gloom of the cloudy day. They could be statues, so still are they, but they emanate an aura of power.

Sandoval stands near the remains of the barricade, talking to a tall woman with two braids hanging almost to her waist. She has a beautiful face, eyes set wide, and an air of command that makes even Sandoval seem diminished beside her. She pauses now and again to give instructions to the soldiers moving around them. Sandoval looks terrible — his face and neck red and swollen, his eyes small with weariness. He can barely keep his head up, but he manages, nodding now and then to the woman and pointing to the barn, the house, and the stream.

Dr. Jemisen appears at her side. "You're awake. How are you feeling? You really shouldn't be up."

"I'm all right. How long was I out?"

"About six hours. It's almost sunset. Not long enough, to my way of thinking. I wish you would go back to bed."

"Who is that?" Lucinda points to the woman.

"That," says Kat, watching the woman with a look of deep respect, "is Amaste, commander of the Eagle."

"The Eagle?"

"The First Nations elite fighting force. It seems they got Sandoval's message. Arrived in the nick of time, as they say. Saved us all."

"Seems like I missed a lot."

"You did. You blacked out. What happened? You lost control of the battle soldier somehow, and then you collapsed."

"The Doctor. Ashburn. He accessed my COR and took 'Xerxes away from me." Lucinda swallows as the dull lump of his absence pulls her down. She looks down the hill to the crater. A tiny figure sits quietly at its edge. Creek.

Kat puts her hand on Lucinda's shoulder. "I'm sorry. That must have been awful."

"He was inside my brain. Then my head exploded and I lost consciousness. I don't know why."

Kat thinks for a moment. "My guess is, however he accessed your implant, he didn't do it very carefully. He must have caused a power surge or short circuit or something — I don't know how it works — which knocked you out."

"That makes sense. The pain didn't start until he was inside me."

"I tried to help, but there was so much chaos, I couldn't get you into the house until the battle was almost over. After Candela…you know…"

She blinks back sudden tears. "Well, the soldiers regrouped and started marching up the hill. We were done for, but dammit, we weren't going down without a fight. Then, out of the woods over there—" she points to the left, up toward the pasture where Artaxerxes had stood beneath the tree — "Suddenly, the cavalry comes bursting out and falls on them from the flank like a lightning bolt. Some of those guys put up a fight, but most threw down their weapons and surrendered. The whole thing was over in minutes. They're over there." Kat points down the hill, and Lucinda sees a dozen or so of Ashburn's soldiers sitting on the ground, guarded by First Nation troops with ion spears. "Most of the Mindworm victims, the berserkers—"

"The Afflicted. He called them the Afflicted."

Kat frowns. "Did he? Well, most of them are dead, but about ten survived. We couldn't kill them. They're victims like the rest of us. We herded them into the barn. That was probably the worst part of today. They're not like you. Like animals."

"He doesn't give them the same treatment I get. Just enough to keep them alive."

Kat shakes her head. "That figures. What a... Well, they're in there now."

"What about him? Did they...?"

"No sign. He vanished before they could get up the hill to where he was."

Lucinda nods. She should be angry, or afraid, but her mind has fixated on the tiny figure of Creek, sitting by the crater. He looks so small. *What is he doing? Who is he inside?* The First Nations troops eye him as they pass to and fro, but give him space.

"Did anyone else, you know, not make it?"

"We're all here, miraculously. Even Bright Swallow, though she won't be moving for a while."

"I'm glad."

"Me, too," says Kat. "Listen — I don't know what to do about these, these Afflicted. How to treat them. They're going to die if I don't do something, but I can't get near them. I'm hoping maybe you have some ideas."

Lucinda nods, but barely registers what she says. *That boy.*

"I'll do what I can. But first, I need your help."

"Sure. What do you need?"

"I need you to teach me something." She explains what she wants.

Kat says, "Not me. Talk to Kimo."

Creek sits by the crater, his feet beside one of the many puddles that fill the hole after the afternoon's rain. Fragments of metal, many smaller than his little finger, dot the ground. There may be fragments of another sort, but he doesn't look too closely. His eyes are focused on the shoe he holds in his hand.

It is smaller than he expected, not much larger than his own shoe, though more delicate. Pale pink leather, with yellow stitching around the eyelets. A smudge of red-brown dirt mars the toe, but otherwise it is surprisingly clean, though worn. He wonders where she got it. Somehow, she always managed to find pretty things — her loose, blowzy dresses, the little clips she would put in her hair. He berates himself for not noticing her shoes before, as if his noticing could have prevented what happened.

He knows almost nothing about her. Only that when she came to John Chaico's, she left behind a story of horror too unspeakable to share, and that in the Duke she found a way forward toward the light, and that though she loved Baby, she loved the Duke more. And that she had always been kind to him. And that when he first saw her, he thought she was the most beautiful thing he had ever seen. She was like a promise. He had never dared to do what he wanted most in the world — to climb into her lap and lose himself, to bury himself deep in the softness of her body, as if he could crawl into her and find the childhood he never had. And now he never would.

Someone sits beside him. Lucinda. He shoots a glance at her, too quick for her to notice, but long enough to see how tired she looks: dark circles under her eyes, her impossible red hair lank and tangled in the damp, her pale skin chalky and tinged with gray. He doesn't know what she wants. He doesn't care.

She doesn't seem to want anything, anyway. They sit for a long time, the silence holding them like a bubble. He wants her to leave, sort of, though he can feel the warmth of her body along his side, and it feels good.

After who knows how long, she touches his knee. He turns and looks at her. She looks nervous, her hands fidgeting. She holds them in front of her like they don't belong to her, like they are frogs or rats or something unpleasant. She takes a deep breath and moves them.

I'M SORRY. It surprises him. The few times she has tried to communicate, she has only used her mouth. He watches her, waiting.

SHE WAS NICE. YOUR FRIEND. She tries to shape Candela's name but only gets it half right. *I LOSE MY FRIEND.* She points at the scattered fragments of metal and plastic littering the ground. *SHE SAVED US. FROM HIM. FROM ME. I'M SORRY.*

She turns her body toward him, sitting on her calves. *I WISH I KNEW HER BETTER. ALL OF YOU. SHE LOVED YOU. I KNOW. MAYBE ONE DAY SHE LOVES ME, TOO. HER LOVE WAS BIG. SO BIG. FOR YOU.*

The words conjure up Candela's warm smile, her lovely face. He blinks back a sting in his eyes, but the image remains. Then it begins to change, to evolve, unlooked for, and unbidden.

Through the dream of Candela, as clear as glass, as if a door has opened in his memory, he sees another woman. She kneels on the floor of that little house, sitting on her calves, her arms spread out to him as he toddles across the floor toward her. *So big! So big!* For the first time since she vanished from his life, he can see her face. Her face is warm as rich wood, smooth and shiny, her eyes enormous, liquid. She has big teeth in a full mouth that spreads in a smile so bright it could light up the dark side of the moon. He can see her. He can see her.

Something cracks inside Creek, like ice on a little stream, frozen through a long winter. One warm day in spring, it gives way, and water moves again, pouring over the little stones and sticks — dark and wet and alive. He has never seen ice, or winter, but out of his frozen heart, grief begins to run, first in a trickle, then in a torrent. It pours out of his eyes, where tears have not flowed since he lived in that forgotten house with his forgotten mother.

A tremendous need swells up inside him, and he succumbs. He could never succumb with Candela, he can never feel his mother's touch again, but he cannot hold the world at bay anymore. He is just a child, after all. A little deaf boy, made hard and old as flint by a world that has no use for him. Just a kid. He buries his head in the chest of this strange woman. This woman who has been kind. He wraps his thin arms around her waist, climbs into her lap — he is small enough that he almost fits — and sobs and sobs, a gushing river of lost love.

She holds him. He is so small. His grief cracks her heart, and she cries too — for Artaxerxes, for her family, her home. For Sebastien.

They cry together for a long, long time. At last, the flood abates. They share a sigh. She holds him.

Chapter 52

Lucinda sits by the fire in the cabin's main room, the family all around her. Creek sits at her feet, playing an inscrutable game with stones and bits of string. They sat in the field for a long time, then he slipped away without saying a word. She thought perhaps that was it, that their relationship — or non-relationship to be more accurate — would return to its previous state. But then he slinked in and plunked himself down at her feet without even looking at her. And here they were.

She doesn't understand what happened in the field. She has no idea if the things she tried to say to him made any sense at all. Kimo had taught her the signs she needed. She had been patient. Lucinda had not. She couldn't explain the strange compulsion to go to the boy, but she couldn't resist it, either, and could hardly concentrate on the brief lesson. Creek's reaction to her had surprised and confused her. Was she pleased? She wasn't sure.

She looks around at the others. Kimo reads her book, angling it toward the light of the fire so she can see. Lamarque sits beside her, staring into the flames, his eyelids drooping now and again. He must be exhausted. Kat sits on the other side of her, Baby on her lap, reading from a tabula and stroking the blanket that wraps the little child, who has finally fallen asleep. Only Sandoval is missing, recuperating in the bedroom down the hall. And Candela. Her absence hangs over them like the leafless branches of a dead tree. No one can speak about her, but she haunts their faces, one by one.

The Eagle departed at sunset, leading the Doctor's soldiers with them in a double file. They promised to return in the morning with supplies and to aid in the removal of the bodies from the field. They left behind two guards to watch the Afflicted in the barn, but that is all. The house is quiet. The fields are quiet. Only the rain on the roof and the crackling of the fire.

Lucinda dwells in the silence, stark and unfamiliar as it is. She has rarely known silence in her thoughts. She feared it. Even here, she kept her mind bubbling, never comfortable unless she had one of the chips inserted in her COR. It didn't matter that they had little value to bestow. They kept the silence away. Now it has returned, and she tries to understand it, and live in it.

Lucinda.

At first, she thinks she must be dreaming, must have nodded off.

Lucinda.

It sounds again. That voice. Her stomach turns. Her mouth goes dry. A wave of fear rolls through her head, making her ears ring.

My dear.

They hear a shout from outside. Lamarque sits up, suddenly alert. Kat puts down her tabula, reflexively draws the sleeping baby closer. There is another shout, then a weird electronic wailing, followed by the sound of two men screaming, suddenly cut off. Heavy footfalls on the porch. Everyone rises and moves together into a tight clump by the fireplace. Ashburn walks into the room.

He looks taller than she remembered. His long, dark coat sweeps against the calf of his robotic leg. He holds a gun in his hands, black and gray. A snaking cable rises from it, over his shoulder, to a small pack. The tip glows red.

"Hello, friends," he says. *Hello, Lucinda.* "Well, well, well. Children and women. I did not expect my plans to be undone by children and women. Though clearly, I should have. It is not the first time. You have set my project back a year at least. Had I known how paltry your defenses were, I never would have bothered with an army. I would have come myself right off, but I never imagined…this." *And I never thought you would betray me. More fool I.*

"In case you don't recognize it, this is a heat weapon. It will melt the skin off your bones in seconds. You at the doorway!" He raises his voice, nodding quickly toward the bedroom down the hall. "You can drop that weapon. I am hard to kill, as you can imagine, and your little family will be nothing but a pile of ashes before you can bring me down." He never takes his eyes off them. "Put it on the ground. Good. Now put your hands in your pants, and join the others. Yes, down your pants. I'm no fool." Sandoval appears through the door, arms stuffed into the waistband of his trousers. His face is red, whether from rage or embarrassment, Lucinda can't tell. He sidles up and stands next to her. Lucinda can smell his fury.

"Excellent," says the Doctor. "Are there any more surprise householders? I killed the Indians outside. Anyone else?"

Lucinda becomes aware that Creek is not in the room. The last time she saw him, he was sitting on the floor beside her. She glances over at Kat. If the woman has noticed it, too, she makes no sign. Kat shakes her head.

"Good. All right. I need my equipment. It's why I came, after all. And I need her." He gestures at Lucinda. "Surrender her to me, show me to my equipment, and you live." *Step away from them, my dear.*

"No," she says aloud.

Step away if you want to live.

Her pulse races with fear, but she can smell his desire. Though it sickens her, she speaks to him in his mind. *Horace.*

He cocks his head, surprised. *Yes. Lucinda.*

You don't need to kill them.

I think I do.

If you kill them, you kill me, too. Aloud, she says, "Spare them. I will go with you. I'll show you to the equipment."

"You'll all show me."

No, whispers Lucinda. *Leave them be.* She turns to Kat. "I'm sorry. I need to go with him. He's won. I need the medicine to survive, so I need him. I'm sorry." She can feel Sandoval's anger through her back. Kat just looks at her, her face unreadable. She turns again to Ashburn. "We can lock them in the back room. They won't try to get out. Will you, Dr. Jemisen?"

Kat shakes her head. "Sandoval?" The man's mauled face mottles with rage, but he shakes his head as well.

Ashburn regards her skeptically, his head tilted to one side. She knows he cannot read her thoughts, only speak to her in her mind, but she feels naked under his gaze. *Do this for me, Horace. You have what you want. You have me. Let me have this.*

"Very well," he says. "Let's go." He gestures with the weapon. They move as a group toward the door of the back room. Lucinda stays with them, making sure Ashburn can't fire without hitting her. Just before she closes the door, she catches Kimo's eye and makes the signs she learned from Candela. *TRUST ME.* She pulls the door shut, turns the key, and shows it to Ashburn.

All right, let's go. She walks past him, brushing his arm lightly with her hand. *This way.* She leads him not to the lab room, but out into the yard.

Creek stands in the yard. He's not sure what he's doing. As soon as the others sat up, he sensed trouble. As they rose and clumped by the fire, he slipped down the hall to the back and climbed out the window, following instinct — run, hide, survive.

He creeps around to the front. The bodies of the two Firsters sprawl on the ground, twisted and smoking, almost unrecognizable. He scurries past them.

He makes out the back of a tall man standing just inside the ruined entrance. He recognizes the heat weapon. He's seen one before, when the warband destroyed John Chaico's school.

It's over. They're all going to die. Everyone always dies. He should just run into the night, like he's been meaning to do for weeks. Candela is gone; there's nothing left for him. Why doesn't he just leave? He stands there, willing his feet to move.

Lucinda comes out onto the porch, the man just behind her. She sees him and gestures urgently, her hands tight against her body. *Get away! Go!* He darts towards the barn, hiding in the shadow of the wall.

The machines are in the barn, Lucinda whispers. She only has the shreds of a plan. They pass the bodies of the fallen guards. The stench of charred flesh makes her wretch.

I'm sorry about that, he says. *I hate to upset you. But it was necessary. I'm all right.*

They arrive at the door of the barn. Ashburn passes her and reaches for the handle. Lucinda catches a glimpse of Creek, peeking around the corner of the building, his face no more than a smudge in the gray darkness. Their eyes lock. They connect. It all comes into place. She makes a low gesture. *Watch and wait.*

"Horace." He turns. She looks up into his twisted face. *I'm sorry. I'm sorry I disappointed you. I got confused. They had my medicine, and I didn't know what to do. I made a mistake.*

He smiles. *I know. But this is better, isn't it? Connecting like this? It will be all right. I might even spare your "friends" after all.*

Please do. They don't matter, but no more killing.

Only what is necessary. He turns back to the door.

"Horace." She steps into him, pulling him to face her. The smell of him almost makes her gag, but she stifles the urge. "Why me? You have been so kind to me from the beginning. I've let you down, but still, you don't turn me away. Why?"

Her intimacy befuddles him. The captain of men falls away, and he becomes just another boy, like all the boys she has known. Marcus, Jerome, Peter. Sebastien. *Poor Sebastien.*

He touches her hair like it is made of smoke. "Who can say, my dear? You awaken something in me, something that I thought had died a long, long time ago. A hundred years, or more. You are beautiful, of course, but it's more than that. I had a mission, but now I have a calling. I want to make the world beautiful for you. And perfect. Whatever the cost."

The little smile comes easily to her. She touches his chin and releases him.

He turns back to the door, grabs the handle, and slides it open. Before he can enter, she grabs him once more by the waist and pulls him back to her. "Horace. I'm sorry I was afraid. I'm so lucky."

Ashburn holsters the weapon, takes her head in both his hands, and kisses her on the lips. It takes all her strength, but she endures it. Low and to the side, she gestures to Creek. The boy slips along the front of the barn. Ashburn releases her and stares into her, wonder and lust battling on his face.

"Lucinda."

"My dear," Lucinda says. With all her strength, she shoves him through the doorway. He trips over the little boy, curled up behind his feet, and goes sprawling onto the dirt floor of the barn, his back banging painfully against the shoulder pack of the weapon. His mouth pops open in pain and disbelief.

"What?"

"Thank you," she says, and holds up the Butyrate Inhibitor that had hung, until a moment ago, on his belt. His eyes go wide. *What have you done?* She slides the barn door closed, draws the bolt, and takes a step back.

The boy gets to his feet and moves in beside her. They watch the door. She puts her hand on his shoulder. She is glad he can't hear, as the Afflicted — roused by the smell — fall upon the man within. The heat weapon fires, but the noise cuts off almost immediately, and something bangs against the wall and clatters to the ground. Ashburn doesn't scream, but she can hear him grunting and gasping, the sounds of tearing cloth, flesh pounding on flesh, cracking bone. Louder than all, his voice calling out in her brain. *Lucinda, Lucinda, open the door, how could you how could you save me save me save me Lucinda, Lucinda, Lucinda—*

And then it stops. Her mind goes silent.

Chapter 53

Lucinda smells the air as she comes outside. Cold again today. She heads back in and grabs a blanket to wrap around her. Three days of cold now. She can't remember it ever being this cold. No rain, either. The asperity of the air draws her outside again and again. Her soul clears, and her silent mind calms when she inhales the sharpness.

The farm is quiet at last. The Eagle finished its work last night and departed for good. There were no recriminations for the death of their guards. They covered them in simple shrouds of orange cloth and bore them away. They built a pyre for the bodies of the Doctor's soldiers and the Afflicted up on the north pasture. She doesn't know what they did with Ashburn, but she imagines his corpse laid across the top. She wonders if he would rejoice at that. Burning like a Viking king.

This is the problem with her silent mind. It wanders into dark places, and she can't stop it. When her COR was full, it was easy to channel her attention to things that kept her calm. Now, her brain moves where it will, often stabbing her with sudden guilt (*the Enclave…her family…*), or regret (*Sebastien…Artaxerxes…*). Still, she refuses to put in a module. She dwells in the silence and the shadows that accompany it. She tries to *Be*.

Kat comes out of the barn, the Inhibitor strapped to her waist. She approaches Lucinda. "They're resting. Another treatment and they'll be as safe to be around as you."

"You think I'm safe?"

Kat chuckles. "Well, I don't think you're going to bite me in the face. I have something to show you."

"What?"

"After the…after the thing. It's good, and we'll need it."

Lucinda nods. They look out over the browning field. "It's cold," says Kat.

"Yes."

"Nice."

Sandoval comes out of the woods above the house. His face is still blotched with red streaks and scabs, but he no longer walks with that stooping pain. He calls to them. "We're ready. Get the children."

Creek follows the others into the little clearing. For all the death he has seen, he has never seen a funeral. He carries the pink shoe. The others carry other articles that once belonged to her. Lucinda has Baby hoisted onto one hip. She struggles with him. He looks huge in her small arms. Creek remembers how well he fit in Candela's big, soft embrace. He belonged there.

Sandoval stands beside a shallow grave. A spade sticks in the ground beside him. There is no body, of course. A small mercy that the explosion left no remains. People take their places in a loose circle around it, and he steps back to join the circle. They stand there for a long time. Nobody knows how to start. Creek doesn't want to be there. He wishes he could go.

Dr. Jemisen begins to shape. *EVERYONE HAVE SOMETHING? WE'LL PLACE THINGS IN THE HOLE ONE AT A TIME, AND SAY SOMETHING YOU REMEMBER ABOUT CANDELA. WE'LL GO AROUND THE CIRCLE. OKAY? I'LL GO FIRST.* She leans down and places a brown ribbon into the grave. *CANDELA, I REMEMBER YOUR BEAUTIFUL HAIR.* She steps back.

Lamarque lays a green scarf next to the ribbon. Tears roll down his face, two bright lines against the darkness of his skin. *SHE WAS PRETTY,* is all he manages to say. He steps back into the circle and wipes his face.

Kimo goes next. She holds a precious treasure — a fragment of mirror about as big as her hand. Candela kept it wrapped in an old scrap of wool, but would take it out now and again to adjust her hair. Nobody knows how she came by it. The Duke would have known, and Creek has an unexpected flash of his long, pale face with that wide grin he would crack open at a moment's notice. He focuses hard on the mirror to push away the slavering, wild-eyed phantom that follows it like a zombie rising in his mind. The mirror. Candela let Creek hold it once. He stared into his own eyes, not recognizing what he saw as himself. He gave it back to her and never asked to hold it again. It scared him.

Kimo lays the mirror on top of the scarf. *WHEN SHE WAS HAPPY,* she shapes. *IT WAS LIKE THE SUN WAS SHINING ON ALL OF US.*

Lucinda hands Baby to Lamarque. She mumbles something, her eyes flicking from the grave to the people and back again. She seems to be apologizing, and then thanking them. *For what?* She doesn't have anything to put on the grave. It makes sense. She didn't know Candela. Then she folds her arms across her chest and looks at the ground.

Sandoval looks at Creek. Creek looks back at Sandoval, waiting. The man lets out one of his familiar, tight-lipped sighs, reaches down and picks up a piece of cloth from the ground behind him. It's a dress, patterned with tiny purple flowers. Candela wore it more than any other, her favorite. Sandoval lays the dress down in the grave, spreading it out as if to summon the absent body that should fill the shallow depression. He steps back. He says *SHE WAS JUST A KID. SHE DIDN'T DESERVE THIS. JUST A KID.* He looks down, muttering to himself.

All eyes turn to Creek. Now he wishes he hadn't waited until the end. He feels exposed, picked out, as though somehow he has been elevated to chief mourner. He wants to disappear, or run away, or sink into the ground. The shoe burns in his hands. Tears spring into the corners of his eyes. He blinks twice, hard, and lays the shoe in the hole, not at the foot, but in the middle of the dress. It seems important for him to put it there. He returns to his place and stares at the ground. He has no words, so he says nothing. He can feel all their eyes on him. He waits it out.

After a long, long moment, Dr. Jemisen signals to Sandoval. He pulls the spade out of the ground and scoops up a shovelful of dirt from the pile beside the grave. His face like a cloud, he tosses it gently onto the dress. Dr. Jemisen kneels and touches the clothes. She mouths something, gives a little smile, taps the ground, and rises. Without a word, she walks out of the clearing.

Lamarque hands Baby back to Lucinda, and he and Kimo kneel together, touch the ground, and follow Dr. Jemisen. Lucinda falls in behind them.

Creek waits. He knows Sandoval is watching him, waiting for him to go. He just looks at the shoe. A bit of dirt has fallen onto the toe. It looks like ashes. He waits.

Sandoval nods stiffly and picks up another shovelful of dirt. He starts to fill in the grave. Creek watches as Candela's belongings disappear into the earth.

At last, the man finishes his work. He walks past Creek without looking at him. When he is sure he is alone, Creek reaches into his pocket and removes the little ornament they made in that other life — so long ago, it seems, yet scarcely a season has passed. Candela smiles from the center of the crystal, her cheek pressed up against Baby's plump and open face.

Creek lays it carefully on the mound, then steps back. He regards it for a long time. Then he picks it up again, returns it to his pocket, and heads back down the path to the house.

Lucinda sits on the edge of the cot in the lab. Kat has asked her to wait. Her nerves are rattling, but she pushes aside the urge to plug in a module. She carries the case in the pocket of her sweater — a crutch, she knows, but it helps to know it is there. She soothes her mind by watching the lights blink on the machines that surround her. They remind her, oddly, of the few remaining leaves on the trees by the stream, waving and shaking in the breeze in fathomless complexity, ordered and chaotic at the same time.

Kat comes back into the room with Kimo in tow. The girl goes to the shelf, takes a small silver box in her hands, and carries it to the little table by the bed. Lucinda recognizes it as a Recreate. Her friend Tabby's family had one — the only one in the Enclave. When they were kids, they would sneak into her dad's workroom — he ran the Chemical Division — and make idle little things with it. The manual included a dozen or so projects you could try — jewelry, simple circuit boards, even perfume one time. Then her dad found out and locked it in this closet. He didn't like them wasting valuable resources on trivialities. She wonders what happened to it. Ashburn didn't find it when he destroyed the Enclave. Or at least he never mentioned it to her.

Kat gives her a warm grin, resting her hand for a moment on Lucinda's knee. "I wanted you to see this." She and Kimo fall to, filling the Recreate with a variety of materials from the shelves and drawers — little wafers, liquids, powders — carefully checking items off a long list on Kat's tabula. At last, they finish, and Kimo spends a few minutes programming the device. "You'll have to show me how to work it," says Kat, "but for now, it will be quicker if you just do it. No reason to drag this out longer than necessary." Kimo finishes inputting instructions and steps back. The button on the top of the Recreate turns bright green. "Will you do the honors?"

Lucinda reaches out and taps the button. Blue lights chase each other around the surface of the box. After five minutes or so, a little chime sounds, and the small door at the base of the cube slides open. Kat removes a small vial filled with clear liquid. She holds it up for Lucinda to see.

"You did it?" Lucinda swallows the lump in her throat.

Kat nods. "I did it. Thanks to you and Dr. Rolfus. I actually cracked it a few days ago, but there has been too much going on, and you were fine, and I had to stabilize the patients in the barn first, anyway."

"Is it a cure?"

"It's a therapeutic vaccine. It should eliminate the virus from your body, and provide you with immunity from contracting it again. That's the hope, anyway."

"Is it dangerous?"

Kat shrugs. "I don't think so. I mean, there is always a risk with any treatment. Especially a new one. Human bodies are complicated. Before the Collapse, they had a whole series of stages a drug like this would go through before you stuck it in someone's arm — with animals and controls and all sorts of stuff. We can't do that anymore. You're the test subject. I don't believe anything will happen, but I can't *promise* you. How do you feel about that?"

"Does it mean I stop getting the treatments every couple of days?"

"It does."

"Then let's do it."

"I'll watch you closely. If all goes well in the next forty-eight hours, I'll give it to the patients in the barn."

"Then what?"

"I'll monitor your progress. For a while, anyway. I think this will work, and then you'll be done, and I can focus on getting it out to the people who need it. Hopefully, the First Nations can provide me with enough materials. Are you ready?"

Lucinda nods. Kat takes the vial and loads it into a syringe. "Take off your sweater." Lucinda complies, surprised at how nervous she is. It's cold in the lab, and she shivers. "Don't worry. I've gone over it again and again. It's going to be fine." Kat swabs her left arm with alcohol. "Okay, Lu. Can I call you Lu?" Surprising herself, Lucinda nods. *Since when does she let people call her Lu?* "Are you ready to make history?"

Chapter 54

Creek carries the last box from the lab out into the yard and deposits it by the cart. Lamarque scoops it up and jams it in between another box and the bag containing Dr. Jemisen's few belongings. Kimo works on the other side, tying down one of the machines with a piece of cording. Dr. Jemisen stands by the front, talking to the two Firsters who brought the cart from the village. They belong to the Eagle, and Creek feels intimidated by their sleek leather uniforms and piercing eyes. There are six soldiers on the farm, including Amaste, the captain, who is talking to Lucinda and Sandoval over by the barn.

He wonders if he should go with her. A life on the road, distributing the vaccine to people with Mindworm, traveling from place to place with no end in sight — sounds appealing, or at least familiar. He's not so thrilled about the Mindworm part — I mean, those people are unpredictable as all get out. But he understands the life — always moving, independent, free to go his own way if the occasion demands. It makes more sense than staying here, in one place, doing…*what exactly?*

Not that Dr. Jemisen would take him. She's bound to tell him that it's too dangerous, that he has a home here, blah, blah, that the road is no place for a kid. As far as he can make out, the two Firsters have been assigned to travel with her by the Eagle, and they look tough as tree trunks, so how dangerous could it be? Besides, he's lived closer to the edge than she *ever* has, and he's made out okay. Who is she to tell him what danger is? And he could be useful — carrying stuff, keeping lookout, all kinds of things. Couldn't hurt to ask.

But Creek doesn't ask. Something holds him back. Maybe he's too shy. He doesn't, as a rule, put himself forward. Or maybe it's something else. He doesn't know. He watches her converse with the Firsters, not trying to guess what they are saying, just observing the movements of their faces and hands. He feels as if his legs have taken root in the soft earth of the yard, and he could no more go over to her and ask her to take him than he could sprout wings and fly into the clouds.

She gives the soldiers a nod and a laugh, and shakes their hands. As they head over to the barn, she crosses to him and Lamarque. Kimo finishes what she is doing and joins them in an awkward line.

EVERYTHING SET?

Creek nods.

THANK YOU, ALL. I'LL BE BACK IN THE SPRING TO CHECK UP ON YOU. I KNOW YOU'LL LISTEN TO SANDOVAL — HE'S A GOOD MAN, AND KNOWS WHAT HE IS DOING. AND LOOK AFTER LUCINDA FOR ME, OKAY? SHE'S GOING TO NEED HELP FROM SMART YOUNG FOLKS LIKE YOU — SHOW HER WHAT YOU KNOW ABOUT THE WORLD. SHE'S NEW TO IT.

Dr. Jemisen leans down and gives Kimo a big hug. The girl, on tiptoes, holds her tight, her eyes shut. She moves to Lamarque, who already has tears streaking his face. They embrace, then break apart. Lamarque wipes his cheek.

She turns to Creek and looks into his eyes, asking for consent. He returns her gaze, neither accepting nor forbidding. Apparently, she takes this as permission, because she wraps him up in her arms, squeezing him tightly. She smells like butter, which he has only had once in his life, but the memory fills him as he breathes in her scent. He feels a damp prick in his eyes and blinks it back. After a long moment, she releases him and takes him by the shoulders, giving him a deep look. Then she steps back.

TAKE CARE OF EVERYONE, OKAY?

He frowns. He nods. *OKAY.*

"You don't mind taking them?" says Sandoval to the Commander. Lucinda looks up at them, feeling out of place. Amaste is almost a head taller than she is, and carries herself with a ravishing confidence. She feels small and insignificant, like she might disappear into the ground. She almost wishes she could, then shakes herself. This is not like her. *Get it together.*

"Not at all. The Nipmuc have agreed to tend them until they have returned to health, and we have provided them with medicine, provisions, cots, and a tent. The Eagle will remain in the area at least until the summer, though we will be concentrating on the coastal areas. A sizable contingent of the Doctor's forces remains near Fall River, though we don't know who, if anyone, has taken over after his demise."

"Thank you," Sandoval says. "If you need any intel on the area, please ask me. I've been scrapping in this part of the world my whole life."

"That would be very helpful." She eyes him appraisingly. "We have our scouts, but an insider's view could be invaluable. You're welcome to come with us, if you like."

Lucinda gets a pulse of unease. She hasn't figured out how she feels about Sandoval, but the idea of him leaving her here with the children makes her heart flutter, and not in a good way.

He glances at her, too quickly for her to read his thoughts, then over to where Kat is talking with the children. He pauses for a moment, considering. "It's an attractive offer," he says at last. "But I think I'll stay."

Amaste nods. "If you change your mind, let me know. At the very least, come up to the camp and we can talk for an hour or two. We won't be heading east for at least a week."

"Sounds good. Thank you for the supplies." He gestures to the pile of crates stacked alongside the barn.

"You're welcome. We're happy to help. I expect you to pay us back."

"With what?"

"With your intelligence, with your labor, and your loyalty. This land is now under the control of the First Nations, and you have our protection as long as you respect our ways and our people. Chief Soaring Hawk is now our representative in this valley, and you will bring any concerns you have to him. You can also discuss what services you can provide in exchange for goods until you get things up and running here. Sound good?"

Sandoval smiles. Lucinda can hardly believe it. She has never seen him smile. His hard face brightens. He looks ten years younger, softer, more approachable. "Sounds very good. Thank you!"

Amaste nods. Behind her, the door to the barn opens. Two soldiers lead the former Afflicted out into the yard. They blink in the bright light of a white sky. They still look ragged and weak, but the madness is gone from their eyes; in its stead, a haunting sadness. Lucinda wonders if they will ever be whole again. She turns away as the First Nations soldiers lead them to several open carts, where they take their places, silent and ashamed. A shaggy voice, familiar but strange, calls out "Lucinda." She turns back at the sound of her name.

"Sheena?" She didn't recognize her friend *(ex-friend)* at all. Sheena's once-plump face is thin and drawn, her skin gray and blotchy, her eyes big and lost as a lamb's, her curly hair straggling and lank. Lucinda crosses to the cart. "Sheena," she says again.

Sheena stares into her face. Lucinda can barely stand to see the weary agony behind her eyes. "You're alive," Sheena says.

"So are you."

"Yes."

"How are you feeling?"

"I'm all right. You?"

"I'm doing well."

Lucinda wants to say *I'm sorry. I'm sorry I was such a bad friend. I'm sorry I ghosted you. I'm sorry I saw you in the infection line and didn't do anything. I'm sorry I betrayed you and the rest of my people.* The words don't come. "You'll like it with the First Nations," she says instead. "They are good people. They'll take good care of you."

"You live here now?"

Lucinda pauses, unsure. "Yes, I suppose I do."

"Maybe I'll see you again."

"I hope so." *Is that true?* She doesn't know. Of all the people from her past, Sheena is the last person she ever thought to see again. Life is so uncertain. One never knows who will rise up and walk with you into the future.

The cart begins to move. "I'll see you," says Sheena, and smiles. Lucinda almost recognizes the girl she knew, were it not for the aching sadness that hangs around her.

"Yes. Take care."

The Eagle soldiers activate the robot horses that pull the wagons. They begin to roll away, out of the yard. Lucinda makes herself speak. "Sheena?"

"Yes?"

"I'm sorry."

The girl gives a confused little grin. "What for?"

"For everything. Just everything. I'll see you."

The carts make their slow way up the north pasture toward the hills. Lucinda gives a little wave, which Sheena returns, and heads back to Sandoval.

"Who is that?" he asks.

"Someone I used to know. We need to change your dressings. Come on inside."

They gather around the fire. It's a cold night, colder than any of them can remember, and even though the breach in the front of the house has been covered with a large, plastic tarp, the air bites, and they huddle as close as they can to the flames, each wrapped in several layers of Nipmuc blankets.

The room is thick with silence. Lucinda misses Kat's cheerful voice, her easy conversation, always keeping the energy moving in the room. Kimo and Lamarque sit together in the big chair, cocooned in a single blanket, the boy's head on the girl's shoulder, his eyes lost in the flames, her attention focused on her book. Baby sleeps in the little crib beside the fireplace. Creek sits again at Lucinda's feet, leaning against her knees, his little hands busy mending a rip in his coat.

No sound except the crackling of the fire, the whisper of turning pages. Lucinda swims in the quiet, her mind still, her heart still, the press of the boy's back against her legs reassuring her of her place in the world.

Sandoval comes into the room. "I think you should see this," he says. He moves in front of the fireplace and kneels down. *GET UP. YOU ALL NEED TO COME OUTSIDE.* As he rises, he bumps the crib, and Baby stirs, a little, sleepy mewl. "It's all right. Bring him. He should see this, too."

Lucinda stands, the blanket still draped around her shoulders. She lifts Baby out of the crib and gathers him to her side. With her other hand, she reaches for Creek and guides him beside her. Kimo and Lamarque rise as a unit — Lamarque yawning a huge yawn — and they shuffle together toward the entrance. Sandoval pulls aside the gray tarp, and they file out onto the porch.

As Creek steps through into the night, his heart almost stops. The sky above is heavy with clouds, but they end in a tumbling line just above the eastern horizon, where the full moon, hanging clear between the dark heavens and the trees, limns the cloudbreak with silver-white radiance.

The world is transformed. Thick snow blankets the fields, candy-coats the branches of the trees, smoothing and purifying the landscape into something rich and strange. Large, puffy flakes tumble from the sky, dancing in the tender breeze. They pile on the fenceposts, on the roof of the barn, on the ruins of the barricade, burying the past, making everything new, and beautiful, and perfect.

Creek has never seen snow. None of them have. He doesn't even know the word, or that such a miracle could happen. One hand creeps up to Lucinda's, and she takes it, her fingers warm and soft. The other stretches out before him. In the glow of the lantern that hangs from the door post — beside the little sign that gives their home its name — he watches the snowflakes land on his open palm. Most vanish in an instant, but a few remain, their impossible crystals winking and sparking in the gentle light.

THE END

Thank you for reading HOPE. I hope you enjoyed it.

If you have a moment, please help other readers find
HOPE by leaving a review on Amazon, Goodreads, Bookbub,
anywhere!

You can leave a Goodreads review here:

Also, get the latest news about new releases, special offers,
prizes and more by
Subscribing to my email list!

The cadaver opens his eyes to the sound of music. Dissonant, atonal — dislocated pings and chimes and throbbing lows. The chaos of it pushes his brain to create order, the thing he prizes above all else. Slowly, it restores to him his sense of self. The fog of his long sleep lifts. He looks around. The same ceiling of gray metal, the same squares of light illuminating the small chamber. His faceless robot attendants move in slow concert, disconnecting him from the machines around him with graceful precision.

He is not, in fact, a corpse — though he has lived like one for the last forty-three years. Every six months or so, he will rise and hobble to the small desk in the corner of the room, where he will write — long hand — the history of his life and the fall of the world he once knew, once dominated. Even more rarely, he will have his attendants wheel him to Central Control, where he will peer into the monitors that circle the huge round table, trying to glean what passes in the world above. They are mostly blind, the stations they connect to robbed of parts and power, but a few still function. Like a peeping tom, he spies on the chaos and suffering of the stragglers who fight for survival among the ruins.

Mostly, he sleeps, dreaming uneasily — sometimes of his wife and daughter, but more often of endless processions of weapons and fevered meetings with white-faced men over deployments and supply lines. The dizzying, final crash of all he loved.

As he dresses — slowly, stiffly — his yellowed eyes fix on the tattered flag secured to the wall of his chamber. It once flew outside the New States Department of War. His true home. What was the name of that young man who retrieved it? Prior? Priker? He can't remember. He had praised the boy's bravery in the frenzy of the retreat. Not to his face — the poor kid had been vaporized along with the rest of the rear detachment — but in his mind, he paid him what honor he could.

A door slides open, and another cadaver shuffles into the room — gray and gaunt, sunken into a uniform now several sizes too large.

The corpses eye one another across the room. "Good morning, Cragg," says the first.

"Good morning, Prendergast," the newcomer responds.

"Are the others awakened?"

"All except Branford. He's dead."

"I'm not surprised. He was always weak. No matter. Tell them to assemble in Central Control. I'll be with you shortly. We have much to discuss. It is time."

Cragg nods and leaves without a word.

Oliver Prendergast, Director of Advanced Weaponry for the New States of America, pulls the knot tight on his red tie. He looks at the flag on the wall.

"It's never too late, my girl," he says. "To bring you back."

Virgo hangs in balance over the mountain stream, spear raised, elbow cocked, still as stone. She cherishes moments like this: the crisp autumn sun strong and steady; the unchanging, ever-changing rush of water over rocks; the quiet in her mind. In times like these, she can almost remember the universe of Joy she once sailed through, for fifteen uncounted years. The vibrating peace of it. The stillness humming with life. The simplicity. Her body suspended, almost forgotten, her mind focused on nothing and everything at the same time. She doesn't try to force such moments to come — she left that universe behind of her own free will — but they feel like home.

A speckled trout has swum out of the current into the little pool beneath her feet, just as she expected. It noses among the shaggy weeds along the bank, searching out a water bug or minnow, a late-morning snack. The fish turns its side toward her for an instant, and she strikes. The long, thin tip of the spear flashes into the water, with barely a splash. She pulls on the line to retrieve the missile. The trout flops and twists, but the prongs of the spearhead (which she carved herself during the long winter nights) hold it in their death grip, and it cannot escape. She watches it struggle, the blankness in its eye mirrored by the stillness in hers.

The noise rouses Cincinnatus, spread out in a spot of sunlight on the bank. He raises his shaggy head and looks at her with placid disinterest, his huge pink tongue lolling, then relaxes with a deep sigh. His days of chasing squirrels or chipmunks have long passed, and he bathes in the warm sun as in a bath. Virgo raises an eyebrow at him, nothing more, then works the trout off the barbed spearhead and drops it into her basket. That makes four. *Good enough.*

She takes a small detour on her way back to her camp, up a narrow path through a stand of birch and western maple to a broad flat rock, covered in pale lichen. At the end of the rock, the land falls away in a steep decline, so that as she looks out across the valley, she is at the same level as the tops of the trees. She loves the change in perspective. For most of life, trees are all thick trunk and heavy boughs, towering above her. Here, she is among the highest branches, spreading their dryad fingers into the air to catch the first rays of the sun. She can almost imagine herself a bird, perched alone above the dangers of the dusky ground.

Near the edge of the rocky shelf stands the cairn she built for Tender. After the pyre she made for him had burned to nothing (which took the better part of two days), she had picked through the gray ashes for what remained. Most of him had been consumed, his molecules released to fly into the sky and dance among the stars. But his hardened alloy chassis, his android bones, remained. They looked like nothing at all — a mess of blackened tubes and struts, more like a wagon frame or a disassembled bookshelf than a man — but they were all that was left of him. Virgo gathered them up and carried them here, stacked them neatly, and covered them in a pile of white stones she carried up from the stream bed. She thought that he, too, would have enjoyed the view. *Not enjoyed*, she reminded herself with an inner grin. He would have found it *interesting, unexpected.*

She thought of him often, though no longer daily. He was, in a real sense, her father. He had selected the zygotes that made her, he had implanted them in her mother's womb, he had managed her birth, fed her, changed her bath, exercised her body, and maintained her in the protocols of Joy for fifteen years. When the Spa was destroyed, he had saved her, protected her, and brought her west. And in that final moment, when she chose the magical uncertainty of life over the security of mindless pleasure, he had given up his own existence so she could have hers.

She can't remember much of those few months they had lived together in the world. Images, sounds, impressions. For most of it, she had been as an infant — innocent, without language or experience to ground her memories. But as her mind began to shape, she recognized, and remembered, more and more. She can recall the tumult of those last few days with perfect clarity, down to the words that were spoken, the explosions of violence, the sudden painful departure of Aureleo, her first friend. *What had become of him?* She hadn't thought of him in many days. He had said he would return when he had found his mother and sister. He never came.

A tabula, about the size of her two hands, lies atop the cairn. Battered by rain and buried in snow, it no longer functions. Tender had left it for her when he passed. It contained her history — all about the Spa, and her ancestors, and him. It even had a simple version of his personality that would speak to her in his voice. But it wasn't really him. It had no memories, no shared experience. It wasn't a part of the life they had lived together. After a few months, it just made her sad. She absorbed all the information it contained about her past — she had an almost perfect memory now — and then left the tabula here, with the rest of him.

Virgo replaces the device on the pile of stones, carefully, almost reverently. She knows she did the right thing, letting him go, moving on. As she looks out through the treetops, she wonders if she should move on from here, too. She has lived in her little camp above the Lakota village for almost two years now. They still send supplies up to her, but she hardly needs them. She has learned to hunt, to fish, to forage. She rarely sees anyone from the village. Her quiet mind is comfortable in the silence, and Cincinnatus provides her with all the companionship she needs.

Or so she thought. Lately, a vague unease has drifted up into her mind, like a call she only hears when asleep, or like the pull of a distant magnet that vanishes when she turns to face it. She looks out over the mountains and wonders if somehow her future lies out there, if she has stayed long enough, learned enough, prepared enough for some new chapter that she can't imagine. She can't see much point in just heading out into the wilderness, though. To what end? What would she find out there besides danger and death?

She shakes her head and gives Cincinnatus a little poke with her toe. He has found another spot of sunlight, of course, and plomped down in it without hesitation. He ignores her at first, so she pokes him again. He rolls up onto his feet with imperturbable resignation. They head back down the hill.

Virgo senses something before she reaches her camp. Perhaps the silence is deeper, perhaps an unfamiliar energy fills the air, she doesn't know. But something puts her on her guard. She has never been attacked, but she knows of at least two women from the village who have been. She once saw a solitary man making his way across the slopes to the south, a rifle strapped to his back. The world still has people, if only a few, and most of them would kill you for a piece of bread. She draws her knife and creeps forward, Cin padding along beside her, more comfort than protection.

As she comes into the clearing, Virgo sees a figure seated by the firepit in front of her tipi. She relaxes. It is a young woman, not much older than herself, with dark hair and a serious, round face. She wears the uniform of a First Nations soldier — close-fitting leggings in dark brown and green, and a short jacket with fringe along the arms. Some of the soldiers decorate their uniforms with beads or feathers, but hers is largely unadorned. The woman turns toward her as she approaches, and stands.

"Are you Virgo?" she asks.

"Who are you?"

The woman raises her hands, palms outward. "My name is Sara Estevez. I'm also called Little Cloud. I've come to find you."

"Why?"

"You know a boy named Aureleo, yes?"

"Yes." Virgo's heart starts thumping.

"He's in trouble. Big trouble. I thought you should know."

Lucinda pulls back her hood as she enters the market. The rain, which had been pounding down all morning, has finally let up. Lucky for her, the Nipmucs she traveled with had a covered wagon, so she is relatively dry, unlike many of the people at the fair. But everyone is used to getting soaked, so no one gives it much notice.

Concord Market has grown over the last few years. It started as a place for vagral caravans to meet up. They had chosen the location because it was a kilometer or so off the only passable road into the ruined city, a dangerous stretch haunted by bandits preying on migratory Steaders looking for a place to settle. Here, they were relatively safe, could exchange news and supplies, and help each other out with repairs.

Recently, now that the First Nations were patrolling the roads, more and more people were coming to trade — still mostly junk and scavenge, but also crafted goods and services. Homespun, tools, repair and refurbishment, weapons and ammunition. An informal group had sprung up to manage the increased traffic, giving information to visitors and resolving disputes between vendors out of an old ranger parked beneath the stone obelisk that marked the center of the market.

350 years old, it still stood as tall as the nearby trees, its inscription eroded but readable: *Faithful Unto Death*. Lucinda found it vaguely sinister. She understood it meant to commemorate the honor of someone

(she didn't know who — the brass plates that once lined the base had long ago been pried off for re-use), "faithful even until death." But to her, it sounded more like "faithful *to* death," like a summons to one of the Death Cults that had formed after the Collapse, and still threatened the peace and safety of the Steaders.

She never liked coming here. For one thing, it was an overnight slog from the farm, even with the Nipmuc to help. For another, it jittered with a fractious energy that made her nervous. She wasn't used to it. Had never been used to it. She had spent her life in the cold but placid world of the Hamilton Estates Enclave, and then in the quiet retreat of Hope Farm, where they would go days without speaking, where most conversations were conducted through flying hands and the gestures of Shaping. Here, the air buzzed with chatter, and the bubbling frenzy of acquisition. Everyone was constantly looking over their shoulders, on the lookout for a bargain, or a thief, or a band of men with guns.

And then there were the unwelcome discoveries. She had come in the spring to find some pipe for a privy Sandoval was building in the long hallway (so nice not to have to troop to the outhouse in the rain), and some fresh needles. As she was sorting through one junk dealer's goods, she came upon a brass artifact about the size of her head. She recognized it immediately as the finial from the gazebo in the Enclave's central square. Dented and blackened, the "H-E" in curlicued script was as familiar to her as her own hands. The pit of her stomach dropped into her heels, as the unbidden memory of that terrible day of fire and death rolled over her, pursued by a plunging guilt. She had stood by while the Doctor's army destroyed her home, and walked through its ruined streets like it was nothing in the world. She would never forgive herself for that.

She shakes off her gloom with the last of the rain, and gets about her business. She has come for cloth and clothing. The kids are all growing too fast, especially Lamarque, who had shot up like a cornstalk in the last six months. She scans the crowd of vendors, looking for a particular ragpicker who always has the best stuff.

Lucinda spots her at the end of a row and heads over. She keeps her head down and her hood up to cover her thick red hair, but she can feel the eyes of men crawling up her body, drinking in her pale cheeks and hands. She stands out among the normal folk here — Niners mostly, with warm brown skin and dark hair. Whelites like her are few and far between anymore, and she is paler than most.

Nobody bothers her, though. *Small mercies.* And the ragpicker greets her kindly. She has a tight-wrinkled face and lively eyes, and always seems cheerful. Lucinda wonders how she could be so happy. How many bodies has she stripped in her time, how many burnt-out settlements, how many Steader corpses felled by plague or animals or accident? But her goods are clean and folded and free of holes, and Lucinda would never press her on where they came from. Clothes are clothes.

The apples she brought for trade — blotchy but big and juicy — are worth a lot, and Lucinda gets trousers for both the boys, several shirts, two jackets, and even a little flowered dress for Kimo. The ragpicker tells her she made it herself from curtain fabric, and Lucinda chooses to believe her. Most days, Kimo dressed for farm work like the rest of them, but she had a love of pretty things, and Lucinda warms at the thought of the happy twinkle the dress will spark in her bright black eyes.

As she turns away from the ragpicker with a grateful smile, Lucinda's attention is drawn to a small crowd that has gathered on the far side of the clearing. A loud voice is speaking, in a singsong. She drifts that way, in spite of herself, curiosity winning out over caution.

"...can remember those days, can't you, old-timer? Enough power for everyone, running water, order, safety, laws? It's been a long, dark time, but those days are coming again. I tell you, they're back. Where have they been? Well, that's a damn good question. Preparing. Building. Investing. It takes time to recover from those losses — the wars, the disease, the violence.

People lost their way. We all lost our way. But our leaders never lost sight of that one noble goal — to restore order and prosperity to the Nation. To rebuild the Nation. To give us something to belong to. And now, they are returning with the bright promise of a new day."

Lucinda reaches the back of the little crowd. A young man, whelite like her, blonde, stands behind a table — an actual plastic table (most of the vendors pile their goods on boards or crates). Behind him is a banner that looks new-made, actually manufactured. It has an image of a flag that she recognizes as the emblem of the New States: ten stripes of red and white behind a blue circle with ten stars, and an eagle in the center. The New States had dissolved more than forty years ago. Above the flag are the words, "Join us in Patria," and below it "For a New Life!"

"Who'll come with me? Patria has everything — sanitation, food, a school. Just like things used to be."

"It just sounds like a refugee camp," says someone in the crowd. "And we know how long those last."

"It's not like that at all," says the young man. "You've got the strength of the government behind you, police to keep the peace, and soldiers to protect the people."

"The First Nations are making things safer on the roads," says another voice.

"And who are they? Outsiders. From where? Somewhere out west. You really want them telling you what to do? What's the price you're going to pay for your so-called safety?"

He comes out from behind his table, his arms spread. Something glints on his forehead. Lucinda sees that he has a small silver disk, about the size of a walnut, in the center of his brow. She can't see it well, through his hair. She wonders what it signifies, what it does.

"Listen, my friends. Patria is for *you*. For *us*. For the people who have lived here for hundreds of years. It's a new beginning that takes us back to the way things used to be, the way things should be. There are even shops, a rec center. You've all wondered what it was like to live in one of those fancy Enclaves. Well, now you can. Only this one is for you. For the people. Now, who's with me?" He holds up a tabula. "All you have to do is sign the loyalty pledge, collect your things — or your family, if you have one — and meet us here at sundown. The caravan—" he points to a large vehicle parked beneath the trees behind him—"will take us all to paradise. Who's first?"

The crowd hesitates for a moment. Then a short man with a gruff face and a thick beard steps forward. "I'll give it a try. Why not? Can't be worse than what I've got." He moves to the table and bends over the tabula. A line forms behind him.

Lucinda backs away and turns to go. The whole scene makes her uncomfortable. Something doesn't sit right, but she can't put her finger on what it is. Too good to be true, she supposes. She looks around for her Nipmuc friends and sees them in a small huddle near the edge of the market.

Just as she begins to go to them, a woman bursts through the crowd that has gathered. "Where is he?" she shouts. "Where is he?"

The young man ignores her, bent over the tabula with one his recruits. Without hesitation, she sweeps around the table and grabs him by the collar. "Hey! Watch it!" he says.

"Where is he?" she says again, almost spitting into his face. "He went to trade. He went to your so-called town to trade. He wasn't going to stay. That was five days ago! What did you do to him?"

"Listen, lady," says the young man. "I'm sorry about your man. I don't know anything about him. He probably got waylaid on the road. You know how it goes."

"My brother saw him go in. My brother saw him go in! Through the gates. He waited outside. For more than a day. He wasn't going in." She turns to the crowd. Tears streak her face. "We heard things, about what happens in there. I didn't want him to go. He said he'd be fine. He was just going to trade." She wheels again on the young man. "Where is he? Where is he? Where is he?"

She falls on him with a fury, beating on his chest. He tries to push her off, but she is stronger than him, and they stagger back into the table, knocking it on its side.

Four men in dark grey uniforms appear out of the caravan. They surround the woman with swift precision and pull her off the young man. She struggles and screams, but she is no match for them. They drag her into the caravan and up the stairs. Lucinda can see that these men, too, have silver disks on their foreheads. It is over in seconds.

The young man gets to his feet and sets the table back on its legs, gathering the tabula from the ground. "Sorry about that," he says, grinning. "Crazies. I don't know what she was talking about. That's not the Patria I know. The gates are open. People come and go all the time. Now, who's next."

The crowd hangs back. Lucinda doesn't wait to see what happens next?

Thank you for reading this sample from **LOVE**,
the third book in the **Novels of the New Frontier.**

Look for it in November 2026!

For information on the release, and to get the inside scoop on the
world of the New Frontier,

Join my mailing list!

ACKNOWLEDGMENTS

Boundless thanks to Elbert Joseph and Johan DeBesche, who gave me invaluable insights into Deaf culture and the realities of communication for Deaf and HoH people. I hope I rose to the challenge you put to me. My brilliant and generous cover designer Kerry Ellis. My editor Amy Lisane — thank you for the friendly nudges and gentle reminders. To my writing buddy Jessica Taylor, who asked the right questions during the early drafts of this book. Brian Cali for giving me great ideas about Mindworm. Maria Cali for her thoughtful responses and questions as a beta reader. Ben Galley for all his advice and depth of knowledge. Spencer Evett for throwing himself into the enormous task of recording the audio book, and thus becoming a de facto proofreader. And of course, my incomparable wife Kelli Edwards, who not only gave me brilliant advice about how to make the book better, clearer, and more true, but also provides me with the unstinting support that keeps me going in my writing and in my life.

ABOUT THE AUTHOR

B.R.M. Evett spent his life as a professional actor working in theaters around the world. His play Albatross, co-written with Matthew Spangler, was nominated for the 2015 Elliot Norton Award. He grew up in beautiful Cleveland Heights, Ohio. He now lives by a quiet pond outside of Boston with his wife and their dog, Zeppo. He studied Classics at Harvard College. His first book JOY was shortlisted for the 2024 Rubery Book Award.

Get the latest news about new releases, special offers, prizes
and more by
Subscribing to my email list!